This was the world.

The blue waters of the Mediterranean were at the heart of it. The world was the islands in this sea and the lands that ringed its shores. Journey was by water, across the sea, and up the rivers of fresh water that fed it.

This was the world where bold warriors battled with bronze swords. Without bronze there could be no warriors—just as without tin there could be no bronze. Copper alone was too soft to make a warrior's weapon. Therefore no journey was too difficult, no effort too great, to obtain the tin that transformed the abundant and malleable copper into noble bronze.

Only the boldest warriors dared to voyage to the ends of the world, to venture up the rivers to find this tin. Only the bravest dared to go beyond the land-rimmed sea, out through the narrow straits into the storm-filled Atlantic beyond. To sail north in the cold fog, to the icy island in the ocean where, with heroic effort, the tin could be found.

This was the world one thousand and five hundred years before the birth of Christ.

The Greek cities were in command of the one side and fought through the whole of the war, and in command of the other side was the king of Atlantis, which was an island once upon a time, but now lies sunk by earthquakes.

—Plato, *Critias*

STONEHENGE
WHERE ATLANTIS DIED

HARRY HARRISON AND LEON STOVER

TOR

A TOM DOHERTY ASSOCIATES BOOK

Maps copyright © 1983 by Tom Doherty Associates.
Drawn by Jacques Chazaud

Copyright © 1972, 1983 by Harry Harrison and Leon Stover
Portions of this book were formerly published as *Stonehenge*.

A Tor Book

Published by Tom Doherty Associates, 8-10 W. 36th St., New York City, N.Y. 10018

First printing, September 1983

ISBN: 0-523-48073-3

Printed in the United States of America

Distributed by Pinnacle Books, 1430 Broadway, New York, N.Y. 10018

for
our wives
Joan Marion Harrison
and
Takeko Kawai Stover
who built Stonehenge
with us

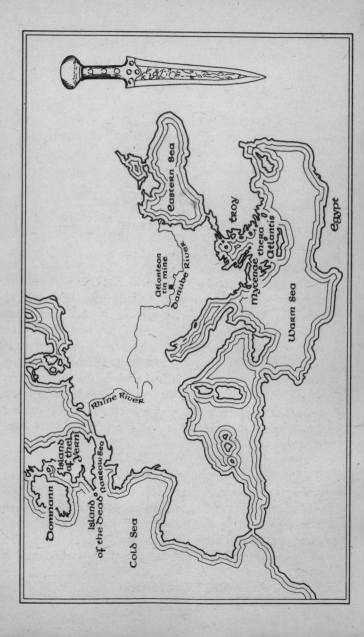

BOOK ONE

1

Britain, 1480 B.C.

The wind swooped out of the wooded hills to the north, driving a scud of fine snow before it. It rushed through the tall, dark trees of the forest, rattling the bare twigs and bending the tops of the evergreens. Here and there in the endless forest it crossed clearings, man made, with short stubble in the frozen furrows and squat buildings leaking feathers of smoke to be snatched away by the wind. Over a ridge it moved and down into an open-ended valley well cleared of trees. Here the wind pressed close to the ground and moaned about the squat sod buildings and tore fragments of reeds from their roofs.

Lycos of Mycenae walked with his chin bent into his chest to keep the stinging snow from his face, wrapping his white wool cloak more tightly about him. His conical helmet of rows of boats' tusks offered protection from sword blows but not from the weather. He stopped under a low lintel and pushed open the door of the last building. The air inside was as cold and damp as that outside, and it stank.

"What happened?" Lycos asked.

"We don't know," Koza said. A gray-haired and scar-red warrior, his bronze half armor bore the traces of much hard use as did his sharp-pointed bronze helmet. He squinted in the dim light as he looked down at the man who lay bubbling and moaning on the dirt floor of the hut. "One of the boys saw him at the edge of the forest and told me. He was unconscious, just like this. I dragged him in here." A short, compact man in stained, brown garments. Dying.

"Do any of them know who he is?" Lycos asked from the doorway, not interested in entering the foul-smelling hut.

"He's not one of them, he's an Albi," Koza said. "That's all they can say. They're frightened. One of them thinks he may have seen him before, but he doesn't know his name. They're all stupid." The small boys crouched together in the boxlike bunk, among the matted furs, looking on fearfully, their eyes round white splotches in their dirty faces. They shrank even further when Koza talked about them.

Koza did not like this. He poked his toe into the man's ribs with no effect. The man's eyes stayed closed and a pink froth dribbled from his lips. Fresh moss had been pressed into the great wound in his chest, but it could not stop the flow of blood that oozed out and snaked in thick streams down his ribs. Koza had fought in a great number of battles and had seen many men die, so it was not the familiar presence of death that troubled him now.

"Leave him," Lycos ordered and turned to go. He halted and pointed at the boys, who shied away at the gesture. "Why aren't they working?"

"One of the tin streams has been flooded," Koza fell into step to the left and slightly behind Lycos. "We can't dig in it until the water goes down."

"Then put them to work on the charcoal kilns or to pounding ore; there's plenty for them to do."

Koza nodded agreement, uncaring. They were just

8

Donbaksho boys sold into bondage by their parents in exchange for a few gifts. The wind whirled the snowflakes about them; spring was coming late this year. The sun was a glowing cold eye close to the horizon. They strode through the half-frozen mud and long drifts of white ashes to the welcome heat that surrounded one of the furnaces. Under the lean-to a pile of burning charcoal, mixed with the ore, had been heaped into a cupped depression in the ground. It needed a forced draft, and when Lycos appeared the two boys, who had been half-heartedly leaning on the pair of bellows, began to apply themselves with great energy; sparks glowed and scattered wide. The bellows, each made from a length of wood fastened to an entire pigskin with its legs kicking in the air, squealed with restored life.

"This one will be finished soon," Lycos said, squinting into the pile of red coals with a professional eye.

"I don't like that Albi coming here like this, wounded. None of them live that close. Why. . . ."

"They fight with each other and die. Has nothing to do with us."

This was dismissal enough. Koza reluctantly left the heat and went to his own quarters to get his bronze-studded shield and sword. A dagger and half armor were safe to wear in the security of the settlement—but nowhere else. A foot beyond the protective embankment a man had to be armed and walk with caution. There were bears out there that would attack if they were disturbed, and wolves, often in packs, that considered men just another welcome source of meat after the long winter. Boars, savage killers in the thick brush. And men, the most dangerous killers of all. A stranger was an enemy. Once you left the home circle all men were strangers.

Mirisati was sitting on his heels just below the top of the embankment that had been thrown up to seal off the end of the valley, his heavy shield at his side while he traced circles in the dirt with the tip of his sword.

9

"I could have killed you," Koza growled. "Squatting down like you're enjoying a good bowel movement."

"No, you couldn't," Mirisati said with the indifference of the young for the concerns of the old. He sat and stretched, then climbed to his feet. "I heard you coming one hundred paces off with your knee joints squeaking and your armor rattling."

"What have you seen?"

Koza squinted through the thin curtain of falling snow. The land before him was bare the full width of the narrow valley that held the settlement, tufted with grass now brown and dead. Beyond this were heather bushes backed by the dark curtain of the forest that covered the Island of the Yerni from east to west, from the sea-washed beaches of the south to the fogs and swamps of the far north. The valley was wrapped in silence. The only movement was a flock of crows that rose up and swept away out of sight.

"I've seen just what you are seeing now. Nothing. No one is coming here. I wish they would. Butchering a few of these savages would be a change."

"Nothing? What about the one with the hole in his chest the boy found?" The dying man's presence still troubled Koza.

"Who knows? Better, who cares? They just like to kill each other. And I can understand that. What else is there to do in this cold land?"

"The Albi don't fight."

"Tell that to the dying one. If you want to talk to me, tell me about the sun-warmed stones of Mycenae. What a distance we have traveled from that happy place! My arms ache just thinking about it, but I would start rowing tomorrow if it meant we could return. Fifteen days across the green water of that cold ocean to the Pillars of Herakles. Thirty days more on the blue waters to the Argolid. The first olives will be ready for the pressing by then."

"We'll leave when we're ordered to leave," Koza grum-

10

bled. He had no more love than the other for this Island of the Yerni. The wind drew the falling traceries of snow aside for a moment and he saw the dark silhouettes of the birds settling down into the forest. They were roosting for the night—but why had they moved? Had something disturbed them?

"You better go back and start the boys in the hut working again. Orders from Lycos. And when you see him, tell him that the underbrush is growing up here again. We'll have to clear it back."

"Always looking for new labors, Koza?" Mirisati was in no hurry to return to the camp.

"We've had attacks here before. The Yerni stay away now because we killed all of the ones that tried. And they'll try again someday. That brush is protection for them. Men could lie out there, get close."

"You have bad dreams, old man. My dreams are of a superior sort, of warm sun and olive groves and cool wine. Fine Epidaurian wine, so rich you must thin it twenty times with water. And then a girl, not one of these Donbaksho sluts whose wrappings you have to cut away to be sure it isn't a boy or an old man, but a honey-skinned girl who smells of frankincense."

"You won't find any of that out here," Koza said, gesturing at the shadow-filled forest.

"No, I don't think I will. Is it all like this—the whole island?"

"The parts I've seen. We went out there two summers ago; Lycos had dealings with the tribes. Forest everywhere, too thick to get through except on the high downs. Almost a five-day march to reach the tribes where the big stones are. Dig like moles, these Yerni, circles and banks and hills and burial mounds, then stand these stones around, great ugly things."

"Why?"

"Ask them. This one tribe, Uala's, where we went that time, they have them in a big double circle, blue stones

11

with their tips painted red like big pricks stuck in the ground. Dirty-minded people. . . ."

"What was that?" Mirisati pointed his sword at a clump of heather in the darkness below the beach trees.

"I didn't see anything." Koza stared hard, but nothing was clear in the fading light.

"Well, I did. A fox, perhaps a deer. We could use a little fresh meat in the stewpot." He climbed to the top of the embankment to see better.

"Get back here! It could have been anything."

"Don't fear the shadows, old man. They can't hurt you."

Mirisati laughed and turned to jump back down. A sudden, whispering sound cut the air. The spear buried itself deep into the side of his neck, hurling him over and down with a clatter. His legs were spread wide, his eyes wider with surprise. He reached up for the wooden shaft and died.

"*Alarm*!" Koza shouted. "*Alarm*!" over and over, beating his sword against his shield.

There were no more spears. But when he looked cautiously over the top of the ridge, he could see the men running forward now from the shelter of the forest, silent and fast as wolves. Naked, even in this weather, except for short leather kirtles. One man, ahead of the others, held a spear which he hurled at Koza, who dodged it easily. There were no more; they used spears only for hunting. The others came on, round shields on their left arms, brandishing stone battle-axes in their right hands. Some had daggers about their necks; all had whitened hair and stiff white moustaches. There were a great number of them. As they reached the foot of the ridge they cried out, *Abu-abu*!, piercingly, a scream meant to drive fear into their enemies so they would flee. Koza stood firm.

"Yerni!" He bellowed it out and heard the alarm being shouted behind him. They would fight now. His heart beat strongly in his chest as he saw more and more of the near-naked men emerging from the shelter of the trees. The snow had stopped and he could see their mass stretching the width of the valley. Never before had he seen so many of their warriors together at one time. This was an entire tribe or more.

Heavy running footsteps sounded behind Koza and he knew he was no longer alone. Well, then, this would be a battle.

When the first of the warriors were puffing up the slope, he leaped to the top of the embankment and shook his sword at them.

"Sons of goats! Come meet a Mycenaean!"

He raised his shield so the battle-ax bounced from it, then plunged his sword into the man's stomach. Not too deep; he was too experienced for that. A twist and a pull had it out. Even before the first Yerni had dropped, Koza's sword was chopping the neck of another man, his shield pushing aside an ax. Then another and another, until the blood ran wetly from his sword onto his arm. Something struck sharp pain through his leg so that he almost fell; with the edge of his shield he knocked that attacker away. But others were behind him. Many of them. Too many of them. They ran by on all sides, howling in high voices.

He fell only when his legs were too butchered to support him, and even then he rolled and chopped upward with his sword, wounding and killing those he could, only stopping when his helmet was torn away and an ax crushed in his skull. A dagger was pressed to his neck, sawing through it, severing his head from his body.

More and more of the screaming tribesmen ran by, and the snow was trampled by many feet and soon stained and splashed with red.

2

Mycenae

In the gray dawn the city was as sharply etched as a silhouette against the sky and the blur of distant hills. Its presence commanded the valley all about it; the paths between the trees and fields led to it. The hill on which it sat was gently rounded at the base, but angled up steeply at the top to the thick-walled and impregnable city. As the first light colored the stone, the great gate under the rampant carved lions was swung open by invisible hands. Threads of smoke from the many cooking fires within the walls rose straight up through the motionless air. A boy leading a goat came slowly along the rutted road between the fields: men and women with baskets of produce appeared down the lanes. They halted when they reached the road, stopped by the sound of sudden hoofbeats, staring with dumb curiosity at the two-horse chariot as it rumbled by them.

In the open gateway high above, the guards looked down with interest as the horses clattered on the stones of the ramp leading up to them. The charioteer was in a great hurry. One of the horses slipped and nearly fell; the rider lashed it forward. Since the sun was only newly risen the man must have been riding by night, a dangerous thing to do, and one that evidenced a most unusual need for haste. One didn't hurry in Mycenae; the seasons came and went, the rain dampened the earth and crops sprang up, the animals were slaughtered and the young ones grew. There was no reason for unseemly haste by night, no reason to risk crippling and killing a sacred horse.

"I know him now," a guard called out. He pointed his bronze-bladed spear. "It is Phoros, cousin of the king."

They drew aside, raising their weapons in salute to his rank as Phoros came up. His white cloak was black with blown spittle from the stumbling horses, and he appeared no less tired himself. Looking to neither right nor left he drove the exhausted animals through the tall opening of the gate, under the carved lions, and past the royal grave circle into the hilltop city of Mycenae. Slaves hurried out to hold the horses while Phoros climbed stiffly to the ground. He staggered at first, his legs so fatigued from the ride, and had to lean against the great stone wall. The ride was a nightmare better forgotten; he was no charioteer and he entertained a secret fear of the noble beasts. But he had driven the creatures, despite this fear, just as he had driven his rowers that last day along the coast, forcing speed from them despite their exhaustion. The king must be told. There was a trough here for the horses and he bent wearily over it and filled his cupped hands again and again, splashing the water over his face and arms. It was still cool from the night, and it washed away the dust and some of his fatigue. Water dripped from his hair and beard, and he wiped at it with the tail of his cloak as he climbed the steep ramp to the residential part of the palace city. The muscles in his legs loosened as he went along the paths by the kitchen gardens, past the workshops and houses where the people were just stirring. They came to their doorways and looked on curiously as he hurried by. Then he was at the great palace itself, climbing the smoothly dressed stone steps to the entrance. The door with its hammered bronze covering was open, and the oldest house slave, Avull, was waiting, bowing and clasping his knob-knuckled and shaking hands together. He had already sent a slave running with word to the king.

Perimedes, war king of the Argolid and master of the House of Perseus at Mycenae, was not at his very best this morning. He had slept fitfully the night before. The wine perhaps, or the dull ache of old wounds or, more surely, Atlantis.

"Oh, the bastards," he muttered to no one and to everyone, slumping low in his great chair and reaching for

15

the figs in the basket on the table before him. He chewed on one, and even its rich sweetness could not sweeten his mood. Atlantis. The name alone stung like a thorn or a scorpion's lance.

Around him the day's work of the great megaron was already beginning. With the king awake no one sleeps. There were occasional hushed voices; no one dared to speak too loud. On the elevated round hearth in the middle of the chamber the fire was being built higher to cook the meat, the fire he himself had kindled years before when the palace and this megaron had been first built. The thought did not warm him today, just as the figs could not sweeten him. Under a nearby canopy his two daughters and some house slaves were carding fleeces and spinning the wool into thread. They stopped talking when he glanced their way, turning their attention more closely to their work. Though his face was set in anger, Perimedes was still a handsome man, heavy browed, with a thin-edged nose above a wide mouth. He was well into middle age, yet his hair and beard were still as brown as in his youth, and there was no thickening of his waist. The white scars of old wounds made patterns on the tanned skin of his arms, and when he reached out for another fig it was obvious that the last two fingers were missing from his right hand. Kingship was something hard won in the Argolid.

The slave, Avull, entered at the far side of the megaron and hurried over to him, bowing low.

"Well?"

"Your cousin, the noble Phoros, son of. . . ."

"Get him in here, you son of a chancred goat. This is the man I have been waiting for." Perimedes almost smiled as the slave hurried away to usher in the ship's captain.

"We need you, Phoros. Come here, sit by me, they'll bring us wine. How was your voyage?"

Phoros sat on the edge of the bench and looked at the

polished marble tabletop. "Uncle Poseidon in his might drove our ship quickly all the distance."

"I'm sure of that, but it is not details of the seafaring that I care about. You have returned with the ingots of tin?"

"Yes, but a small amount, less than a tenth of a ship-load."

"Why is this?" Perimedes asked quietly, a sudden premonition darkening his vision. "Why so little?"

Phoros still stared at the table, ignoring the wine in the gold cup that had been set before him. "We arrived during a fog; there is much fog off the coast of the Island of the Yerni. Then we waited until it had cleared before we could sail along the coast to the mouth of the river we know. I beached the boat there and left men to guard it, then followed the overgrown path to the mine. We came to the place where the tin is stored, but there were no ingots there. We searched nearby and found some, but almost all were missing. The ingots are kept close to the mine."

Phoros looked up now, staring squarely at the king as he spoke.

"This is not the word you wish to hear. The mine is destroyed, all there are dead."

A wave of quick whispers died away as those nearest in the megaron passed the word backwards as to what had been said. Then there was silence and Perimedes was silent as well, his fists clenched, the only movement a heavy pulse that beat beneath the skin of his forehead.

"My brother, Lycos, what of him?"

"I don't know. It was hard to tell. All of the bodies had been stripped of armor and clothing and had been there many months. The animals and birds had done their work. There had been hard fighting, a battle with the Yerni. All the heads gone, not a skull. The Yerni take heads, you know."

"Then Lycos is dead. He would never surrender or be

17

captured by savages like that.''

Anger burned a knot of pain in his midriff and Perimedes kneaded it with his hand. His brother, the lost tin, the dead men, the Atlantean ships, all coming together; these were dark, unhappy days. He wanted to shout aloud with this anger, to take his sword and kill something, someone—fight back. He might have done this once, when he was young, but a wisdom had come with the years. Now the anger stayed inside of him and he squeezed it with his fingers and tried instead to think what should be done. The pain did not go away.

''Is it true? My kinsman Mirisati is dead?''

Perimedes looked up at the angry man before him. Qurra, first among the chalcei, the workers in metal. He must have come directly from his furnace when he heard the news, because he was wearing his leather apron, burned by many sparks, and soot was on his arms and smeared across his forehead. Forgotten, the stubby tongs were still clasped in his right hand.

''Dead, certainly,'' Phoros said. ''Everyone at the mine must be dead. Mycenaeans do not become slaves.''

Qurra, an emotional man, shouted aloud in pain. ''What ruin is upon us! The mine is gone, our people killed, my kinsmen slain.'' He shook his tongs angrily. ''Mirisati is dead, to whom you promised your younger daughter when she comes of age. . . .'' The words ended in a fit of coughing. The chalceus always coughed from breathing his metal fumes, and many died because of it.

''I did not kill him,'' Perimedes said. ''Nor my brother Lycos. But I will see that they are avenged. Return to your furnace, Qurra, you serve us best there.''

Qurra started away, but called back over his shoulder.

''And tell me, noble Perimedes, how long will my furnace burn with the mine closed?''

How long? This was the question that gnawed at Perimedes' vitals the most. Had he been too ambitious? Perimedes thought. No, there had been no other course open to him. As long as the Greek cities of the Argolid warred one with the other, they remained weak. Lerna fought Epidaurus, Nemea sank the ships of Corinth. While at the same time the ships of Atlantis sailed freely where they would and grew rich. Only the united power of the cities of the Argolid could challenge that ancient power. The rocky plains of home had been tilled and bore fruit, but never enough. Across the sea were the tempting riches of many lands, and his people already had a taste for these riches. Bronze-armored warriors with brazen weapons could take what they willed. Bronze made them. They ate bronze and drank it because they would be nothing without it. Soft golden copper was everywhere, but that was not enough. With a technique known only to them, the chalcei blended the copper with the gray tin in the burning throats of their forges. The result was noble bronze. Of this bronze Mycenae forged weapons to conquer, more weapons as gifts for the other cities of the Argolid to bind them all together.

Without bronze, this loose union would fall apart and they would war with one another as they had always done. The sea empire of Atlantis would rule as it had always ruled. Atlantis had all the tin they needed. Their camps and mines were along the Danube. Mycenae had tin; not as much, but they had tin. They had to travel the length of the warm sea to the cold ocean beyond, to that distant island, to get it, then bring it home the same distance. But they had it, and Mycenae had bronze.

Mycenae no longer had bronze.

"The mine. We must reopen the mine."

Perimedes spoke the words aloud before he saw that another had joined them, a short, brown man. Inteb the Egyptian, now wearing a robe of thin white flax instead of his usual rough working clothes. Gold thread was set into the edge of the robe and there was a collar with precious stones about his neck; his black hair was oiled and glistening. Looking at him, Perimedes remembered.

19

"You are leaving us."

"Very soon. My work here is finished."

"It is a work well done, you must tell your Pharaoh that. Here, sit, you will eat with me before you leave."

The women quickly brought plates of small fish fried in oil, cakes drenched with honey, salty white goatsmilk cheese. Inteb picked delicately at the fish with a gold fork taken from his pouch. A strange man, young for his work, though he knew it well. He came from a noble family, so in a sense he was the ambassador for Thuthmosis III, not only a builder. He knew things about the stars, as well, and could read and write. He had supervised the building of the new, massive outer wall of the city. As if this were not enough, through his craft, he had erected the great gate and mounted above it the royal lions of Mycenae. It was well done indeed—nor had the price been too high. There had been agreements. Thuthmosis III, busy with his wars in the south, would no longer be troubled by the Argolid raiders who sank his ships and burned his coastal towns. An arrangement between kings.

"You seem troubled?" Inteb asked, his voice bland, his face emotionless. He freed a fish bone from between his teeth and droped it to the floor.

Perimedes sipped at his wine. How much had the Egyptian heard about the tin mine? There should be no stories going back to Pharaoh of Mycenaean weakness.

"A king always has troubles, just as Pharaoh has troubles; that is the way of kings."

If the comparison between the ruler of this brawling city state and the mighty ruler of all Egypt troubled Inteb, he did not show it; he took a honey cake in his fingertips.

"I am troubled by the dung-flies of Atlantis," Perimedes said. "Not satisfied with their own shores, they come here and cause dissension among us. Their ships appear along the coast with weapons for sale, and our little squabbling princes are only too eager to buy. They know little of loyalty. Mycenae is the armory of the Argolid.

Some forget that. Now there is an Atlantean ship at Asine in the south, a floating bronzesmith's shop, doing business in our waters. But it will not be there long—nor will it be returning to Atlantis. My son Ason led our men against it as soon as we heard of its presence. You may tell Pharaoh of this. You have my gifts?''

"Safe aboard my ship. I am sure Pharaoh will be pleased.''

Perimedes was not so sure. He talked of equality among kings, but in his most innermost thoughts he knew the truth. He had seen Egypt, the cities of the dead and living, the teeming people and the soldiers. If that power were turned against Mycenae, his city would cease to exist. Yet there was power and power—because Egypt was so great it did not follow that Mycenae became small. It was the first city of the Argolid and the mightiest, and that was something to be proud of.

"We will walk together before you leave,'' Perimedes said, rising and buckling on the square-shouldered royal dagger of Mycenae. Graven on its long and narrow straight-edged blade was the scene of a royal lion hunt, incised with gold and silver and niello. Its pommel, a peculiar rounded cap of solid gold upon a golden stem— another royal insignia, this one vegetative.

They walked side by side, with the slaves rushing ahead to open the coffered doors of bronze. It was not by chance that they passed by the roofed mushroom beds just inside the palace walls. Perimedes paused and looked on with a critical eye while the gardeners prepared a fresh bed, laying down the layer of cow dung, then scattering the tree bark over it. As they moved on, Perimedes bent and picked a mushroom, twisting it in his fingers as he walked. It was white crowned and pale stemmed, with lacy edges. He broke off a piece and sampled it, extending some to Inteb. The Egyptian also ate it, although he really did not like the musty flavor. He knew everyone else thought it delicious.

"This is history,'' Perimedes said, pointing to the dung
21

and the mushroom beds, and Inteb, being a diplomat, managed not to smile. He knew that the mushroom was held in great esteem here. Myces they called them; they shaped their sword and dagger hilts to their form and had even named their city after them. Mycenae. Though he found it hard to understand why. Perhaps because of the *maleness* of the shape of the things, always an important concern with these kinds of people.

"The royal mushrooms," Perimedes said. "Perseus found them growing here and named the city for them. We have a long history, just like Egypt, and like Egypt we have those who can read and write and keep our records."

Perimedes paused before a wooden door and hammered on it until it screeched open. The elderly slave peered out, blinking into the sunlight, a soft clay tablet in his hand. An Atlantean, from the look of him, no doubt captured; so much for Mycenaean culture, Inteb thought. He, who had visited often at the library in Thebes, with its papyrus scrolls neatly shelved in a complex of rooms larger than this entire palace, pretended interest in the tottering piles of baskets filled with unsorted tablets. He tried to ignore the squashed ones on the filthy dirt floor. Probably vital records of cauldrons and wine jars and fire tongs and footstools and other things of equal importance. He doubted if he would tell Pharaoh of this.

But before they could pass through the doorway, there was a cry, and they turned to see two men in armor half carrying a third man between them. He was coated with dust mixed with blood, his mouth gaping in the agony of near exhaustion.

"We found him this way, crawling on the road," one of the men said. "He has word; he is one of those who marched with Ason."

Once again the coldness possessed Perimedes. He could almost hear the words the man would speak—and he did not wish to hear them. This was a day of evil. If there were a way to remove this day from his life, he would. He seized

22

the man by the hair and crashed him against the wall of the archive building, shaking him until he gaped like a fish drawn from the water.

"Speak. What of the ship?"

The man could only gasp.

One of the slaves came running with a jar of wine and Perimedes tore it from his hands and dashed the contents into the exhausted man's face.

"Speak!" he ordered.

"We attacked the ship—the men of Asine, there. . . ." He licked at the wine that streamed down his face.

"Asine, what of them? They fought by your side, they are of the Argolid. The Atlanteans, tell me."

"We fought. . . ." He choked the words out one by one. "We fought them all. . . .Asine fought with Atlantis against us. . . .They were too many. . . ."

"My son, Ason, in command. What of him?"

"He was wounded. I saw him fall—dead or captured. . . ."

"And you returned? To bring me this word?"

This time the king could not control the anger that flooded through him. With a single motion he drew his dagger and plunged it into the man's chest.

3

Tiryns was already dropping behind them, with only the tops of the buildings set on the hill behind the seaport still visible. The sea was smooth here in the Gulf of Argos, and the ship moved easily on its way under the quick dip and pull of the oars, echoing in their motion the slow beat of the drum. On the starboard side the coastline slipped by, bright green with new growth. But the touch of the sun was welcome, gentling the morning coolness of the air.

Inteb leaned against the rail, staring unseeingly at the bubble of foam and rush of water beneath the counter, unaware as well, of the brawny form of the steersman a few paces away. It was spring, and the storks would be crying in the reeds along the Nile, and he would soon be home. Home after three years' absence, to the heart of the world and of civilization, away from the dirt and the petty bickering of the barbarian Mycenaeans. He had done his duty, as distasteful as it had been at times. Some men were great generals and fought wars, serving their Pharaoh in that fashion. Though violent death was the usual reward, it was still an easy thing to do. Soldiers tended to be simple men because of this, and a little brutal, which was only natural, considering that butchery was their trade. Thuthmosis III had need of these men. Yet he also had need of Inteb. Victories can be won without wars, and they both knew it. It was this knowledge, despite his natural feeling of revulsion, that had forced him to bow to his king's will and voyage to the barbarian world. His personal cost may have been high, but the victory had been a cheap one for Thuthmosis. Inteb did not begrudge him that victory. For the services of one noble—a few slaves, a handful of gold, some gifts—a war had been averted and the coastal raids on Egypt stopped. Mycenae was the stronger for his having been there; but he felt that these years had been plucked from his life and lost to him.

But not completely. In all those months of musty wine, winter rains and scorching summer sun he had found one thing, one memory that it would not be a distinct pleasure to forget, one man whom he could call a friend. The friendship had been perhaps one-sided, since Ason knew him only as one of the very many who dwelt in the palace, and gave him no pride of place. Strangely enough this did not bother Inteb; love did not have to be returned to still be love. He had been happy to sit at the feasting and wine drinking, sipping his own while the others swilled, watching them grow nobly drunk. They were a rough, unruly,

24

violent group of men, the nobility of Mycenae, and Ason could hold his own with any of them. Yet he was something more, a man destined to be a king, who had inherited his father's sharp turn of mind, who was more than just a foul-mouthed barbarian. Perhaps Inteb had imagined all this, but even that did not really matter. It had made the years bearable. Though he had not said so, he had been as shocked by the news of Ason's death as had been Perimedes. The strength of Atlantis had brushed aside this great warrior and crushed him like an insect. It was faintly disturbing that he would soon be in the land of his friend's murderers. Aroused by this thought, he saw that Tiryns had now fallen from sight astern and the gulf had opened out. They were rising and falling in the heavier rollers of the open sea. The captain had just emerged from the cabin and he signaled to him.

"What is your heading?"

"We change course east into the rising sun, lord, as soon as that island you see there is abeam. Beyond that is another and yet another, the Cyclades they are called, though I don't know the names of all of them. They reach all the way to the coast of Anatolia; we are never out of sight of land, though always in deep water. After that we follow the coast. There are few hazards as long as the weather is calm, and there are many friendly ports we can reach if there are storms."

"Neither my safety nor comfort is under discussion at the moment, captain. Do not presume. I have done my share of sailing, so it holds no horrors."

"I did not mean—forgive me. . . ." The captain's fists were calloused and scarred; the crew lived in fear of his ready blows. Yet now he moved his shoulders in greater fear of this nobleman, friend of the Pharoah.

"What I would like to know is whether we will pass the Atlantean island of Thera on this course?"

"Yes, surely, it will be clearly off to starboard after Ios falls behind us; it is one of our landfalls."

25

"We will go there."

"But just this morning you told me Egypt; those orders you gave me—"

"Were for the ears of the men of the Argolid who report back everything that is said to Perimedes. You sail the ship, captain. I will deal with kings. Set sail for Thera."

The ship heeled over as they reached Spetse, and its wake cut a great white arc in the blue water. Perimedes would not know that he was on his way to the court of Atlantis, son-killing enemies of Mycenae. He would be angry if he discovered it, and the years of labor to effect the friendship with Egypt would be in danger. Therefore the polite ruse. On the other hand, Atlas, sea king of Atlantis, might be slightly annoyed if he discovered that his Egyptian visitor had recently been dining with an enemy. He would probably be more astonished at the bad taste displayed. The tiny warring states were like fleabites on the thick hide of Atlantis, to be either scratched or ignored. Singly or together they did not pose any threat to the countless ships or the home islands of Atlantis. Atlantean vessels sailed where they wished in these seas, along the mainland shore, trading as far away as Egypt. It was even said that the glories of their court were on a par with those of Egypt, but Inteb would believe that after he had seen it for himself. As much as he wanted to return home, he had welcomed the message in the boxed scroll that the captain had given him. Its waxen seal had been impressed with the cartouche of Thuthmosis III, fifth king of the Eighteenth Dynasty, by his own hand. The orders were simple: a state call at the court of King Atlas, a renewal of the ties of friendship. There were gifts aboard the ship for the king, long elephant tusks of ivory to be presented with great display, as well as fine textiles and pots of spices, gold work and scarabs, and little blocks of white veined alabaster and amethyst from which court artisans cut the official seals of the far-flung Atlantean bureaucracy. Of more importance to both Atlas and Egypt were the bales of papyrus, smooth

26

and white. It was only the year before that the first papyrus had been sent to Atlantis, along with scribes who knew the practiced use of reed pens and ink. By now the Atlanteans would be aware of the superiority of papyrus over the clumsy clay tablets for record keeping and would welcome the new supply. But gifts were a two-way thing, and Inteb had instructions to mention in the right places that timber would be well received in treeless Egypt, cypress wood in particular. This would be done.

On the third morning the round bulk of the island of Thera lifted out of the sea. Inteb had dressed carefully in his best white flaxen robe, jeweled collar, and gold bracelets, then had sat quietly as the slave had oiled and combed his hair. This was to be a state occasion. The captain was wearing a clean tunic as well, and had made some attempt at a rough toilet; clots of blood spotted his face where he had shaven with a none-too-sharp blade.

"Have you sailed here before?" Inteb asked.

"Once, lord, many years ago. There is nothing like it in the whole world."

"That I can believe, if the reports are true."

The island was a green gem rising from the blue sea. Groves of olive trees and date palms marched in ordered rows down to the shore, with freshly planted fields set between them. The white buildings of the villages could be seen among the trees. A fishing village stood on the shore, in a cove with red sand beaches where small fishing boats were drawn up. For a moment, in a gap between the hills, Inteb had a glimpse of a city on a hill far inland, colorful buildings rising one above the other. Then the helm was put over as they headed west around the island.

"Down sail," the captain ordered.

There was an ordered rush at this command. Some of the sailors untied the lines where the bottom corners of the large square sail were secured to the siderails; it spilled the wind with a great flapping, and the ship slowed. Others had released the horsehair-and-hemp hawser that ran to the masthead, that had acted as a backstay to the mast. This ran through a greased hole in the top of the mast. When they had eased off the hawser the sail lowered in great flapping folds. After it had been tightly wrapped about its yard, then laid the length of the deck, the captain ordered that the mast be unstepped and taken down as well.

"What is the reason for this?" Inteb asked. He had never seen it done before at sea.

"The island, lord; you'll see." He was too busy to say more, and Inteb restrained his curiosity and did not bother him.

Massive oaken wedges kept the mast secure in its socket, and they had to be knocked free with heavy mauls. There was much shouting, as well as a good deal of cursing in a variety of languages, before it was lowered safely and secured in place beside the sail. In the meantime, the ship wallowed in the troughs of the waves with a decidedly uneasy motion that produced equally uneasy sensations in Inteb's middle. He muttered a quick prayer of thanks to Horus when the men finally clambered back to their rowing seats and unshipped their oars. They were under way again and turning a rocky headland of the island when a great cleft in the shore came into view. It was as though a god had struck it with a giant war-ax and cleaved the soil and stone. Its sides rose straight up, and deep into the land it ran. The captain stood by the steering oar, guiding them around the headland and into the cleft itself.

The thin clear note of a horn sounded above the hissing of the waves as they broke against the stones of the channel wall. Inteb shaded his eyes with his hand and could make out the forms of helmeted soldiers on the cliff high above, dark against the sky. Lookouts certainly, to herald the approach of any ships. And more than that. It took very little imagination to see the rows of boulders that could be levered over to fall on any unwanted ships in the channel below. There might be buckets of burning pitch, as well. Atlantis could defend herself here.

Another turn and the sharp cliffs fell away suddenly, as though they had passed a barrier, and the channel became narrower and very straight. There were tilled fields close by on each side, and the peasants stopped work, leaning on their mattocks to gape at them as they glided slowly by.

"A canal?" Inteb asked. The captain nodded, looking ahead and resting one arm over the steering oar.

"So I have heard said. They brag a lot, these Atlanteans. But it could be true. That cleft through the hills, they couldn't have done that, but this part would be easy enough to dig, given enough time and men."

Straight as an arrow's flight the channel ran, towards the rising hills inland. There was no sight of the city now, but another ship came into view in the canal ahead. Seeing it, the captain ordered in the oars and steered for the bank. The other ship approached swiftly, until they could clearly see the jutting horns above the bow and the glare of the yellow eyes painted beneath them. It was an Atlantean trireme a full 40 paces long, its banks of white oars dipping and rising in perfect unison like a great bird's wings. Then it was upon them, sweeping alongside, towering over them. The drum was like a heartbeat, the oars moving in time with it. There must have been fifteen or more oars in each bank, far too many to count as the ship slid by. A sailor in the prow looked at them curiously, as did two more on the mast, but otherwise they could have been invisible. The officers, magnificent in bronze armor set richly with enamels and gems, with high plumes on their helmets, ignored them completely. As did the fat merchants sitting under an awning on the stern deck, laughing together, lifting golden cups with jeweled fingers. Wealth and strength on easy display. The high stern and great steering sweep moved by, then a flurry of foam marked the ship's wake. It was past and gone, and they rocked in the waves raised by its passage.

"Fend off that bank," the captain shouted, and the ship was under way again. He pointed ahead. "There, lord, you see why we unstepped the mast."

A black hole opened up in the hillside before them. The canal ran into it and vanished. The rowers became aware of it, too, and looked over their shoulders and muttered together and missed the beat. The captain raised both fists over his head and swore at them in a harsh voice that could have been heard the length of the ship during the most savage storm.

"Sons of noseless whores, lice upon the stinking hide of beetles in a sun-blown corpse! Tend your rowing or I'll flay every one of you alive and make a sail of your poxy skins. We are coming to a tunnel, no more. I have been through it and it runs straight, but is narrow. Watch your rowing or you'll be breaking oars, or worse. We'll be through quickly enough if you don't fear the dark."

The black mouth swallowed them up. It was most frightening for the men who were rowing because they saw the tunnel entrance fall behind them and grow smaller, all light vanishing with it. The earth could be engulfing them, the underworld consuming them. The beat of the drum echoed from the rock around them, rolling and fading with the sound of thunder.

From the rear deck, the far entrance was clear once their eyes grew accustomed to the darkness; a bright beckoning disc. The captain steered for it, shouting encouragement to his men, but stopped when his voice echoed back like mad laughter.

The moments of entombment passed quickly enough, and they slid out into the sunlight again, amused at their fears now that the tunnel was behind them. Inteb blinked in the light, and all but gaped at this scene they had burst upon so suddenly.

They had entered a circular and land-locked lagoon. Inteb realized for the first time the complexity of the island. Thera was really a hollow mountain, perhaps an ancient volcano that vomited out its lava and left an empty center for the ocean to fill. But there was a circular reef within the crater—they had penetrated it in the tunnel. And here, at the heart of everything, lay a lagoon. It was rimmed by low hills on all sides that ran down in gentle slopes to the water. Grapes grew richly in this sheltered bowl, and the green shoots of the spring-sown crops were already high. Porticoed villas as well as simpler dwellings were half shielded by the tall trees. In the lagoon was an island, connected by bridges to the shore, almost filling it so that the lagoon became a moat of surrounding water. Moored on this island were the ships of Atlantis, row after row of them, almost too many to count. Triremes and beaked warships, fat-bellied merchantmen and swift galleys. Behind the ships were the busy docks and warehouses, while beyond them rose up the hill and the citadel that Inteb had only glimpsed for a moment from the sea.

This was the metropolis and royal city of Atlantis.

The rowers stopped, gaped, the ship drifted, and Inteb felt the same awe and wonder that they did. Up the side of the conical hill the buildings climbed in wave after wave of color, tier upon tier of neat three-storied cubical mansions. They were faced with decorative tiles in a dizzy mixture of blue and white and red, luridly trimmed with shiny horizontal bands of precious metals, roofed with sparkling white cupolas. All of these nestled at the foot of the palace that held mastery of the summit, its lengthy bulk colorful and dazzling in the sun. Brilliant red pillars, tapering downward in the Atlantean style, rose above rank after rank of stepped-back loggias. The roofline and porticoed state entrance were adorned with outsized bull-horn emblems, glinting a blazing metallic red. They were sheathed with orichalc, that noble alloy of gold and copper.

"Who are you and what is your business here?" a hoarse voice called out in bad Egyptian. "Speak!"

Inteb looked down over the rail at a guard boat which

had approached unseen while they were gawking at the city. A dozen rowers slumped over their oars and on the high stern deck were armored and greaved warriors, as well as an official in a white but badly stained smock. He had some bronze badge of office about his neck that was almost completely hidden by a straggling gray beard. His head was bald and sun-reddened, and he squinted up out of a single eye, the other being only a raw wound in his head. As he opened his mouth Inteb spoke first, leaning over the rail so his jewels and gold bracelets could be seen. He had heard Atlantean slaves talking in Mycenae and the language was not too different from Mycenaean, so he spoke in that tongue.

"I am Inteb of the household of Thuthmosis the Third, Pharaoh of Upper and Lower Egypt. I come here at his bidding to bring his words to your master. Now *you* will speak."

There was more than a hint of anger in these closing words and it had the desired effect. The man abased himself as best he could on the tiny deck, while trying to look up at the same time.

"Welcome, welcome, lord, to these waters and to these sacred precincts and the court of Atlas who is king of Atlantis, master of Thera and Crete, Milos, Ios and Astypalea and all the islands within a day's sail, and of all these ships in these waters. If you will follow, I will lead you to a berth for your ship."

He muttered something to his rowers, and the guard boat darted away with the Egyptian ship following slowly behind. Around the island they went, towards what appeared to be another tunnel. Only when they had entered it did they see that it was a channel cut through the land and roofed over with heavy timbers. Bars of sunlight lanced down from square openings in the wooden ceiling above. The captain pointed up at them.

"More defenses. They have boulders up there, right at

the edge. A ship trying to get through here gets holed and sunk.''

This passage was shorter than the first tunnel, and the other end was close at hand. From above they could hear the rumble of chariot wheels and the clatter of hooves and stamping feet. Then they emerged into yet another ring-like body of water that sat like a moat around the islet that was the heart of Thera. They tied up at a mooring where great steps of black and red stone led down into the water. Standing above it was a colorful wooden canopy, shielding the landing from the sun. It was painted a bright crimson, and in the center a pair of enormous, gilded bull's horns stretched out, stylized like those atop the palace building. Inteb saw the waiting ranks of warriors and the litter chair and knew that the word of his arrival had been passed swiftly ahead. As the mooring lines were thrown, he spoke to the captain.

''Break out the gifts from Pharaoh and have slaves bring them after me. Don't let more than half your men ashore at one time. If you must drink and whore yourself let it be known aboard where you are.''

''How long will it be before we sail, lord?''

''I don't know. Days surely. I will send a messenger when I am ready.''

More horns roared like the god of bullfrogs when Inteb stepped ashore, blending with the thunder of great wooden drums with the hides of bulls across their ends. He was bowed to and led to the palanquin, which was lifted by eight slaves as soon as he was seated. There were running sores on their shoulders where the poles cut, and their skins dripped with sweat as they climbed the winding steps up the hill, but Inteb noticed none of this. He was looking at the people and the buildings of this city so different than any he had ever seen before. Thebes was grander, but in a different way. Atlantis was a clash of color that almost hurt the eyes, of brilliant paintings on white plaster that

33

made a jungle of unreal birds and leaves. There were living creatures in this jungle as well, bluish-furred monkeys climbing on the rooftops and porches. Inteb had seen these strangely human beasts before, but never ones of *that* color. From where did the Atlanteans import them? Other animals too, donkeys bearing loads, cats watching from the open windows. Most curious of all were the elephants, which seemed to roam at will. They were totally unlike the great African war elephants that he knew; these were as small as horses and far lighter of skin. The people made way for them and occasionally would reach out to touch their thick hides for luck or for blessing.

Then they were on the summit of the acropolis, and the soaring white masonry walls of the palace rose before him in a majesty that did indeed rival that of Egypt. As his chair touched the pavement, the lofty state doors of bronze swung open and he was bowed through by servitors in royal blue robes.

Within was a vast colonnaded hall lined on both sides with ranks of ebony-black Nubian guards, another Egyptian export, holding upright spears and dressed in leopard skins. Ahead, another great hall that ended in a broad stairway, all dimly lit with soft light that filtered down from clerestories above. There was chanting in the distance and the smell of incense and a half silence broken only by the burden-heavy steps of the slaves who followed him. Strolling by were slim-hipped men, dressed in tight-fitting short garments, who looked at him as curiously as he did at them. On the walls were frescoes of these same youths clutching the horns of charging bulls, dancing in the air above them. More paintings of odd fish and many-armed squid, as well as waving underwater plants—then flowers and birds. Women passed, as strangely attractive as the men, wearing many-colored skirts arranged in tiers, tiny hats perched high on their elaborately curled and combed hair, their bare breasts full and cupped out before them, nipples tinted blue. There were other women who were dressed for the hunt; the royal hunting preserve was well known, and they would be on their way there. They wore calf-high leather boots that were brightly painted, and short green skirts ending above the knee and held at the waist by a wide, bronze-studded leather belt. A supporting strap from each side of the belt crossed in the middle of the chest and passed over each shoulder. Since they wore no upper garments, this served to outline their bare breasts and draw attention to them. Inteb thought it slightly disgusting. Then there was sunlight again as they emerged into the roofless megaron at the heart of the palace.

Word of Inteb's arrival must just have reached King Atlas, who appeared to be holding court, seated on a high-backed alabaster throne against the far mural beyond the hearth. Clerks with clay tablets were being hurried from his presence while a prisoner in wooden fetters was being pushed out by his armored guards. Inteb drew back into the shadows until the disorder ceased, to make a proper entrance as befitted his rank and mission. The prisoner, naked except for a breechclout, was bruised and filthy with caked-on blood. One of his guards thumped him in the ribs with the pommel of his sword to move him faster, and the prisoner stumbled, then looked back over his shoulder to curse the man.

Inteb stood stunned and unmoving.

It was Ason, son of Perimedes, prince of Mycenae.

This time the guard hit harder and Ason slumped and was half dragged from the atrium.

4

"This is a very fine wine, my dear Inteb," King Atlas said, patting him on the arm at the same time, as though to assure him of the truth of the words he spoke, his fingers ringed and jeweled, fat and white and swollen like thick sausages. "It is from the fields on the south slopes behind Knossos. The skins are left in the ferment to provide that rich purple as well as the indescribable flavor. It must be thinned by water ten times, that is how strong it is."

The tall amphora, half as high as a man, was tilted so the wine would pour out slowly, not taking with it too much of the oil that floated on its surface to seal it from the air. A beaten golden bowl decorated with scenes of the capture of a wild bull was filled part way, then one of the serving slaves bent over it with a sponge to sop up the golden globules of olive oil. Only then was it placed on the low table beside Atlas who, as honor to his guest who sat at his right hand, poured the cool water into it himself and then filled a cup for Inteb, who sipped and nodded.

"A pleasure to drink, royal Atlas, and doubly pleasurable taken from your own hands."

"You shall have some for Pharaoh. Ten amphorae—no, twenty—a more significant number and one with greater power."

Atlas nodded, smiling, and sipped at his wine, pleased with himself. A great, quaking jelly mountain. As a young man, Inteb knew, he had been a bold sailor, taking his ship to the Golden Horn and into the Eastern Sea beyond, and up the river Danube that ran into it, further yet to the north where the trees grew high and close together and blocked out the sky. Where men fought with stones and were covered with fur and had tails like animals, or so it was said. If that bold warrior was hidden somewhere inside the present bulk, there was no sign of his existence. Rolls of doughy flesh, white as that of a drowned corpse, hung like wattles below his neck and drooped from his forearms. He was hairless as a shaven priest, lacking even eyebrows and eyelashes, and his eyes, almost hidden behind the swelling fat, were of a color between green and blue. His mouth smiled a lot, though his eyes never did. His lips drew back into red-painted bows, disclosing a dark mouth containing only a few browned stumps of teeth. As a final touch, as though the gods had shaped this man in some mysterious humor of their own, his cheek and one ear were colored an inflamed reddish purple, though luckily this was his left side, now facing away from Inteb. He must have surely been one of the bravest, when young, to have survived with these multiple marks of heavenly displeasure upon him. In Egypt, even though of noble birth, he would never have lived, but would have been cast adrift on the Nile soon after birth for the most sacred crocodiles to eliminate.

"Tell me of Egypt," Atlas said, looking slyly out of the corners of his eyes, then quickly away.

Inteb was sipping his wine, and he smacked his lips loudly afterward to show his pleasure. And thought quickly. Just because this man was as white-larded as a sacrificial swine did not mean that his thoughts were fatty too; he had ruled the sea empire for three decades. Few men had ever done that. He knew something, or he guessed something, which meant that truth would be the best concealment. Inteb was well versed in court intrigue and took pleasure in dipping into it once again after all the desert years.

"I do not have much to tell, royal Atlas; I have been traveling and have not seen my home for many months."

"Really? Very intriguing. You must tell me of these travels."

"They would bore you, for I was among barbarians much of the time."

"Tell me in any case, for there are pleasures and interests everywhere. Rough wines are good on the hunt, fresh-killed boar fine when roasted over a campfire.'' The cold eyes flicked sideways again. ''Young boys with sweet round bottoms good anywhere, hey? And big-bellied, big-breasted girls almost as good.''

Inteb had speared up a morsel of meat with his golden fork, dipped it into the savory sauce and was chewing on it. The truth, there was no way to avoid it.

''Most of the months were spent in rock-girt Mycenae on an errand for my Pharaoh.''

''Building their walls high to battle Atlantis, Inteb?''

He did know, Inteb thought, and has been leading me on.

''Surely not to fight Atlantis, great Atlas, who rules the seas and the shores wherever she wishes to venture. You can certainly have no interest in this miserable tribe on a sun-baked rock, who rear up walls only for battle with the other tribes and squabbling villages. But you know of this already. You must have the godlike eyes of Horus.''

''No, only spies who can be bought for goat droppings. You would be surprised of the word they bring me.''

''After the glories of this court, nothing could surprise me,'' Inteb said, bowing his head as he spoke. Atlas laughed and seized up an entire roast chicken, dripping with honey.

''Your Pharaoh is well served, Inteb. I wish I had men in this court who would do my bidding just as well.'' He tore the chicken in half with a single pull, then chewed while he talked, bits of meat falling from his lips, honey running down his chin. ''Perimedes can sting like a horse-fly. Your Pharaoh was wise to buy him off with great walls and gates that Mycenae's own slaves had to labor to build. His ships raid elsewhere now because of this.''

''But not in Atlantean waters?''

''Of course not—I did not say he was stupid. So I am not troubled by your labors in Mycenae. Though I surely hope you bathed well after leaving that cesspit. . . .''

38

"And anointed myself with sweet oils and burned the soiled clothing I used there before venturing to mighty Atlas' court."

They both laughed at this, and Inteb felt relieved—but still on his guard. The young Atlas who had been captain and warrior was still concealed inside the gross bulk beside him, the only sign of his presence the coldness of those tiny eyes. But now he wielded more weapons than simple force of arms; there was a smell of intrigue about the megaron of Atlantis that was faint, yet clearly detectable. The rich merchants and shipowners lolled at ease on the cushion-covered stone benches set against the walls of the room, beneath a colorful and realistic fresco of sportive dolphins. They bent forward casually to take a drink or a bite of food from the tables placed before them, calling aloud to each other. Yet they were never relaxed. Like lions resting after the hunt and the kill, they were still ready to spring up again at any instant. And all the time they talked, their eyes moved about so they would miss nothing, returning time and again to the bulk of Atlas on his throne against the wall, the center of concern for them all.

The head clerk from the archives was reading a list of royal receipts to the king, speaking loudly enough for all to hear. No court poet in rich Atlantis, but a clerk instead to chronicle the larder.

". . . and three ewers, six tripod cauldrons, and three wine jars, oil, barley, olives, figs, stores of wheat, livestock, wine and honey; all these gifts of the merchant, strong Mattis, just returned from a lengthy voyage."

The merchant referred to—*strong* must have meant his appetite, because he was round as a melon—stood and bowed towards the king, who raised his wine cup in salute. The list went on.

"Then six wine-mixing goblets, three boiling pans, one ladle, two fire tongs, eleven tables, five chairs, fifteen footstools. . . ."

It was endless, and Inteb paid no heed, although the others listened with half an ear, nodding when something out of the ordinary was mentioned. More food was brought to them in pretty dishes, the latest of many. First had been the flying things, tiny grilled birds just a mouthful each, as well as larger fowl, then meat from the chase. Now the ocean was giving up her bounty: blue-black mussels in their shells, squid in their own ink, tiny grilled fishes, great boiled ones. Fish was a great favorite in this sea kingdom—and almost as attractive as the women. The guests found their attention divided. Some Atlantean women dined here as well, their bare breasts a little sticky at times from the appreciative caresses of the diners. They were almost forgotten now as the seafood courses arrived.

While Inteb was looking at the diners, examining them, he realized suddenly that he was being watched in the same manner himself by the youth who sat to his right: Themis, Atlas' third son. Inteb smiled into his wine cup and felt himself already being enmeshed in the intrigues of this court.

Themis was a handsome youth and obviously knew it. Slim hipped and wide shouldered in the Atlantean tradition, he wore the tight, short wrappings about his loins that showed the muscles of his legs to their best advantage. His chest was bare, smooth and hairless, yet strongly muscled as well. Despite this proudly displayed strength there was a sensitivity to his face, the thin, arched nose and full lips, that showed he was less of the animal and more of his father's son. A hammered-gold band held back his straight, dark hair and disclosed a well-formed forehead. When he caught Inteb's eye, he raised his drinking beaker in greeting.

"You seem to be examining our court with critical eyes, lord Inteb. I imagine it must be far inferior to the fabled glories and wealth of Egypt that you are so used to?"

"I am more used to dung and rancid oil of late—but you misunderstood. That was admiration in my eyes, even wonder. Without speaking ill of Egypt I can still say that your city, this palace, are a miracle to behold. Your paintings almost shock my eyes. We like order in our art and feel secure and rested by the forms and decorations we know. But your painters drown me in a sea of birds, flowers, plants, animals, fish—there is no end to the variety. And there, those bull leapers, I feel they could spring down from the wall and turn cartwheels at my feet, or that great mottled bull might leap and gore me.''

"You have seen the bull dancers then?''

"Never. I hope to some day. You are a bull leaper yourself?''

"You can tell?'' Themis laughed and shrugged his shoulders so his muscles moved smoothly under his skin, well conscious of Inteb's admiring eyes upon him. "And more than that. I am the first boxer in this city.''

"I do not know of this; even the word is strange to me.''

"Then you must see this noble sport before you leave. Imagine, two warriors, stripped, with their bodies glowing with oil. They face each other, solid leather wrappings about their fists, strike and defend themselves from blows that would kill an ordinary man.'' Themis drank some wine, then picked up the conical beaker from the low table before him. "Do you know this game?'' he asked, shaking the beaker so that it rattled loudly, then upending it.

"We have it in Egypt, though perhaps the rules are different.''

Themis lifted the beaker to reveal the three dice.

"A six, a three and a two, not bad. The rules are simple enough. The highest number wins. The best you can get is an Aphrodite, three sixes, and the lowest is a dog, all the ones. Shall we play?''

Before Inteb could answer he became aware that King Atlas was addressing him, and he turned to him as quickly as any other would in that great room.

"Look, my dear Inteb, have you ever seen a more unwholesome sight than that?''

41

Inteb looked at the prisoner who stood before Atlas. Wooden shackles weighted his arms and legs; a guard stood on either side of him. Battered, filthy, bloody, naked, a ruin of a man. Ason, son of Perimedes, prince of Mycenae.

For the entire evening Inteb had been preparing himself for this. That single glimpse of Ason that he had had, unknown to Atlas, had warned him of what would surely come. He knew that Atlas would never resist the opportunity to parade this prisoner, whom Inteb would surely know, from the city he had left so recently. So Inteb's reaction was no sudden thing, but had been carefully considered and weighed. He looked Ason up and down, and his expression did not change in the slightest.

"It appears to be Ason, son of Perimedes. Is there any reason why a man of noble rank is being treated in this manner, great Atlas?"

Silence followed instantly as the smile oozed away from Atlas' lips and his face sank into cold and deadly lines. He stared at Inteb, his gaze as fixed as that of a poisonous serpent. Inteb looked back no less steadily. Atlas was Atlantis and ruled supremely—but Inteb was an Egyptian, sent in friendship by Pharaoh, and a reminder of this was not out of order. Egypt was at peace with both Atlantis and Mycenae and was above any differences they might have. Atlas seemed to realize this, too, because he did not speak at once. When he did the smile had returned ever so slightly. There was, however, nothing except cold hatred in his eyes.

"Noble? Noble cock on a mountain of stable sweepings perhaps, but nothing in the eyes of Atlantis, my little Egyptian. Yes, he is of that quarrelsome hill tribe that we talked about earlier. . . ."

"You—here!" Ason said in a cracked voice, recognizing Inteb for the first time. "Traitor. . . ." He tried to leap forward but was pulled back and forced to his knees by the

42

guards. Atlas rumbled with laughter, his bulk quivering with the strength of it.

"Do look, Inteb. The creature does not even understand what you say, that you attempt to take its side. That was very brave of you, Inteb, but you waste your bravery on something like this. Filth-ridden barbarians."

"As good as your get of pigs!" Ason shouted, coughing, writhing in the grip of the guards.

The room roared with laughter. This display was too funny for words, and even Inteb smiled slightly to show that he was as civilized as they were, enough to appreciate a good joke. Atlantis and Egypt, they were civilization, art and culture, completely different from the animal people outside their gates who scratched in the dirt for their food with pointed sticks and who were inferior in every way. Perhaps the rockpile of Mycenae was lord of the other rockpiles and dungheaps—but that meant nothing here. With every angry word from his mouth Ason proved them correct, and they laughed the louder, and Inteb had to smile as well.

"Kill. . . ." Ason spluttered.

"Kill swine as long as they are not armed or armored," Themis shouted, and they laughed anew.

"Good as any dog digging in the garbage heap," someone called out, and through the laughter Ason tried to turn to face his new tormentor, grating his teeth in frustrated anger.

"You. . .all of you. . .whoresons! With my sword, I'll kill. . . ."

"Sword?" Themis raised his eyebrows in mock astonishment. "We would give you a sword—but how would you hold it with your paws?"

The laughter was overwhelming now, and Ason tried to shout over it but his voice could not be heard, and the sight of his working mouth and blood-engorged face only sent them into greater paroxysms of pleasure.

It ended suddenly. One of the slaves, bearing a great glazed bowl of fish stew, passed down the row of diners. Ason, fettered and bound as he was, managed to get his legs under him and, as the slave passed, he sprang forward dragging his guards with him. The slave went down, the bowl struck and burst asunder, drenching Themis with its burning contents. Slave and guards tangled together, and from their midst Ason burst, falling across the low table, crushing it with his weight and reaching as far as he could to lock his fingers onto Themis' neck.

There was shocked silence for an instant—then shouts of outrage burst out. The two guards kicked the slave aside and seized Ason, clubbing at him, trying to pry his fingers from Themis' throat, where they were sunk deep into the flesh. Almost unconscious, Ason still gripped tighter, until a wildly swung sword pommel caught him in the temple, and he shook all over and was still. Then he was dragged face down out onto the floor and one of the guards held his short sword in both hands, blade down, and raised it high in the air to plunge the point down between Ason's shoulderblades.

"Wait," a hoarse voice said, and the blow stopped.

Themis stood up, rubbing at his throat while gobbets of fish fell from his stained clothing.

"He is not going to die that easily. He attacked me, so he is mine to kill. Am I right, father?"

Atlas drank his wine and dismissed the entire matter with a wave of his hand. The entertainment was over, and he had had his fill of the hill barbarian. Themis turned to Inteb, still shaking with fury.

"You asked about boxing. Tomorrow I will demonstrate this skill to you. In the open arena, in fair combat, I am going to beat this creature to death before your eyes."

5

Ason awoke to darkness, not knowing if it were night or day in the black hole where he had been imprisoned: not caring. The various aches in his body had now merged into one gigantic pain of outrageous proportions that seemed to be centered about his head. When he started to sit up the agony leapt upon him like a waiting animal, dropping him back to the unyielding stone floor. The next time he tried he was more careful. He now knew the pain as an enemy he would defeat. He ran his hands over his body and could find no new wounds, or rather none of any importance. Then, with utmost care, he touched his fingers to the throbbing pain in his temple, to the contused swelling there.

Now he could remember, the banquet, the taunting—the attack upon the most annoying of those buzzing insects. He smiled into the darkness. The head was well worth it; what a pleasure it had been to lock his fingers into that throat.

It was night. It must be night if he were imprisoned in the same place he had been before. The acrid reek of dung was in his nose. The same place, the bull pens. The lion of Mycenae trapped in the stables of the bull of Atlantis. But not dead yet. He dragged himself painfully across the floor to the trough of running water in the rear. It was cool and he buried his face in it, then his entire head, holding his breath as long as he could while it leeched away some of the pain. Then, a bit at a time, he managed to work himself up until he was sitting with his back against the cool stone wall.

He must have slept in this position, because more time passed, and when he opened his eyes again there was a ring of light about the great wooden door and he could hear the scraping of the bars being pulled back. There was time to close his eyes and shield them with his arm before the light lanced in as the door swung open. Heavy military sandals tramped in and he blinked up at the dim forms that stood over him. There was no point in resisting now, and he permitted himself to be hauled to his feet and to be dragged from the pen. Death was very close; he wondered vaguely why he was still alive after this length of time. But the pain in his head destroyed all capacity for thought and he went where he was led.

What happened next was most surprising. He had heard of the Atlantean baths—many stories were told of the wonders of this city. But this one at least proved to be true. Well guarded, with two armed men before and two after him, and one on each arm, he was taken to a lustrous chamber where light filtered in through clerestoried openings in the walls high above. A terra-cotta tub, higher at one end than the other, stood in an honored place in the center of the floor. An attendant came forward bowing and waving him towards the tub while the guards drew back to the entrance.

"Here, sir, if you please, use this step." He stripped Ason's loincloth off with practiced skill and held his arm while he climbed into the empty tub and sat down. The attendant clapped his hands sharply and a slave brought in an immense jar of water, freshly heated and steaming, and set it in the hole in the clay counter next to the tub. With a dipper the bath attendant poured water over Ason in soothing streams, his words coming as steadily as the water.

"Water, such perfect water. Atlantis is blessed with flowing springs that are guided close by through channels and pipes, a wonder to behold. Hot springs and cold, sir, which are blended here."

There was a sponge in a niche in the wall which he used to scrub Ason with, ever so gently, removing the dirt and clotted blood, then pouring more water over him as a rinse. The water cleansed Ason's wounds, and his aches were washed away along with the caked-on filth. He stood when he was instructed, climbed out to lie upon a cool slab of stone where the attendant poured scented oil onto his skin and hair and worked it in with supple fingers. The soreness was kneaded from his muscles while more oil was applied to the still-open cuts. Under this treatment, the worst of the pain had ebbed away by the time the man began to shave him with a sharp obsidian blade, and he was half asleep when someone else stamped into the chamber and stood over him. Ason opened his eyes to see a face of unsurpassed ugliness. The nose had been broken, apparently many times, one eye was almost closed by scar tissue, both ears torn away as well as part of the lower lip, so that the man's clamped teeth peeked through. His hair was gray and cropped short enough to reveal even more scars.

"Do you know about boxing?" the man asked in a harsh voice that exactly matched the face. Ason blinked, then shook his head *no*: he had no idea of what the man was talking about.

"No. I didn't think one of your kind would. Then you had better listen to old Aias and everything he says. Learn fast. If you don't make a good show out there, last awhile before you are killed, it will be my head as well. Do you hear me, stranger?"

Ason did not bother to answer this time but closed his eyes instead. A sudden agony of pain lanced through him and he sat up, pushing the attendant to the floor, clutching his side and expecting to see a gaping wound there. Nothing was visible except a reddening area of skin. Aias smiled down at him—an ugly sight with the hanging flap of lip—and clenched one great fist and held it out.

"That is boxing. Your first lesson. In boxing the hands are closed to make fists and with your fists you hit the other man. In the arena you will have the leathers around your fists to make them harder and to protect the knuckles, which break easily." His own were knobbed, scarred, and deformed. "There are many good places to hit a man, but I have no time to show them all to you. For you it will

47

be best to try for the middle of the body or the head. Now—stand and make a fist and hit me."

"Give me a sword and I'll hit you."

"No swords here, mountain man. This will be done the Atlantean way, and you will be killed with great style by Themis, who is a master of this sport."

His fist lashed out suddenly and caught Ason a light but painful blow on the point of his jaw, rocking back his head and sending the pain surging through it again. Roaring with anger, Ason jumped for the man, swinging a powerful blow that the boxer easily ducked.

"No, not like that; you're not hacking with a sword. Throw your fist as if you were throwing a spear. Better, better, but still not good enough. Don't leave yourself so exposed so that I can do *this*. Hurt, didn't it? Themis will do worse. I hear that you poured hot food on him and tried to throttle him. Themis is not a man to take an insult like that lightly. He will butcher you, mountain man."

Ason backed off, his fists still before him, still wary.

"Is that the man who wishes to fight me? Isn't he a son of Atlas?"

"He is. But also a mighty boxer, which is more important to you at this time. Do you wish to die out there like a quaking slave or like a man?"

"I wish to kill Themis. Show me more."

There was too much to learn—and no time to learn it in. The guards looked on and laughed while Ason pursued the squat form of the boxer about the chamber, flapping and swinging his arms like a crane's wings, getting little result for all his efforts other than an occasional lazy blow to his ribs. But the exercise had cleared his head, and when the boxer left he poured a jugful of water over his head, laughing when his guards cursed at the water slopping about their feet. He made no protests when he was once more dried and rubbed with oil. The attendant dressed him in a high-waisted, tight-fitting breechclout of layered leather, then strapped on boots of the same hard leather that reached up to midcalf. There were no manacles this time, but all the guards had their swords out when they led him from the chamber.

"Put up your swords," he said to them. "We have the same destination. I wish to meet your worm-infested prince in combat."

He meant what he said. He would have preferred to fight with bronze dagger or sword, even the war-ax these Atlanteans favored. But a weapon was just the means to the end; it was the battle he lusted after. There was no thought of defeat—or rather there was always the thought of death. It was not to be feared or welcomed, but was eternally there. You killed the man who fought you. If you wounded him deeply he would die in any case, so it was only right to finish the battle that had been started. When two men fought; one died. Sometimes both of them. The weapon was of no importance. The battle was.

For Ason the world was a simple place and his pleasures equally simple. He seized the opportunities that life presented just as they came, taking the same sharp pleasure from the hunt and spearing of a wild boar as from the possession and embrace of a woman. Both were over with quickly. He always had good friends to drink with, who would fight beside him. It was in battle that he found the greatest pleasure of all. Nor was there any shortage of conflict in the Argolid. Ason's earliest memories were of screaming men outside the walls, of wounded men, dead men, and of blood-drenched bronze swords. His first toy had been a small sword—and it was not a toy. He had not had it a day when he had chased and killed a shoat and brought its bedraggled body to his father in triumph. Soon there was larger and more dangerous game to pursue, and finally, after he had come of age, the most dangerous game of all. He had a spear, and he had poked it in under the lip of an Epidaurian helmet and through the man's eye. His only reaction had been surprise at how easily the man had died, far easier than some of the stag he had killed.

Women found him attractive, as did men. His blue eyes were clear, his skin unwrinkled. His brown hair and beard, when trimmed and combed as they were now, were very much the color of amber. If his nose was slightly large, it was no more a deformity than the beak of a hawk, which it did resemble. His teeth were white and sound; they could be little else on the simple Mycenaean diet. A jagged scar across his chin was one with its many fellows that lay a white tracery over his tanned body. In the past he had walked—and run—for a day and night, and had still been able to do battle at the end of that time. He had the muscles for it, smooth, tough muscles that moved easily under his skin, that were not knotted and protuberant like those of men well past their prime. That he was intelligent could not be doubted. In that he was like his father, Perimedes. But he used his wit only to enable him to fight better. He never thought to question at all why he was fighting. Some day he would have to, when Perimedes was dead and he was king of Mycenae, but as yet he had no reason to. Now there was another battle ahead, and he walked to it as easily as he had walked to any other conflict during his twenty-one years of life.

"Stand here," one of the guards ordered as they seized him by his arms. There was an arched opening ahead, through which he could see a large courtyard covered with sand. Then the scarred boxer came up carrying a large handful of leather straps.

At that same moment a far-off rumbling sounded, as if some monstrous animal stirred deep in the earth. It shook the ground beneath their feet. The walls moved, columns quivered, and bits of plaster twinkled down in dusty motes.

Ason jumped forward, towards the safety of the open air outside. Strong hands grabbed and pulled him back.

50

"Don't be frightened, mountain man, you're not dead yet." The guards laughed while Aias began to lace the leather straps around Ason's hands in a practiced manner. "Atlantis is too well built to fall down when Poseidon Earthshaker causes a little rumbling in the terrestrial guts. You'll live to fight Themis and he will kill you, so your moment of destiny is not quite yet."

Their obvious lack of fear relaxed Ason for the moment. He knew that many of these islands had quakes that threw the buildings down, even flows of molten rock that burst from the ground and buried them. These stirrings in the ground must not be rare if they thought so little of it. He watched while his fists were sealed in a casing of thin leather. Then a lead plate was fitted and bent into place over his fingers and knuckles, secured there with a broad band of thicker leather.

"It's called the hammer," Aias said as he put another strip of lead into place on the other fist. "Even with leather fists it takes some time to kill a man. This is when the hammer is used." Shrill horns sounded from outside and he hurried to finish the wrappings. "That's the signal. They want you now. Die well, mountain man. Many would consider it an honor to fall before the fists of a prince of Atlantis." He smiled a twisted grin as he said it.

Ason's hands hung heavily, as clumsy as dumb hooves. He looked at them and thudded them together. He would have preferred other weapons, but these would have to do.

"Out," one of the guards ordered, stepping forward and prodding Ason in the back with his sword.

Without turning, Ason swung one of his fists behind him into the man's middle. The guard gasped and folded over, his sword clattering onto the stone flags. Before the others could move, Ason walked forward, alone, into the arena.

The courtyard was immense. The palace surrounded it on three sides, while the fourth was cut off by a low wall with a drop of some kind beyond. A large stairway broke

51

the central wall, flanked by bright red wooden pillars that were wider at the top than on the bottom. More pillars framed the balconies and openings above, many of them adorned at the top with the gleaming golden double ax of Atlantis. A colorful crowd, both women and men, were at all the balcony and window openings, but Ason was only distantly aware of them. What he saw were the sword and ax men around the wall of the courtyard, near every doorway. And the man who stood alone on the sand.

Themis. Dressed just as Ason was, and shining with oil—with his fists hanging at his sides in swollen clubs. He started towards Ason, pacing slowly, and Ason went to meet him.

"I shall not talk to you, just kill you," Themis said and swung his fist.

Ason jumped backward, lessening the force of the blow so that it bounced from his shoulder. He swung his own fist in return, a mighty blow that would have killed a bull had it connected. But it whistled, harmless, in the air as Themis dodged it.

Then bright pain shot through Ason's side, and he sprawled helplessly back onto the sand. There was the distant roar of voices.

"Stand up," Themis said. "That was only the beginning."

Ason rose shakily and the slow butchery began.

Blow after terrible blow struck him, bruised him, shattered him. He could not hit the wavering form of Themis, nor could he reach him. Just once he fell forward and managed to clutch the other man, to strike a single heavy blow in his side, then he was hurled away and the hammering attack to head, arms, body, chest, went on. Ason had no way of measuring the time; it was long, just long, and still he swung ineffectually, and the clublike blows struck in return. Blood ran from his face into his eyes and was salty in his mouth. Blood covered most of his body, and the yellow sand stuck to it when he fell. Then a blow

52

struck him down, even harder than the others, hit in the middle of his body and paralyzed him so he could only lie there like a fish on the shore, gasping for air. Themis turned to the king and the crowd watching above.

"This is the sport," he shouted. "Every blow struck where it was intended and in the manner desired. But that is over. Now it is the time of the bone-breaker. I shall snap his bones as I wish, his arms and his ribs, and then I shall blind him and destroy his face and only then, when he knows what has been done to him, shall I kill him."

His final words were drowned in the sea of hoarse voices. Yes, they wanted to see this, see this skill and sport to remember it and talk about it in years to come. This was a very good day for them all.

All except one. Painfully Ason rolled over and pulled his knees under him, fighting the pain and shaking the blood from his face, and rubbing his eyes with his forearm so he could see. No way out. No way to bring this man down with him. This was not how he preferred to die, and this thought hurt more than all the blows.

Under his knees the ground shook, and he dropped forward onto his hands to steady himself. The voices roared even louder in his ears. Had he weakened that much?

When he saw a section of the great building tear loose and slide to the ground, he realized that the great sound was outside of him and that the world was shaking beneath them all.

This was no tremor. This was an earthquake of the kind that rocked cities and leveled them.

Still not comprehending completely, Ason blinked up at the shaking wall and crumbling columns. People were screaming in panic, some dropping into the courtyard, some falling heavily from the upper windows. Brass sheathing ripped and tore away, while pieces of stone cornice broke free. A massive length crashed into the sand near Ason, broken fragments biting into his skin.

It *was* happening. All hesitation vanished in that

instant, and he sprang forward, getting his clumsy fists under a carved length of stone as long as his forearm. With all his strength he heaved at it, muscles hard as the rock itself, lifting it into the air and over his head. Themis was coming towards him again, arm back to strike a killing blow.

But Ason struck first. Even the raised, padded fists could not stop the falling stone. Down it came, crushing into Themis' head, felling him in that instant, stretching him out silent and unmoving, with the jagged end of rock buried deep in his skull. But even as Ason turned to flee he heard his name bellowed above the thunder and screams, and looked up to see Atlas leaning from the balcony above.

"Kill him for me! Kill that Mycenaean!" he shouted, and a young noble in bronze armor sprang from the box, falling heavily to the sand with the weight of all his metal. He stood, drawing his sword, starting towards Ason. Two of the warriors in the arena were also running towards him—the others were lost in the mob—and Ason did the only thing he could do. He turned and fled.

The dark opening of a doorway was before him, and Ason fell through it. Clouds of dust made it difficult to see; he stumbled over the fallen debris on the floor. Around him the palace groaned like a living thing. There were sharp cracks as the heavy beams built into the stone structure bent and snapped. Rubble filled the stairwell ahead, so he turned and with his clubbed hands followed a wall that led to a larger room full of wreckage but clearly lit by the sunlight that poured in through the fallen ceiling above. He circled the mound, climbing the wreckage, looking for an exit. There was none. There was a harsh cry as the first of his pursuers appeared in the doorway, blocking his escape.

Bronze helm with high, blue, horsehair plume. Bronze shoulder guards and breastplate over heavy leather, a leather kirtle and bronze greaves on his lower legs. And a heavy, glinting, sharpened and deadly bronze sword raised high to cut him down.

Bloodstained, near naked, Ason ran to attack.

The warrior stood waiting, coldly, then brought the sword down in a sharp cut that would catch Ason at the base of the neck, half decapitate him, kill him.

Ason raised his bare left arm, as though to ward off this unstoppable blow that had all the other's weight behind it.

The sword struck his fist.

At the same instant, Ason's right fist swung around in a hammer blow that caught the man on the side of his head, below the helm, felling him like an ox. He moved, tried to stand, and Ason struck again and again with his right hand—his left arm now hanging limp and dead—striking the same spot on the helm, bending and denting the solid bronze until the man lay still.

He scrabbled at the fallen sword with his gloved hand, but could not pick it up. He was tearing at the leather and laces with his teeth when the other two men appeared in the doorway. Ason backed away slowly as they came after him, one slightly behind the other. There would be no escape this time. With a sword he would have fought them, but not fist against swords. They came on.

The second man shouted aloud in pain, writhed and fell, and Ason saw that someone was bent over him, pulling a dagger from the man's back. At this the first Atlantean turned, uncertain, and Ason hurled himself upon him, driving him down by the weight of his body, beating at him with his right fist. The man roared and struggled to pull away, to free his sword, and managed to writhe clear. Raising his sword arm in just the right manner to allow the already reddened dagger to slip up through his side, between his ribs and into his heart. Ason rolled over, still ready to fight, to look up at the Egyptian.

"Inteb!"

"We have to get out before all Atlantis falls about our heads."

"Cut these damn things from my hands first so I won't have to bear them to the grave with me."

Inteb did not pause to argue. His dagger was well tempered and razor edged, slipping easily through the bindings on Ason's right hand. The leather fell away, and Ason stretched his numbed fingers before reaching over and seizing the wrist of his dangling left arm. While he had been fighting for his life he had forgotten this arm. It felt as though it had been split down to his wrist. Which it might have been. The sword had hacked through the glove, and Inteb cut the few remaining strands of leather and pulled them away.

The hand was swollen and inflamed—but uncut. Inteb held out the lead plate, which was deeply scored but not chopped through. This and the thick leather had stopped the sword before it reached Ason's hand. Ason worked the fingers back and forth, ignoring the pain this produced, but could find no broken bones.

A greater tremor shook the building. They heard the tumble of falling masonry and thin screams in the distance. More of the ceiling tiles fell in on the far side of the room. Inteb quickly wiped his hand and the bloody dagger on the tunic of a dead Atlantean, then pointed to the mound of rubble.

"We might be safer climbing out here instead of trying to get out through the building, the way we came."

"Help me to get this armor off first," Ason said, pulling at the thongs that held the dead man's greaves in place.

"We don't have the time. . . ."

"This is full armor, the best. No one will stop us when I am wearing it."

There was truth in this—and Inteb knew that arguments would avail him nothing. So there, in the center of the

56

toppling palace, they stripped the corpses and Ason put on his armor.

"Here, take this other sword," Ason said. "And the man's helmet. Quick."

"What good to me? I'm no warrior type."

"You killed these two."

"From behind. Cowardice. I have no knowledge of these things. I've never killed anybody before."

"Yet you followed me here, fought beside me, saved me."

"I didn't mean to. It's just that. . .I didn't plan anything. Sitting there and watching Themis batter you to death. . . . When you killed him, instead, and these men went after you, I went after them."

"Why, why?"

Inteb smiled at that. "Why? Because I respect you, Ason. You are a fellow prince. You in your realm, and I in mine."

They climbed the mound of stone and plaster at its highest spot. Inteb succeeded in bracing himself against a fallen beam while Ason clambered on his shoulders and clumsily, one handed, pulled himself through the opening. With his good hand he easily pulled Inteb up after him. Around them was the ruined palace, walls still collapsing as the quakes continued. A hot wind blew through the skeletal ruins, while pieces of ash fell from the sky, burning their bare skins.

"I have an Egyptian ship here," Inteb said. "If we can reach it we are safe."

"Show me the way."

They were the only living things in the ruins. The Atlanteans had fled, though an arm sticking from the rubble and the occasional crushed body were evidence that not all had escaped. They scrambled through the broken remains of the palace, avoiding the gaping holes that dropped to lower stories, and finally reached the now deserted courtyard. Steps led down from it to a lower garden where red columns and stylized bull horns lay fallen among the flowers and trees. From this terraced garden, atop the hill of the acropolis, all of the island of Thera could be seen below them. Stretching down the hill were the ornate buildings and temples—now mostly fallen in a jumble of ruins—with smaller buildings below. Then the ring of water of the inner harbor where ships were pulling from the shore, coming together in the mouth of the canal that led through the ringlike island to the wider outer harbor. At this distance little damage could be seen there, though there was the same jamming of vessels into the canal that led to the open sea.

From the far northern slopes of the island there rose up a white cloud, a climbing mountain of smoke that was already drifting overhead and dimming the sun. It billowed and rose, higher and wider all the time, brightened with rapid flashes of lightning. Thicker, evil-looking black smoke boiled about the base, bursting with explosions that sent arcing streamers of white out in all directions. One of these smoke trails shot towards the acropolis with powerful speed. The black dot at its tip, a gigantic boulder, grew to huge size in an instant before crashing down to blast into more rubble the already shaken ruins of the buildings. Horrified survivors ran down the hillside. Below them harbor waters were seething with fallen pumice.

There were other people here, in the dockside ruins of the town, dead in the streets, or digging out from their collapsed houses. Through the crooked nightmare streets of chaos the two men ran, headed always towards the waterfront and safety. Others were also fleeing in that direction, and at times they had to struggle through the jam of people in the narrow alleyways.

The docks themselves were empty of life. All the ships and boats had gone, and the people who had not sailed were fleeing across the bridges to the doubtful safety of the outer part of the island.

"We came this way," Inteb shouted. "My ship is moor-

58

ed on the other side of those buildings.''

One of the large buildings had fallen and completely blocked the main thoroughfare, and they had to detour around it, climbing carefully through the tottering ruins of smaller structures. A small elephant lay crushed by a fallen wall, almost dead, just the tip of its trunk moving helplessly from side to side. Then they were back at the water's edge by the collapsed ruin of the great ceremonial mooring. The roof had fallen in, and the gilded bull's horns drooped like lowered spears into the water.

The mooring was empty. The Egyptian ship was gone.

6

"There!" Inteb shouted "I see it going into the tunnel, out to sea, the last ship.''

It was low in the water, loaded heavily with passengers, and a sheen of armor was visible on the stern deck. The captain had fled without Inteb—or had been forced to leave at sword's point. It did not matter which. Ason pointed.

"To the bridge, then. We'll have to follow the others.''

Inteb raised his fists in impotent fury as the stern of his ship vanished into the covered canal, then he turned to follow Ason. They stayed along the shore, which was relatively clear of rubble, lowering their heads and shielding their faces against a sudden fall of hot particles of ash. The wind was blowing more strongly now and they leaned into it. There were moans of pain and shrill cries for help from a dock they passed, but they ignored these as they had all the others they had heard since leaving the palace. But one of the voices rose above the others and Ason stopped suddenly.

"Mycenaean—I call to another Mycenaean!"

Ason stumbled out onto the wooden dock towards the wreckage of a long, narrow galley. It was half underwater and had been abandoned. The galley slaves, clamped to their benches, had been left to die. It was one of these who had called to Ason, who stood on the dock above, looking down at the man.

"You are Tydeus, son of Agelaos. We have fought together."

Tydeus looked up, filthy and naked, the water almost to his waist. He had to shout to be heard above the wail of the other slaves, who were howling at Ason in a half-dozen tongues.

"I was taken at Asine, as you were, and prisoned here since. A wooden clamp is upon my right ankle; your sword can cut it."

Ason drew his sword, but Inteb pulled him by the arm and he stopped, angry. He could not leave a Mycenaean here to die. But Inteb was interested in more than a single life.

"This galley is only half foundered. If it can be bailed out we have a ship."

"Little chance of that," Tydeus said. "We were loaded, heavy, ready to leave, when great boulders fell from the sky. The biggest struck near the stern there, right through the bottom. They panicked and fled. Left us here." He laughed humorlessly. "The overseer was the last one off, tried to get by me. I grabbed his leg, pulled him back. We choked him and passed him along to stuff into the hole. Not much of a man alive, not a very good plug dead."

Inteb looked at the body that was submerged up to its shoulders. The man's head bobbed as small waves rocked the galley, mouth wide open and eyes still staring with horror.

"He appears to be a fat man," Inteb said.

"A pig," the nearest rower said.

"Then he will close the hole well, even better when he starts swelling up. And we can push cloth in around him for a better seal."

Word had passed in quick whispers and now all the slaves were silent, staring at Inteb, awaiting his word.

"That seems to have stopped the sinking. I'll take care of the plugging, the rest of you start bailing. We may have a ship that can get us away from here, at least to Anafi or Ios, the nearest islands. Shall we, Ason?"

"Of course. There'll be no other ships for us." Ason jumped into the galley and let Tydeus guide his sword to the shackle that held his ankle.

No time was wasted now in freeing the other rowers. They bailed with their hands where they sat. Tydeus ran to the ruins of the nearest buildings and returned with buckets, clay pots, anything that would hold water. He brought flaxen sailcloth, as well, from a looted ship's chandler; Inteb cut it into lengths with his dagger. He wadded the rags and pushed them into place around the corpse. It bobbed and gaped sightlessly at the hurried activity until finally it fell over as the galley was bailed out. Some of the galley slaves were dead; those in the prow had been drowned when it had gone under, and one in the waist had been brained by a falling stone. The surviving slaves ignored them and bailed frantically, hunched over beneath the fury that exploded in the sky above. The air was thick with dust and almost unbreathable. With painful slowness the galley rose in the water while the hot wind sent it banging into the dock.

"Enough," Inteb finally said. "Some can keep bailing. All the others must row now while we are still in smooth water."

Ason hacked the bow line with his sword, then ran back the length of the ship, between the slaves who were unshipping their oars, to cut the one at the stern. The figure of a man loomed suddenly above him and Ason raised his sword until he saw the other was unarmed. His face and head were caked with dried blood. Ason slashed at the line.

"There is room for one more aboard your ship, mountain man.

It was Aias, the boxer. Ason slashed with his sword but the man jumped nimbly back.

"Stay and die, Atlantean, we don't need you."

"No Atlantean, but a slave from Byblos. Used as a punching sack by the nobility. I see dead men aboard. Let me take one's place and row with you."

The line fell free and the galley began to move out.

"Come, mountain man, I did you no harm other than to tie your leathers and show you how to box. The palace fell on me and I was left for dead, but my head is too hard for that."

As Ason turned away and the oars dug in, Aias leaped and fell sprawling on the foredeck. He grinned up out of the red mask of his face as Ason spun about.

"Kill me if you wish. I would be just as dead if I stayed on shore."

"Take an oar," Ason said, dropping his sword into its slings. Aias laughed hoarsely and seized the nearest corpse, hurling it from the rowing bench to the deck, using it as a footrest as he slid the oar into its socket.

They were the last ship to leave. The sky was dark as dusk now, the hot wind sending waves before it across the water so that the rowers had to bend all their strength to their oars to move the galley against it. Only when they reached the canal was the force of the tempest cut off. The galley moved quickly through its dark length, while falling rock crashed and rumbled on the wooden covering above their heads. Then they were through and out into the choppy waves of the outer harbor.

It was like the aftermath of a naval battle. On the far shore three ships had been beached, half sunk, holed by falling rock. One had been careened already and men were working desperately on repairs. A mast projecting above the surface showed that at least one other had not been so lucky. Further on, the last ships, at least half a dozen, were jammed into the entrance tunnel of the canal. Oars crashed together and were broken as they fought to reach safety.

"Slow the beat," Ason called out when he saw what was happening, and Tydeus, who had taken the dead overseer's position at the drum, dropped the count.

They could do nothing until the ships had struggled free of each other and opened the way for them. And with every passing moment the volcanic eruption and earthquake worsened. Stones of all sizes were falling almost continuously now and the water foamed with their impact. Still worse was the hot ash now darkening the sun and falling in suffocating clouds. It coated the decks and formed thick mud in the bilges, making it almost impossible to catch a breath. Heavy sulphur fumes rode with it, and the men coughed and spat as they breathed it in.

"Look!" someone shouted, and they turned to see a fat-bellied merchant ship destroyed in an instant. It had pushed its way forward by weight alone and was at the mouth of the tunnel when the rock descended, half the size of the ship itself. In that brief moment, as the unstoppable mass struck the ship and plunged into the water, it was turned into broken fragments that vanished from sight in the maelstrom the rock's fall had caused. A black wave of water surged out, crushing the nearest ships, bearing swiftly down on the galley. They were thrown up and up to its summit then down into the trough as it passed at rushing speed. Water poured over the sides. Then they were level again, bailing frantically.

There were no longer any ships blocking the tunnel. Wreckage and half-foundered ships bobbed and scraped against the rock wall. A single ship, low in the water, limped into the tunnel and was gone. The galley went after it, pushing through the wreckage and the cries of drowning men. One man swam to the galley and clung to an oar, reaching up to the gunwale, holding on. The nearest tower, still clamped in his footstock bent double and sank his teeth into the fingers, ground down hard until they vanished. Then they were into the tunnel and darkness closed around them.

"The tunnel's blocked, fallen in!" a man shouted, and Ason called out even more loudly above the panic-stricken voices.

"No—I can see the other end. It's the sky that is dark, but the tunnel is still there."

They went even slower, feeling their way when the oar tips brushed the rock walls. Then a gust of mephitic air laden with ash blew over them, and they knew they were almost through. Finally the canal opened out ahead, and beyond that the safety of the open sea.

The men at the oars did not seem to mind what was happening now, and Ason took no notice of the banks on each side, but to Inteb this was in many ways the most terrible part of a nightmare journey. For there were people there, whole families, lining the banks. They had come running from the farms and the villages seeking some escape. Their wailing was louder than the thunder in the clouds above as they reached out their hands, clutching towards the ship sailing by so closely, so unreachable. While all the time the volcanic ash fell in silent torrents from the sky until each of them, man, woman, child, was coated with it, until they were all the same: dusty, yellow figures transformed into living statues. Mothers held their children out to be taken; the ship continued on by. The other Atlantean ship was ahead of them in the canal, and there were wails as it, too, passed them by. Some people hurled themselves into the water to reach it, but few could swim. Only one man was afloat when the galley reached him, but an oar struck him full in the face and he vanished from sight.

On and on they went, between the endless rows of staring, yellowed figures, some still shrieking, others struck dumb with despair, and Inteb tried not to see them, longing for the escape of the dark cleft in the hills ahead. Waves were surging and splashing against the rock walls here, while the ocean beyond would be even rougher.

"Stop the oars," Ason ordered. "Step the mast and break out the sail."

They did it quickly. The sail was not a large one, meant more to aid the rowers than to move the ship by itself, but it would be vital in the open sea. As soon as it was rigged, the beat started again, and they sailed from the rift into the sea and away from Thera.

Into a growing storm. There was rain now mixed with the volcano ash; the sky wept thick mud upon them. The wind increased and they had a fierce struggle with the mud-coated sail, taking in two reefs to keep it from blowing away. Behind them Thera belched out ash and stone and thundered at their escape.

"The wind is wrong," Ason said, hammering his fist on the rail. "From the north. It will wreck us on Crete if we are not careful, and we'll all be dead or back in Atlantean hands." He squinted at the sky and at the dimly visible disc of the sun. "It will help if we sail northwest, or even west. But we'll have to row as well."

By sunset the wind had not lessened; if anything it had increased. Half the men rowed while the others slept, sprawled in the mud. The ship had been well provisioned and nothing had been touched when the crew and passengers had fled. They drank water, pouring it down their dry throats, ate bread, cheese and dark green olives. Ason collapsed on the cot in the tiny cabin and lay, unmoving and exhausted, while Inteb rubbed sweet oil into his cuts and bruises. Now exhaustion and pain overwhelmed him; his left hand was swollen like a melon, the fingers like sausages. He cradled it against his chest and dropped instantly into the black well of sleep.

He awoke to darkness and the frantic movement of the

65

ship; the creaking of the timbers around him and the howl of the wind outside. A hand was on his shoulder and Inteb spoke, shouting to be heard.

"We are close to shore. The breakers, we can hear them on the rocks. The rowers are exhausted, I don't know how much longer we can keep on."

Ason shook his head, trying to drive away the dulling pain and fogginess, then staggered to his feet and felt along the wooden ribs for the amphorae lashed there. His fingers found the silver cup tied by a thin chain to the handle of one of the tall containers. He plunged it in and drank deep. It was wine, not water, but he drained the cup twice and felt the better for it.

On deck the wind struck like a hammer. The rain seemed to have stopped, but the wind was stronger, tearing off the tops of the waves and sending the scud flying before it. Nothing could be seen in the enshrouding darkness, but between gusts a distant booming could be heard off to port.

"It seems to be louder now," Inteb called out.

"Is the sail still holding?" Ason asked.

"We had to lower it before it blew away."

"Raise it again. Oars alone will never hold us off that shore."

One man was lost overboard when they raised the sail; there was a single wail as the wind caught him and hurled him into the ocean, then nothing more. That is how close the end was for all of them, just the strength of their arms and the thin wooden hull of the ship keeping them from the hungry sea. A single reef was all that could be let out of the sail, but it helped. This and the labors of the oarsmen kept them off the unseen shore.

The night was endless. The men rowed to the point of complete exhaustion, then rowed still more. When there was no strength left in their arms to pull the heavy oars, they bailed until they were able to row again.

Dawn came upon them unaware. Because of the layers

of clouds, there was no color in the sky, just a growing awareness that forms could be dimly seen. Then, in shades of gray, the water-logged galley appeared to view with the men slumped over their oars. Far fewer than had been there at sunset the night before. Tydeus stood solidly at the steering sweep, where he had been all night. Aias looked up from his oar and grinned his hideous gap-lipped smile at Ason. For all his years, he was one of the few men still rowing, slowly but steadily.

Off to port, no more than 20 stadia away, the dark bulk of Crete rose out of the sea. Behind them it was black and jagged and still topped at the horizon, but ahead it seemed to be cut off abruptly. Inteb looked up from bailing when Ason called to him, pointing off the port bow. Inteb blinked to focus his red-rimmed, totally exhausted eyes.

"There, is that the eastern tip of the island?"

Inteb joined him on the deck, trying to make out details in the half light.

"It's hard to tell. It might just be a headland. We'll know soon enough."

"Once we clear it we will have sea room and we can run before the wind if we must. No chance of being wrecked on that shore then."

Even as he spoke there was a sharp crack, and the line that raised the sail and acted as a backstay broke and snapped loudly over their heads. It had borne the increasing pressure of the wind all night against the sail. It had finally been too much. Without this support the mast bent dangerously, pulled over by the bellying sail.

It happened in an instant, and there was a stunned moment before the exhausted men could react. Ason was the first. He pulled his sword and ran for the bar-tight lines that secured the foot of the sail. Before he could reach them there was a splintering crash as the mast snapped like a dead stick and began to fall.

Ason hurled himself aside and the mast crashed past

67

while the sail buried him in its folds. By the time he fought free it was all over.

The mast, though still attached by the lines, plunged over the side of the ship, pulled by the weight of the sail, splintering the rail and crushing one rower as it went. Now, with the sail gone and the rowing stopped, the wind was carrying them down towards the rocky flank of Crete where the spray from tall waves could already be seen leaping high into the air.

7

Once more, from the depths of their strained bodies, they had to find the energy to seize the blood-stained handles of the oars. To row again. The wind was driving them towards the rocks, and now they could no longer count upon the sail for any aid. They rowed. The dead weight of the mast and sail in the water slowed their progress—but also made it more difficult for the wind to drive them ashore. They left it all there, hanging clumsily over the side, and bent to their oars.

They rowed. Heads down, pulling, not stopping, rowing for survival. They were moving slowly along the shore—yet it was rushing closer towards them all the time. Details could be seen: rocks standing out in the surging surf, trees overhanging the edge high above. They rowed. One, then another, falling from exhaustion, unconscious, only to awake and seize the hated oar again. The headland reached far out into the sea, a gray arm waiting to seize them, and the final few minutes were the worst. They were actually in the surge of breakers from the rocks, white foam all about them, when they struggled by.

Ahead was the open sea, with the island of Crete cutting sharply away from them in an immense bight, curving out to a distant, smaller headlead. They could weather that one easily.

"Cease rowing," Ason called out, his voice cracking with the dryness of it, too weary to rise and get a drink.

"And now, mountain man?" Aias asked from the seat opposite, where he leaned on his oar. "We are both a long way from home."

"Now?" Ason stood and stretched his aching muscles. "Now we drift. Unless you can think of something better."

Aias shrugged and looked at his palms. Even his leathery hands were blistered and bleeding after the night of effort. "I've had enough rowing for awhile, I'll say that much." He leaned over the sides and let his hands drop wearily into the water.

They ate on the rear deck, mixing the wine with water, then drinking it greedily. Someone had brought up a pithos of olives, which they dipped into and ate by the handful, and there was a wheel of hard cheese that they tore chunks from and chewed. Basic fare, no more and no less than they were accustomed to. They ate greedily. Even Inteb had his share, his hunger masking for the moment the pain of his flayed palms. Tydeus was relieved at the steering sweep and he dropped down beside them on the deck, sprawling as exhaustedly as the others.

"You are the seaman, Tydeus," Ason said. "Your father, Agelaos, had a great ship; you must have sailed on it?" Tydeus nodded, his mouth filled with cheese. "What is our course—and what do we do next?"

Tydeus squinted at the sky and the receding shore.

"We don't return to Mycenae this way," he said.

"That I was sure of. What lies in this direction?"

"Deep water, monsters that eat ships, nothing."

"There is always something. We can't even row to Crete to surrender—if we should want to—we are well past the island. What other islands lie in this direction?"

"None."

The word was coldly said and drew a responsive shiver from the circle of listening men. To sail a ship meant to sail along a coast or, as in the closely spaced Cyclades, to sail from island to island. One island was always in sight ahead before the last one dropped astern. At night, or in case of storms, the ship could be pulled ashore on some beach. What else could be done? The ocean was a vast waste, more empty of landmarks than the emptiest desert. If you sailed out upon it how could you return? A man could tell directions from the sun—but what happened on cloudy days? To leave the security of a shoreline was madness. And now they were leaving Crete behind, the undying wind forcing them away from its shores. If a man were to look ahead he would see nothing except heaving water, nothing at all.

"Then we are lost," a rower said. "And will die out here."

"The wind will die first and we can return."

"And if it does not?"

"A moment," Inteb said, and their voices stilled. He took out his dagger and knelt, drawing on the wooden deck with its point.

"I am no ship's captain, but I do know about the parts of this world. I am learned in mathematics and geography. I am also an Egyptian, and I sailed from Egypt, and I will show you how it was done. We sailed along this shore here, in a line like this. Past cities and islands until we reached the Argolid and the port of Tiryns here." He had scribed a half loop upon the deck, a half circle, and now he pricked the boards at the center of the loop.

"From Tiryns we sailed to Thera, and now we have passed Crete and are going in this direction, into the emptiness of the sea." They watched in silence as he slid the blade further on until it touched the spot where he had started.

"There you see it, Egypt and the Nile, Thebes. They are all there, somewhere on the far side of the water, in that

70

direction." They followed the direction of his pointing knife, saw nothing, and turned back to him with widened eyes.

"But—how far?" someone asked. Inteb shrugged.

"Forty skene, eighty skene. I don't know. But if we continued south far enough we shall come to that shore. And it seems we have very little choice in the matter. We cannot return, even to Crete and the Atlanteans, not against this wind. Crete will soon be out of sight—and then what do we do? Ride before the storm, that is all, and instead of praying for the wind to die pray that it blows until we reach the African shore."

There was nothing else they could do. The sea was rough and the storm continued with frequent heavy rain squalls passing over them. But the sail and broken mast acted as a sea anchor in the water so that they rode easily before the wind. Ason stayed awake with a few others, to steer and bail, while the others slept where they dropped. The day passed, and the night, until by dawn of the second day the wind had fallen and the seas died down. Ason was still awake, leaning on the steering sweep, when the sky lightened in the east. Stars appeared through rifts in the scudding clouds. Inteb came on deck a few minutes later, blinking at the strange red light that lit the sky and bathed everything in a bloody glow.

"What is it?" he asked. Ason shook his head.

"Sunrise. But I have seen nothing like it before."

In the growing dawn the entire sky was aflame. Not only in the east where the orange globe of the sun was rising above the horizon, but wherever its rays struck. The disappearing clouds were on fire, burning and vanishing in their own combustion. They all watched silently, and only when the sun was higher in the sky did the consuming display lessen and disappear.

"I have seen something like that once, in the desert," Inteb said. "It was during a sandstorm and the sun was as red as that coming through the clouds of sand. Perhaps the

71

dust thrown up by Thera. But so much, impossible to believe.''

"I believe what the gods will, they will. It is their sky.'' Ason drooped tiredly, half supported by the sweep, the phenomena in the sky forgotten in his weariness. Inteb looked at him, concerned.

"How is your hand—and the wounds?'' he asked. Ason flexed the fingers of his left hand. The skin was purple and black, but the swelling had died down.

"Better, everything better. The cuts have caked in their own blood the way they should, and even my head does not bother me this morning. There are other things to think about. No wind.''

"We can begin rowing then.''

"In which direction?'' Ason asked.

"That is for you to decide. There are still light airs from the north. If we return we must row against them all the way. Towards Crete. While ahead lies Africa.''

"How far?''

"I can only guess, no one knows. Further, closer, who can say? A decision will have to be made.''

"I have already decided. We go south.''

With the sun to port they began the long row.

The tangled mass of sail and mast was cut away and drifted astern. Watches were assigned and an inventory of their supplies begun. If the men had any doubt about the wisdom of this decision to go on they kept it to themselves. Half of them were slaves and the sons of slaves, capable only of taking orders, knowing nothing else. The rest were fighting men, warriors from all the cities and countries that bordered on the sea empire of Atlantis. Men from the Argolid, Mycenae, Tiryns, Asine, from the far islands of Ikaria and Samos, and even more distant Byblos and Tyre. They spoke different tongues and were of different races, alike only in one thing: Each of them had fought Atlantis and been defeated, captured and enslaved, shackled to this galley. Destined to labor hard on poor food for a few years until they sickened and died and were cast overboard. Ason had freed them from this and saved them from destruction on the exploding Thera. In doing this he became their leader and, being simple men, they would simply follow where he led. Spitting on their palms, they bent to their oars.

Inteb sat in the open doorway of the cabin and scratched marks onto a fragment of broken pottery, recording his inventory of the ship's supplies. Sitting here he could also keep track of the galley's course, marking how the shadows fell across the deck outside, telling him both the time of day and the direction of their sailing. When they ventured too far to the east or west he would call out instructions to the steersman to point them south again. Ason had slept well and now sat inside with his bronze sword and a whetstone, working out the nicks and putting a better edge to it. A cup of wine mixed with honey sat nearby, as well as some raisins.

"Raisins," Inteb said, ticking off his list. "Barley meal and cheese, olives, olive oil, and some dried fish with the worm in it. We won't starve. Wine and water, though some of the water is beginning to stink already. There are ship's supplies: thread, cloth and needles to mend the sail we no longer have, tar for caulking and wood for repairs. But there is nothing we can do with them until we reach a shore. The overseer has swollen nicely and is still making a fair plug, though he is beginning to smell more than the water, and no one will sit near him when they row. Some chests that belonged to the bronzesmiths who had deserted, and to the captain."

"What's in them?"

"The chalcei's tools for working bronze, the usual thing. Some jewelry, a lot of clothes, then a chest with a seal that I broke. It has three swords and four daggers in it, part of their stock in trade. Nothing else of real importance."

Ason looked into his cup. "How much wine and

water?" he asked.

"We won't be thirsty for awhile yet."

"How long?"

"If we are careful ten, maybe twelve days. But the fish will have eaten away the overseer and we'll have sunk by then."

"You are in a cheerful mood today, Inteb. Will we reach land before that happens?"

"Hawk-billed Horus may know, or your gods who watch from Olympus—but how can I tell? The sea may be too wide to cross, we may go in circles forever, a storm may come and swamp us. Could I have some of that wine? I feel a need for it."

Ason handed over a silver cupful and Inteb buried his nose in it, drinking deeply, hoping the strong fumes would burn the thoughts of death from his brain. He stared into its depths, seeking some omen there, then drank again. Ason looked up at him, aware of the sudden sadness.

"Do you feel the end so close? Yet you were the one who told us how we could go on."

"To speak of a decision in the abstract is one thing, to do it is another matter. When I am asked to build a wall or a tomb I draw a plan. I do not have to build the thing myself. I may even turn my design over to another builder and go away. He will see that it is built. I do not have to be personally involved with what I design. So to design a voyage that has never been done before is one thing, I am very good at that. To take the voyage is something completely different."

"That is a new way of looking at things."

"Different from yours, strong-thewed Ason. To you, I imagine, the thought and the deed are one; the thought of the battle begins with the battle."

"You begin to sound like my father."

"Perimedes leads the Argolid, as well as Mycenae, because he thinks of more than just the battle. He thinks of alliances and high walls and bronze for the swords men must fight with." Sudden memory struck Inteb, and he looked up. "Your father's brother, Lycos, I heard of him before I left the city. He is dead."

"How could you know? He was far away—I cannot tell you where."

Inteb glanced out at the deck, then shouted a course change to the steersman before he answered, wondering how much of the truth he should tell.

"You have known me for three years, Ason. Do you call me friend and think of me as a friend of Mycenae?"

"Yes, I suppose I do. But you were in Atlantis. . . ."

"Sent by Pharaoh, on his mission. I told them nothing of my work in your city."

"I believe you. My belief is strengthened by the two men you killed to aid me. But why are you asking this now?"

"Because I know far more about your city than you may realize I do. The megaron of your father covers all Mycenae. People gossip and talk; nothing is secret long. I know there is a mine on a distant island in the cold sea and that all of your tin comes from there. Your uncle Lycos was killed there and the mine destroyed. Perimedes did not take the loss lightly."

"No, he would not. My father is a maker of mighty plans. His holy bronze is a big part of them. Poor Lycos, what a cold and wet place to die. I sailed with him, when he went back there, but I returned on the ship with the tin. He stayed on, swearing no one could root the tin from the earth as he could, but it looked simple enough. There were others to do the work. Did many die with him?"

"All. Your cousin Phoros returned with the word."

"Old Koza, he showed me how to use the sword. Mirisati, we were friends. They should be avenged, ten to one at least, put the whole island to the sword." Ason thought deeply about it, forgetting even the wine while the shadows lengthened.

They rowed all that day and into the early evening when the stars came out. Inteb pointed out the guide stars to the steersman and told him to keep them always behind him, but the sky clouded over soon after and they had to take in the oars. Then, except for the man on watch, they slept, and were awakened at dawn by heavy seas and rain. This storm lasted for two days, and it was all they could do to stay before the wind, bail out the galley and keep it from foundering. On the third day the storm blew itself out, but the seas were still high and the sky clouded over. A feeling of despair, as dark as the clouds above, hung over the galley. That was when Ason had to kill the slave from Aleppo.

He was a dark man with olive skin, as dark as an Egyptian, with long black hair that he kept tied in a knot on one side of his head. Where he was born there was nothing but hills and a river, with dry desert beyond, stretching away to the end of the world. Until the Atlanteans had captured him, he had never seen the sea, and until this voyage had never been out of sight of land. There was wine mixed with the water now—he had never tasted that before either—and it did strange things to his head. When they did not row, and water poured over the side and sloshed over his legs, something seemed to swell up inside of him, bursting out of his mouth as a scream, driving him to his feet.

"Row!" he shouted. "Go back. To Crete, the Atlanteans. We will die here."

"And which way is back?" Ason asked, looking down on him from the deck above. "We will row only when we know which way to go."

"Now, we must—"

"No."

The man from Aleppo jumped to the walkway and swung the heavy bailing bucket at Ason, catching him on the thigh and sending him staggering back. Ason was unarmed, his sword in his cabin, but Inteb was close by. He seized the Egyptian's dagger and, when the man raised the

76

bucket again, he reached out the dagger like a shining deadly finger and drove it into the man's throat, twisting it so that the major blood vessels were severed. A push sent the man over the side, and only his blood rose again to the surface. Ason went and put on all his armor and sword and did not take them off again.

That day was the worst, because the sky did not clear. But soon after dark the stars came out and they rowed, looking at the stars that marked the north above the stern, and told each other how to find them, shouting at the steersman and cursing him thoroughly if he strayed from the proper course.

The overseer's corpse lasted two days more before its obvious state of decay became too intolerable. And the hole was beginning to leak around the edges. A thin and broadshouldered young man named Pylor from the island of Kea said that he had much diving experience after the sponges that grew offshore there, and he volunteered to look under the galley. A line was tied under his arms and he dived and came up quite soon after.

"Lots of fishes," he reported. "And not much of that whoreson left below the waist, except for hanging bones. He's been used up."

Tydeus, who had experience in patching ships at sea when they could not be properly careened on a beach, showed them how to make a mat that could be slung outside the hull. They took the largest piece of sailcloth they had and sewed rope ends and rags torn from good clothing to one side of it. Lines were attached to the four corners of this and, with much shouting and pulling and a number of dives by Pylor, it was passed under the galley and over the hole and the truncated corpse of the overseer. The rags and rope ends faced the hull and would mat together to form a temporary patch. Once this was in place, all that remained was to pluck the corpse from the hole and put a wooden cover inside the ship. Boards were cut and shaped for this and held together with bronze pins, but there were few volunteers to remove the noisome plug.

"I'll take one arm—who'll have the other?" Ason asked. Some of the men actually leaned away when he looked around at them, and Inteb managed to be out of sight in the cabin.

Aias laughed at their squeamishness, and pushed them aside and went to stand beside Ason. "I've hugged women and boys and sheep to my body, mountain man," he said. "This will be the first time for a stinking corpse, but I have a mind to try it to see what it is like."

A single strong heave did it, and the overseer's corpse bobbed astern in a flurry of fish, while Ason and Aias washed their arms over the side. Very little water came in around the patch, and the wooden cover was quickly secured in place and sealed with pitch. After that only a slight amount of water leaked in. No one wanted to think what would happen to these makeshift repairs in case of a storm.

One day was very much like another after this and Inteb recorded their passing by making marks on the inner wall of the cabin. He measured out the water and food himself while Ason stood close by, or slept in the doorway so no other could enter. There was no more open rebellion, though sometimes the men whispered together after dark. One of them tried to talk to Aias, but the boxer struck him on the side of the head and he was unconscious the best part of the day.

The water began to run low and tasted increasingly foul and Inteb mixed more and more wine with it, of which they had a greater supply. Most of the men were unused to this, and with the heat of the sun many babbled and others fell down and had to be propped over the benches with their faces out of the bilges so they did not drown.

It was on the twelfth day that they sighted the dark line of what might be clouds low on the horizon before them. They rowed then, all of them, without being told, and the line grew darker and larger and was not clouds at all.

"The coast, it must be," Inteb said, and the galley rocked wildly as the men stood to see for themselves. Ason settled his sword in its slings over his shoulder for the first time since the man from Aleppo had been killed. They were as one again, drinking and laughing together, and any thoughts of mutiny were left behind in that trackless sea. There was a shore ahead, land, any land, it did not matter. The endless voyage was over and the boldest were already bragging about it to each other. They were already remembering it as being twice as long as it had been, and their memories would improve with age.

It was Tydeus, at his accustomed post at the steering sweep, who first saw the sail. A dot to begin with, perhaps a rock, but as it grew clearer he called to the others. They crowded up to look until Ason ordered them back to the oars. But Aias remained on the deck, staring at it as though it were a face he remembered, even tugging away the drooping scarred flesh over his eye so he could see better.

"That dark sail, the way it is set. I know them. The men of Sidon."

"I know the Sidonioi," Inteb said. "They are traders, silver bowls and fine textiles, I've bought from them myself."

Aias had the scarred rocks of his fists clenched, crouching forward.

"Yes, they trade with Egypt," he said. "And Atlantis—because they have to. But we know them in Byblos and they are known all along the shores of the sea wherever they sail. Traders when they must be, pirates by choice."

"They'll butcher us for the stores of the cabin and the wood in the hull."

The ship moved swiftly towards them, swooping down to the attack like a dark bird of prey. This was something that Ason felt he could take care of. No armored fists here, or sinking ships to deal with, but the straightforward threat of arms that could be met in the same way.

"Inteb, open the bronzesmith's chest and give weapons to those who know how to use them. The rest of you, quickly now, bail water into this ship."

They did not stop to ask why but did as they were told. The orders were definite, and as the dark ship came closer the galley sank deeper in the water. The men with the swords bent low and hurried to conceal themselves in the stern cabin and under the narrow foredeck, while those who had the daggers sat on the rowing benches and hid the weapons beneath them. Aias refused the offer of a sword and held up a clenched fist.

"My weapons are with me always," he said, dropping onto the bench nearest the cabin. "What will you have us do?"

"Take them by surprise," Ason said. "Put your ankles back into the stocks and close them, as though you were locked in. Take in most of the oars. Look sick, that should be easy enough. Look dead if you are afraid to play-act. The mast and sail are gone, the ship waterlogged, you are slaves who have been deserted. Let the men of Sidon see a ripe fruit easy for the plucking so they will be unprepared. When I call to you we will all attack at once. We will not stop until they are dead. One ship will leave here, one crew alive. It will be ours."

Aias, perhaps from his many battles in the arena before the crowds, gave a fine performance. He had boxed with nobles whom he could have slain in moments, yet had managed to lose to them, and in doing so proved their superior skill. Now he collapsed on the bench, calling hoarsely to the approaching ship, while whispering at the same time to the men in the cabin.

"They're coming on steadily, using oars with the sail furled. Men hanging over the sides, pointing and shouting. Helms on some of them, but no armor that I can see, swords and spears. They're taking in the oars now, drifting close."

There were guttural shouts from the dark ship that loomed above them, drifting down upon them. High stem posts rose fore and aft, darkly painted, and just as dark was the sail now furled, angling across the mast in the high lateen rig. There was more shouting and laughter, and then the galley shuddered as the ship bumped against them. Feet thudded onto the cabin roof while another Sidonioi jumped down to the foredeck with a line, bending to tie it securely. Others boarded once the two ships were lashed together, tall dark men with black hair and beards, their hair held back by a circlet about the head. And Ason still waited. Until now they had ignored the galley slaves, and he wanted as many of them aboard as possible before he made any move. Then a man appeared in the doorway whose robe was dyed purple, unlike the plain white of the others, and he held a richly decorated sword in his hand.

Ason plunged his own sword into the man's middle, kicking the body out of the way as it fell, seizing the sword from the limp fingers, roaring the lion roar of Mycenae.

The rowers rose up and killed the men nearest to them. Aias lashed out a fist as a dark-bearded warrior turned towards him, hitting him so hard that he crashed into the next man, toppling them both over; before they could recover Aias hurled them both into the sea.

After the first surprise attack the men of Sidon rallied and stood back to back with their weapons drawn. They were bold fighters and did not retreat, but shouted instead for help from their ship. More men climbed over the sides to join them, and the fighting became fierce and deadly.

Ason's sweeping sword cleared the rear deck and then, instead of joining the battle in the ship below, he mounted the rail and clambered up the side of the black ship. A spear stabbed down, but he lowered his head and it glanced from his helm. Before it could be drawn back for a second blow he stabbed upwards with his sword, impaling the man, then pushed his body aside to climb to the deck above. Seizing up the spear to use in place of a shield, he shouted aloud again so everyone could hear him, then, like a farmer cutting grain, began to scythe his way slowly down the deck.

A warrior in full armor cannot be stopped. Another armored man may fight him, and the better will win, but no one else. Spears rebound from his chest, swords from his helmet, the solid bronze of his greaves keep his legs from being cut from under him. Ason was made for killing, as methodical and unstoppable as waves crashing on a shore, looking from under the rim of his helm and putting his sword into the soft and unprotected bodies of those who stood before him.

He thrust and cut and moved steadily down the deck. The men who had attacked the galley tried to return to save their own ship, but were cut down from behind when they did. A wail of despair went up from the survivors, yet they did not stop fighting. Powerful men and good swordsmen, they fought on, singly and together, fewer and fewer of them, the last man fighting as ably as the first, dying with guttural curses on his lips.

It was finally done, the last drop of blood shed, the last corpse stripped and heaved over the side. The men of the galley had suffered, but not heavily. The simpler cuts were washed with oil and sea water until they closed. But a heavily bearded, silent man from Salamis had been cut deeply in the stomach, and he held the lips of the wound together to keep his insides from falling through. He made no attempt to stop the blood. Bleeding to death was the least painful way to die and they all knew it. They brought him wine, although he could only touch it to his lips, and sat and talked and joked with him until his eyes finally closed and he slumped.

Ason had mixed the wine himself and saw to it that they all had some. Then, while they were still laughing and cursing, filled with victory, he called to them from the high rear deck. His own mind had been made up ever since they had first sighted this ship, and he had waited only for this moment to tell them.

"I know this shore," he called out. "I sailed here once. In that direction, some days sail, is Egypt. You can go there if you want to, you can have your share of what we find aboard this ship and the galley."

There were excited shouts at this, because looters had already plunged into the holds and come up with cloth and flasks of oil, even ivory carvings, which were highly valued everywhere. Ason could feel the rise of their emotions, and at its peak he called out again and pointed his dripping sword in the opposite direction, west along the shore.

"You can do as you will—but I am going that way, to the west, and I ask the best of you to come with me. Past the Pillars of Herakles to the Island of the Yerni, to avenge my uncle and my kinsmen who were killed there. We will bring back tin, enough to fill a ship, tin that is more valuable than gold or silver—and you will have your share. So now I ask you, men who sailed the ocean where no one has ever gone before, who battled and killed the men of Sidon, are you afraid of anything? Will you sail with me to the lands few men have ever seen—to return home rich? Who is with me?"

There could be only one answer, a roared cheer, again and again. How could they refuse? They could do anything, they knew it, anything! Ason dropped his sword to the deck and threw the spear into the air with his other hand, catching it as it dropped in his right, drawing it back farther and farther. Then he threw with all his strength, hurling the spear west towards the low afternoon sun. Up it arched, thrumming as it flew, with the sun driving golden light from its bronze head, as though it would reach the sun itself. It was only a speck when it hit the water and vanished, and the men were still cheering.

Ason bent to pick up his sword, and when he straightened up he saw Inteb looking at him with a half smile on his lips.

"You planned this, didn't you?" he asked.

"Yes. I have been thinking about it ever since you told me about Lycos and the others. A ship will have to go to avenge them and get the tin—and we have a ship right here, along with a crew. It would take weeks to return to Mycenae and set out again, and why should we? We are well on our way to the western sea. My father has talked enough of tin, so even I know that Mycenae must have it and now, soon, at once, while Atlantis still licks her wounds. They lost many ships and warriors on Thera, perhaps even Atlas himself is dead, though that is too much of a blessing to expect. Now we must fight them—now we *can* fight them. For that we must have the tin."

"When you say that you sound like Perimedes."

"He is the king and I am his son. But what about yourself, Inteb? I don't think I heard you cheering with the others."

"You will always have my cheers, Ason; they do not have to be delivered at certain times. We are close now to Egypt, where my home is, and I have high honors due from Pharaoh. Shouldn't I return there?"

"Should you? You could come with us. You have become like my right hand, and I love you like a brother."

"And I love you, Ason, but not like a brother." He took him by the forearms and leaned his cheek against Ason's rough cheek, damp with sweat and specked with drying drops of blood. "I love you and I will go with you wherever you wish me to go."

BOOK TWO

1

The trees and thick undergrowth came right down to the water's edge, green and damp, breathing a moist breath upon the laboring men in the ship whenever a trickle of breeze penetrated the jungle barrier. Skirting the cliff, crawling along like a great waterbug, the black ship made its way against the current. The oars spraddled out like a waterbug's legs, driving it painfully forward. The great sail was furled, since what little wind there was blew in the wrong direction. They pulled at the oars, grunting and cursing when they had the breath, staying as close to the shore as they could where there were backwaters and where the current was not as strong.

Across the width of gray channel, north of them, there rose up the even grayer and sky-touching rock of the Pillar of Herakles. They had been amazed when they first saw it, had crowded the rail to look and shout and describe it to each other. Now they were sick of the sight of it. Strain as they would, hour after hour, the brooding shape dropped painfully slowly behind them. Ahead were the cold waters of the western sea, and they rowed with all their strength to reach them. A bucket over the side would bring the

85

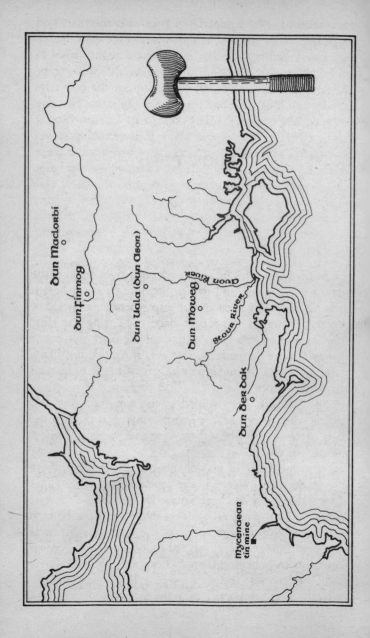

Dun Maclorbi

Dun Finmog

Dun Uala (Dun Uaor)

Dun Moweg

Uaon River

Stour River

Dun Der Dak

Mycenaean
tin mine

water inboard to be dumped over sweat-drenched skin and heads burned by the sun. It was colder water than the sea they knew, and not as salty, but it was a mighty labor to reach. None of the voyage, since taking the Sidon ship, had been this hard. Now they sweated out the easy days and the rich food they had consumed. Since that first day the wind had been fair. They coasted Africa, watching it slip by them, pulling up on shore in the evening to get fresh water, to sleep. Many times they had hunted there and dined on meat. Ason's arm was the strongest, his aim the best. He could bring down a deer with a spear cast none of them could approach. It had been an easy voyage, without equal. At night they could laugh at all the old tales they had heard about the dangers and labors awaiting ships that sailed these waters.

Then the wind had failed them. Just as the current turned against them, so did the airs that moved above it. For three days they had remained ashore waiting for the wind to change; it never had. Like it or not they had to row.

They were getting very little pleasure from it. For an entire day, from dawn to almost dusk, they labored at the oars, until they were through that channel of rushing sea water and into the open sea beyond. Here they could use the wind to tack across to the opposite shore. Just before sunset the breeze died completely and they rowed, much more easily now, until they found a sheltered bay on the rocky coast. The men ate hungrily, for the first time since that morning, and were asleep soon after.

In the cabin, Ason poured olive oil into the stone lamp, floated a wick upon it and lighted it. "We must now think about our course," he said.

"Without charts?" Inteb asked.

"Lycos had no charts, but he found the way and explained it to me. From the Pillars of Herakles we sail north along the coast until the land ends. . . ."

"And the world as well—and we sail into chaos."

"You are in good spirits today, Inteb."

87

"It comes from leaning on the steering sweep while everyone else rows. Let me pour you some wine."

Ason smacked his lips over it and then stretched mightily, hearing his joints crack. He had rowed with the others all that day. "Get a piece of that broken pot, and the thing you use to scratch on it, and we'll make a chart."

Inteb placed the articles on the table before him and looked up expectantly. Ason made a fist of his right hand, then opened it out partway and stuck his thumb up in the air.

"This is it," he said.

"Is it a problem of some kind?"

"No, a chart." He placed the back of his hand against the fired clay surface. "Now scratch around it, outline it clearly."

When it was done he admired the incised line and tapped it at the bottom, near the base of his smallest finger.

"This is the strait of the Pillars of Herakles. The thumb points north. So first we sail west along the base of the hand until we come to the knuckle of the little finger. Then we turn north and sail along the outline of the fingers. The knuckles of the fingers are the mouths of great rivers. There are four of them, just as there are four fingers, and we must pass them all. After the last we come to a large headland, and that is where our course turns east and we sail along the top of the hand to the base of the thumb. Still following the hand, we turn north again, and as the thumb curves out so does our course slowly change from north to northwest. It is all here in the hand."

"And when the limit of the thumb is reached?"

"It is time to cross the sea to the Island of the Yerni. When the coastline turns away from the direction it has been following, to the east again, we leave it and sail north. There is a small island there off the coast, Uzend is its name, and we sail between it and the mainland whenever there is a following wind. North, due north, for just one day and one night if the wind is good and the sky clear, and then we come to the Island of the Yerni and the land of the Albi.''

"Different tribes?"

"Very different, but you will see."

Ason took off his tunic and lay on his stomach while Inteb poured oil into his hands and kneaded the great muscles of Ason's shoulders and back. Ason was snoring long before he was finished.

The pleasant voyage continued with little to mark one day from another. They passed the mouth of a large river and saw a small craft of some kind fleeing up it, but did not bother to follow. The country looked mountainous inland, but was fertile enough along the shore. They filled their water skins at streams, then hunted the deer and wild pigs that came there to drink.

Only one additional time, in all of that long voyage, did they see any trace of other men. It was a pale column of smoke that rose straight up into the cloudless sky. They beached their ship and stalked their human quarry in silence, as they would any other wild game. The fire had been made in the lee of a large artificial mound twice as tall as a man, which concealed their approach. A family gathering on a picnic feast was grouped about the fire, roasting a whole ox before a wall of stone slabs facing that side of the mound, and they all ran shrieking with fear when the armed men burst upon them. Ason and his men roared with laughter as they dragged the ox back to the ship, laughing even louder at the timid faces peeping out from the surrounding brush. There was nothing wrong with the voyage, nothing at all.

When the north-south coast ended, Ason carefully followed the chart they had made. It took them along the coastline to an immense bay and to the headland beyond.

"This is the place," Ason said. "I remember the shape of that island. There is a stream there with a sandy bay where we landed and filled all the skin bags with water. Then we sailed away from land."

"We have had enough experience of that," Inteb said. "And for a far longer distance."

Although the men were not anxious to leave the comforting presence of the shoreline, they did not worry too much about this last stage of the journey. Since the day they had captured the Sidonioi ship the sailing had been good, with fair winds and smooth seas. There was little rain this time of year. The voyage had been easy—and riches were waiting at the end of it.

For seven days the wind blew from the west and they remained in the tiny bay. The drinking water was taken aboard, the rigging checked, the worn lines replaced. Any open seams were caulked. With all the work done that could be done, one of the men made nets from twine, and they trapped the fat birds that roosted in the trees. They ate them baked in mud in the embers of their fire. On the morning of the eighth day Ason awoke before dawn and went on deck to smell the air. Aias was there, on watch, leaning against the rail. He dampened a finger in his torn-lipped mouth and held it high.

"From the south," he said. "Is that the wind we are waiting for?"

"The very one. Rouse them up."

Once again they pulled away from a shore into an empty sea, although this time it was done deliberately. The steersman faced aft so they would sail away from land. Inteb carefully noted the sun's course to be sure they were heading correctly. The sea was easy, with long swells that they rode up and over and down. White-winged ocean birds followed them out from shore, screaming sharply and diving for fish in their wake. They sailed briskly before the wind, paying no heed to the thin, high clouds that sprang up in the afternoon. It was only towards dusk that the clouds thickened. But the setting sun could be clearly seen, and they kept it carefully to port and searched the empty sea ahead for the sight of land, wagering as to who would see it first.

At sunset, with little warning, the storm struck. The wind increased and clouds quickly covered the sky; the sea rose. These waves were a kind they had never experienced before, so from the very beginning they were in danger of foundering. The low-sided galley would have gone down at once, and even the larger and more seaworthy Sidonioi ship could do little more than run before the storm. With the smallest amount of sail possible she still plunged her bow deep into the waves, while the rigging hummed and creaked.

Tydeus stood at the steering sweep, squinting ahead through the lashing rain to see the white-foamed tops of the waves as they rushed by, steering by the feel of the ship and the wind. Ason was beside him when Inteb came on deck, working his way to them along the rail to keep from being blown overboard.

"Get into the cabin!" Ason shouted, reaching out his arm to steady the Egyptian. Inteb held to him so he wouldn't fall.

"It's worse in there. The ship creaks and groans as though it were dying. I expect it to go to the bottom at any moment."

"We are still before the wind, and as long as we keep bailing we'll keep above the water."

"Your sword," Inteb said, realizing that it was strapped over Ason's shoulder for the first time since they had been at sea. But he was not wearing his armor. Inteb took sudden fright. "You would never go on a voyage without your sword—even to the underworld. You think that we are going to drown, don't you?"

"I think this is a very bad night."

"Is it the end?"

"Only Zeus knows that. He will show us soon enough. We have run before the wind for all of the day now, and part of the night. The wind blows to the Island of the Yerni and we have no way of turning aside. Now go to the cabin."

"No. I must stay here."

As frightening as the deck was, with the black waves rising up suddenly, foam flecked, to break hissing down the sides or to disappear back into the darkness from where they had emerged, the cabin was far worse. There every heave and falling away of the deck felt like the beginning of the last plunge to the bottom. It was unbearable. Inteb thought of the sunlight and warmth of Egypt and of all that he had left behind. If he were lost at sea, how could his body be preserved and entombed so he could voyage after death to the Western Land? It could not, that is what the priests said. To be lost at sea was the worst kind of death to suffer. He used to laugh at the priests, but that was easier to do on solid land, during the day. He was not laughing now.

The end was sudden. The only warning they had was a sudden booming, louder than the roaring of the storm, and the quick sight of white spray leaping high before them. Then the ship struck the rocks, was impaled, broken, destroyed. The men thrown into the sea or trapped in the crumbling wreckage.

Before he could realize what was happening, Inteb was hurtling through the air, falling into the icy ocean. He tried to scream but his mouth and nose filled with water, water all around him. He was drowning. He did not know it. He rolled onto his side spewing out salty sea water until together and he was aware of the other man's form close by. Inteb coughed and choked the water from his throat, sucking in a great lungful of air. Something dark and large rushed upon them, striking him across the side of his head.

After that he had only the most confused memories. Ason was there, or someone, holding his arms, his clothing, and something hard dug in under his arms. The water was over his head much of the time, and he breathed that in as much as he did the air, coughing, weaker and weaker each time. Then it all ended in a flurry of white

92

water, spray, and something hard tearing and tearing at his body as he turned end over end, finally stopping struggling and sinking down to die peacefully in the darkness that now rose up to overwhelm him.

2

Inteb awoke, coughing again and again, unable to stop, until his throat was raw and his eyes closed with the pain of it. He rolled onto his side spewing out salty sea water until he was empty, drained. After this he was too weak to even open his eyes, although he remained conscious, feeling the hard ground under him and aware that he was shivering with cold and exhaustion. His eyes were grainy with sand, the lids so stuck together that he had to rub to open them.

A gray sky, low overhead, with blowing clouds. He lay on rough ground tufted with clumps of grass, in a small hollow. His last memories had been of the sea, the storm, the water closing over him. How had he come here? Certainly not by himself. Ason?

"Ason," he called aloud, struggling to his knees, and then in near panic, "*Ason!*"

Could he be dead? Inteb stood swaying, then climbed the low ridge. From here he could see a stretch of beach with the waves still rushing strongly up it, then bubbling back. Not far offshore the black wet backs of a bank of jagged rocks broke the surface of the sea. He knew what had happened the night before. But how had he come here? He shouted again and heard an answering hail from down the beach. Ason appeared, dragging something long and dark, and waved to him. They met on the damp sands. Ason threw down the broken piece of driftwood and seized him by both arms.

"It was a bad night, Inteb, but we are alive, and that is

93

something to be glad of.''

"Others. . . ?''

"None. The ship hit those rocks out there and flew apart at the blow. We went into the water together, and the steering sweep almost took our heads off coming down on top of us. But I used it to save us in the end. It held us up until we washed ashore. I called; there was no one else. I pulled you up there out of the wind and searched, out in the water as far as I dared go. Nothing. They must have all gone down with the wreck. Not many could swim, I suppose.''

He dropped heavily to the sand, leaning his head forward on his knees. He had not slept and was very tired. He had been the leader and captain and responsible for the crew. And now they were all dead. His muscles ached and the sword was a cold weight across his back.

"Do you know where we are?'' Inteb asked.

"On the coast somewhere, I'm not sure. We sailed along it last time I came, and one place looks very much like another. No sign of people here, or villages. Or food. Nothing came ashore from the ship. Just broken wood. We had better start walking.'' He climbed to his feet.

"Which way?''

"A good question. Until the storm it seemed we had a good following wind, but it could have veered after dark. Walk east, that must be right.''

Ason gave one long look around at the deserted beach and fang-tipped rocks that had destroyed the ship, then turned left and led the way down the shore. The sand was soft and easy on their bare feet: their sandals had been torn off by the sea. Inteb followed, down the beaches of the trackless coast. They had only walked a short time when they came to an inlet that was too deep to cross. Turning inland, they followed it away from the ocean. Inteb had a sudden thought, and bent and filled his palm and tasted the water.

"Just brackish," he said. "This must be the mouth of a stream. If we follow it upstream, there should be fresh water."

The stream twisted and narrowed until clear water was running over moss-covered stones. They lay on their stomachs and drank their fill. Ason sat up, wiping his mouth on his arm—and was suddenly still. Inteb saw him draw his sword.

"What is it?" he asked. Ason pointed.

Low, wooded hills rose up from the downland, and through the branches could be seen a bare hilltop beyond. On the summit of the hill was a rounded construction of some kind. There was no one in sight. After a moment Ason led the way there, sword ready. They passed through the grove, following an overgrown path, and emerged on the hillside below the raised hummock of the structure. It was made of heaped earth, and a line of stone slabs were visible at one end. The biggest one in the center appeared to be a sealed doorway.

"It looks very much like a tomb," Inteb said.

Ason nodded agreement but kept his sword in his hand as they mounted the hill, only slipping it back into its slings when they realized that they were the first visitors here in a very long time.

"It is a tomb," Ason said. "I've seen this kind before." He bent to peer around the edge of the central slab covering the entrance, but could see nothing except darkness. "There will be a room in there, a burial chamber formed by upended boulders that hold up the big ceiling slabs. Dried bones, grave offerings, gold perhaps." He pulled at the heavy stone.

"Very much like Mycenae, in a far cruder way. Must you open it?"

"No, no reason to. Let's get back to the beach."

The sun burned through the clouds and felt warm on their backs. They walked on until it was near midday. It was Inteb who called a halt, pointing to the curved beach ahead of them. He drove a stick into the sand and peered at its shadow quizzically.

"We seem to have turned north," he said, "and if this beach keeps on as it does we shall soon be walking west, back in the direction we came from. Could we be on a peninsula or a neck of land?"

"Possibly, but I don't remember any shaped like this. But there is a lot of coast; it's a big island. It goes north no one knows how far. This could be a part of the land I haven't seen."

"I'm going to see what lies ahead," Inteb said, scrambling up a grass-tufted dune, tired of walking and only too aware of the rumbling emptiness of his stomach. He reached the top, looked around—then bent over and slid quickly back to the beach.

"Someone coming along the shore. I dropped down as soon as I saw him—I don't think he saw me."

"Just one?" Ason asked, slipping his sword from the slings.

"Absolutely. I could see the length of the beach. He's alone."

"There is nothing to fear from one man."

Sword swinging easily, Ason strode down the sand. Inteb, feeling none of this same self-assurance, lagged behind. He caught up with him as they came to a rocky spur that ran out into the sea, and Ason stopped there. There was splashing as someone moved out into the water. They heard grumbled curses as a high wave surged up and broke against the rock. Inteb stepped back—the splashing grew near. The tendons in Ason's hand stood out as he closed his grip on the pommel of the sword. A man waded around the end of the rock and faced them—as startled as they were. A familiar, scarred and battered man.

"Aias!" Ason shouted and plunged his sword into the sand before striding into the water to embrace the boxer.

"Well met!" Aias shouted in return as they clasped

each other, there in the sea with green water surging about their legs.

"I thought you dead with all the others," Ason said.

"You are returned from the grave. If I did not feel your solid flesh I might think you a spirit. But there are three of us now—unless that Egyptian on the shore is a wraith come back from his Western Land?"

Inteb began to laugh with the others until he was struck by a sudden and terrible thought. How had the boxer come here?

"Aias," he called out. "Have you been walking along the shore?"

"Ever since the sun opened my eyes this morning. I was alone on the sand. No one else. Thirsty and hungry. Still am. Started walking along the beach and have been walking ever since. Not that I found anyone. . . ."

"Did you turn back?"

"Never." They waded ashore and stared down at Inteb who had dropped to the sand looking deathly ill.

"Then you realize what this means?" Inteb said. "We have been walking, too—in the opposite direction."

Ason understood at once.

"An island. We have been wrecked on an island."

"And a desolate one at that," Inteb said, some of the same desolation in his voice. "We met no one along the shore, found nothing except that stream."

"Then you found more than I did. If you know where water is, show me the way."

"We found a tomb as well," Inteb said, standing. "This is an island of the dead."

"There may be people inland." Ason slipped his sword back into its sling and led the way down the shore. "If there are, we will find them. There must be people here."

There were none. Inland among the low hills they found more tombs, even a group of older mounds with the earth partly weathered away, exposing the roof slabs of the stone burial chambers within. None of them spoke aloud again the words Inteb had spoken, but the words were easy to hear, even unspoken. An island of the dead. From the highest hill they could see water on all sides and a dark bulk on the distant horizon that might have been the mainland. Nothing else. When the shadows began to lengthen they returned to the stream beneath the first tomb they had found and lay down to drink their fill of the cool water, again and again, in an attempt to allay the hunger.

"What do we do?" Aias asked, and they turned to Ason. He shook his head slowly, staring out towards the darkening sea.

"I imagine we shall die."

After being plucked from the sea like fish and thrown on the beach?" Inteb said. "It seems a strange destiny to survive all that only to die from an empty gut."

"We can eat." Aias pulled a long stalk of grass through his fingers and looked at the few wild grains that lay on his palm. "Not well. But I have eaten worse. Eat these seeds. Catch birds."

"Fish perhaps," Inteb added. "Water and food, we can survive."

"Why?" Ason asked. "We can live like wild animals without fire or shelter, drinking this water and chewing these dry seeds. Why? Death will come in the end no matter what we do."

In the silence he spoke aloud again Inteb's words.

"This is an island of the dead."

3

Aias walked, head bowed to the streaming rain that ran from his hair and beard and dripped into his already soggy clothing. He trudged along at the water's edge dragging the driftwood after him, a length of splintered branch that he had found on the shore. The waves broke, hissing up the sand and around his ankles. There was the rumble of unseen breakers on the rocks offshore. Aias walked on, turning inland from the beach on the path his feet had made during the many journeys back and forth here. The path wound up through the boulders to a larger jutting overhang of stone, with a natural shelter underneath it. Stuffed in here were the pieces of driftwood Aias had found: limbs and logs, branches and a single length of carved thwart from the wrecked ship itself. This and the steering oar were the only reminders that the ship and the drowned crew had ever existed. Aias pushed the pieces of wood aside and made room for himself out of the rain.

He was not exactly sure why he was collecting the wood here. There was nothing big enough to build a raft with, nor even any creepers to tie it together with. They could burn the wood if they could find a way of striking up a fire. No outcrops of spark-making pyrites, either. And they would need a fire or they would surely die during the coming winter on this desolate island, this far north. Winter would kill them quickly; summer was making too slow a job of it. He looked down at the plaited leather thong about his waist, at the bends and creases on the hanging end where he had shortened it, day after day. The grass and sedge weeds were no diet for men. The few birds they had managed to snare were only feathery memories. How long had it been? He rubbed at the new beard on his face. A long time. The Egyptian would know, a man of learning who must still keep track of the dates even in this barren place, mumbling and marking hieroglyphs on a little wooden tablet. He had worked it out that it was the month of Mesori and that the Nile had already risen. As if that mattered here. As if anything mattered except staying alive. They were all getting weaker and the Egyptian was the weakest of the lot. Probably die first. Well, that would mean meat for awhile. He had eaten man-meat before and did not like it. But you could live on it, yes you could.

99

After a time the rain stopped falling. Aias' legs had become stiff. He climbed out and stretched, hearing his joints snap, his muscles aching from the damp. Water dripped from the bushes, the gray sea was the same leaden color as the sky. He turned his back on it and walked back through the low, rounded hills to their tomb. A fit dwelling place for men who would soon be dead, though he never thought of it that way.

This was the first tomb that they had found, the biggest on the island and high enough to stand erect in. The opening sealed only by a single large slab of stone. They had levered it aside before hesitatingly entering this home of the dead. An ugly statuette of a goddess lay in the rear. There were bones everywhere. The older ones were crumbling to dust, while some of the more recent ones still had bits of mummified flesh clinging to them. They had cleaned house by kicking all of the bone and rubble to the far, dark end of the tunnel-like grave. Mixed with the bones were golden grave goods, collars and pins, useless decorations that meant nothing on this island, though they would have been well received anywhere else. At first they had kept them close by, but they were in the way in the cramped quarters and had soon been thrown in with the rest of the rubbish. Aias still wore a gold armlet, but only because it offered some cheer in the grayness of the island.

The other two were already there when Aias crawled through the entrance. They were bent over something.

"Look!" Ason called out, holding up a brown bird whose legs had been caught in their snare. It fluttered helplessly, terror in its large round eyes.

"How shall you divide it?" Aias asked squatting down, as eager now as the others.

"We are the wrong number," Inteb said as Ason drew his sword and whetted the edge against his thumb. "Remember the trouble with the last bird. If we were two we could half it, quarter it for four."

"And a feather each for four hundred," Ason laughed.

Three grown men on the edge of starvation, bent over a mite of a struggling life that could provide only the tiniest amount of nourishment. But their bellies growled for it. The sound must have been in the air for some time before they became aware of it, drowned out by their voices. It was Ason, the hunter, who cocked his head suddenly to one side—then held his finger to his lips. They froze, motionless and silent, and the distant moaning could be clearly heard.

If it had been night they would have been sure that the spirits of the dead they had expelled from the tomb were coming back to reclaim it. There was a dirge of death to the sound, the wailing of the dead, and like dogs they felt the hairs on their necks and down their backs rise. Inteb shivered, not from cold.

"Voices," he whispered. "It must be people, chanting."

Voices, getting closer, louder, and soon words could be heard. Ason strained to make them out, then nodded his head.

"Listen. You can understand the words. It is the old-fashioned language of the bards, not quite the same, but you can make out what they are singing."

The same phrases, over and over again, a ritual chant. Clear now, louder and closer, coming towards them up the side of the hill.

> Back, back to the womb of the mother
> Inside, inside, the earth and the hill
> Dead, dead, sleeping inside you
> Born, born again out of the tomb.

Ason had his sword in his hand, crouching, ready to defend himself against any attacker, human or inhuman. Aias closed his fists, and his simpler yet equally deadly weapons were ready. Inteb huddled where he was.

The bird fluttered wildly on the sandy floor and, before anyone could reach it, freed its wings from the snare.

Peeping loudly, it flew by them, the woven grass strands dangling, and out of the opening of the tomb.

There was a sudden silence as it burst from the opening and the chanting stopped. For a long, long instant Ason endured this threatening silence—then scrambled forward bellowing like a bull. Whatever was out there was better faced in the open. He swung his sword in short arcs before him and jumped to his feet outside with Aias just behind him.

Screams and cries, thudding feet, the sudden sight of people running, brown backs vanishing from sight. In a moment all except two of them were gone. And the long bundle dropped at their feet. A man, old, gray haired, brown garbed from head to toe with the hood of his cape down over half his face. He was shouting distractedly, resisting the young girl who pulled at his arms. She leaned away in panic, yet would not desert the old man.

"A funeral procession," Inteb said peering from the tomb's mouth, pointing to the fallen corpse sewn into uncured hides.

"And more frightened of us." Ason lowered his sword. "Not a warrior among them." He stalked down to stand before the old man. The girl stopped tugging and stood helplessly beside him now. Her hood had fallen back in her struggles and her rich black hair hung to her shoulders. Her eyes were as dark, her skin olive, her lips red and trembling. Ason reached out and lifted the man's hood that concealed his face. The old man cried out.

"Who is it? Who is there? Naikeri—what has happened?"

Ason took one look and let the concealing hood fall back into place. Something sharp and heavy had been crashed into the old man's face. It had destroyed the bridge of his nose and his eyes, blinding him, leaving only an inflamed scar the width of his face. When Ason did not speak, the girl whispered, hoarse with fright, into the old man's ear.

"One man, three men, coming from the tomb. They are armed with bronze swords. . . ."

"Who are you?" Ason broke in.

The old man straightened up. He might have been a warrior in his time, because he was well muscled though slight of build.

"I am Ler of the Albi. If you are a bronze-sword man you may know of me."

"I know the name of Ler of the Albi. It was told to me by my uncle Lycos who said your people aided him at the mine."

Ason kept his sword ready and looked about. He knew nothing about these strange people—they might be the very ones who had destroyed the mine. Ler wailed in sudden agony.

"Oh, dead, all of them dead, slaughtered like animals, rivers of blood." He shook his fists at the sky and writhed in torment, tearing at his clothing. Ason turned to the girl, Naikeri. She was standing quietly now that they had been revealed as men, not spirits.

"What is he raving about?"

"The Yerni. They attacked us, killed all the men, my brother on the ground there was the last, and he was many months dying. My father was blinded. They killed your people too, everyone at the mine."

Ason dropped his sword into its slings; they appeared to share a common enemy. Now that the sudden emergency had ended, the significance of the funeral procession was driven home to him.

These people had come to this island from some other place. The survivors of the shipwreck would not die on the barren island.

"Where do you come from?" Ason asked. Naikeri pointed back over her shoulder.

"From home. We always come here to bury our dead, at

103

least our dead of rank. We must come a long way, yet we still come. The distance does not matter, since this island is sacred to us because one time long ago our people lived here. Many are still buried here in these tombs." She grew angry with sudden memory. "You have torn this tomb open and gone into it to steal the offerings—like that!" She pointed to the gold armlet Aias wore.

"You have a ship?" Ason asked. Naikeri began to shout.

"Thieves and tomb robbers. . . ." She gasped and was silent as Ason reached out and seized her jaw in one hand, his corded fingers biting deep.

"*Do you have a ship?*"

She stepped back when he released her, rubbing at the white marks on her skin where his fingers had clamped down. "We come in coracles. We row along the coast and then out to this island."

"You have brought food with you?" She nodded. Ason smiled and slapped at the hollow of his stomach. "Call your people out of hiding—we won't hurt them. Then we will have some food and after that you can bury your brother. We are hungry and he is not. He can wait."

Aias laughed aloud at this and even Inteb smiled, coming all the way out of the tomb and joining them. But Naikeri was angry. The lines about her eyes and her tight-clamped mouth showed it, though she said nothing. Turning her back on the intruders, she murmured softly to her father, quieting him, then sitting him on the ground beside the skin-wrapped corpse. He huddled there, swaying with grief, touching the body, as Naikeri turned and went away down the hill calling out to the hidden people. They emerged one by one, frightened women and girls, dressed alike in brown cloth. A few men, all old, limping hesitantly and blinking up at the strangers through rheumy eyes. No warriors, no young men. As the three strangers came down the hill, they moved aside and did not look at them directly, but peeked instead around the edges of the hooded capes they all wore.

"Take us to these ships of yours," Ason ordered, and Naikeri led them to the beach. There were ten round dark mounds, shaped like beehives. They were all well above the reach of high tide. The girl went to the nearest.

"Like no boat I have ever seen," Aias said.

Inteb was interested and helped Naikeri turn one over. It was light enough to lift, a hemisphere of sewn-together skins that had been stretched over a framework of thin willow boughs. They were woven and tied together to form a latticework structure. The skins had been painted with pitch to waterproof them. On the sand beneath it was the coracle's cargo: bundles, baskets and wide-mouthed jars. Naikeri held out one of the jars and Ason pulled out a sausage as long as his hand and almost as wide.

"Meat!" he shouted, and bit into it while the others crowded close. It was rich beef, smoked and dripping with fat. Leathery and delicious. They chewed and chewed until the grease ran down their chins and coated their hands. When Naikeri left they scarcely noticed.

They poked through the rest of the cargo, sipping the brackish, tarry water in the skins, then trying the sticky lumps of cold, cooked gruel. There was even a paste made of crushed berries and nuts. They thought everything delicious. Sated at last, Inteb and Aias stretched out on the sun-warmed sand, patting their rounded stomachs and laughing at the sharp pains the unaccustomed feast brought on. Ason stood, looking out across the sea. His first wild happiness had died down and now he could think about what lay ahead. While they had been trapped on the island there had been no future; just existence and the avoidance of death. That was over now. These clumsy-looking coracles must be seaworthy or the Albi would never have reached the island. They would be leaving soon. He would take up again the mission that they had all sworn to with such enthusiasm that day.

They would land on the inhospitable shore, as dimly

105

seen as a cloud on the horizon. Then he must reopen the mine that was so vital to Mycenae, and avenge the Mycenaeans slaughtered there.

And do all this with a single Egyptian who knew nothing of battle. And a scarred boxer who preferred his fists to a sword. Ason reached to touch the pommel of his sword. He had that. With it in his hand he feared no man. If Zeus had wished his death he would be dead by now, as dead as his companions in the sea. Instead he had reached this shore and would soon reach the land over the water, the Island of the Yerni.

With his sword.

The savages there would soon discover what even one Mycenaean could do.

4

From the first moment that the coracles put to sea Inteb was sick. The clumsy things bobbed up and down on the surface of the water, spun in circles, leaked. Loaded with a small amount of cargo, each coracle held two people, three at the very most. Ason and Aias soon managed to learn to control the stubborn craft, though at first they simply spun about in one place when they chopped at the water with the stubby paddles, laughing at their own efforts. Inteb never even touched a paddle; as soon as the bobbing craft left shore his insides heaved and he hung over the side voiding his stomach. After that he was carried as cargo, slumped in the bottom and awash with water, with the rowers' feet sometimes resting on him when they moved. Not that he cared. Pain, even death would have been a relief from this rocking sickness. The sky spun and moved overhead, and he closed his eyes to keep it from sight.

The crossing—from the Isle of the Dead to the western-

106

most tip of the Island of the Yerni—took the better part of a day, even though they left at dawn. After that they slowly worked their way east along the coast, rowing most of every day and pulling into shore at dusk to eat and sleep. Guided by the old men, they stopped at a series of campsites that must have been in use for generations, mostly isolated beaches, cut off from the land beyond by high cliffs, accessible only by sea. The Albi were secretive by nature, not particularly afraid of other people, but preferring to go their own way.

One day blurred into another, strenuous work by daylight and exhausted sleep at night, until even Inteb lost track of how long the voyage was taking. It was only a little after noon one day when they put into shore at the mouth of a wide stream.

"What is wrong?" Ason called to Ler, who was being helped from his beached coracle by his daughter.

"This is the landing place. We are close to home now."

The coracles were quickly unloaded and inverted, their cargoes divided up among the younger girls and children. Once the others had been loaded with their burdens, the stronger women and the old men lifted the coracles, holding them on their backs, almost vanishing inside their rounded forms. Aias wanted to carry one as well, but his offer was turned away; their habit of keeping to themselves was not easily broken. In single file they started up a barely discernible path alongside the stream, towards the dark curtain of the forest.

Rain had been threatening since early morning and the sky was low, pressing against the tree tops until the tallest of them vanished in the mist. Dark, alien trees with flat and pointed leaves. Thick oak for the most part, broken by stands of beech and the occasional white arrows of birch trees. The ground beneath them was almost impassable, a tangle of undergrowth and hedge thick with the spikes of thorn. The track they were following wound along the grassy bank above the stream, rising and falling, first to avoid the marshy land at the water's edge, then the impenetrable forest. They walked on without stopping, silently, bent under their burdens, while the land itself rose steadily. At one point the stream gushed over a rock ledge in a small waterfall and broke onto the rocks of a rapid. There was a stiff climb here and the coracles were passed up from hand to hand. The land above changed suddenly, giving way from unending forest to cleared downs and meadows. The path was more clearly seen—and there was the smell of woodsmoke in the air. But little could be seen after that because the mist turned to rain. They plodded on, soon soaked and chilled.

It was nearing dusk when the first of the great mounds loomed up out of the rain, rising like a small mountain from the flatness of the moor. A burial tomb, but much larger than the ones on the island where they had been wrecked. The line of marchers wound around it, then past another mound, and the houses came into view. Their gabled, thatched roofs reached almost to the ground and the raised earth bank that surrounded them. The wattle-and-daub were walls held up by logs with their bark still upon them. Small tilled fields were behind the houses, divided by piled stone walls. Smoke seeped out from openings under the gables of the buildings. As they approached, someone whistled, high and clear with a peculiar warble on the last note. At this signal people appeared in the doorways and moved down towards them. Without goodbyes the file broke up as they went their separate ways. Ason stopped and waited until Naikeri and Ler had reached him.

"How far is the mine from here?" he asked.

"The mine of Lycos? Not far," Naikeri said. "You can walk there and back in half a day."

"Someone must show us the path."

"In the morning. It is too late now and it is raining. You will have to stay there all night, and there is no shelter."

"We wish to go now."

"Speak for yourself," Inteb said, sneezing and rubbing at his nose with his knuckles. "We have been so long on this voyage that one more night will not matter. And I find the thought of a fire most comforting."

Ason would have gone on had he known the road, but he could not, in the face of the resistance of the others. Reluctantly he permitted himself to be led to Ler's house, one of the largest. He bent over to enter through the small doorway. A fire was already burning, a clay pot was boiling in the embers. They seated themselves on low wooden benches near it to dry out, while an old wman hobbled about with bowls of gruel. It was tasteless, but hot and filling, and they spooned it down. Ler sucked at his and sat afterwards, rocking, his sightless face towards the warmth of the fire. When he had finished he called for beer, and a great covered crock was pulled from a hole in the ground. Only after he had dipped out and drained a cupful did Ler wave the others to the crock. It was fermented milk, sour and sharp with a bitter aftertaste, yet still it contained the same seeds of drunkenness as did wine. Here in his home, his sorrow softened by beer, Ler was more of the man he once had been.

"You will go to the mine in the morning," Ler said. "It was once our mine, but Lycos gave us many gifts and we let him use it. We will use it again now, for there is also copper there."

"No," Ason said without hesitation. "It is a Mycenaean mine, you just told me that."

"You have no need now for its rich metal. Nor do you have any boys to work the mine for you. They are all gone now, most of them dead, and it will be hard to find others to go back there."

"If Lycos did it—then so can I."

Ler smiled wickedly, forgetful in his own blindness that the others could see.

"Then you do not know. It is I who found the boys for

Lycos, children of the Donbaksho in the forest out there. They come to us for their woodsman's axes. We make it possible for them to clear their forest fields. Lycos gave me a gold cup and many other things to get the boys. Do you have a gold cup?''

"You will have a gold cup, even more if you can find the boys.''

"I would like to hold that gold cup now. I cannot see it, but I could touch it with my fingers and feel its weight. When can I hold this cup?''

"Soon.''

Ler, half drunk now, cackled with pleasure and groped under his bench until he found what he wanted. First a hardwood ax handle, then the double-edged stone ax-head, drilled through neatly from top to bottom. "Here is another kind of ax, a battle-ax, the kind we trade to the Yerni. They don't know where to find rare stone like this. Far better than anything they can make. Worth taking to the afterlife. Here, see for yourself, see how sharp it is. You see my ax. Now I will see your gold cup.'' He laughed again and belched resoundingly.

Ason turned the jadite blade over and over in his hands; but there was nothing to say in answer. He had no cup, no treasure. Nor any warriors to fight beside him. Nothing. Yet he had to open the mine—and find and kill those who had murdered his people. This old man could help. These Albi had no leaders. But Ler was old and re-spected, about as close to a leader as anything they had. If he could be persuaded, why then something might be done.

More beer was passed around. The men began to sweat comfortably in the heat of the fire, then to sing. Old Ler sang the loudest of them all. The rain beat on the thatched roof in a continual hushed roar. Ason sipped at his beer, stared down into it, trying to see the future through a haze of fatigue and heat, memories and hatreds. One man against an entire land?

Ler's voice dwindled and vanished as he slumped and fell off the stool. The old woman hobbled over and dragged him to a lockbed built into one wall, then rolled him into it with Naikeri's aid. Naikeri had sat silently in the shadows all evening, listening but not speaking so they were scarcely aware of her presence. Aias leaned back against the rough wall singing to himself with his eyes closed, drunk to extinction but happily unaware of it. Inteb swayed when he sipped at his mug and looked at Ason over the rim of it.

"We are here, Ason, after a journey none will believe."

"There is no one to tell it to in this lost place."

"Perimedes will send a ship and you will have men to aid you in reopening the mine."

"How can I be sure of that? My father will send a ship—but when will it be here? Will it come at all, through the dangers of the deadly seas? Must I simply sit and eat pap and drink soured milk until it does arrive? These questions are tearing at me, Inteb, and I see no answers. I am a prince of Mycenae, a warrior of the Argolid, ready to fight and win, or die. But how can I fight without warriors and with one badly nicked sword? How can I get aid without treasure for gifts? You are the wise man, my friend, can you answer these questions for me?"

Inteb's head bobbed loosely and his speech was thick. "Count upon me, I'll help you, always help you, Ason. My love for you will aid you. I could be in Egypt now at Pharaoh's right hand watching the bountiful Nile rise— but look where my destiny has led me. Yet I am not sorry, not sorry." He began to weep, and weeping fell asleep.

The fire burned low, and the air was thick with the smell of fermented milk and smoke; Ason could not bear it. There was a pressure inside him, a knot of desire to fight someone—but whom? There was no one he could fight. Still clutching the stone axhead, he rose and pushed out through the door, jarring his head on the low doorway as he went through. Outside, the rain was still falling and

111

there was the rumble of thunder in the distance. He stood there in the rain, facing up into it blindly, not knowing whether to curse his fate or pray for aid.

Ason was suddenly aware of a motion nearby, of someone standing close by him. He turned about swiftly and stood ready, the axhead raised. Lightning crashed in the forest and in its quick flare of light he saw that it was Naikeri. He shook his head as the darkness descended again. Was he now afraid of women?

"I can help you," she said in a low voice, coming close.

"Go away," he answered, turning his back on her.

"I know you Mycenaeans," she said, moving to stand before him. "Women must be sick creatures in your land, the way you despise them. You must make yourself understand that is not true here. Among our people women are like men in many ways. Since my father's blindness it is I who speak in his name. I can be of aid to you."

"I want no woman's help."

"You'll get no other kind here," she shouted angrily. "Keep your pride and the mine will stay closed, your countrymen unavenged. Decide now. Which will it be?"

She spoke the truth, Ason realized. He was far from the Argolid. Strange lands bred strange ways.

"Why do you want to help me?" he asked.

"I don't. I need you, as you need me, to exact my own vengeance. I want you to kill Yerni. My people won't do it. All of my people are weak. My father is blind. They want to go farther into the forest, avoid any more trouble. I don't. I want to stay here. We have always traded in peace, even with the Yerni. We will do it again—when the ones who did this are dead. Your enemies are my enemies. I will aid you in their destruction."

"The mine must come first. You will get the boys to work there?"

"Yes. Will you have warriors to kill the Yerni?"

"Many. They are on their way now. Men who do killing of a kind you have never seen."

112

"Then reopen the mine—and kill Yerni!"

Her shouted words were drowned in the closer roll of thunder as the lightning blazed again through the rain. Darkness fell instantly, but her image was burned into his brain. Head back and wild eyed, the rain streaming from her glossy hair, soaking her clothing so that it clung tight to her full woman's body.

His hands went out to hold her—and he could feel her muscles grow hard under his grasp. She did not struggle as he forced her to the ground, but her voice was cold and sharp as a knife's edge.

"If you take me, you must take me by force, brave prince. Is this the only way noble Mycenaeans know how to make love?"

"No," he said, pushing her away angrily, sending her sprawling into the mud. "All I want from you are those boys to work the mine. See to it."

He slammed back inside, out of the rain. Disturbed and annoyed and not really sure why.

5

Ason was awake at first light, yawning and stretching as he pushed out into the misty dawn. He could hear the pigs snorting after acorns in the woodland that began just beyond the kitchen garden. Above the rising mist the sky was clear, with the full disc of the moon riding high above. A good omen perhaps, Artemis keeping watch so early after dawn. There was a stir in the house behind him, then smoke began to rise from the opening in the thatch, as the hearth was fanned to life. The day had begun. Perhaps more than just the day: the future. The mine.

He went back inside and shook Aias awake. The boxer just groaned and rolled over. Ason planted a solid kick in his ribs. Aias stumbled to his feet, swaying and cursing, blinking about for someone to hit with his clenched fists. Ason left him there and went to Naikeri, who was bent over the fire.

"I'll need some sandals for my feet," he said. "They are bleeding from the rocks."

"There are none here big enough for you, but I can make some that will fit. When are you going to the mine?"

"Now, this morning. Be quick with the sandals. We will need someone to guide us."

"I will show you the way."

By the time preparations had been made for the journey, most of the others were awake. Ler's snores vibrated loudly from the lockbed, while Inteb still slept exhaustedly among the blankets and tumbled furs. Ason left him there, gave Aias a stone tree-felling ax to carry, and followed Naikeri from the house and down the path between the fields. They left the Albi settlement and passed through the outlying clearings where long-horned cattle grazed, watched by dark and silent boys. The trail entered the forest, rising and falling as it followed the ridges between the trees. By the time the sun had climbed halfway up the sky they were sweating heavily. Aias groaned.

"This is no way to treat a sick man," he said.

"You are sick from the drinking."

"The cause is not important, just the fact that I am ill, perhaps dying."

Despite his complaints he kept up with the others. When they stopped for a drink at a stream which widened into a pool by a beaver dam, he took one sip of the water, sighed—then fell full length into the water. The beavers slapped their tails with alarm and disappeared. When Aias emerged, streaming and shivering, he claimed to feel much better.

They went on, Naikeri keeping her eyes carefully on the

trail they were following, going slower and slower until she stopped and pointed at the ground. Ason knelt and could make out a broken twig on a low bush, as well as other signs that someone had passed here. "There are Donbak-sho not too far from here," she said. "We could see them now, find out about the boys for the mine, they could tell others."

Ason was reluctant to turn aside. He had come so far and his destination was so close. "Why must it be boys?" he asked. "We can find people later to work the mine. Or slaves."

She shook her head, not knowing what he was talking about.

"Who else would do this kind of work except boys? There are many of them and they are not needed. What are you saying?"

They were wasting time. Perhaps there were no slaves in this land. Nor had he gold to buy any, or soldiers to capture and guard them. Like it or not, he must follow where this girl led.

"All right. Do what you want."

Naikeri appeared not to hear his angry tone and led them into the thicker forest. The sunlight vanished as they worked their way through the undergrowth and around the boles of the tall trees. It was hot, with all movement of air cut off, with insects humming irritatingly about their heads. Their path took them down a steep hillside into a valley, through a thick stand of massive-trunked oak trees, gnarled and ancient. It was cooler here, and they went more silently on the damp moss where a spring oozed out of the hillside, so quietly in fact that they surprised a boar rooting and snuffling for acorns in the fallen leaves. He looked up and snorted, as surprised as they were, yellow tusks flecked darkly with loam, small eyes red and angry. Aias shouted and threw the ax, but the boar whirled on his sharp-hooved feet and vanished into the undergrowth with a last flick of his tail. The ax missed and Aias cursed as he groped about under the thick bushes for it.

When they reached the valley floor they could hear a sharp thudding from ahead, regular as a heartbeat. It stopped and the silence was broken a moment later by the crackling descent of a falling tree. They went on, along a well-marked trail now, until they reached a clearing in the endless forest. On the hillside was a low, rush-roofed, square building with mud-dabbed walls. It was surrounded by small fields where knee-high, green-tassled grain rustled in the breeze. Three women were tilling between the rows with sharp deer-antler picks. They were bent double, bare to the waist in the warm sunshine, wearing only leathern skirts, their pendulous breasts swinging as they worked. They looked up and gaped at the newcomers. One of them called out in a high-pitched voice.

"Wait here," Naikeri said. "I can talk to them better if you are not close by."

Ason and Aias dropped to the ground in the shade and looked on, as children tumbled from the house and stood sucking at their fingers in the dooryard. There were a number of them, of all ages, alike only in their lack of clothes and the smears of dirt on their pallid skin. On the slope, high above, there was a sudden motion as two men burst into view, running heavily and carrying their stone-headed axes in both hands. Their shoulder-length hair blew free. Like the women, they were naked to the waist and drenched with sweat. When they saw there was no danger they slowed to a plodding walk, looking constantly at the two strangers as they came up to Naikeri, whom they knew. The women watched from a distance as the two men and the girl squatted and talked. She was being forceful and they grunted in response, shaking their heads and scratching deep under their hair with their thick fingers. In the end one of them stood and went to the house and pushed the children aside to grab a boy. He did not want to come but the man cuffed him, then dragged him by the ear back down the slope. There was more talk until they all stood and Naikeri left them, the men looking stolidly after her as she walked away.

"They are hard to talk to. Some of the boys came back, but others were killed at the mine."

"I didn't notice any shortage of replacements in that house," Ason said.

"There are enough boys, here and in other places. But the cost will be high. They have broken one ax this year and want a new one. That will take months of grinding. This one even wants a copper adze head if he is to get the boys for us. We have the mold and I think there is enough copper, but my father will not like it."

"But you will still do it?"

"Of course. You know that."

Ason believed her. He looked at the solid width of her thighs and flanks as she led the way out of the valley again, her muscles working steadily under the brown strands of her skirt. With her hair and skin she looked like one of the peasants at home, shorter perhaps, one of the workers in the fields. But here she was something else, a person of rank among her own people, able as well to talk to the Donbaksho men and make them listen. Just as he had listened and been convinced. Things were very different in this country, so far from the Argolid. He must learn the new ways. He would have preferred to lead his armored men into battle and take what was needed. No men, no armor. A way would still be found.

It was nearly noon, the air thick with the heat of the day, when they emerged from the forest again. This time at the mouth of a valley. Small shrubs were growing here, but the tree stumps and high grass showed that this area had been cleared once, and not too long ago. A dirt palisade sealed the mouth of the valley. Though it had been six years and he had been only a boy, Ason recognized the place at once. The mine.

Now he pushed the others aside and climbed the slope that he remembered only as raw earth. Where he and the

117

others had labored and sweated, digging and carrying dirt to heighten this defense. From the top he could see the end of the small valley where Lycos had worked so hard, torn so much wealth from the ground.

Ruin. The buildings jagged burnt shells with fallen-in roofs, weed-grown and already sinking back into the earth. The raw gash in the ground was still there, as well as the heaps of useless stone and dirt. But even these were already sprouting with grass and weeds, would soon vanish from sight. The hollow logs that took the water from the stream and carried it under the palisade had jammed with leaves and dirt. The water, no longer able to escape, had formed a marshy pond reaching back almost to the diggings. A pair of ducks, frightened by his sudden appearance, flapped heavily up from the water and flew away.

Ason did not notice them. He was seeing this place as he had known it before, busy with activity. He was trying to remember everything. His uncle, proud of what he had built, had taken him by the hand and explained it all to him. He remembered being bored, wishing he could go hunting instead with the men who went out for deer. But he had learned despite himself, watching what the boys were doing, working alongside his uncle when he charged the furnaces, the final vital step that he would allow none of the others to do.

Here was the tin stream, like a captured rocky rivulet in the soil. Lycos thought much about this and had taken him up to the hillside above and chipped off a chunk of the reddish rock, pointed to the black granules it contained. There was tin in the rock here, but it was easier to go down. To find it in the dry stream below where it had been washed out of the softer, weathered rock by the rains of untold years. It was close to the surface, even on the surface at the narrow top of the stream, but this area had been picked clean years before. Now they had to dig beneath the soil where the hidden stream of black stones and sand fanned out. The wooden tye was still there, though badly rotted and in need of repair, still with heavy granules of tin in it where the dirt had been dumped and the water of the brook had washed the lighter soil away. Not that all the tin was this easy to find. Most of it was sealed in larger chunks of rock which had to be broken with hammers to free it; the grooves and holes in the outcropping of rock where it had been pounded were clearly visible.

And the furnaces were still there. That was the important thing, because the secret of their construction was unknown to Ason. They looked simple enough, each one a cone-shaped hole in the ground, with a smaller hole for the bellows cut in from the side to meet its base. But Ason had no idea of how they had been made, or what the hidden design that had shaped them was. But they were intact—and he knew the art of charging them. The tin could be mined and smelted; it could be done. Perimedes would send a ship, sooner or later, to reopen the mine. They would find it in full working order again, with a rich harvest for Mycenae.

"Killed them all," Aias said, and Ason realized for the first time how many bones there were in the camp.

Human bones, skeletons, most of them with the skulls missing. No armor or weapons, though sun-bleached scraps of leather and cloth fluttered here and there.

"There are Mycenaeans here," he cried aloud. "We will avenge them." In sudden anger at the bitterness of the death of his kinsmen, so far from high-walled Mycenae, he tore his sword from the slings on his back and whirled it brightly over his head.

"Vengeance!" he howled, over and over. "Vengeance!" and his lips curled back with the hatred that filled him, and he clenched his teeth until they grated together. Men would die, many, many.

On the hilltop, high above, the man squatted in the shade of the stand of beech trees. His body was concealed by the undergrowth and only his head was visible through

119

an opening in the wall of shrubbery. He made no move that might be seen; his face appeared part of the light and shade of the forest.

Silent as a painted statue. His skin painted white with chalk, and chalk rubbed as well into his light blond hair until it was whiter still. Although his cheeks and chin had been plucked smooth, the hair on his upper lip had been allowed to grow into a great drooping moustache. It had been combed out on both sides and worked with clay and chalk, until it was stiff and hard, white as an animal's horns. Or a boar's tusks. Under the solid moustache his lips parted in a grin and he licked them greedily. He had come a long way and waited a long time, until he had almost given up all hope of the treasure he had been promised. Now it would be his.

A tall, well-muscled man clad only in a short leather kirtle that stopped above his knees, decorated in front with a pelt of fox fur. He wore a bow on his back, a clutch of arrows tied in with it, and held a hunting spear in his hand.

He laughed deep in his throat as he dropped slowly from sight and turned and made his way back through the undergrowth. Once among the trees he stood and began running east at a steady, ground-eating pace.

His name was Ar Apa and he belonged to the teuta of Der Dak on the high downs.

6

Tired, running with sweat, limping from a stone cut on his foot, stumbling from the effort of walking and running day after day, Ar Apa came within sight of the walls of his dun late in the afternoon. Two half-grown boys were close by, driving home the cattle after a day's grazing on the down. The sight of the animals' great eyes, smooth muscles and sleek hides quieted him and made him forget his fatigue. He walked among them, calling by name the ones he recognized, rubbing his hands on their warm flanks and feeling the hard strength of their long, sharp horns. They were sleek and fat now, recovered from their nearly fatal winter leanness. He smiled at the beauty of them. One of the boys, running to head off a straying calf, got in his way, and Ar Apa slapped him so hard on the side of his head that he fell and rolled, stumbling to his feet and sobbing as he ran on. Ar Apa waved to the other boy, who came forward hesitantly. His eyes were frightened and suspicious behind the mat of long blond hair that fell to his shoulders, half covered his face.

"Water," Ar Apa shouted. "Or you'll get twice what I gave the other one."

The water was hot and foul after a day in the leather bag, but he only sipped a little to wet his throat, then poured more into the palm of his hand to mix with the chalk he had pulverized there. His mustaches were bedraggled and broken and he had to work the fresh paste into them to smooth them back to their original firmness. He sat on the ground and grunted while he worked at them, then rubbed the remaining white water through the already stiffened mat of his hair. The cattle had gone on to the enclosure of the dun walls, their steaming dung the only mark of their passing. He broke a nearby clod with his toe: well formed, solid—they were eating well. Very good. Wiping his hands on his kirtle, he took up the spear, the bow and arrows that had fed him during his long vigil, and followed the cattle. Breaking into a fast trot as he came within hailing distance of the wattled walls, shouting so they could hear him.

"Ar Apa comes, what a man, what a runner, what a hunter! He has run a hundred nights without stopping, killed a hundred deer without stopping, drunk only their blood and eaten their raw flesh without stopping. What a

121

man. Ar Apa, Ar Apa!''

He smiled happily, almost believing himself, so well did he shout, trotting down into the ditch that fell below the chalk embankment that surrounded and defended the dun, taking a short cut directly to the entrance to his own apartment. If anyone had heard his boasts, they made no sign, but since they had been mostly for his own benefit he did not mind. It was doubtful if even the loudest war screamer could have been heard over the evening bedlam inside Dun Der Dak. Striding through the doorway from his rooms into his mother's, he looked out from the woman's second-story balcony onto the scene below.

Cattle milled about, the cows lowing with the weight of their full udders, while the sheep, their red wool whitened by chalk dust, moved bleating between their legs. Women were milking the cows and ewes into squat clay pots, screaming at the younger children who ran among the animals, seeking out lumps of dung to use as missiles to hurl at each other.

Ar Apa nodded appreciatively at the rich scene, the bursting life, and only turned reluctantly away when he remembered the urgency of his message. He put on his hair belt and slipped the handle of his stone-headed battle-ax into it. Then he slowly made his way along the high chalk bank that encircled the dun. This gave entrance to all the men's quarters on the outside of the ring of apartment dwellings, an unbroken ring except for the main entrance. Der Dak's rooms were here, spanning the entranceway, first in pride of place, where he could look down and see all those who came and went. But he was not here now. Ar Apa peered into the darkness and called, but there was no answer. He went even slower as he retraced his steps back along the top of the bank, around the outside of the wicker work of the apartment walls and past the openings of the other men's quarters. There were voices inside many of them. Outside the next doorway, asleep on a wolfskin, was a man named Cethern. He was getting old

122

now for a warrior, ready for marriage, but still a great fighter. Cradled under his right knee was a man's severed head, yellowish and shriveled beneath the film of cedar oil that it had been soaked in, stinking a good deal despite this embalming treatment. Cethern opened his eyes, which were red and inflamed, and smacked his lips many times as though trying to get rid of a taste he did not enjoy. He had been drinking ale all day. His breath declared that, if not the discarded pot and his squat little drinking cup. Ar Apa sat down on his heels by him.

"Ar Apa has been away many nights," he said. "Running all the time, killing boar and hunting deer."

"Cethern killed a champion from Dun Moweg," the other called out hoarsely. "Chopped him down after battling fifteen nights without a stop in the middle of the Stour River, cut off his head, here is his head, have you ever seen a head like that? Moweg's champion."

Ar Apa had seen it too many times, and he let Cethern talk on while he pulled over the pot and saw that there was still some ale in the bottom. He drained it. "Der Dak is not here," he said.

Cethern shook his head and grunted *no*, sighing as he dropped down.

"And the other, the one, who is there. . . ." He did not speak the name, but shrugged his shoulder in the right direction.

"He is there." Cethern said, showing no desire to talk too much about him either. He closed his eyes again.

There were things that had to be done. Ar Apa breathed out heavily and stood, brushing his hard moustaches with his knuckles, clutching his ax. Even more slowly now, he followed the walkway in a complete circle around to the first door on the other side of the entrance, the place of honor next to Der Dak's, and looked inside. Its interior was invisible now, with the sun gone and night upon them.

"Come inside, strong Ar Apa," a voice said from the

darkness, speaking with a strange accent and a wet lisp. "You have come with something to tell me, something *important* to tell me?"

Ar Apa held even more tightly to the haft of his ax and blinked about the darkened chamber. There were hangings of cloth here and chests, as well as a sweet smell that he had never known before. And an even darker movement in the rear. A person, a man, the one they called the Dark Man whenever someone, drunk enough, dared to speak his name aloud.

"The gift. . .," Ara Apa said, the words not coming easily.

"I have many gifts, rich gifts, gifts you've never seen before. And I have a gift for you if it pleases me. But you must please me, Ar Apa. Do you please me? You took a gift from me, an amber disc rimmed with gold, made by the wonderful craftsmen that serve in great Dun Uala. And you told me you would go to the west, to the place where all the men with swords were killed, to wait there and see if anyone came back. Have you done this? Have you seen anything?"

"I have done this! I have run a hundred nights and slain a hundred boar and eaten a hundred deer, all this I have done! I have gone to the valley." Boldened by the sound of his voice, he told all the things he had done, or wished that he had done, or heard that others had done, or even imagined might be done. The Dark Man listened in silence. In the end Ar Apa finally told him about the two men and the girl who had come to the burnt-out settlement, how one man had waved his bronze sword and sworn so loudly that, on the hill above, Ar Apa had heard him clearly. Then his voice ran down and he was silent, coughing and spitting onto the floor and looking back over his shoulder through the doorway where the first stars were now appearing.

"You have done very, very well," the Dark Man finally

said. "You have told me that which I wanted to hear, and you have told me what a great hunter and warrior Ar Apa is, which I wanted to hear as well, since I am honored to be among such great warriors. Now—here is your gift."

There was a rattle of bolts in the darkness and the squeak of hinges. Ar Apa walked forward with his hand out, everything else forgotten in his greed, and felt a cool hand, soft as a child's, touching his, and something cooler was pressed into it.

"It is gold, all gold," the Dark Man said. Ar Apa hurried out and looked at the wonder in his palm, clear and shining in the moonlight. Solid gold, heavy and precious. Already fixed to a necklace. A haft and an ax in gold big enough to cover his palm. A wonder beyond belief.

Filled with the joy of it, Ar Apa went down to the great hearth in the center of the dun, down to the sound of much shouting and loud talk, with the flames of the high-leaping fire casting moving light upon the ring of pillar stones that embraced the scene. As he stepped into the circle Ar Apa brushed his hand against his own red-tipped pillar stone, higher than he was by several heads. He gained strength by the touch. An ox had been killed and had roasted most of the day until now. The skin was black and crackling and gave off a mouth-watering odor that hung in the air, heavier than smoke. Urged on by much shouted instruction, some of the newly initiated warriors struggled to lift the ends of the green pole. It had been thrust down the steer's throat and out its bottom. They staggered with the steaming carcass, until the pole rested between two wooden hurdles. The older warriors were already calling out and boasting as to who should have the honor of cutting the meat and taking the choicest piece. Cethern would cut it as he always did, but not before the others had their say.

"I am a champion," Nair said, jumping to his feet and beating his ax against his shield. There were sharp cries which he ignored, shouting even louder to drown them out. "*I* claim the right to carve the roast. In the raid against Finmog's teuta I cried out in the night outside the dun. When the warriors ran out I killed the first ten with my ax, killed the next ten with my ax and took their heads, and another ten and another ten. . . ." His voice rose with each repetition, and he jumped and stamped on the ground until Cethern himself began to howl and beat on his own shield. He was hungry and out of sorts this evening. He wanted to eat without the extended ritual of boasting that would last until the meat was cold.

"I am Cethern, I am the best, I am the killer of men, the stealer of cows, the dealer of death, with death in my hand, and death in my ax, and death where I go." Carried away, he spun in a circle, swinging his ax so that the men in the front had to fall back shouting angrily, and Nair growled in his throat and went to sit down in the back.

"Cethern the killer; a hundred men dead in an eyeblink, and all their heads at my belt; a hundred times a hundred dead in a night, and all of their heads making a pile as high as my pillar stone; and all their cows my cows, and all their bulls my bulls, and all their deaths my deaths. The strongest, Cethern, the killer, Cethern, the murderer, the blood-letter, the terrible. . . ."

"The great empty skin of air," Ar Apa shouted.

There were appreciative cries at this, and some laughter, and Cethern howled with rage and looked about for the man who had insulted him. Ar Apa pulled a shield away from the man next to him and pushed through the crowd. He had listened to Cethern boast before and had been as angry as the other men, but like them had kept his silence because he knew that Cethern was as good as his boast. But not tonight. The glow of the golden ax still burned in his eyes, and any man who could win an ax like that was as good a man as this bragging fool.

"Boasting fool!" he shouted aloud, and the men roared with answering shouts. This was going to be a battle. "I'll cut the meat. *I* am the champion. I ran a hundred nights, killed a hundred deer, beheaded a hundred boar—all in a single night." He circled about Cethern, who was growling and spitting as foam collected on his lips.

"Ar Apa's father was witless, he had no mother, he is no man, he has no balls. . . ." He choked on his own sputum and Ar Apa shouted back.

"I am the killer, I have an amber disc bound with gold, I have a two-headed gold ax, I talked with the Dark Man, I cannot be stopped!"

He swung his ax around in a swirling blow, but Cethern jumped back and raised his shield so that the ax bounced from it. Everyone was shouting now. Speaking the Dark Man's name aloud was very bold, and they appreciated it, and so did Cethern, who moved away again to dodge a blow. The women and children were running up to huddle behind the seated men and watch, their eyes round. Silent figures in the darkness.

"Ar Apa is a liar," was the best Cethern could say, swinging a blow himself that the other dodged.

"Look, look!" Ar Apa shouted, seizing his ax haft in his teeth as he backed away, reaching for his belt and the small bundle pressed against his skin there. He unwrapped the necklace from around the golden ax and held it high, to glow redly in the firelight, then plunged it away again at the appreciative shouts. Cethern rushed at him and caught the blow on his shield and spat his own ax into his palm.

After that the serious fighting began. If Cethern was the better axman, he was past his prime and had drunk a lot that day. Ar Apa was strong and angry, pushed into ferocious attack by the golden ax, elated at how the others had cheered at the sight of it. He rained down blows upon his opponent, pushing at his body and trying to tangle his legs, all the time hammering with his ax as if he were chopping a tree. It was all Cethern could do to keep his shield up to catch the blows that crashed upon it. He was

127

never able to free his own ax from the pressure of Ar Apa's shield. They went around the fire like this, thundering and straining, shouting wordless curses at each other. Almost in desperation, feeling the flames at his back, Cethern pulled his ax away and swung a sharp quick blow up under the other's guard that caught Ar Apa on the thigh, drawing blood. Ar Apa sprang back, and the men shouted even louder.

Still possessed by anger, Ar Apa was not bothered by the wound for it infuriated him even more. He felt the numbness in his leg muscles, and saw his own red blood, and shrieked with fury, an ear-splitting blast that silenced all the others. Even Cethern hesitated a moment and peered over the top of his shield.

Ar Apa threw his arms wide, hurling his shield away from him so hard that it flew over the men and fell among the squealing women. Then he seized his ax in both hands, raising it above his head, leaping in at Cethern. He did it all in an instant, unthinking, possessed by fury that overwhelmed him. Cethern crouched and raised his shield, drawing his own ax back for a counterblow that he knew the other could not avoid.

The ax came down with such force that Ar Apa's feet left the ground. Striking the hide-covered wooden shield, splitting it, driving through with such force that the shield struck Cethern on the forehead and he fell. He was half stunned, and rolled about trying to get back to his feet.

He never did. Ar Apa raised the ax high again and brought the polished sharp weight of the blade down on Cethern's forehead. Through the bone and into his brain, killing him instantly.

All the warriors were shouting again, pummeling each other with elation while Ar Apa strutted before them, waving his battle-ax around and around his head with such joy that bits of gore flew from it and spattered them. Then he threw his ax aside and stood over Cethern, straddling him, pulling the man's bronze dagger from his necklace. A rich object this, one of the very few owned by any warrior in the whole teuta, and sharper than anything else was sharp. Clutching it in both hands, pressing and sawing through the dead man's neck until he had severed his head, and the ground beneath was soaked with blood. Then he stood and tucked the long hair into his belt so that the severed head dangled there, the last blood draining down his leg.

Numbed by success, he walked stiff-legged over to the roasted ox and with the dagger, still dripping with gore, cut from it the champion's portion for himself.

7

"I'm sure it's ready now," Ason said. "See, there's no more ore on top of the coals." He bent over to peer into the glowing mound, squinting into the shimmer of rising heat that was clearly visible in the warm sunlight.

"Patience," Inteb advised, brushing at the charcoal smudges on his arms and hands. "The walls of Mycenae were not raised in a day, nor is tin drawn from stone in a few brief moments. That was the fault the first time we tried this. Don't you remember that the coals were still glowing when we raked them aside?"

"How can we be sure?"

"We cannot. But it does no harm to wait."

Ason did not have the patience to stand idly by and watch while the smelting continued. His temperament was completely different from that of the builder Inteb, who could wait quietly while stone was worked to his design, while buildings and walls were raised. Leaving the Egyptian by the furnace, Ason walked over to the tin stream where Aias lolled on the grass nearby, apparently asleep.

That he was not was proven when the two boys fell to whispering and stopped their digging. Aias had a small pile of rocks to hand and a good aim; the boys shrieked as the missiles hit them, then fell to shoveling again with deer shoulderblades. They scooped the gravel to one side, then filled their basket with the deeper soil that contained the gray-black nuggets. When the basket was filled, they pushed and dragged it to the sloping wooden sluice of the tye and dumped it in. The water from the spring ran over the muddy mixture as they stirred it with their hands so the lighter particles would be washed away. There were still not enough boys. These should have returned to their digging while others picked out the black pebbles, while still others pounded them into fragments. The boys worked faster under Ason's gaze, putting the wet ore into baskets before hurrying back. They would break up the walnut-sized lumps later.

Everything about the operation was makeshift, but was the best they could do with the limited labor available. If they had had treasure, bronze, gold, they could have bought more boys; only Naikeri's hatred for the raiders had carried them this far. There were rough lean-tos for sleeping, just slanted roofs of boughs and branches. They cooked over an open fire; they drank plain water. But they were mining ore. The earth-covered mounds of the charcoal-making fires were burning well. And if they had charged the furnace correctly this time, they would have their first tin. Ason resisted the temptation to return to the first furnace and went instead to help Inteb with the dirty work of charging the other furnace that they had prepared. It was just a round depression in the clay, sloping toward a hole in the center the size of two cupped hands. A mound of charcoal had been heaped in there, topped with pulverized ore, then ignited. The bellows boy was called over to pump air into it, leaving the other furnace to burn itself out. Lycos had smelted tin this way, and Ason remembered how he had done it. So far all they had produced was an evil mixture of charcoal and slag. And tin was what they needed, tin. Through his harsh thoughts he was aware of someone calling his name, and he looked up to see Naikeri standing on top of the granite-studded wall of earth that sealed the valley.

She was wet with perspiration, her hair matted and moist, her mouth gaping as she tried to catch her breath. "The Yerni have been seen near my father's home and he is frightened. He will not stay any more but is taking everything and fleeing to our people in the west. He is very afraid that this time he will be killed and all of us destroyed. He thinks the Yerni have gone mad as rutting deer and he will not stay where they can reach him. You must come with me and stop him."

"Let him go. It means nothing to us here."

"Nothing!" She spat the word and clenched her fists with anger. "How is this mine open, why are you digging for tin? It is all my father's wealth that did this. His gifts to the Donbaksho brought the boys here. He provides your food. Even a copper adze head. I made him cast it in his blindness to get what you needed. And now you scorn him. Where are the dead Yerni warriors you were to kill in your vengeance? Where are their heads? You take everything and give nothing—and then say my father is nothing."

Ason turned away from her and folded his arms and looked at the mine workings, not hearing her. If she were not so important he would have silenced her. But he could not. Neither could he lower himself to trade angry words with a woman. He waited until her voice had stopped, then turned back.

"What can I say to Ler that would make him stay?"

"Say that you will protect him, that you will kill Yerni. Talk to him of vengeance for his dead sons and murdered people. Perhaps you can anger him to vengeance; I cannot. He wants only to run."

Ason did not like it. He was needed here at the mine.

There would be long arguments with Ler and promises made that he might not be able to keep. Endless talk and no action; he hated this. Yet he had to do it. If talk could take the place of warriors he would have to talk—because he had none to stand behind him.

"I'll come," he said reluctantly. "I must tell Inteb what is happening."

There was no other course open. With a long last look at the dying furnace he led the way out of the camp and along the ill-defined path. He went at his fastest pace and could hear Naikeri behind him panting to keep up, which made him smile.

Well away from the mine the trail dipped downward from the open heathland, to pass by the edge of a thicketed marsh. As Ason worked his way down the slope he felt, with a hunter's instinct, that there were eyes upon him. There was game in the fenland, deer and boar to be sure, but mainly water fowl and small game. But this was different. He looked ahead and stopped, pulling his sword from the slings as he did so. Naikeri nearly ran into him.

"Why do you stop?" She had to gasp out the words. Ason pointed down the slope with his sword.

At the bottom, at the very edge of the boggy thicket, in the sedge grass, stood a man and a hulking, wolflike dog. Both as unmoving as stone. The man was short and dumpy, with a pasty white skin that was rounded with fat over the muscles below. They were close enough to see that he wore only a breechclout of red fox fur. His legs were encased up over the knees in waterproof boots made from the skin off the hocks of a wild horse. Gripped in one hand was a thin spear tipped with a bone point, with a pendant snare below. At his waist, hanging in a net, were a gutted hare and a brace of dark-feathered duck.

"Who are you?" Ason shouted, brandishing his sword. At the sound of his voice, the man splashed back into the depths of the bog. Naikeri shouted a harsh, strange-sounding word and pulled at Ason's arm.

"Put away your sword," she said. "It is one of the people from the deep fens, the Hunters they are called. They trade with us and do not make war like the Yerni. He is here for a reason. Let me go first and talk to him."

Ason lowered his sword—but did not return it to its slings—as Naikeri went ahead. The dog growled deeply and showed its fangs as she came close. The Hunter hit it in the ribs with the haft of his spear, pushing the beast behind him. Naikeri sat down on her knees, and the short man, after looking up at Ason, stepped up on the grass and sat down on his heels. They talked for a long time, and Ason was getting restless before Naikeri called out to him.

"Put your sword away and come down, slowly. He has much to tell us."

The Hunter and his dog looked at Ason with identical suspicion as he approached and sat down cross legged on the ground three paces away.

"This man is Chaskil," she explained. "I have met him before many times, and he speaks our tongue as well as his own."

Chaskil seemed reluctant to speak any language. He stared at Ason, dark eyes peering from beneath fatty eyelids. His face was flat and his nose was depressed without a bridge, his hair black and lank. After a long while he turned away from Ason and looked into the distance. When he finally spoke, his words were heavily accented but understandable.

"I am Chaskil and she is Naikeri and you are Ason, or so she has told me. I am Chaskil of the Hunters who have hunted here forever and we talk about it. We hunted here when it was cold in all seasons and we talk about it. The Albi came and we talk about it. They came to the moors and they do what they must do, and we do what we must do, and we talk about it. Then the Donbaksho came to the forest with their tree-killing axes and we talk about it. Then the Yerni came to the downs with their cows and man-killing axes and we talk about it. We talk about a tree-killing ax." He fell silent and fingered his hunting knife, a row of tiny, delicately flaked chips of flint set in a shank of antler. Naikeri had experience with these solitary, hidden people and knew how to speak with them. Ason was baffled and thought the man mad.

"We talk about it," she said. "We talk about the Yerni and we talk about the ax. Do we talk about your ax?"

Chaskil stirred at her words and shifted his weight so he could lift his left foot. Under the sole of his horse-skin boot was a broken piece of greenstone, the type of rare jadite that the Albi ground and polished for the making of battle-axes, as well as wood-working axes and adzes.

"That's a piece of broken axhead," Naikeri said. "An Albi axhead. Is it your axhead?" He nodded. She went on: "The Albi are friends of the Hunters. We give them ax-heads so they can make dugout canoes. So they can go fishing along the coast. They give us help. They guide us in our trading travels. They tell us things they have seen. Have you seen something?"

"We talk about the Yerni. We talk about my axhead."

"You will have a new axhead as soon as one can be made. You will come to my father's house as you always do, and we will talk of it there. But you do not go to my father's house, but instead meet us here. Why is that?"

"We talk of Yerni."

Ason had a sudden thought. "Are there any nearby?" he asked. Chaskil turned to look squarely at Ason.

"We talk about Yerni who killed a Hunter. Who watch the place where you dig in the ground and make smoke. We talk about Yerni who hide and watch. . . ."

"Waiting for me to leave!" Ason shouted, springing to his feet. "They have been watching, they know my sword, they waited for me to leave. . . ." Then he was pounding up the hill and over it, back toward the mine. Naikeri talked briefly to Chaskil, then hurried after him.

After the first burst of anger, Ason slowed down and

forced himself to go at a steady run that would take him back to the mine without stopping, without exhausting himself. As he jogged through the shadows of the high trees he found himself smiling with anticipation. If the Hunter were right this was his chance for revenge. Yerni—that was something to look forward to! He hastened to the meeting with all his heart.

When he neared the mine he slowed down and went more carefully. If they were hiding nearby he did not want to disturb them. As he approached the base of the hillock that sealed the valley, one of the boys burst over the top of it. Running as if death were at his heels—and at the same moment Ason heard a high shrieking.

"They are here!" Ason shouted in return and ran as hard as he could, sword ready. The valley and the mine opened up before him, changed drastically in the short time since he had left.

The rain shelters over the furnaces were knocked down and burning. The boys were gone. And Inteb's body lay on the ground, half in the water running from the lye. Near him was the body of a stranger; further up the valley was another.

Howling with anger, Aias stood halfway up the valley wall where he had climbed, hurling stones down at three Yerni, who were trying to climb up after him. They were shouting even louder at this unnatural way to fight and were trying to get up high enough to reach him with their stone-headed battle-axes. One of them climbed ahead of the others and instantly regretted it when Aias leaped down beside him. Long before he could swing his ax around, the boxer's fist lashed out against the side of his head, and he fell and tumbled down the hillside. Then Aias had scrambled higher again, calling back insults. He had not gone unscathed himself; his chest and arms were wet with blood.

Ason ran quietly and was almost upon them before they were aware of him. The last man Aias had knocked down the hill was stumbling to his feet and groping for his ax. He saw Ason coming and shouted a warning. He raised the ax but died a moment later when the point of the bronze sword tore out his throat. The other two spun about to attack Ason. He smiled and let them come.

He could have killed them quickly, but he wanted them to die knowing who he was and why he was doing this. The sweat started out from their faces and they swung wildly as he cursed them. One tried to rush him, and Ason slashed his legs so badly that he could do no more than rise to his knees.

When he had told them what he wanted them to know, Ason attacked and killed each of them quickly. Then went back to make sure that the other two Yerni were dead as well. Both had fallen victim to Aias' fists. The nearest one lay with his eyes open, a great bruise on the side of his head, which was twisted around at an odd angle. His neck had been broken and he appeared to have died at once. The other lay on his back, rolling from side to side and clutching at his head. Aias must have hit him squarely on the nose, breaking it all over his face, and he was just regaining consciousness. He shook all over, and his bloodshot, blackened eyes opened when Ason pushed his sword against the base of the man's throat.

"Who are you?" Ason said.

The Yerni looked wildly about him and reached for the sword, but dropped his arms back when Ason pressed harder.

"Nair," he gasped, choking under the sharp pressure.

"Where are you from?"

"I am—of the teuta of Der Dak."

It meant nothing to Ason. He shook his sword angrily and kicked the man in the stomach. "What are you doing here? Why are you raiding this place?"

"The man—Dark Man-gifts—the Dark Man."

He rolled sideways suddenly, slapping at the blade at the same time. Ason lunged but his sword only stabbed

136

into the ground. Before he could lift it again, Nair was upon him, grappling him and pulling a bronze dagger from his necklace. Ason grabbed the man's wrist before the thrust could go home. His own sword arm pinioned the same way. They strained, face to face, Ason smelling the man's foul breath, the reek of his unwashed body. Over his shoulder he saw Aias running up, his fist drawn back for a decapitating sweep.

"No," Ason called out. "He is mine."

Aias stopped, but stood ready. Ason did not try to bring his sword around for a cut; it was a clumsy weapon at these close quarters, but instead bent all his strength to turn the dagger aside. Slowly, shaking with the effort of the struggle, the point was turned away from his own skin and forced back towards the midriff of its owner. Nair looked at the approach of the blade, his eyes starting from his head. He put all of his strength against it, but still it turned and turned until the point was touching his skin. He never thought to release the dagger, but instead held it in his own fist as Ason fought against him until, with a single convulsive effort, he plunged the weapon home deep up under Nair's breast bone. Ason held it there for a long moment as the man writhed and died, then stepped away so the body could fall.

8

Inteb was not dead. His head was bruised and raw where an ax had struck him down, but he was still breathing. Naikeri had arrived in time to see the last man slain, looking on with pleasure at this first payment of the vengeance she had worked so hard for. She now sang softly to herself as she tended Inteb, bathing his head with cool water from the stream.

Ason sat down heavily next to the corpse, stretching the strained muscles of his hand.

"They came after you left," Aias said. "They must have been watching. They came yelping and howling up the valley, very sure of themselves. They knew who was here. Inteb was unarmed, tried to run. They chopped him down. I broke that man's neck before the Egyptian could be killed. All the boys ran. I threw my club at one of the Yerni then hit him in the nose. Another one hit me. I ran too. Up the cliff there. Then you came back." He grinned through the blood and bent for a handful of water to wipe his face.

"Round up the boys and get them back to work," Ason said. "Put up new shelters." He went over to look at Inteb, who now had his eyes open and was blinking dazedly.

"Yerni. . .," he said weakly, then tried to look around.

"All dead. But one of them talked to me before he died." Naikeri looked up when he said this. "What is the teuta of Der Dak? That is what he said."

"Der Dak is a bull-chief of one of the tribes of the Yerni," Naikeri said. "One of the five tribes; five teuta that fight against each other all of the time. If the Yerni have any allegiance at all it is to their bull-chief. Der Dak's teuta is the one closest to us. These men must have come from there; Dun Der Dak is four days' walk to the east. Why did they come? Did Der Dak send them?"

"He talked about someone called a Dark Man. Is that one of their chiefs?"

"I have never heard of him, or anyone by that name. Perhaps it is one of their gods."

Inteb groaned and sat up. "You came back in time, praise Horus," he said weakly. "Are they dead?"

"All of them, and no thanks to Horus. A man stopped us, some kind of hunter from the forests around here. He saw the Yerni watching us."

Ason turned about to face Naikeri. "And why weren't

138

your people watching out for raiders? You seem to know when your own places are threatened, but not when the mine is."

"My people have other things to do than spy for you. We work hard and must defend ourselves. And what about my father—you said you would see him?"

"Your father! Your people! I cannot defend him and them and this mine, and smelt tin, not one man by myself. I am needed here."

"If you do not help my father, you will have no more food, or boys—or a mine. What do you choose?"

What could he choose? He had to have the help of the Albi. But how could he guard them all from the murderous Yerni raiders?

"Why don't you stop the raids?" Inteb asked, answering his unspoken question. Ason turned to listen. "The girl told you that the Yerni have never acted like this before. Apparently the different tribes of the Yerni make war on each other and trade with the Albi. A sensible arrangement. But someone has stopped being sensible and is sending out these raiding parties. Find out who it is, kill him. The trouble will stop."

"But who is it?"

"Der Dak!" Naikeri said. "Who else could it be? The men of his teuta do not make war without his orders. They fight alone, that they do any time. But they would not come this far, all together, unless he told them to do so. Go and kill him and the trouble will be over."

"Battle my way through his entire following of loyal warriors? I can fight one man, but not all of his men."

"Perhaps you won't have to," Inteb said, touching the side of his head and wincing. "This arrangement of the teuta with its bull-chief and warriors sounds much like one of your cities of the Argolid—"

"You dare compare noble Mycenae or Tiryns to these stinking savages!"

"Patience, kind Ason, I compare only the lines of

139

authority. I have dwelt in many places and I find that people are very much the same everywhere. They have rulers and gods, and among the people there are those who kill and those who are killed. Those who lead and those who follow. Let us profit from this experience."

"I could call this Der Dak out and kill him and that would stop the raids." He looked at Naikeri. "Do they speak as your people do? Would they know what I was saying? The one I killed seemed to understand me."

"Their talk is a little different, some words are different, but they will understand you. I can tell you some words so they will understand you better."

"What is it that they are most proud of?" Inteb asked.

Naikeri thought for a moment. "Their fighting ability; they always brag about that, and how bold they are, and how fast they can run, and how many beasts they have killed. Oh yes, and how many cows they own. And have stolen. They love their cattle more than their women, I have heard. And their jewelry—the gold torcs and bronze daggers they get in trade. They are very vain."

"If I leave in the morning will you show me the way?" Ason asked.

"With all my heart. If Der Dak's men killed my people, I want to be there when you slay him."

Aias came up and called to them. He had two battle-axes in each hand, three twisted gold bars around his neck and a bronze dagger hanging there as well.

"From the bodies," he said.

"For the mine," Ason said. "We will not have to depend upon Ler's bounty now."

"I will take the axes," Naikeri said. "They are Albi made. You take the torcs and the dagger. Wear all of it. Only that much treasure will give a warrior high enough standing among the Yerni to challenge a bull-chief."

"The furnace," Inteb said, climbing slowly to his feet. "We have forgotten, and it should be finished by now."

They hurried to it, watching closely as Inteb raked the

ashes away from the little pit underneath. He pried into it, but could see nothing but the crumbled ash. Ason grabbed up a singed length of fur sopping with water and wrapped it around his hand. He groped about in the bottom, drawing something out with a great hissing, dropping it as it burned his fingers.

A disc of silvery crackling metal, convex on the bottom and flat on top, thick and heavy.

"Tin," Ason said. "At last. It can be nothing else."

Naikeri and Ason left Ler's house at dawn the next morning. At first the old man ignored them and was intent upon moving his own belongings at once. Naikeri shouted and pleaded with him, and after a time he listened. In his blindness he would really prefer to stay in the place he knew, so in the end they prevailed. If Ason defeated Der Dak, the raids would cease and he could live in peace. He wanted to believe that and they convinced him.

There were a number of wooden chests that had been dug up from under the dirt floor. He rooted through one of these, heaving aside a small boulder carved all over with shapes for the open-casting of various types of copper axes and adzes. He came up with a bronze skullcap, its plume socket empty. It was lined with padded leather, profit of a trade of years previous. It was not the helmet of a nobleman, but it would do. Ason also had a thick hide tunic that might help turn a blow, and he had one of the round Yerni shields. And his sword. That alone was more important than all the rest together.

Their path took them across the high moors, along a trail marked by generations of travelers' feet. It had rained during the night, and the air was filled with the pungent smell of loam, damp earth and heather. A hawk moved in silent circles over a copse—then folded its wings and dropped like a rock, soaring high again with some small animal in its talons. The sun was warm but the air cool, a day for doing things. Ason hummed tonelessly to himself.

141

Naikeri led the way, carrying a backpack filled with the food they had brought. She walked at a steady, tireless pace, her legs moving smoothly, the thrust of her buttocks visibly working between the open spaces of her yarn skirt, strands of brown wool that ran from her narrow waist to tight bands that gathered them together on her thighs. Ason looked at this and felt a stirring, a desire long unsatisfied.

When the sun was overhead they turned off the well-marked path and went down the bank of a small stream, to a place where they could eat and drink. Wordlessly, she took a piece of sun-dried meat from her pack and gave it to Ason. He chewed it and cupped water from the stream with his hand to wash it down. They sat in silence, but when she looked up she found his eyes upon her. He looked away.

Many things about the world Ason knew, many more were mysteries. The doings of women would always be a mystery. Naikeri, who had pushed him away in the night, now called him to her in the heat of the day.

When he was done with her he went to wash in the stream. Naikeri slowly pulled her clothing back into place. Ason wanted to leave, but she did not rise from the spot where their bodies had pressed the tall grass flat.

"Do you have a wife in this far-distant land that you come from?" she asked.

"It is time to leave."

"Tell me."

"No, no wife. This is not the time to talk of these things."

"This is the time. You are the first man who has ever had me. If you want me—"

"I want you when I want you, nothing more. Put any other thoughts away from you. When the tin is mined I shall return to the Argolid. When I marry it will be a woman of a noble house. That is the way it must be. Now get to your feet."

She was angry and did not stand, pulling away from his hand when he reached for her.

"My line is the oldest of the Albi—you saw our tomb. If we had queens I would be one. . . ."

"You are nothing," Ason said harshly, dragging her to her feet. When she spoke now all emotion was gone from her voice.

"Then I will not be your queen. But I am your woman; no other shall have me now. I am strong, you know that. I can help you, warm your bed at night."

"If you wish." Ason was already moving off towards the track they had left. Naikeri looked grimly after him, then shouldered the pack and followed in his footsteps.

The first days were the easiest. They would rise before daybreak, and as soon as it was light enough to see the path they would set out, stopping only with darkness. But on the third day, Naikeri led them off the trail and up through a stand of silver birch trees to the top of the hill. They had to force their way through the thick undergrowth, and at the top they crawled the last distance to peer out from under the hedges there. Just below them the open downs began again, a vast plain, covered with grass for the most part. A herd of dark cattle grazed here, watched by some boys. A man lay sleeping nearby with an axe and shield close to hand. Beyond them was the rounded form of a circular building.

"Yerni," Naikeri said. "They must be of Der Dak's teuta because his dun is the closest, out there. His people are on the plain on all sides of the dun where he has his warriors and cattle. If we are seen he will know about it quickly enough, and you will have to fight all of them at once if you are not here for trade. They do not like strangers on their lands."

"We must get close to the dun without being seen, so that I can call out their bull-chief. How will we do that?"

"Move only by night."

As long as they avoided the widely scattered boolies and circular cow-pens there was little chance of being discovered. A dog barked when they passed one isolated homestead, but dogs bark at a lot of things and they were not seen. The waning crescent moon rose later, and by its light they moved faster along the cow-paths. Naikeri had been this way before, by daylight, and seemed to have no difficulty in finding her way by night. Well before dawn she pointed to a curving shadow on the plain ahead.

"Dun Der Dak," she said.

Following a fold in the ground, they crept close and hid behind the earthern mound of a tomb, no more than a spear's throw from the dun. The dun was surrounded by a rubbish-heaped ditch. This ditch had been the source for the embankment of chalk rubble that rose from its inner edge, shining white in the moonlight, high as a man. The wooden part of the dun had been built against this chalk ring. Ason could make out only a length of overhanging roof and the dark blank of the walls beneath.

"Those are the warriors' quarters on the outside," Naikeri said, pointing to the building. "There are doorways into it from the top of the mound. That is where the men live. The cattle are kept inside the dun, and the women and children live inside as well—on the other side of the men's apartments."

"Is that the only entrance?" Ason asked, pointing to the dirt ramp that crossed the ditch to an opening in the structure.

"Yes. It is closed with bars at night so the cattle won't stray. Der Dak is there, above the entrance."

Ason grunted and settled down in the gulley to keep his vigil until dawn, his drawn sword in his hand.

9

When the first gray light tempered the darkness, Ason took out the jewelry removed from the slain Yerni. He put the biggest torc in place, then hung the bronze dagger about his neck, Yerni style. Naikeri handed him the skullcap helmet that she had rubbed with sand during the night. It shone and glinted when it reflected the gold of the rising sun. He took the shield in his left hand, the sword in his right, then turned to face the dun.

"Stay here where they cannot see you," he ordered, glancing back at her. "If I am killed you must return and tell the others. If I win I will send someone out for you. In either case, you will not let yourself be seen unless you are called by name. A hero with a single woman for a following is something to be laughed at, not feared."

Ason then turned away to face the dun and did not look back again. He waited, silent and still, until the sun had cleared the horizon. Sounds of morning bustle arose from inside the walls before him and he could see people moving about. With the naked sword in his hand he strode forward alone, against the dun and all the fighting men inside of it.

No one noticed him until he was a few paces away from the entrance. A woman and some of the older boys were there, tugging at the bars to let the cattle out for the day. She looked up and squealed, and Ason stopped.

"Der Dak!" he bellowed at the top of his lungs. Then "Der Dak" again.

The boys and the woman ran away while shouted voices raised questions inside the dun. Warriors were coming out of the doors on the mound above like ground squirrels from their holes. A dog, a great dark animal with matted fur, caught Ason's smell and ran at him, barking and showing its long fangs. A single slash of the sword dropped it in a silent, dirty heap. Ason raised his voice again.

"Come out, Der Dak, so I can kill you as I have killed your dog. You will be easier to kill than your dog. You are a coward made of dung, a woman wearing a stolen goat's pizzle tied to your filthy loins. Come out and face Ason, the man who will kill you."

There was a roar of anger from the first doorway, drowning out all the other voices. Der Dak leaned out, clutching the sides of the opening in his hands as he peered down. His hair rose high in a stiff white-chalked mane, and his moustaches were just as long and white, reaching down to his shoulders and curling outward. He had just awakened, naked, boiling with rage.

"Who is it that invites a quick death like this?"

"I am Ason of Mycenae, first son of King Perimedes, my father. Come out, murderer of my kinsmen, and face the man who has come to kill you. Come out, coward—to your death."

Der Dak was chomping his jaw with rage now at the insults; a froth of saliva wet his lips. Plunging back into his quarters he prepared for battle.

Ason had no thought of the others, but Naikeri was well aware of them. From her hiding place she watched with concern as the warriors emerged one by one. Most of them carried weapons but did not appear ready to use them. They gathered on the top of the mound, shouting loudly to one another and pushing for a good position to watch the coming battle. None thought to interfere. They looked forward happily to the contest and shouted for the women to bring them mead. They called out loudly when Der Dak emerged ready for battle, his shield on his arm, a great stone-headed ax in his hand. He jumped to the ground, and when he came forward Ason saw what he wore on his head.

A Mycenaean helmet. Dented and badly cared for with most of the high-arched plume of horsehair missing, but a Mycenaean helmet nevertheless. It could have come from only one place. The massacre at the mine. From his uncle, or one of the others.

Der Dak howled wordlessly and rushed in. The battle began.

The bull-chief was a powerful man. They were evenly matched. He had fought and killed many men, and their heads now sat above his doorway. His axhead was twice the size of any other and he had the strength to wield it. Wearing armor Ason would have been immune to any attack and would simply have cut the man down when he came close. But now it was the Yerni who wore the bronze helm and had his shield before him, as impenetrable as any bronze.

Ason thrust, but the shield pushed his sword aside. Then he had to draw back and raise his own shield to catch and deflect the ax. It struck with a boom like thunder, and pain tore through his arm.

They circled each other, spitting curses, swinging their weapons in ruthless attempts to batter through the other's defenses. It was a wild battle with no quarter given, no quarter asked. Soon they had no breath for cursing, gasping in air, their bodies running with sweat. And blood.

Der Dak drew first blood with a backhand swing of the great ax that glanced from Ason's shield, slashing him in the upper arm, grazing the skin. It did not hurt much and was no hindrance, but the blood ran freely and the watchers shouted happily at the sight. Der Dak grinned and intensified his attack. Ason gave ground, glancing down at the blood, gaped, lowering the shield as though the arm were weakened. Der Dak saw this and pushed even harder, sweeping his ax down with a force that would strike through the lowered shield.

Ason had been waiting for this blow and was ready. Instead of trying to avoid it or raise his shield, he held his sword above the shield to catch the blow.

147

It did, just below the axhead. Before the ax could touch the shield or drive past it the axhandle struck hard on the edge of the sword.

Bronze cuts wood.

The handle was severed, the axhead thudding to the ground, and Der Dak was left with the useless length of wood in his hand. As he gaped at it, Ason's sword point whirled around and up like a swooping bird to find its nest in the pit of the bull-chief's stomach. Sliding in deeply until the point rested against the man's backbone.

Der Dak threw his arms wide, his shield bouncing and rolling away, and gave a single last hoarse shout of pain before he folded forward and died.

Ason stood over the slumped body and hurled his shield away as well. Naikeri had told him about the customs of these people. They took heads. Severed them with a bronze dagger kept only for that purpose. Sawed off slowly: a man's neck is a very strong thing. He would show them a better way to do their butchery. In a screaming arc the sword came down, driven by the strength of both his arms.

Der Dak's head rolled away from his body.

The cold anger still possessed Ason. He threw his bronze skullcap to the ground, bent and pulled the Mycenaean helmet from the severed head and put it on. The stiff moustache made a ready handle. He seized Der Dak's head by it, then strode towards the warriors on the mound. Those who were armed made no move to raise their weapons as he stood before them.

"Der Dak is dead!" he shouted. "Your bull-chief is dead. Who is it that will take his place?"

The warriors looked to one another, each waiting for another to speak. They all knew the ritual by which a bull-chief was chosen, everyone knew that. Explaining it to this angry stranger was another thing altogether. Ason shook his bloody sword in the direction of the nearest of them and the man muttered, "It will be done. There is a way of doing these things."

"Good. Then it is no concern of mine. Lead me now to the Dark Man. He is the one who next sees my sword."

It was a door like any other in the dun. Ason kicked it open and strode in, ready for anything. But the room beyond was empty. Someone had left in a hurry; household objects were strewn about, a clay jar lay broken on the floor, nothing else. A heavy odor still hung in the air and there was no other sign of the occupant. Ason poked his sword in among the jumble of furs. Nothing. As his anger seeped away he became aware of his wound for the first time. As well as the fact that he had not really planned anything other than the death of Der Dak. What now?

The warriors made way for him when he came out and went to Der Dak's rooms, still swinging the former owner's head. There were withered human heads and a rotting boar's head—with polished stones for eyes—on a ledge above the doorway. Ason swept them all down with a single cut of his sword and kicked them bounding into the ditch. Then he put Der Dak's severed head in their place and sat down under it.

"Bring me food—and something to drink," he called out.

There was silence for a moment, and he kept his hand on his sword, then one of the warriors repeated the command to a woman nearby. Ason relaxed his tense muscles and took up a piece of fur to clean his sword with. Naikeri stood before him.

"You should have waited," he said.

"I saw what happened. You have won. My people have been seen here before, and these warriors pay no attention to a woman."

"Sit in the back out of sight."

"What are you going to do now?" she asked, moving past him into the apartment. "It stinks in here."

"I am going to eat."

"And after that?"

149

He only growled in response because he had no answer. A serving girl sidled up, put down two bowls and hurried away. One contained pungent fermented milk and he drained most of that before turning to a bowl of soft cheese. He was scooping it with his fingers when one of the warriors came and stood before him.

"I am Ar Apa." As soon as he said it he sat down on his heels. He was silent a long time. Finally, when Ason did not speak but continued eating, he struck himself on the chest. "I am a killer, I am a hunter, I ran for a hundred nights and killed a hundred deer, I killed Cethern after a battle that lasted ten nights and his head is above my door."

"Did you kill my people at the mine?" Ason asked, coldly, tired of the bragging. Ar Apa spread his empty hands.

"Der Dak did that. And others. Many from Dun Uala. They were given rich gifts then went all together to the mine. Many did not return."

"Did Uala lead them?"

"Uala led them, but that was not why they went." He looked uncomfortable. "*He* gave them gifts, even before they went." For all his bragging, Ar Apa was loath to speak the name and only pointed his head over one shoulder.

"The Dark Man?"

Ar Apa nodded and began boasting again. Ason did not listen, the words were repeated after awhile in any case. But he did hear Naikeri's whisper from behind him and he nodded agreement. He repeated her words aloud.

"You wish to be bull-chief?"

Ar Apa did not answer the question directly; if he did so he might appear to be challenging Ason, and he had already seen more than once what the bronze sword could do.

"There must be a bull-chief," he said.

"That is true. There will be a bull-chief."

BOOK THREE

1

With summer past, the nights grew cooler, and most mornings the hoarfrost silvered the blades of grass. It was now just past dawn and the sun shone between the tree trunks around the clearing of the mine, casting long shadows across the ground. The air was still and the first trickle of smoke rose straight up from the fire, pointing a gray finger at the cloudless blue sky. Aias hunched down close to the flames, putting dry wood on it and stirring it to life with a stick. Yawning, then scratching under his arm with the other end of the same stick. His face was still loose with sleep and his torn lip hung even lower.

There was the squealing of wood on wood and Inteb came out of the reed-thatched hut built to replace the lean-to, bending low to get through the door. He had a blanket clutched tightly about his shoulders and he hurried over to sit across the fire from the scarred boxer, crouching so close that the blanket smouldered and the reek of singed wool filled the air. Inteb shivered, his dark Egyptian skin now a grayish blue.

"Not yet winter and already my bones are beginning to ache with cold," he mumbled. Aias smiled crookedly.

"This is nothing. The days are still warm, sun hot. But the winter will bring snow, white and cold. As high as your head perhaps."

"May Ra in his wisdom melt it before it falls, then guide a Mycenaean ship here well before that season of snows. This is not a kind country."

"Kind enough to me, Egyptian. Far kinder than your land is to a slave. Handful of grain, hot sun, die young. I have meat to eat here, every day. More than in my entire life before. And women. That one who cooks for the boys. Thighs and rump as fat as a cow's!" He clapped his hands together with pleasure at the memory. "What handfuls of flesh to hold to. Lows like a cow, too, when I put it to her. A fine country."

Inteb widened his nostrils with distaste and pulled his smouldering blanket end from the fire before it took flame.

"Stay then, Aias. Take no insult, but you are a coarse man and fitted for this coarse country. There are other pleasures that you will never know. Perhaps you are happier never to have sampled them. Good wine, fine food, sweet friends, civilized pleasures, all the things that I long for. There are headier pleasures in this world than that fat-rumped cow you service."

"Some of us like that kind of thing." Aias belched deeply, as though to make the point.

"I am sure you do. But as a wise scholar said: a man for love, a boy for pleasure, a woman for duty. I feel no duty towards the women here, and the boys are filthy and would give no pleasure."

He did not add that only a great love could have brought him to this place. But that was not to be discussed with this scarred slave, hawking and spitting into the fire before him. The sun cleared the lower branches and the face of Ra shone warmly on his shoulders and head. An early breeze stirred the trees above; an oak leaf floated down to fall almost at his feet. Inteb picked it up and

152

admired its many-pointed shape and the burning fall colors it held within it. Behind him the hut door squealed once again and Ason came out to join them by the fire. The smell of Naikeri's flesh was still warm on his skin. Inteb turned away from it, picking up a piece of wood for the fire.

"Good sailing weather," Ason said, squinting up at the sky. "Smooth sea and easy rowing."

The ship. Thoughts of it were foremost in their minds these days. He spoke for all of them.

"We'll have tin for it," Aias said, looking towards the abandoned lean-to where they now stored the silvery disks. Over 480 of them, the shining evidence of their labors since the middle of summer.

"It must be on its way now," Inteb said, seeking reassurance.

"You know that better than I do," Ason answered. "You were there when the message was brought to my father. My memory is filled with his endless stories of the importance of tin to Mycenae. We can be sure that Perimedes dispatched a ship just as soon as he could. Weather has delayed it. We have seen what the ocean can be like. It will be here, and when it arrives we will have the tin for it. There will be chalceus aboard to work the mine, warriors to protect it. Our job will be done."

"Then we can return in it—when it returns," Inteb said, unaware of the yearning in his voice. Ason hesitated before he answered.

"Of course. Is there any reason to remain in this cold place at world's end? There is wine in the Argolid waiting to be drunk—and Atlanteans impatient to be killed. I would do both. There is nothing here for me."

He glanced up at the hut as Naikeri emerged carrying a short-legged tray. It was laden with bowls of thin ale and strips of cold meat from the deer they had roasted the night before. The tray was set on the ground next to Ason, who helped himself first. Aias leaned over and took a bowl, sipping loudly, breathing out happily afterwards. Inteb chose a piece of the lean meat and chewed slowly on its end.

"The time of samain is here," Naikeri said.

"I know nothing of this," Ason mumbled through a mouthful of meat.

"I have told you. This is the time of year when all the cattle are brought into the duns by the Yerni. Some are slaughtered. My people go there and trade, while others come from far away to trade. It is the most important time of the year for all of us."

"Go and watch the cow butchers, I'm not interested."

"Other important things happen. This is when there is a new bull-chief. This is the time when Ar Apa will become the new bull-chief."

Ason was silent, chewing the tough, sweet meat. Ar Apa. He would expect Ason to be there when he became bull-chief—he might not even become bull-chief if Ason were not there. These barbarians knew nothing of kingly strains and noble succession. There was no order in what they did. They seemed to pick their chieftains for the biggest mouth and strongest arm, if they picked them at all. It would be best if Ar Apa were the new bull-chief. Ason knew him, and he knew Ason. Knew the strength of Ason's arm and feared him. If he ruled the dun there would be no Dark Man to cause raids on the mine. Ason had fought in enough battles to know the value of the flanks and when to protect them. The dun and the grazing lands of Ar Apa's teuta lay between the mine and the other Yerni tribes to the east and north. Raiding warriors would have to pass through them on the way to the mine. It would be best if Ar Apa were the new bull-chief. The mining and smelting would continue while Ason was gone so the time would not be wasted.

"I am going to the samain gathering," he said aloud.

"You cannot go alone," Naikeri said.

"What I do is no business of yours, Albi woman. I'll not be taking you, that is for certain."

She gazed back as firmly as he glared at her, unfrightened by his temper.

"I will go with my people, we always go to trade at samain. But you are a great chief and they have heard about you. A great chief does not travel alone at a time like this."

There was truth in what she said, but he would not tell her that.

"Perhaps you should come with me, Inteb. It sounds a sight worth seeing."

"It sounds like a boring bloody day in a butcher's abattoir—but I'll go with you. A king should have retainers. More than one. Aias can be your sword bearer and I'll be your seneschal."

"Aias will be needed here to keep the boys working."

"They won't work very hard without you here to supervise. We must all go to show the Yerni that the long arm of Mycenae stretches this far. Remind them not to forget that. We'll go armed and armored—and who is to know that I flee at the first sound of battle? Or that this scarred hulk throws away his weapons to beat people to death with his fists? Do we all go?"

"I suppose we do. Though someone should stay with the mine."

"Why? If the boys run away we go to their parents and have them dragged back. The tin is useless by itself so the discs are as safe as rocks just lying there. No one on this island knows what it is good for; they think us mad for mining it. I have seen some of them biting it and looking at their toothmarks and wondering what it is. Too brittle for weapons, too dull for jewelry. They have no way of knowing that we use it to make the bronze they covet so—and even if they did know they are incapable of smelting the metal themselves—" Ason had a sudden thought

155

and interrupted him with a lifted hand.

"What if the ship comes while we are gone? We must stay."

"My people are along the coast," Naikeri said. "They will know when the ship comes and they will tell those aboard where you are. And take them to the dun if you have not returned."

"Then we go?" Aias asked.

"We have to," Ason answered.

"Butchery and coronation," Inteb said. "Blood and drunkenness. Fighting and feasting. Repulsive."

"Sounds good," Aias said, his split lip twisted into a tooth-revealing grin.

2

They set out in the early morning. Ason wore his sword and freshly painted leather armor, the round shield with its polished bronze bolts on his left arm. His bronze dagger hung about his neck in the Yerni manner. The dents had been hammered from the recaptured Mycenaean helmet, but the missing tufts of horsehair could not be replaced in this land, where the only horses were stunted, soft-maned ponies that were hunted for food whenever they were found. But Ason had killed wild boar with his spear, fast dark brutes even more deadly than the boar of the Argolid, and their hair was thick enough to fill the gaps in the helmet's crest. Nor was there shame attached; the wild boar was as respected here as the noble horses of home. The Yerni warriors stiffened and whitened their long moustaches with clay to resemble the boar's tusks, stiffened their hair for the same reason. There was no shame and much honor in bearing that boar's crest.

Aias was impressive as well in his leather armor and

bronze skullcap, the one that Ason had first worn to battle against Der Dak. His leather half armor resembled Ason's, though of course was not as elaborately decorated. Among the effects belonging to the slain leader they had found a bronze-headed ax of the type used for chopping down trees. But it could be used for chopping men as well, was carried with that intent.

Inteb, the least warlike, wore simple leather and carried a plain wooden shield covered with heavy hide. But his stone ax was well made, as good as any the Yerni boasted. He had a small pack with food slung over one shoulder, while Aias bore the larger bundle with gifts for the new bull-chief.

By nightfall they were tired and did no more than eat their food and roll into their cloaks, their feet towards the fire. Inteb woke just once during the night when Aias got up to put on more wood. The air was so cold it burned his eyes and he had to blink to clear away the tears. Above him in the black bowl of the sky the sharp points of the stars reached down clear to the horizon. A shooting star burned its arc across the darkness and vanished soundlessly beyond the hills. In the distance an owl hooted like a lost spirit. Inteb shivered and drew closer to the warm bulk of Ason, breathing deeply and regularly beside him, drawing strength from his presence. But for this man, he would be Pharaoh's advisor in court at Thebes, in his rightful place instead of here on this freezing ground in this lost land. What folly had brought him here? He smiled at the thought and slipped back into sleep, the smile still on his lips.

By midafternoon of the fourth day they saw the chalk mound and the wattled walls of the dun rising from the flat plain ahead of them. Twice that day they had passed herds of cattle being driven in that direction; the herd boys and cattle both rolling worried eyes in their direction. Keeping well out of the path of the armed men. The guarding Yerni warriors scowled and fingered their battle-

157

axes as they passed. Now more cattle were visible ahead, milling about in temporary pens that had been thrown up around the dun, raising clouds of dust in great billows.

The path they followed was thick with cow droppings as it wound between the low She Mounds that surrounded the dun. Here were buried warriors from the entire teuta, returned to the Earth Mother, awaiting She of the Mounds to escort them to the Land of Promise. This cemetery was the life center of the tribe, where the annual assemblies were held and all other great events: the planning of cattle raids, the initiation of new warriors. And the raising up of bull-chiefs.

When they had passed the last cattle-pen they saw that a large crowd had gathered outside the walls of the dun. Some sort of ceremony was in progress. There was a high-pitched wailing that set the teeth on edge. A man's voice could be heard shouting above this sound.

It was a burial, that much was clear when they drew closer. The death house had been built, a wall-less structure that was no more than a pitched roof made of small logs, leaned against a low ridge pole. Just high enough and long enough to hold a single body. Women and boys had been laboring for days to loosen the earth around the death house, hammering in deer antlers to pry the hard chalk up in lumps. Now their work was finished and the warriors, already drunk, listened in appreciation to the tall man, impressive in a long white tunic, who was chanting in a loud clear voice. His hair was gray and shoulder length, his beard full. But the hair had been plucked from his upper lip so he had no moustache; only the Yerni warriors had these. At his feet was the decapitated corpse, the head carefully tucked beneath the right arm, glistening with oil and draped with a boar's skin. Next to him a man sat squat-legged, blowing strongly into a wooden mouthpiece that was fitted to an inflated skin. He puffed energetically until his face grew red, blowing the skin up like a tin-smelting bellows. But the stream of air, instead of serving some useful purpose, was blown through a hollow length of bone that had been pierced with a row of holes. This produced a continuous squealing noise that rose and fell in pitch—but never ceased—as the sweating man opened or closed the holes with his fingers. Supported by this sound the shouted chanting could be clearly heard.

"He led the warrior's life, the good life that never ends. Died he in battle, shouting he died, battling he died, died as the Good Striker made man to die. Dying this way he cannot know death but instead has put his foot along the warrior's path that leads to Moi Mell. Now we send him to Moi Mell and She of the Mounds will make his path easy. Now he goes to the place of youth forever, where there is no pain and there is no death, where there is no sadness, where there is no beginning and no end. Where there is no envy, where there is no jealousy, where there is no pride, where there is no fear. It is a place of plenty he goes to, with flocks and herds as far as can be seen and to them there is no end. There is a pig long-roasting there, so big that forty men cannot lift it, and he will have the first cut from this pig. There are beakers to drink from, which are never empty. This is where he goes and this is where we send him."

The bone and bellows thing squealed louder. The warriors shouted until they were hoarse as the corpse was slid into the death house. As soon as the last logs had been put into place to seal it, they began to shovel the loose chalk with the flat shoulder blades of deer, each trying to outwork the others. The mound of chalk rose until the house was covered, the warriors reeling with exhaustion and drink. Ason found it wonderful to watch and turned reluctantly away only when Ar Apa appeared beside him.

"You are here," the Yerni warrior said, and there was more than a trace of relief in his voice. Apparently the succession to bull-chief was no easy thing. Ason's presence might assure that station for himself.

"Who are they burying?" Ason asked, his attention still on the ceremony.

"Der Dak. Samain is the time when a bull-chief is buried."

Ason looked at the completed mound, now crowned with a stuffed bull, with renewed interest. "It was summer when I killed him. I thought he must have rotted by now?"

"Our druids know many things. They know what has been and what will be, and they heal the sick. They painted the body every day with cedar oil so it is firm just as you saw it now. You must come and drink."

Ason would have stayed to listen but Aias smacked his lips together loudly while Inteb turned his back on the crude ceremony. This rough embalming bore little resemblance to the sophisticated Egyptian technique he was familiar with, which rendered a corpse as impervious to corruption as a block of wood. They went past a long rack of flayed sheep carcasses and through the entrance into the dun.

Noise, confusion, color: protesting animals, shouting people. The inside of the great, spacious dun was a riot of activity as tumultuous as any feast day in Egypt or funeral game in Mycenae. The Yerni warriors were here, strutting through the crowd with their axes and shields, touching their knuckles to the proud, white stiffness of their moustaches. Their women were here, as well as numerous children, the smallest of them naked, all of them dirty, playing underfoot, rolling cylinders of carved chalk. But there were strangers too, dark Albi with their packs and trade goods, Donbaksho staring about with wide eyes, bearing poles on their shoulders hung with plump hares and fowl. And others too, blond men of a kind Ason had never seen before. They were warriors; that was clear from their cow-horned bronze helmets and the long daggers that slapped against their legs. Heavy gold bracelets hung on their wrists, and huge gold link-fasteners closed their cloaks. Yet they carried great baskets on their backs like slaves, while their women bore even larger packs. They were setting these down, but none had been opened as yet. Ason wondered with interest what goods they might contain. Then a pinch-waisted beaker was put into his hand and he lowered his head thirstily to the ale.

"Look there!" Aias called out, eyes wide with wonder. "I've never seen that before."

A strangely dressed man had jumped up onto a bulging wicker structure made of intertwined small branches and willow wands. The women who were still weaving it screeched at him, but he dodged their grasping fingers and worked his way out upon it to the center of the structure that bent and creaked beneath him. His leather kirtle was so long it reached almost to his ankles, his cape so short it was just a fringe at his shoulders. Almost a mockery of a Yerni warrior's thigh-length kirtle and long cape. Black mud or charcoal was smeared on his hands and face and rubbed into his hair, which had also been worked up to a black point above his head. He fell and rolled on his back like a great dark beetle, black-soled feet kicking in the air, and everyone watching roared with laughter.

"The druth, the druth!" the crowd shouted, and people came running from all directions to see the fun.

The druth rolled easily back to his feet and then howled with mock pain and hopped about on one foot, holding the other in his hands and licking at it with his tongue like a dog with a thorn in its pad. One of the women reached for him, but he evaded her hand and fell onto all fours, and barked and panted and howled at her, until the crowd howled answering laughter and she ran away. In quick succession, then, he did realistic immitations of a bull, then a cow, finally a calf looking for its dam and a warrior looking for the calf. This last drew shouts of appreciation, even from the warriors, who saw everyone but themselves in the strutting, swaggering, moustache-twisting, image. When the laughter had died down the druth rooted about in his sagging kirtle, extracting a number of carved wooden

161

apples. They had been painted red and yellow and glistened brightly when he tossed them into the air. One after another, he threw them high above his head, hurling up a second before he caught the first, then another and another until the watchers were dizzy at the sight. They gasped with wonder at the number he could keep in the air at the same time. Ason and Aias shouted with pleasure along with the rest, and only Inteb, who had seen this and more besides in the court of Thuthmosis, was silent, sipping at his ale.

When they had finally tired of the druth's performance, Ar Apa led them to the fire pits where the smoking carcasses of sheep and cattle gave off rich odors of fat and meat. The women were hacking off strips and chunks of meat with their flint knives. These were seized instantly by the many grasping hands. Ar Apa pushed and cuffed the crowd aside, then directed the slicing of the best cuts from the flanks for Ason and his followers. When they had their meat he dug into his wallet and produced a handful of white crystals, mixed with crumbs of dirt, and held it out to them.

"Salt," he said proudly and sprinkled some onto their meat. Ason felt the saliva flow in his mouth as he chewed. Some of the visitors must have brought the salt for trade; he had to get some before he returned. The salt meat brought back his thirst, so then there was more ale. He was beginning to find out why samain was the event of the year.

Angry barking and fierce growls drew their attention. They clutched their cups and followed the others to a crowd on the far side of the dun, pushing through to stand in the front rank.

"Are those dogs?" Inteb asked, keeping a firm grip on his ax.

They were fierce and unruly beasts, heavily pelted with curly dark fur, and large as bears. Ason had heard of them, but never seen them before. Yerni wolfhounds that had been bred to hunt wolves and wild boar, brought here for dog racing in the funeral games. Now the two hounds wanted each other, pulling at their collars so that it took all their masters' strength to hold them back. Their lips were drawn to reveal bright red gums and the polished ivory fangs of their teeth; spittle flew as they howled with rage. The two owners were shouting wagers and curses over the growling roar of the animals, and finally agreement was reached. The watching circle pushed back and the great beasts were released. They flew at each other.

They were evenly matched, savage in their rage. They locked in a growling tangle, then fell apart, snapping and darting at each other. Then they clashed again, muzzles buried in thick fur, worrying through to the flesh below. This went on until one of them managed to slash the other's leg open with its great fangs. Blood spattered the dust now, and the fight would only have resulted in the wounded beast's death if the owners had not rushed in and called for help to separate the animals. Ax butts and spear hafts finally drove them apart; the wagers were paid. Sharp yipes of pain resounded as the loser beat his animal mercilessly for the defeat.

There was almost too much to see, too much to do. Albi traders had come across the narrow sea from the green island of Domnann to the north, to bring their worked gold and bronze. The Yerni warriors crowded about offering everything that they had for the pieces they valued the most. The horned men, Geramani they were called, from across the sea to the east, had more things of value than the precious salt. Warm brown lumps of amber, some with miraculous insects buried in their depths that could be seen when held up to the sun. They also had well-worked bronze daggers. Ason turned one over and over in his hands beneath the watchful eyes of its owner, wishing that he had something to barter with. In their packs they had brought Egyptian beads as well, and Inteb laughed when they were pointed out to him.

"They and I are a long way from home," he said, holding one of them in the palm of his hand and squinting at it. He handed it back without saying any more until they were out of earshot of the Geramani. "Inferior work, badly glazed, not fit for sale in Egypt. More than good enough for this crude part of the world."

There were many things to eat: fresh apples and plums, sweet pieces of honey still in the comb. Yerni sausage that they had never tasted before, as good as any in the Argolid. Rich with lumps of fat and meat, sharp with salt and some kind of seeds, smoked over the fire until it had grown hard and nourishing. And mead that had been flavored with hazel nuts to drink, fermented from honey, fermented heather-berry juice, and more ale, and more and more. Before the sun touched the horizon their stomachs were full, their eyes full, as well, of strange sights, their ears deafened by sound.

"Look!" Aias said, pointing at a crowd gathered across the dun, a sudden light of happiness appearing beneath his sagging eyelids.

Two men were grappling on a cleared circle of sand, each straining and sweating to toss the other to the ground. They wrestled, trying for holds, pummeling each other with their fists at the same time. Once they broke free of each other and swung in a flurry of ferocious full-armed blows, most of which did not connect. Aias grunted in contempt. Finally one of the big men—they were both tall and massive Geramani—managed to get a grip on the other's leg and, striking with his fist at the same time, succeeded in driving his opponent to the ground. Half of the watchers cheered; the others mumbled while they paid their wagers. Aias shambled forward and called out hoarsely, his words clearly heard by everyone.

"Great wet bladders full of suet, both of them! These two aren't fighters, just women with tits on backwards. I spit on them both." His words took practical form when he actually did launch two great gobbets of saliva at the

Geramani, catching one on the belly and the other on the side of the face. They howled with fury, and would have leaped upon him had they not been restrained by their admirers.

"Angry, are you? Want to kill me, do you?" Aias shouted back. "Come on then. Both at once. Knock them both down, I will—who wants to wager against that?"

There were plenty of offers, and Inteb and Ason took them all. They would be killed if they lost, for they pledged all they had, as well as a number of things they did not have. But they had faith in this stocky dark man, a head shorter than his giant opponents. He strutted up and down in front of them while the bets were made and goaded the Geramani to greater fury.

The battle began. At the shout to start the two Geramani lurched forward—clawed fingers extended—and Aias ran away. There were cries of anger and catcalls as he trotted about the circle, with the angry men running after him, reaching for him wildly. Silence descended when he stopped suddenly and one fist lashed out, fast as a striking snake. It caught the first man in the pit of the stomach. All the air went out of him with a rush, and he folded slowly to the ground and lay still.

"One," Aias called out. "Come, you're next."

The remaining fighter was more wary now. He crouched low, moved in slowly, trying to grapple the boxer before those murderous fists could strike him down. A blow to the side of his head rocked him, and another caught him in the ribs so that he staggered and almost fell. But he did not, leaping forward instead and grappling Aias to him. This was well done, and the fight almost ended there. The Geramani was the stronger of the two, and kept Aias's arms pinned to his sides as he bent him backwards towards the ground, slowly and surely. Aias struggled against the unwelcome embrace and, just as it seemed he would fall, managed to work one arm free.

That was all that was needed. He smiled out crookedly

at the crowd, bunched his fist—and drove it around in a short hard arc that ended in the small of his opponent's back over his kidneys. A shiver went through the man's great frame and he staggered. Before he could recover, the fist struck again in the same spot and the man bellowed aloud with agony, throwing his arms wide. Aias stepped away and relieved the pain by striking him so hard on the side of the head that the Geramani was unconscious before he hit the ground.

"Now they know something about Atlantean boxing," Aias said as he stepped over the two unmoving bodies to help in collecting the wagers. There were some grumbles about the unorthodox manner of the victory but these were stilled quickly enough at the sight of a great closed fist. It was a profitable day.

Nor did samain stop at sunset. The fires burned higher, their wavering light washed the walls of the apartments and the milling crowd within the circular enclosure of the dun. From the darker corners there came muffled squeals and laughter as women, visitors and Yerni alike, with no trade goods other than those they were born with, worked to earn small tokens and gifts. Torches of burning reeds lit up the displays of gold and jewelry, stone axes and fine flint knives, bronze daggers and amber discs—as well as simpler offerings of game and fowl, salt and sweet fruits. There was something for everyone.

More important events were in preparation. A fire had been laid in the largest pit in the center of the dun. Women brushed the ground around it until it was fairly free of animal droppings, then scattered oak and laurel leaves all about the pit. Two post holes next to the fire were cleared of a year's accumulation of debris, and a pair of upright logs, each as tall as a man, were inserted in them under the first druid's instruction. They had been hollowed into a semicircle at the top to support a shorter log that was placed across them to form a horizontal lintel.

When this free-standing archway had been completed the druid himself applied a thick wash of chalk water until the wooden structure was as white as bone. While he was doing this the Yerni warriors began to arrive. They were dressed in Albi cloth, wearing all their finery, fully armed. They sat themselves around the fire. Even before they had all arrived, one of them, goaded by impatience, was on his feet and declaiming in a loud voice what a fearless and dangerous fighter he was. The choosing of the new bull-chief had begun.

By the time all the warriors were there, the fire had leapt up higher and hotter, so that they sweated under its golden light, shouting for ale and swaggering about to display their golden torcs, bracelets and rings. The noise was loud and continuous, many times drowning out the one who was speaking, but no one seemed to care. The act of speaking before the assembly was the important thing, not the empty content of the familiar and repetitious brags and lies. They shouted loud insults at one another and, one after another, sprang to their feet to strut about the fire banging their axes on their shields, boasting of their exploits at the top of their lungs. This went on all night, without a break, with some warriors dozing where they sat, waking often to shout again and reach for the ale. Ason pushed through to the inner circles of warriors and called out insults as loudly as the rest at the most outrageous lies, and no one thought to question his presence there. Inteb watched from outside, sipping the sweet mead which was very much to his liking, until he fell asleep. Aias, his wallet bulging with the profits of the day's exploits, fresh blood and new wounds on his scarred skin, went seeking greater physical success among the women. He had been admiring the tall, full-breasted and blond Geramani women all day and now managed to lure one away from the firelight with his rich gifts. He gave her some solid memories to take back with her to her northern

167

forests.

By dawn most of the Yerni warriors were sprawled out, asleep in the dust, or nodding dazedly while Ar Apa strutted up and down before them, calling out the glories of his strength of arm in a loud hoarse voice. He had husbanded his energies and had given only short speeches during the night, saving himself for this final effort that would impress his dazed and half-drunk warriors. It was succeeding. In the small hours of the morning he had risen and begun his harangue, shouting down anyone who tried to interrupt him, even knocking back with his shield one drunken warrior who tried to speak at the same time. His powers of oratory were no better or worse than the others, but he did have an enviable staying power that made them nod their heads with respect before they fell asleep. When the sun had burned off the morning mists, risen clear of the eastern horizon, he was still being enthusiastic about the strength of his arm and all his other matchless talents. He stopped for a deep breath, then shouted his war cry over their silent heads.

"Ar Apa Abu! It is time for the fire passage and the purification of the cattle."

The Yerni warriors stirred and called back happily at this. They downed the last dregs of ale in their cups, then went to relieve themselves against the wooden animal pens until the reek of urine was strong in the air. When Ason awoke, Inteb and Aias were both at his side. They went to join the others outside the walls of the dun, looking on with interest as the Yerni women and children joined the men in dragging out the two great wickerwork structures that had been completed the day before.

Lying on their sides they resembled great open-ended baskets twice as tall as a man, sagging and of irregular shape. They were thrown down outside, one each side of the entrance to the dun, and ignored while five wretched men were dragged from some place of imprisonment in the animal pens that lined the walls below the second story apartments. Their legs must have been bound, because they staggered and fell until goaded to their feet at spear point. They rose with difficulty, since their hands were still tied behind their backs. They were Yerni warriors—that was obvious by their garb and whitened moustaches and hair—though none whom Ason had ever seen before. Ason called out to a nearby warrior who was shouting threats at the prisoners; he had to spin him around before he could get an answer.

"Them? Thieves, creeping thieves. Came to steal our cattle at night, but we saw them. From Dun Finmog—but they won't be going back there!" He laughed aloud at his own wit and turned away to throw lumps of cow dung at the men, just as the others were doing.

The prisoners were led outside the walls and, guarded closely by spear and ax men, had their hands cut free before they were pushed into the wicker structures, three into one and the remaining two into the other. Once they were inside, the shouting Yerni fought for places to grab at the upper edge of the open end until their weight was enough to pull the basketlike structures upright. With the open ends flat on the ground, it was obvious what they were.

Heads. Bull's heads. The nostril openings were painted red with ochre, the eyes were black circles with red centers. Long, naturally curved boughs formed the horns. And, crude as they were, the wicker structures were clearly bull's heads. Pronged stakes pinned them immovably to the ground while armloads of wood were heaped around their bases. All of this was ordered by the druid who had presided at the funeral of the day before, assisted by two younger men garbed in the same long robes. The captives clutched at the branches that penned them, staring out wild-eyed at the druid when he screeched at them. The crowd grew quiet.

"Silent snakes on your bellies you came here. Creeping

stoats in the water you came here. Spirits of the night you came here from Dun Finmog—and we know why. The cattle of Dun Finmog are scrawny and fall down sick and die, and your teeth chatter in your head with fear. You know that the finest cattle are here, the fattest cattle are here, the sweetest-fleshed cattle are here. So you came to steal our cattle—but our warriors are here, too!" A loud cry went up at this, and there was a great clashing of clubs on shields, and a rain of oaths. The druid went on without pause.

"A hundred and a hundred of you came, and a hundred and a hundred of you were killed, and your heads made a pile higher than the dun. But five were taken because it was right to capture some, because it was near the time of samain and the purification of the cattle. That is why you are here."

There were more shouts that ceased instantly as the druid drew himself up and slowly lifted his right foot from the ground until he stood balanced on one leg.

"One foot," he called out and then raised his arm even more slowly.

"One hand," he said, much louder, as he pointed at the penned men.

"One eye!" he cried at the top of his voice and cocked his head as he closed his left eye. "Die, burn, die, die, die!"

That was the end of the ritual, and the pleasurable part began. Warriors ran with burning brands from the fires, thrusting them deep into the dry wood around the two great wicker figures. The men inside coughed as the smoke rose, then began to scream as the first flames burned at their legs. They climbed up inside the heads to escape the heat, and the watchers shrieked with laughter until tears ran from their eyes. The women and boys were then driven away from this enthusiastic scene and formed a double row to the nearest cow-pen. The gates to this were opened and, lowing with fear, the cattle were driven down this road and through the gap between the wicker figures that were now burning fiercly. The men inside were just charred lumps, no longer complaining. By the time the last of the chosen cattle had been driven through the purifying passage into the dun, the fires had burned low and the excitement was over.

One by one the Yerni warriors swaggered back to the circle about the ashes of the council fire, picking shards of meat from between their teeth, careful only to avoid stepping on the bowls of milk placed in the dun entranceway to feed and retire the dead souls; it was getting chilly out there in the cemetery as autumn approached, and they always wanted to come on home at samain with the cows. The warriors called out loudly for ale. Ar Apa had arrived before all of the others and was standing now in front of the whitened arch. This was no accidental location. When one of the warriors came too close he raised his ax threateningly. The man hesitated—then went to sit with the others. But when Ar Apa saw Ason he waved him close.

"Will you sit by me?" he asked.

"What does that mean?"

"That you are sitting, you do not wish to be bull-chief yourself. That you are sitting by me, that you will support me."

Ason thought a moment before he spoke.

"I will support you now and you will become bull-chief. You will not forget this?"

"Never!" Ar Apa's eyes were wide with excitement and he crashed his ax against his shield. "My memory is the longest, my arm is the strongest—I will not forget."

There were none opposed to Ar Apa's selection as bull-chief—at least none who spoke up before that union of ax and sword. The word was quickly passed as to what was happening, and the crowd grew larger and larger. Ar Apa sat before the henge drinking, nodding in agreement while the druid paced back and forth before him, extolling his virtues and repeating all the feats of strength and skill

171

that he had ever done. This appeared to be very much of a ritual, including the recital of a great list of ancestors going back into the remoteness of time. There were more nods of agreement—and even a few cheers—when events came more up to date with veiled references to Ar Apa's handling of mysterious black forces, perhaps a reference to the Dark Man. There was a pause after the druid had described Ar Apa's mighty companions of bronze, and at this point Ar Apa slowly rose to face the druid.

"Tell us," Ar Apa shouted. "Is there a special purpose for this day? How can this day be more favorable than others? What can it be favorable for?"

There was hushed silence as the druid closed one eye and squinted up at the clouds, spinning in a circle on his heel while he did so, looking for some omens in their shape. He must have seen something, because he stopped suddenly and clapped his hand over his open eye as though the sight had been a terribly strong one. Some of the braver warriors squinted up at the clouds themselves, though most did not, and the silence was absolute.

"There is a shape," the druid said, touching the upright of the henge lightly as though to gather strength from it, not looking at Ar Apa while he did so. "A shape. A shape not unlike a double-edged ax, perhaps a double ax of gold. With darkness behind it. If this day a warrior of a double ax were to stand as protector of his people, he would surpass all others in battle valor. But his life would be short, very short if he did this."

All eyes were on Ar Apa as he shouted the ritual answer. "What care I? I have a double ax. What care I if I live only one night and one day? All will remember me because the memory of deeds done will always endure."

With slow and careful motions, the druid reached inside his loose clothing and withdrew a short length of branch, still with the golden leaves upon it. Oak leaves. He reached up to brush the leaves against the crosspiece of the wooden lintel, intoning the words in a deep voice at the same time.

"I touch the Good Striker, the Destroyer, I touch him."

Then he turned about and let the leaves touch Ar Apa's forehead, calling out at the same time, "*Ar Apa Uercinquitrix!*"

The crowd of spectators roared the words in response.

"Ar Apa Uercinquitrix!"

Now the lefthand upright was brushed by the leaves while he called out.

"I touch the Magic One, he is our Creator—Ar Apa Uercinquitrix." Once again the spectators echoed his words in response as he turned back to Ar Apa and touched the branch to his left shoulder. Ar Apa's head was back, his fists clenched, possessed by the power of his elevation.

"And now I touch *her,* She of the Mounds, our Earth Mother, our Preserver," the druid intoned as he touched the righthand upright, then Ar Apa's right shoulder.

"Ar Apa Uercinquitrix!" they all shouted over and over, their new leader, the new bull-chief, carried away by their enthusiasm as he stood before them, bathed in the welcome wave of sound.

The hand pulled again at Ason's arm and he shook it away. When it clutched him again he turned angrily, ready to strike. Naikeri was standing there. She had to shout to be heard over the roar of Yerni voices.

"One of my people just came and told me. A boatload of large men with horns, they must be Geramani, came to the mine two days ago. They left at once and are gone now."

"What are you saying? What does it mean?" Ason had a sudden cold premonition. "The mine. . .?"

"They destroyed nothing, it is just as you left it. But they did take all of the metal discs that you had left there."

The tin.

Gone.

The days grew steadily shorter, until they were shorter than any days had ever been in the Argolid. The nights seemed endless. Some days there seemed to be no day at all, when the clouds piled thicker and thicker in the sky and wept a chill dampness onto the sodden forest below. Part mist, part rain, from dawn to dusk, so that the day seemed only a gray interval in an endless night. The small store of tin that had been smelted to replace the stolen ingots grew with painful slowness. In the continual damp the boys became rebellious, running away when they were not watched. The charcoal fires grew wet and flickered out. There was no more dry wood to fire them with.

Since the return from Dun Ar Apa, Ason had changed in many ways. He would not admit defeat, at least not aloud, and kept the work of mining and smelting going with a cold ruthlessness. Before dawn each day he was out in the forest with their heaviest bronze ax, cutting wood for the ceaseless appetite of the charcoal kilns. He slept little, many times spending the entire night tending the smelting fires, almost drawing the tin from the ore by the strength of his own hands. He did all the physical things needed to keep the mine in operation, but he never talked about Mycenae or the ship they had been expecting. With winter upon them they could no longer expect the ship. No one would face the cold storms of the ocean at this time of year. Without a ship their mining was a useless labor. Did Mycenae even still exist? Had the union of Atlantis and the other cities of the Argolid pulled down the remaining warriors of Perimedes, leveled his city? It was possible. Anything was possible. They could stay here, smelting their few miserable discs of worthless tin at world's end, until they grew old and died and that would be the end of it. Ason would not talk about these things, nor would he even answer when others mentioned them.

Aias seemed happy enough with this new existence, but Inteb could never forget where he was. He worried at the fact like a sore tooth, hurting himself and wincing but not stopping for all of that.

"We could die here and no one would know or care—a terrible place to die."

He panted saying it, exercised with his unaccustomed labors at tree felling. In the past months he had gained some skill with the bronze blade, chopping into the tree trunks at the proper angle. He went now with Ason into the forest, to help him—and to keep warm with effort. The rains had stopped finally, only to be replaced by the white chill of frozen snow. There was not much of it. It fell from time to time, lying in the hollows and making little hillocks around the bases of the trees. It was numbing to the touch. Inteb could never get used to it and came to hate its white purity. "Die here," he muttered again to himself. Ason did not answer but stopped to wipe his damp palms on his clothing, then resumed his chopping. The tree trunk squealed and snapped, and they stepped away as it fell with a splintering crash. Ason threw down his ax and drank heavily from the crock of ale they had brought with them.

"I have talked with Naikeri's father, old Ler," Inteb said, hating the silence of the forest, willing to talk to himself if no one else would. "He may be blind now but he has traveled. Knows all about this island and the other one to the north, Domnann, where more of his people live. And he even knows where the Geramani come from. He says that they are the ones who trade with Atlantis— and I believe him. That's where they get those Egyptian beads and the other things. They cross the water from here in their boats, to a great river to the south, some outlandish name I can't remember. That is where they come from, up the river. Far up. He says if you go up this river far enough you come to another river that runs down to another sea. If he is not lying, which he might very well

175

be—or making up the entire story—that could be the Danube running into the Eastern Sea. We know the Atlanteans are all along that river, they mine their tin there, and the Geramani know about tin. Why else would they steal it if they did not? They have traded our tin to the Atlanteans, no doubt. If they could do that—so could we."

He drew back when Ason turned to frown coldly at him, the only sign that he had been listening at all.

"No, Ason. Dear Ason, do not misunderstand. Not that we should sell out to the Atlanteans and trade our tin to *them*; just that we should return that way to the Argolid. Simply return. We can do nothing here. We take tin from the ground—but there is none to use it. You want to return to Mycenae, I know you do. We can do that."

Ason's only answer was the ringing blow of bronze against wood as he turned to the next tree. Sighing unhappily, Inteb shrugged his shoulders and turned to lopping off the branches from the newly fallen trunk.

It was nearly dark by the time they had dragged the wood back to the clearing and dumped it by the kilns, for stacking and firing in the morning. The boys, shivering with dampness and cold, had been returned to their quarters where they were securely locked in for the night. Aias joined them around the fire at the hearth, sniffing the fragrant steam that rose from the pot that stood bubbling at the back of it. Naikeri, shapeless in her many layers of cloth and fur, brought out the large crock of ale without being asked.

"Only two more of these left," she said to no one in particular. This was what happened during winter in the north, as the stored supplies ran out a little at a time. Soon everything would be gone, and if the hunting were not good they would starve.

"I saw deer tracks," Ason said, his thoughts like all of theirs on the same subject. "There is enough wood now

176

for a day or two. I will go hunting in the morning."

"I can come. Carry the meat," Aias said.

"You work here. I need no one."

Nor did he. He needed them for labor, and they did that, but for nothing else. Naikeri cradled her breasts in her arms and wondered why he did not come near her any more. In their closeness, and their apartness, they were all feeling the same thing. Aias spat through his maimed lip into the fire. Inteb was looking unseeingly at that same fire, seeing a warmer land far to the south.

"The son of the sister of my father killed a bear," Naikeri said. "There were two newborn cubs as well. Now he has three pelts. Warm ones." She stirred the thick stew and licked at the wooden spoon. "I have also heard that the warriors of Dun Uala have made the largest cattle raid on the cattle of Dun Ar Apa, and many are dead, and many cows are stolen."

Inteb was the only one who listened. These fragments of gossip and information were passed on by the people of the Albi who moved through the island, winter and summer. They seemed to know a good deal of what was happening—true or not. Inteb would have preferred more civilized gossip and talk, but settled for this because there was no other. He disliked Naikeri intensely, therefore would not answer her. But he could still listen.

"Another boy ran away today," Aias said, and no one even bothered to take notice of that. It was too commonplace.

One evening, after a day spent chopping wood, Inteb and Aias joined Ason around the fire at the hearth. Ason dipped a bowl into the stew and blew upon it before raising it to his mouth. The others did the same. It was hot and good, dried meat and grain with gobbets of fat floating on the surface. The wind moaned outside and blew a white tracery of snow under the ill-fitting door. The last gray filming of daylight was gone. Outside now there was just darkness and the endless forest that stretched out into the blackness on all sides. There was warmth and light only here, and without thinking why, they leaned closer to the fire when the wind blew hard.

Something rustled outside, barely heard above the wind, and Ason lifted his head with a sure hunter's instinct. He half rose, but even as he did so the door burst open, crashing aside, half falling from its torn leather hinges.

An armored man stood in the opening, poised to leap, full bearded and bronze helmed. A long naked blade ready in his hand.

4

The men around the fire dived for their weapons as other armed warriors pushed behind the man in the door, swords ready—and all halted as Ason shouted a single word.

"Atroclus!"

The first swordsman gaped, lowering his weapon slowly, blinking in the dim light of the fire until realization slowly dawned.

"Ason—my kinsman—but you are dead!" He half raised the sword again and Ason laughed aloud.

"Harder to kill than you realize, Atroclus, my cousin. It is a tale long in the telling how I came here. But first—what of Mycenae and of my father? Sit and speak to me."

Atroclus came close to the fire, shaking the snow from his white wool cloak. Five other men followed him in until the room was crowded, putting their swords into their slings and calling out to Ason, who greeted them all by name. Naikeri silently gave them ale and withdrew to the shadowed alcove where she slept.

"You know of Thera?" Atroclus asked. "It was told that you died there."

"I escaped, as you see. Was the island destroyed—and Atlas with it?"

"We would all be happier had it been. There were many deaths on the island, many ships were sunk, but Atlas and his court escaped to Crete. For eight days the ground roared and blew out flame and ash until the island was covered with it, but there it ended. People have returned and life goes on again, though we have heard that the ground still rumbles with some hidden complaint. All of this has enraged Atlas, who it is said feels the explosion was directed against his person. He wages war all along the shores of the Argolid. His men have already sacked Lerna and Nauplia. Perhaps he seeks treasure or captives to appease his gods, we don't know. We know he battles with us and Mycenae is sore pressed. When he heard of your death, your father mourned and grew older. But when war came, Perimedes put aside his mourning to lead us in the fighting. There has been much blood shed, many friends and warriors you will never meet again. It was late in the year before a ship and men could be spared to come here. We were a long time on the ocean road with the winds and weather against us. Twice we had to careen and repair the vessel. Four men died in the passage. But we have come. Now—tell us of yourself and your presence here?"

"Told simply enough, but a question first. You have more men in the ship and a chalceus among them to work the mine?"

"Seventeen men more and *three* of them chalcei!"

"They will find the mine open, some tin, the smelters burning and charcoal ready. We have not been idle."

They talked late into the night. All of the ale was gone

before the Mycenaeans rolled themselves into their cloaks and slept on the dirt floor. Ason pulled the coverings from Naikeri and took her, brutally and suddenly, so that she made a small scream of pain. He laughed and did not stop, and Inteb, awake and hearing everything, pulled his own blanket over his head to try and cut out this sound he loathed.

Ason was up before dawn. As soon as it was light he roused Atroclus, and together they went down along the stream to the sea, where the great ship was beached. Here there were more greetings and, wonder of wonders in this cold place, warm sweet wine from Mycenae, from amphorae lashed in the cabin. The ship had been hauled up far above the highest tides, and now they took what supplies and food they would need and left two men to guard her while all of the others went to the mine.

"Things will be different now," Ason said, leading the way along the familiar path. "There will be more boys to work, more men to cut wood, and the chalcei to see that the smelting goes as it should. By spring there will be a load of tin that will be so heavy we will have to throw all of the ballast out of the ship. We will return to Mycenae, the Argolid will be united again, Atlas will be driven into the sea and sent to its bottom this time."

The men of Mycenae complained mightily of the bitter cold, yet they worked. Ason put aside his ax for the first time and directed the building of new huts, while the chalcei shook their heads over his smelting techniques and set about their own operations. The days were bright, but the sun had little warmth. Inteb and Ason grew closer once again, talking of the return voyage, while Naikeri withdrew inside herself and would speak to no one. Only Inteb seemed aware of this and he smiled at her back. Things were going very well.

On the eighth day after the arrival of the Mycenaean ship, there was an alarm from the men on guard at the mouth of the valley. Ason, in fine armor now that shone brighter than the weak winter sun, went out with his new and sharper sword to find out what the trouble could be. From the top of the embankment he could see three Yerni warriors standing hesitantly at the edge of the forest peering up at the armed men above them. They must have recognized Ason because they came forward slowly when he appeared. When they were closer Ason saw that it was Ar Apa and two of the warriors from his teuta.

"Ason abu," Ar Apa called out, raising his ax but looking uncertainly at the armed and armored Mycenaeans at the same time.

"My friends are here," Ason shouted back. "There is nothing to fear."

With this reassurance the three men came on and entered the guarded area of the mine. They squatted before the fire in the house and were given food. Ar Apa produced only a token amount of bragging about their journey, before speaking his mind about his true reasons for coming.

"It has been a bad winter. There have been many cattle raids and many warriors are dead. First by men from Dun Moweg to the north of our lands and then from Dun Finmog far north of them. They do not raid each other, or Dun Uala which is in between, but pass instead through the grazing lands of the other teutas to steal our cows and kill our warriors."

Ar Apa beat on the packed earth floor with his ax handle as he said this, almost shouting the last word, and the men with him stamped their feet as well and groaned aloud. The Yerni believed in expressing their emotions at all times, and Ason, who had seen this sort of performance often before, waited patiently for it to end. Relieved of some of his feelings, Ar Apa brushed at his stiffened moustaches and finally continued.

"Now I know why this was done. Now I know who arranged all this and who sits in Dun Uala, giving gifts to people when they do what he wants them to. Now I know." He looked up quickly at Ason, then away.

"The Dark Man," Ason said, speaking aloud the name that Ar Apa still found so hard to say. "He is stirring up trouble again? How do you know this?"

Ar Apa looked up at the ceiling, examining with great interest the hole where the smoke escaped. Then he brushed at his shield, scraping away a hardened bit of mud. Inteb came in and listened silently in the background.

"Someone came to me," said Ar Apa finally, reluctantly. "Uala himself came with some warriors and did not want to fight and wanted to talk instead. The druid made the henges that are made when bull-chiefs meet, and we hung them with our treasure and we talked. He showed me gifts he had from. . .the one whose name you said. We talked. . . ."

Ar Apa's mouth stayed open, but he had run out of words. There was a beading of sweat on his forehead, perhaps from the fire. But Ason now knew the path of the other's thoughts and spoke the words Ar Apa was unable to say.

"They are planning to make another raid on the mine? Like the last one, with many teutas together. That's what it is, isn't it?" Ar Apa nodded and looked away. "You were right to tell me and not join with them. Where is the Dark Man?"

"At Dun Uala."

It was so simple and so right. The chalcei were here now to tend to the mine, freeing a warrior for a warrior's work. This Dark Man, this trouble maker, man or spirit, he must be stopped, or there would be no end to the trouble of the mine. Ason knew how to stop him.

"I have armed men to follow me," Ason said. "Armored and unbeatable. I am leading them against Dun Uala to kill the Dark Man. Will you bring the warriors of your teuta and fight beside us?"

"The Dark Man. . . ." Ar Apa was so troubled by the thought that he spoke the name aloud.

"Uala and his men cannot stand before us. We will kill

them. There will be cattle, revenge, gold and treasure."

"We will join you," Ar Apa said in sudden decision, thinking now only of the treasure of Dun Uala, largest, richest, strongest of all the duns of the Yerni. Saliva filled his mouth at the thought of all it contained, and he spat into the fire and laughed aloud.

5

It was imbolc, the happy time, the first sign that the grip of long winter had lessened even the smallest amount. Inside the duns, in their pens underneath the women's apartments, the cattle and sheep were finishing the last of the green boughs and brush which had been cut for them in the fall. The first grass was beginning to appear. Lambs and calves were born. Life was starting anew and that was something to celebrate. There was fresh milk to be fermented, something to celebrate with. The ale made from the grain of the previous year long since finished, drunkenness only a dim and happy memory. Now, drunk again, the warriors could lie in the sun and watch the women carry out the sheep and cattle. The animals were weak and unable to walk after a winter of short rations and immobility, but would quickly restore their strength on the bright green grass.

Dun Moweg was like all the other duns of the Yerni, with the warriors' apartments on the outside overlooking the ditch. The embankment outside their doors was a fine place to find the sun on the good days, and this was a good day, with plenty of freshly fermented milk. The warriors lay there, with the bull-chief, Moweg himself, sprawled in their midst. He was bragging of past exploits, raids and slaughters, when the armored men arrived.

They came quietly, for all the weight of metal they

carried, while behind them were the white-haired, boar-toothed figures of the warriors of Dun Ar Apa. It was not a nice thing to see, or to have happen, and was very shocking. Imbolc is not a time for cattle raids or warfare and everyone knew that.

"You are Moweg," Ason said, looking coldly from beneath the lip of his helmet at the open-mouthed man on the dirt outside his doorway.

"He is," Ar Apa said coming up to join him. Ar Apa dealt a fast kick in Moweg's ribs that brought him to his feet bellowing in pain. The bowl he was drinking from spilled. Brewed from milk from stolen cattle. Ason pushed Ar Apa away before battle was joined.

Moweg needed very little convincing to change sides. He really had loyalty only to himself. He had received fine gifts from the Dark Man for the raids he had carried out. That was in the past. The future looked even brighter with a victorious assault on Dun Uala, the fat and the rich, the largest dun and the most powerful. How would even that power stand against the might of all the warriors of two teutas—led by these frightening men in their hard armor? He remembered, and it was not a good memory, how much killing just three armored men had done when they had been attacked at the mine. And now there were one, two, three—more armored men, more than on two hands, to fight with them this time.

They all stayed that night at the dun, drinking up every drop of the newly fermented milk. Aias had little work to do now at the mine with the chalcei in charge. He had come with the war party and had promised to use his sword instead of his fists. Inteb was no fighter, though he did look impressive in his borrowed armor. And he would even fight if he had to, to be here, with Ason, away from Naikeri's influence. They sat together by the fire drinking in moderation while the others tasted all the pleasures of imbolc.

"There is no doubt that we will win," Inteb said.

"We must do more than win. The Dark Man must be taken and killed. If he escapes again he will flee to the other teutas of the Yerni far to the north. With his treasure he will cause us trouble, for as long as he is alive. After this battle I want him dead."

"What do you plan?"

Ason sketched a circle in the dust with his forefinger.

"They say that Dun Uala is like the others, just larger. There will be one or two entrances, as well as the warriors' rooms with all their doors. We must take them by surprise, from all sides at once, and stop every one of those rat holes.

"How will you do that? Come up by night and attack at dawn?"

"No. That would be impossible with this great number of men. We would be seen or heard and the warning would go out. What we must do is move fast. They say it is an easy day's march to this dun. If we leave at dawn and go quickly we will arrive ahead of any warning."

Inteb looked around at the drinking men. "They won't like that."

"That is of no concern. Fighting the battle and taking the dun is only half of what must be done. I must have the Dark Man."

The sky was still black when the men were roused up. There were groans and more than one thud as the drunkest were kicked to life. Ason permitted them to eat and drink quickly, so that they were straggling away from the dun at first light. The Yerni complained bitterly about the sad state of their moustaches and hair. Ason promised that they would have time to make repairs before the battle. Then he set the pace, first trotting smoothly, then walking, never stopping. There was some rain in the morning that added to their discomfort, but it stopped by noon when they crossed the river that was the boundary between the land of the two teutas. The hills rose up to a high down, flat and stretching to the horizon on all sides with

185

few trees to stop the eye. They reached the home of one of the retired warriors of the teuta and he tried to run away towards the dun but was caught and cut down. Here they made a brief stop, ate what food there was in the house, then hurried on. Distantly across the plain could be seen the circular wall of the dun with the smoke of cooking fires rising up from it. There was another halt, much to Ason's annoyance, while the Yerni chalked their hair and moustaches before the battle. Then they went on.

The warriors of Dun Uala were on top of the embankment and waiting for them; they had received the alarm. The attacking Yerni stopped to shout insults at the men above them, but Ason was too angry to wait for this ritual and spread his Mycenaeans out in a line so no one could interfere with another's sword arm. He led them in the attack. They went down into the ditch and up the embankment, shields raised when the warriors above threw a sudden barrage of rocks. They each had a supply in a holder in the back of their shields. These bounced without effect from armor and shields. Then the Mycenaeans were among them.

Those who tried to stand were cut down. With steady butchery the swords swung back and forth and men died. Even Inteb, paces behind the others, managed to reach past Ason with his sword and push the point of it into a Yerni stomach. It went in easily, and the man dropped his ax and groaned in a terrible manner and fell to the ground. Holding his middle with both hands that quickly dripped with blood. Inteb felt a little sick at this and stayed behind the others. He was almost knocked down in the rush of their Yerni allies, who now felt inspired to deeds of violence when they saw the enemy being killed so efficiently.

The battle spread into knots of fighting men who shouted and screamed at one another, were wounded and died. The warriors of Dun Uala were numerous, more than the other teutas put together, and they were fighting for their lives. They could easily have won if the armored Mycenaeans had not done their butchery so well. They fought bravely but were killed, and very quickly the survivors broke and scattered in panic. Some of them ran through their rooms into the women's apartments inside the dun with the howling victors rushing after them. Ason stabbed at a man, but only punctured his back slightly, which made him run the faster. They stumbled through the sleeping quarters and out onto the balcony beyond, with shrieking women running on all sides. The wounded Yerni vaulted to the ground below. Ason, in his heavy armor, could only follow slowly by climbing down the notched log. Once on the ground he pursued the man who was now cowering behind a tall, bluish stone that rose like a pillar from the ground. Wounded and in pain, the warrior hurled his ax from him, then fell to the ground and begged to be spared. Ason turned and saw that other warriors were doing the same. The fighting was almost over. Individual battles did continue, in and around the double crescent of great stones that stood inside the dun. But when the other Dun Uala warriors saw what was happening they threw their axes aside as well. The fighting was finished.

"Take me to the Dark Man," Ason said to the warrior on the ground before him, pressing the edge of his bloody sword against the man's skin. The warrior, his eyes round and as white as his chalked hair, scrambled to his feet and hurried out of the entrance of the dun with Ason just behind him. They pushed through the victorious Yerni, shouting with joy as they used their daggers to saw off the heads of the defeated. The women of the dun wailed with anguish on all sides. One warrior, unlucky enough not to have killed any of the enemy, was exacting some small victory by mounting one of the women on the ground among the slain and wounded. A circle of children stood close by, chewing on their fingers and watching.

There was the same dark doorway Ason had seen once

187

before, and the same alien scent. The same absence of any occupant, as well.

"He must be here!" Ason shouted, hurling the warrior to the ground and striking him in the face with the edge of his shield. The man howled and tried to roll away, babbling in answer.

"He was here, I know he was. But someone warned us, they saw you coming, told us, so we took up our axes. Maybe then he ran away—don't hit me—I don't know."

As some of the anger ebbed away Ason began to think again. The Dark Man could not be far away. There could not have been that much warning; he could be followed. Where could he go? To the next dun to the north, Dun Finmog. There was no place else he could find safety. He could be overtaken. Ason kicked the man to his feet.

"Take me on the trail to Dun Finmog. The shortest way."

There was no place to hide on the open plain. Ason ran, ignoring the weight of his armor, while the point of his sword kept the wounded Yerni running before him. They came over a small rise, and far ahead three dark figures could be seen moving steadily away from them. Ason shouted a victorious cry. He burst forward, knocking the Yerni aside, running as he had never run before, forgetting his fatigue and his heavy armor, spurred on by the sight of the fleeing people. One of them must be the Dark Man.

As he came closer Ason could see that two of them were women, their skirts flapping about their calves as they ran clumsily beneath the burdens on their backs. One of them looked back and squawked in terror. The two women stopped and screamed, dropping their bundles to the ground and running off in different directions. The man ran after one, hesitated, ran back to the fallen bundles— then stopped. He bowed over, bent almost double, as Ason jogged up breathing heavily. When he straightened up he touched his hands together before his chest and spoke in a high lisping voice.

"I greet you here, oh noble Ason, son of Perimedes, some day King of Mycenae. All hail Ason."

He was old and fat, his skin dark olive. His black beard was shot through with gray, curled and oiled, as was his long hair, cut off straight above his shoulders. He wore a colorful and richly embroidered cap on his head, brimless and tight fitting, while his ankle-length gown of dark blue was also embroidered in black. There were dark tassels on its bottom and tassels as well on the length of cloth worn like a cape across his shoulders. A richly decorated sword with jewels set into the pommel swung from his waist. Ason lifted his own sword when the man reached for it. But the Dark Man only pulled his sword free and threw it from him.

"Who are you? How do you know me?" Ason asked.

"All men know of Ason of the great deeds. I am Sethsus, he who would help you."

"You are the Dark Man who has been raising the Yerni against me. It is now your time to die." Ason swung the sword high and stepped forward. Sethsus fell back, his eyes wide with fear now, his skin ashen and drained of color.

"No, Ason, champion of the Argolid, you must listen. I have many things to tell you and I can help you. There is gold and rich treasure you can have." He fell to his knees by the nearest bundle and tore it open with trembling fingers, pulling out a handful of golden jewelry that he held out to Ason. "This can be yours, I can aid you."

"Where do you come from—and why are you here with your gold?"

Sethsus was calmer now, with death withheld for the moment. He stood with the golden axes and discs still in his hand.

"I am a simple trader, a man who buys and sells and thereby makes a small profit to live by. My city is Troy, so

189

distant it pains me to think upon it, but I am no longer welcome there. There are such things that you, a mighty warrior, should not bother your head with; politics is one, and the struggle for power, a curse. Others rule there now, Sethsus is not welcome and must travel the ends of the world to stay alive. I have voyaged far and have traded with many along the rivers, in the camps and cities. I came here to this land, to Dun Uala where the trade routes cross. From the east and south they bring amber and bronze and fine things. Here joins the path from the north that brings the Albi, with their red gold from the green island. Here I stayed, using what little skill I have in trading to stay alive."

"You lie to me, great ball of grease from the rotting walls of Troy. I know the people of your city and their tongues are as twisted as a snake's spine. The truth is harder for you to speak than the lies that fall from your painted lips as rain falls from the clouds. Look at this—do you think me a fool?" He reached out and tore the little golden ax from the Trojan's hand. "The double-headed ax of Atlantis. You are here on their bidding."

"That I trade with Atlantis is true; one does business where one can. . . ."

"More lies. You came here for gold, you just said that. Do you *bring* gold with you for that purpose?" Sethsus was wordless for the moment, and Ason smiled without humor, knowing he was coming near the truth. "You were in Dun Der Dak until I came. Not for trade—but to watch the mine. Of what importance the tin? What use the tin?" Anger welled up with the memory of the raid, and he pushed out the sword until it dug into the Trojan's cheek. A thin trickle of blood started forth.

"You had the mine watched, and when I left you told the Geramani, who then came and took the tin. Truth?" He pushed the sword hard until it penetrated Sethsus' cheek and grated against his teeth.

"Yes! Great Baal save me, I speak the truth, only the

190

truth! That I am wicked I know—do not kill me merciful Ason. I sold information to the Geramani so they could take the tin which they value, knowing how to work it. Yes, I took presents from Atlantis, a poor man must take what he will. They do not like the tin mine here being worked for the good of Mycenae. You cannot blame them, can you? It is a matter of policy. I was wrong to aid them, I see that now. But I can change, a wiser man crawls before you, mighty Ason. I can aid you, be of much aid, there are things I know. . . ."

"No." Ason said the word coldly and swung his sword high. "Have you forgotten my dead kinsmen so quickly? The Yerni did that because of you. Die, Trojan."

Sethsus screamed as shrilly as a woman and fell away, raising his hand to protect himself. The sword slashed, catching him in the wrist, severing the wrist so that his hand—still clutching the gold—hung dangling and spouting blood. He looked at it with horror, screaming all the louder, and stopped only when the sword swung again and severed his neck.

6

It was dark by the time Sethsus was brought back to the dun. Leather ropes had been tied about his ankles so he could be dragged, yet even in death the Dark Man still exacted a sense of fear from the Yerni who pulled the ropes, so they ran faster and faster, hauling him over the hard chalk of the plain. When his corpse was stretched out near the council fire no one sat near it.

The looting was in progress. Never had so much treasure been gathered in one place before. The victorious warriors began to squabble among themselves for the gold; others slipped away into the night with their wealth. Ason put a stop to this, and his armored Mycenaeans drove everyone, victor and vanquished alike, into the circle of the dun. Here, amid pained cries, he ordered the dumping of the loot. The invading warriors kept the heads they had severed, as well as personal jewelry removed from men they fought. Everything else was gathered in one place before Ason. He sat crosslegged before the fire on a great black bear skin, drinking ale, chewing on cold and greasy mutton. Inteb sat beside him, exhausted by the day's events, looking on with disbelief as the amber discs and drinking cups, gold collars, armlets, tores, coiled wire, placques and lock-rings, copper daggers, pieces of bronze armor, beads and figurines, mounted before them.

"They work the gold and copper here," he told Ason. "I was in that round building, over there against the far wall," he pointed out through the broken circle of high blue stones. "There is a forge, tools, even a workshop such as we have in Egypt, though not as grand or well supplied, of course. They work stone, too; look there, one of those large standing stones is still being dressed."

Ason chewed on the meat. It had been a good day. The Dark Man dead, a host of the enemy dead, even Uala killed, slain in single battle with Ar Apa who was now swaggering around with the head, bragging to everyone he came across. Uala was old; it had been no great deed. So there was no bull-chief for the dun, and the warriors and members of Uala's family were already squabbling about the succession. It did not matter. Right now he, Ason, was leader of all the Yerni, chief of all the Yerni. They followed him—or they fought against him and died. He was at peace.

Inteb went over to the nearest tall stone, standing out clearly in the firelight, and ran his hand over the surface. It had been worked and smoothed, a fair job on a stone this big. It reached high above his head. Sat square in the ground too—he closed one eye and looked along it—or at least squarely enough. The upper, rounded end had been

192

painted bright red, although the thick pigment had chipped and washed off in places during the winter rains. Two rows of the stones were arranged in the shape of a double circle, not quite completed. Years of labor here. The stone didn't even look local. With a builder's eye Inteb had noticed that the only stone they had seen on their way here were the great slabs that lay about on the plain. Grayish white, a different kind of stone altogether. Inteb walked around the upright column and almost stumbled over the man who sat slumped against it on the far side.

"What are you doing here?" Inteb asked, sharply.

"My stone, mine," the man muttered.

"Come out where I can see you."

The man crawled around the stone, dragging one leg, and fell once more against it. He was a Yerni warrior, one of Uala's defeated men. His moustaches broken, his face drawn. A club had shattered and bruised his leg, it was black with clotted blood. Inteb was curious.

"What do you mean, *your* stone?"

"Mine!" the man answered, some of his spirit returning as he felt the strength of his claims. "I am Fan Falna, the one who kills but cannot be killed, who has eaten the bear, the deer, the wild boar, the horse, killed them all. My stone. A warrior's stone. When I took my first head it became my stone, and I put the head on it, hung my jewelry from it, painted it myself. The women cringe before it and are afraid to look, because it is as big and red and hard as I am." He clutched at his groin when he said this, then sighed wearily and slumped back again. "I am Fan Falna," he mumbled, all spirit gone with the memory of defeat.

"Do all the warriors have a stone like this?"

He didn't answer until Inteb took him by the stiffened hair and banged his head against the stone.

"Only the best, the finest," he sighed again. "Uala, my kinsman, I saw him killed. There will be a burial, but his head will look down forever from some different dun."

Inteb went back and sat beside Ason who was staring into the fire, his eyes growing red from the fermented milk.

"We shall stay here until spring, until the ship is ready to return with the tin," Ason said. Inteb lifted his eyebrows but said nothing.

"The chalcei work the mine, I am not needed there."

"You are certainly needed here," Inteb said, putting his hand on Ason's thigh, on the firm warm flesh. Naikeri was far away and would stay far away. "You are a man of war and wage it as it has never been seen on this island. You have captured a royal treasure here. Now three teutas follow you. You can do what you want with the Yerni and they cannot stop you—in fact they cheer you. Stay here, keep them from more mischief. The Dark Man is dead, but they are still great ugly children and capable of anything. Stay here."

There was a wailing and shouting from the darkness, where a smaller fire had been lit; dim figures could be seen silhouetted against it.

"What is that?" Ason asked.

"The druid, Nemed. He is calling to the Earth Mother," Ar Apa said. "He is calling to her to take the dead, which are hers now. The dead go to her and She of the Mounds guides them to Moi Mell."

"Bring the druid here," Ason ordered.

The Yerni warriors drew away and turned their faces to the darkness, acting as if they didn't hear him. The Mycenaeans laughed at this, and two of them went to drag the old man to the fire. Nemed came willingly enough—he had no choice—but there was hatred in his eyes when he looked at their hands upon him. He was gray haired and had a good-sized belly that bulged through his white robe. A heavy gold lock-ring held back his hair, far better than the leather bindings the other druids wore, and no one had dared or even thought to take it from him. He stood before Ason and looked over his head into the night.

"I know of you," Nemed said suddenly. Everyone close fell silent. "Man from across the waters, with the long bronze knife. You have killed the Dark Man and that is a good thing to do. Because of that I do not curse you for what you have done here. . . ."

"You do not curse me ever," Ason said in a low voice, leaning forward with his hand on his sword. "You obey me because I am not one of your boar-toothed warriors. I am a man who will let your guts out in a moment if you cause me any trouble."

The druid did not answer, but was silent, which was answer enough.

"Your bull-chief is dead. This place is no longer Dun Uala, but Dun Dead-man." The listening circle roared with laughter at the rude joke. The druid did not change expression and continued to stare into space.

"There will be a new bull-chief," Nemed said. "He will be from Uala's family, and that is how he will be chosen; that is the way we do it here."

"That is the way you used to do it here, old man. You will not do it that way any more. Perhaps I, Ason of Mycenae, will appoint the new bull-chief. I may do that. Now go back to your wailing."

The druid was angry. He drew himself up and stood on one foot.

"One foot!" he called out, and silence fell through the dun. A prediction, a prophecy, a curse, this was the way it was done.

"One hand," he pointed.

"One eye. . . ."

"And next you speak—but I speak first!" Ason shouted, jumping to his feet and drawing his sword at the same moment. It stretched out straight to the bulge of the druid's belly and stopped not the thickness of a leaf away.

"Speak, but think carefully what you say. I will not be cursed. This sword has eaten men today and it will happily consume more. Your power is no power against its bite, druid. Remember that, then speak."

There was a long silence while the druid stood, still poised immobile on one foot. Then he spoke.

"There has been an ending in this teuta. Now there will be a beginning. This beginning will have an ending too."

Ason smiled and lowered the sword.

"Well spoken, gray one. Just enough—but not too much. All things end, and that is right. Now go."

The druid left without looking behind and Ason dropped back onto his furs, smiling coldly.

"The men are getting drunk," Inteb said. "And pouring seed into women on every side. There could be trouble during the night unless something is done."

"You are a wise advisor, my Egyptian; I need you."

"I am happy to be needed, my Ason," he answered.

There was very little sleep that night while the warriors, filled with the enthusiasm of victory, drank and ate and bragged about their exploits. The beaten Yerni were defeated in spirit as well as flesh, vanishing one by one into their rooms, the wounded being nursed by their mothers and sisters. Ason sat with the bull-chiefs of the two teutas he had led to the victory, but they would only drink and brag and talk of nothing else until things were done in the proper manner. The hurried attack on Dun Uala had been one thing, taken on in a moment of enthusiasm and greed: a war party, a raid. Now more portentous matters would be discussed, and there was a correct manner for this, as for everything. When the sky began to lighten the chief druid, Nemed, was sent for, and he in turn ordered out the wrights who worked in wood. They cleared the rubble from the post holes where the bull-chief's henge was placed, and when night had ended they put the uprights into position. The bull-chief always sat in this place of honor, the first one to be touched by the warm sun of a new day, his back to the setting sun so that the others would have to squint and shield their eyes when they

196

talked to him. Because the bull-chiefs of two other teutas were here, they would have their own henges—smaller ones of course. Set to each side, with the more favored bull-chief to the right. Holes were dug for these, and logs with their bark removed were dragged from their place of storage under the second-story dwellings. They were thickly stained now with animal droppings, but the white painting would cover that.

Inteb had slept during the night, while the others drank, and now sat awake with the two bleary-eyed Mycenaeans who had been assigned the morning's guard duty. He watched the construction of the henges with great interest. Up until now all the buildings he had seen on the Island of the Yerni had been of the crudest, fit only for the construction of Egyptian chicken coops. The duns themselves were simple structures. Their wooden frames were supported by the main circle of heavy logs set upright in the ground. These logs gained support from the circular bank against which they rested, and were spaced one apartment width apart. This none-too-secure structure was held together by the wooden flooring of the second-story apartments. The walls between the uprights were made of wattle, plaited withes, which filled the space but added nothing to the supporting strength of the structure. Dun Uala was built in the same manner, though it was much larger. As in all the duns, the bull-chief's residence was located in the large second-story apartment that spanned the broad entrance. An overhanging roof gave some protection from the weather and kept most of the rain out of the building. In addition to the main construction of the dun, two circular buildings stood inside the outer walls. They were workshops inhabited by the numerous cordwainers, goldsmiths and wrights.

These people worked in stone too, something that none of the other teutas did. The work was of the simplest, smoothly dressed stones that were set into holes in the hard chalk, but even that was something. And they worked well

197

in wood. Inteb looked on with interest while they shaped the lengths of timber that would form the henges.

Using their stone hammers and wedges, they split away one surface of each log until it was flat, dressing it even smoother with copper adzes. While they did this, other wrights were busy shaping the ends of the uprights. One man in particular, an old man with swollen knobby joints, did the most skilled work. With quick, precise strokes of a short-handled ax he worked around the end of the log until a knob the size of a man's fist was left. When this was done he had the log that would form the horizontal lintel of the henge rolled over to him. After careful measurement he used a hammer with a sharp fragment of a broken bronze dagger for a chisel, to dig out a matching hole, into which the knob of wood fitted as well as a man's finger into his ear.

Under the watchful eye of the druid, Nemed, the posts were raised for the first henge, with much shouting and cursing, being secured with lumps of chalk that were hammered into the hole around them to hold them into place. The lintel crossbars on the top required more labor, so much so that a log platform had to be put together to enable the men to raise the lintel of the largest henge. The prepared log was rolled onto this platform, and the wrights climbed up beside it. Nemed prepared them, shouting the signals that directed them to pick it up, to raise it above their heads, to lift one end after another the extra amount more that enabled the projections of the tenons to fit into the hollows of the mortise holes. There were shouts of victory when this was done, while the builders strutted about, feeling very proud of themselves.

While the construction had been taking place, the Yerni warriors had begun to appear and watch the ceremony. When the wooden troughs of chalk and water appeared, they shouldered aside the builders and grabbed up the tied bundles of grass. Nemed pointed out which were the henges of each teuta. The warriors from each one began to industriously wash the structures with white, shouting to possession of the grass bundles, at the same time dipping out handfuls of the white mixture to daub their own hair and moustaches.

When the assembly began, early in the afternoon, Ason made it very clear who had won the battle. With a show of ceremony he led Ar Apa to the righthand henge, then with his own hands slung Ar Apa's shield from the crosspiece. Moweg was conducted to his station on the left in the same manner. Now they were all watching the largest henge, the empty arch of the dead Uala. Ason walked towards it in a growing silence, drawing his sword as he came close. He turned once in a full circle then looked out at them. The Yerni warriors, his own Mycenaeans, the druids and craftsmen of the dun. Only then, with a sudden and powerful overhand swing, he drove his sword against an upright of the henge. It bit deep into the wood and hung quivering when he released it.

"Mine," he said, and sat down before the archway.

No one spoke up or made any move to challenge his right to sit there, to speak for the warriors of the dun. He had defeated them. Until a new bull-chief was appointed his word would rule.

There were shouts of appreciation now from the warriors, as the bull-chiefs put their spoils on display. The recently severed heads of the defeated were placed on the crossbar of the henge, jewelry was hung from the posts in rich profusion. Before sitting, each bull-chief slung his ax from the henge by his hair belt; the axes were sharp, the daggers shining, the jewelry rich. And Ason's treasure was the richest of all. His bronze armor hung from the henge, his shield glittered from it, his sword impaled it. A flood of gold ran down the whitened wood to the ground. And on top where all could see it, though they only looked with quick glances, then turned away, was the round head of the Dark Man, black hair now unkempt and blowing.

The ceremonies went on for many days, scarcely slowing

at nightfall, or towards morning, since there was always one more warrior of rank who was ready to stand and boast of his victories. Even the warriors of the dun had their turn, for the shame of defeat was over and they were warriors again. They even bragged of feats of arms during that last battle; their recent enemies saw nothing strange in this.

There was squabbling over the division of spoils. Each teuta claimed to have done the best fighting and therefore to have the right to the biggest share. When the tempers rose and insults began, Ason had only to point to the two armored Mycenaeans who always sat by him, a needful reminder of where the fighting strength had lain. Division was made slowly, counterclaims settled, and one argument over a particularly handsome neck torc made from a twisted bar of solid gold was settled by a bloody challenge of arms. Ason thought about the funeral games of Mycenae, where matters like this were contested by means of chariot races, the winner awarded the property of slain noblemen by each local king. His father had unified the Argolid that way, turning inter-city warfare into sporting events, redirecting all military action outward against Atlantis. Foot races might do the trick here, but he doubted it. No one bull-chief had the power to give such awards and make his judgment stick.

No one was even certain of how many nights and days had passed, when there came unwelcome interruption. It was the women and children working near the gate who started it first, shrieking and running. Their noise disturbed the warriors in the outer circles, who turned and strained their necks to see what was happening, shouting inquiries. This uproar penetrated to the center of the ceremonial ring, where Ar Apa was demanding the return of thirty-two cows that had been stolen from his dun. He grated his teeth, stamping with anger at the interruption. The crowd of people surged outwards and was stopped by the warriors, who slowly moved apart to make a pathway for the two people who came haltingly forward.

Naikeri was first, her clothing dirty and scratched where she had thrust her way through the forest. She had a thong in her hand. The other end was clutched by the man who stumbled after her. He had but the single hand that gripped the thong; the other, his right hand, had been amputated. He had lost it quite recently, because the arm was still dark with blood, which also coated the cords that bound the stump tightly at the wrist. He had been blinded as well; the blisters on his cheeks and forehead showed that his eyes had been burned out with hot pokers. His feet were bare, his limbs scratched. He was wearing only a few rags for clothing. It took Ason a few moments to recognize him, and when he did he sprang to his feet and shouted the man's name.

"Atroclus!"

The Mycenaean stopped at the shout and turned empty eye sockets in his direction.

"The Atlanteans have come," he said hoarsely, swaying as though he would fall.

7

The blinded Mycenaean noble was taken to Ason's rooms, the large apartment over the entrance to the dun that had belonged to the bull-chief Uala. Ason would not permit another word to be said until they were behind the closed door, with his own men standing outside of it. Atroclus lay unmoving, his skin pale, his chest heaving as though each breath would be his last. Naikeri had tried to talk, but Ason had silenced her with his raised hand. Now he knelt by Atroclus and raised him in his arms, put a cup to his lips and urged him quietly to drink. He did, thirstily, and Ason lowered him gently back to the soft furs on the bed.

"I am going to die, my kinsman," Atroclus said in a calm voice.

"So shall we all. But tell me first the name of the one who did this."

"That is my reason for being here. There is no place in this world for a warrior of Mycenae whose sword hand is gone, whose eyes are gone as well. When I have told you what I know, you will put your sword into me." It was not said as a question, and Ason responded in the same calm voice.

"That will be done as you ask. What of our kinsmen at the mine?"

"Dead or enslaved. Though it was a good battle. It was some days after you left that we had the warning from the Albi who live in the forest. Two ships of armored men had landed and were on the way to the mine. A man was sent to warn you of what had happened, but it was too late. I saw him killed. We stood to arms and formed a line. The enemy marched up to the distance of a spear cast and we saw that indeed there were enough to fill two ships, and they were three, four to our one. I called to the men to die bravely and to take with them as many as they could of the Atlanteans. They shouted that they would, struck their swords against their shields and stood ready. They fought well, even the chalcei, but all were killed except one chalceus kept to work the mine. This was done on orders, for they were so many they could pick and choose whom they would kill or would save. They had many spears which they threw in volleys heavy as rain. In the end we made a circle and stood together behind our shields, and many of them died before we did. They would not let me die, but pushed me with their shields and prodded with spears until I went down and I was captured. I did not wish it that way. Then a spear was thrust between my elbows behind my back and my arms bound to it. I was taken to the one who had sat at a distance bearing weapons, but did no fighting. His name is Themis."

"Themis the Atlantean, son of Atlas, is dead," Ason said, looking at his palms. "I killed him with these hands."

"No. He lives. He spoke your name and said that you had struck him down once with a coward's blow. When he said this his face became red. He babbled, and there was froth on his lips. He took off his helm and pointed to his head which now has no hair, it all having been removed, and to a gold plate that was held in place by linen wrappings. There was much he said that I could not understand. But he lives—that I can assure you."

"Was the wound here?" Ason asked, touching his fingers lightly to Atroclus' head.

"That is the place."

"Then Themis lives. The blow should have killed him."

"He shouted much about that, about the pain, and how he now cannot box or battle and drags his leg when he walks, and has been made an old and near-dead man by you. There was much about the surgeons of Atlantis and how they drilled away the broken bone and removed it, but I could not understand all that he said."

"I should have struck harder. That blow would have killed any ordinary man."

"Would you had. What was done cannot be undone. I do not think that Themis cares for the tin he captured, or the tin he is mining. That is merely something to do while he remains here. It is you he wants. . . ."

"I want him," Ason said softly, and took Atroclus's hand.

". . . and all else is nothing to him. As the son of King Atlas he commands ships, and brought them here through the spring storms to find you. He tied me and tortured me, did the things you see here to make me speak. Though I am of as noble a line as he, and told him only the truth. He would not believe me, threatened to cut off my sword hand if I did not tell the truth about you. I spoke the same words again, and one of his men with a great ax did this, then tied the cords about my wrist so I would not bleed and die at once. Still he said that I lied, and I would no longer talk to him. When he came close, I bit my tongue and gathered blood and spittle in my mouth, and spat it full into his face. I would say no more. Then he did to me what you see and told the girl to lead me to you, to carry the message that he was here to find and kill you. Though it is my hope that you will be the finder, the killer."

"I will be!" Ason swore and bent to kiss the burnt, blistered cheek of his kinsman.

"Then what has needed to be said has been said." Atroclus swung his feet to the ground and struggled to stand erect. "Your sword now, kind Ason. You will tell them in Mycenae that I died well?"

"None has ever died better."

Ason drew his sword from the slings and held it before him, guiding Atroclus' fingers to the point so he would know where it was. The blinded man raised his head, his lips drawn back from his teeth, and shouted "Mycenae" loudly before he hurled himself forward onto the blade. He was dead before Ason could lower him to the floor.

When Ason came out of the door, he ordered the two Mycenaeans there to remove Atroclus' body and to ready it for burial. Then he stood on the high mound and looked across the plain towards the blood-red disc of the afternoon sun behind the gathering banks of clouds. Two black rooks flew by, cawing loudly to each other, settling in the ditch to pick at the refuse. There was an omen here, but he did not know how to read it. When he turned away he saw that Naikeri was sitting against the wall, waiting for him. She stood and with both hands pressed down her clothing so the round fullness of her stomach could be seen.

"The Atlanteans fought only against your warriors. They have need of slaves, they said, so did not kill us. If they had known I was carrying your child they would have killed me."

Ason started away and did not stop when she screeched after him and finally ran and held him by the arm.

"I am sure this child matters little to you, but it is of some importance to me, do you hear?" He raised his free hand to strike her but stopped when she released him.

"Listen," she said. "Hear what I have to say. I am a woman, which is nothing in your eyes, and also not a Mycenaean, which makes me even less. But I can help you and will bear you a son who will be a warrior like you. There are things about these Atlanteans that Atroclus does not know, that he could not tell you."

"He is dead."

"Alive he could not tell you. There was one man who came with the Atlanteans whom I have seen before. He led them on the path from the beach and stood behind with Themis during the fighting. Once before he came that way with others of his kind, no Atlantean but a trader, a Geramani. He was with the men who took the tin."

Ason swung about and clutched her by the jaw, pulling her to him.

"Do you know what you are saying?" he shouted. She smiled, her smile a grimace as her face was twisted by his fingers, but would not talk again until he released her.

"Of course I know. We all heard that Themis was there to kill you, had come across the world to do so. He shouted it often enough. He was guided here by the Geramani who had means of knowing where you were, just as he knew where the tin was."

"The Dark Man, Sethsus. I killed him too quickly. There are much slower ways of dying. Even dead he attacks me. It was more than the tin he took, but the lives of all those who came to mine it. The tin went to Atlantis, as did word that I was here."

"I am with you still," Naikeri said, putting her arms about him. "You are still my king."

205

"Themis must die. We must retake the mine." He was unaware of her presence.

"I can help. The Albi can watch them, tell you when they leave, or when their forces are weak."

"I have Mycenaeans. I have the men of three teutas to fight with me."

"You have me."

"We must attack. Now."

"I will be with you always."

He pushed her aside, unaware, and hurried away. She fell back against the wattled wall of the dun and watched him go. Was there no end to this killing? Would it stop only when every man in the land was dead?

The ravens rose up, calling loudly, and she shielded her eyes from the sight of them.

8

The summer sun was hot, the wind that blew across the plain as searing as the molten breath from the tin smelter. At night it was cooler, but only slightly, and there was just a brief while before dawn when a breeze came up that could be called comfortable. Then the light would wash the east again, the stars fade, and the great hot trembling sun would lurch over the horizon for another day. There had been no rain for thirty days; the grass was burnt yellow and the streams were only a trickle. The cattle went twice a day to the narrow stream of the Avon nearby. They broke down its banks and trampled in the mud until it was only a bog, with a slow-moving, mud-laden surface in center. The women, when they went to get water for the dun, had to walk upstream a long way before it ran clear. They returned, sweating under the weight of the jars on their heads, complaining in high voices that reached Inteb where he lay in the shade on the bank above. For the most part there was silence inside the dun. The animals lay quietly chewing their cuds, and even the children were still. The copper workers could not fire their forges for the heat, so they also lay in the shadows chewing on straws, talking to each other in low voices. One of the masons had rigged some hides on a frame to give him shade, and sat beneath them smoothing the surface of a bluestone column. He would raise the round, stone maul over his head and bring it down to bruise away some fragments of the column. Then he would wait before doing it again. This slow thud, then a space, then another sharp thud was the only sound, other than the constant high whine of the flies. Inteb yawned and waved the insects away from his face. He almost wished that he had gone with the fighting men to raid the mine. But Ason had wanted him here, to secure the dun until he came back, and Inteb had readily agreed. He as no fighting man; he readily admitted it. Not that there was really anything to do here. With the warriors away, the life of the dun went on as it always had. Each day was like the one before. A door squeaked and Inteb looked up to see Naikeri coming out of Ason's apartments, the large rooms over the doorway that had been those of the bull-chief Uala. Now Naikeri stayed there and no one saw fit to complain. Inteb turned away as she came near him. He pretended to be studying the cattle being driven below. He heard her sit close and he closed his eyes.

"We should talk," she said. He did not answer.

"You hate me, I know that. Nevertheless, we should talk."

Inteb turned to look at her with curiosity. A small, dark woman, cleaner than the Yerni women, not unattractive in her brown clothes and gold jewelry. Though heavy in the breast now, and swollen in the stomach with the coming child.

"I do not hate you, Albi woman. I feel very little emotion at all about you."

207

"But you love Ason. I have seen you kiss him and hold him."

"That I love him is no secret. That you talk about it is a defilement. We will speak of it no more."

Being a woman, she treasured talk of what is forbidden.

"You hate me because I love him too, in a way you cannot. I carry his son."

Inteb smiled at this and slapped at a fly. "You speak well for a savage from world's end, but this is remarkable only in the way that a talking cat would be remarkable. Of interest in itself, of no interest to people. Women are jealous of men and men's love. Well they should be, since they can never attain it. Bear a child in blood and suckle it to life, that is your function, and all you are capable of. These things are ordered."

"Not here, stranger," she hissed the words. "In some strange country where you come from that may be true, but not here. Among my people a person is a person, man or woman, and women of my blood are above all others of the Albi. My people listen when I speak; they obey if I order. And we are here, stranger, in this land, and not back in your Nile I hear you talk about. Ason is here, too, and needs help. We can give him more help together than apart and hating each other. We could. . . ."

"Do nothing. I will say this just once and close my eyes and you will go away. You are a female to bear calves and give milk. You should be out there in the grass on all fours with the rest of the cattle, not here with men making believe you can talk."

He did close his eyes when he was through speaking—but kept one lid partly open to watch her, in case she should try to strike him, since he had had experience with women before. She sat in silence for awhile then slowly stood and went away. He smiled and would have closed his eyes all the way except for the sudden shouting of the herdboys below. They were jumping and trying to climb on the backs of their charges to see better, pointing towards the horizon. From his higher elevation, he could easily see the distant cloud of dust and a line of dark spots moving towards the dun. Men.

"Forus," he shouted, and banged on the door next to his. A grumbling voice answered. "Get on your armor. There are men coming this way."

He went for his own armor and fumbled into it. Through the thin wall he could hear the Mycenaean breathing heavily and cursing under his breath as he rose. He had had his kneecap shattered by a Yerni ax and was in constant pain. He and Inteb were the only defensive force until Ason returned.

Armed and armored they stood together on top of the embankment, Forus leaning against the wall to ease his bad leg.

Bright sunlight shone suddenly from bronze armor. He felt a great thudding in his chest—they might be Atlanteans. Had Ason been defeated? Were they all dead? Now the Atlanteans had come to kill the remaining few of the enemy. The heat of the day drove these fantasies into his head and made the air shimmer so the approaching men were unclear. Forus shielded his eyes and grunted.

"Mycenaeans," he said and slid down to a sitting position to ease his leg. When Inteb was sure of this, he stripped off the heavy armor and went out to meet them.

The Mycenaeans were alone—and fewer returned than had left. Their faces were drawn with exhaustion, and most of them walked with their heavy helmets slung with their shields because of the heat. Ason came first and the others followed, with Aias bringing up the rear and half-supporting one of the wounded.

"Are the Yerni warriors here?" was all that Ason said when Inteb came up to them.

"You are the first."

Ason nodded and would say no more, but walked on stolidly and enterd his own quarters when Naikeri opened the door for him. Inteb felt a sharp stab of hatred for the women, then turned to Aias.

"The others can help their comrade. Come with me and I'll give you some freshly made fermented milk."

"By the great horned bull, those are the finest words I have ever heard," the boxer said in a cracked voice. His face was covered with dust traced through with wet rivulets of sweat. He tore off his armor in Inteb's doorway and dumped an entire jug of water over his head. The first bowl of fermented milk was drained without stopping for breath, and he dropped, gasping, on a couch against the wall and sipped at the next. Inteb sat beside him.

"A lot of fighting, Egyptian," Aias said. "All for not much good. Two evenly matched boxers, that's what it was like. Swing a lot, do damage, no one wins. If we had twice as many men, we could have done it. But every morning there were less Yerni than the night before. They had heads to bring back to their duns, treasure too. They had been fighting a long time. And were in no hurry to impale themselves on the Atlantean swords. There were only a handful from each teuta when we did attack. They ran at the first sight of bronze. We couldn't break their line. Then we took cover in the woods; when they came out we attacked. Drove them back. Nobody wins, nobody loses. In the end Ason saw that, and we force-marched here before the warriors came back alone."

Aias lowered his head after that and slept, not waking even when the bowl slipped from his fingers and spilled the sticky dregs across his legs. Inteb sat, staring across the plain, lost in thought. He was still there at sunset when Ason emerged.

"Aias told me," Inteb said, standing and stretching his cramped limbs.

"There are too many Atlanteans, and the Yerni run. There is little they value at the mine, and they have no desire for swords in their guts. It was no victory."

"It was no defeat, either," Inteb said, trying to find a brighter side to look on, because Ason was in the darkest of humors. Even as he said it, he realized that he was speaking only the truth—and the truth was larger than either of them realized. As they walked to the council circle inside the double ring of blue stones he was silent, lost in thought. Only the smallest fire had been lighted because of the heat. They sat well away from it, Ason at the base of his henge, in his proper place.

"We have been thinking too much of the mine and only the mine," Inteb said. "It hangs before our eyes like a fog, blotting out everything else."

"There is nothing else. Mycenae needs the tin. The tin is at the mine."

"Your father's words—and not wrong words. But there is more that can be said. Mycenae will not fall for want of this bit of tin, not at once. You will get it, but only by admitting that you have done something else, are something else."

"You are talking in riddles tonight, Egyptian, and my head is still thick from the heat of the day."

"Then think of this, and you will find your pulse faster. Here is the land of the Yerni, a rich land, with cattle and sheep, many people, grain for ale, honey for mead, sweet milk and good cheese, great centers for trade where many men gather from far away. Of all the tribes and people in this land, the Yerni are the most warlike and rule where they will—but one teuta is stronger than all the others. And the dun of this same teuta is the richest and the largest, where the traders cross paths and meet. And you, Ason, are king in this land."

"Say more, Egyptian," Ason called out when Inteb stopped, and there was sharp interest in his voice.

"There is much more to say. You could be bull-chief in this dun and none would oppose you. Once you were bull-chief here, you could do what your father is doing with the cities of the Argolid."

"Make all the teutas of the Yerni one?"

"It could be done. You could do it. No longer bull-

211

chief, but king of this land. The king could take the mine away from the Atlanteans. The king could rule a rich country, and as king you could bring the entire land to the aid of Perimedes. Give him an ally as well as a mine."

"Of what use? The distance. . . ."

"The distance did not stop Sethsus from doing Mycenae harm. In the same manner you could do her good. The Geramani are friends neither of Atlantis nor of Mycenae but, like all men, befriend only themselves. Perhaps they can get tin to Mycenae. Perhaps they can guide you to the Atlantean tin mines. Perhaps many things—all of them possible to a king. All yours for the taking."

"I'll take it!" Ason shouted, and laughed aloud. The Mycenaeans across the fire smiled that their leader could be in such spirits. The first of the Yerni warriors, coming in from the darkness, wondered at the sound.

"You must unite the tribes," Inteb said in a rush of words, carried away as well by his vision. "Make them all one tribe, one teuta, give them a nation, give them a city to hew to as the Mycenaeans hew to the great walls of rock-girt Mycenae."

Ason smiled at the thought.

"We are both far from home, Inteb, and there are no Mycenaes or Theras, there is no Thebes in this land. A city of rough wood is all we have."

"Tear it down—they work stone here."

"Enough? You tell me, if we used every stone in these two circles, could we lay the foundation or build a single wall of a city?"

"No, you are right." Inteb laughed. "I saw Mycenae on this plain. But if not Mycenae, a greater circle then. Every bull-chief has his stone, we could make a greater circle of pillar stones, circle within circle perhaps, like the canals of Thera, so every great warrior here could have his stone. And the bull-chiefs' stones would be here and they would have to assemble here, all the bull-chiefs together, and you king over them all."

"I'll need my pillar stone."

"And so shall have it, mighty king. The grandest, largest, most glorious stone these people have ever seen. They will come from everywhere to gape at it. I'll shape it as only Egyptians know how to shape stone, and will raise it behind you here at the council fire for them to stare at, right behind you."

Inteb swung about in his excitement and pointed to the bare ground behind Ason, pointing between the uprights of the henge. And stopped, frozen, his jaw open. A dawning expression of delight swept over his features. He clapped his hands together before him at the strength of it, bending to seize Ason by the shoulders, to pull at him and beg him to turn about.

"Look," he shouted. "This silly little arch of wood these people think so precious, white-painted and adorned, the henge of a little cow-chief. It is nothing. But look at it grow, watch it with your eyes as it swells up higher and higher, wider and stronger, reaching for the sky. As high as one man, two, three—four even. Too wide to span, too high to reach, too solid to move, a henge that will drop their jaws to their chests and start the eyes from their heads."

His hands traced the unborn shape in the sky, and Ason could almost see it there.

"And not wood, either," Inteb said. "Stone, good solid stone, a henge of stone mightier than any. It will be your kingdom and your city, Ason, right here.

"I will build it for you!"

BOOK FOUR
1477 B.C.

1

Unable to contain his excitement, Inteb woke Ason at dawn, shaking at him until he crawled up from the depths of sleep. Naikeri looked on accusingly from the bed beside him, but said nothing when they left. The air was still cool, the morning star bright in the east when they walked out across the plain. Inteb led the way to the area nearby where the great blocks of stones lay about in the greatest profusion. He hurried to the nearest and peered at it from all sides, even dug like a hound to examine its underside at one spot. Ason smiled and sat down on the stone, yawning broadly.

"What do you see?" Inteb asked.

"Stone."

"Nothing more, and that is right because you are a warrior. But as you see skill with a sword in a man, or strength, endurance, other warlike qualities, so can I look beneath the surface of a stone. You know the walls of Mycenae and the lion gate there, you have not forgotten?"

"Never. And I know who built them."

"I am the man who did that, so when I speak now, you

215

will know I speak the truth. Notice the way these great slabs of stone are thrown about on the ground as though left there for our purpose.''

"A great mystery."

"Not at all, we know the same in Egypt. Hard stone concealed beneath the earth, that is disclosed when the dirt is cleared away. Here the rain and wind have done that, exposing this stone for us to work with. Now notice the shape and the straight edges and these little lines here.''

"They mean nothing."

"They do to me. This rock is grained like wood and when worked in the proper manner will split just as wood does. We shall take the two largest columns and shape them, bring them to the dun, where I will seat them in holes in the ground behind the speaking stone. Then we will work and raise up a third stone and place it across their tops high in the air. Everyone will marvel and will wonder how it was placed there.''

"How will you place it there?" Ason asked, looking doubtfully at the immense size of the stone, aware of its incredible weight.

"With skill, Ason, the same skill that raised and fitted the walls of Mycenae. We will begin today.''

Ason lay back on the rock, still cool from the night, dozing as Inteb scouted among the great white slabs of stones, nosing in and out like a questing hound. He finally raised Ason with a shout, then led him through the stones to a long slab that rose chest high.

"This is it," he said, slapping it with the flat of his hand. Ason looked on doubtfully.

"You are a master builder, Inteb, that cannot be denied—but what can you possibly do with this giant of a stone that bulks as big as a ship, bigger than the largest stone in the walls of Mycenae?''

Inteb smiled at the question and they climbed up onto the slab. It stretched away from them. Not only as big as a good-sized galley, but shaped very much like one, bulging out towards the center and narrowing at the far end. Inteb paced it out, and it was four paces wide at the widest, and over ten paces long.

"As high as five men, perhaps higher," Inteb said proudly. "This top side, you will notice, is flat and will need little dressing, and we must hope the bottom will be the same. The two outer sides must be straightened and that great bulge knocked away."

"Do we have the lifetime for that?" Ason asked unbelievingly. "Do you propose that all that stone be removed here, without the tools and instruments and devices I saw you employ in Mycenae? Can it be done?"

"I will do it, Ason, and if you wish I will do it *today*."

Ason cocked his head with unbelief, searching for the joke or the lie—but there was none. When he realized this he roared with approval. Seizing Inteb by both arms he embraced him.

"If you can do that, I can certainly do a far easier thing. I will seize this land and rule it as my kingdom. The Yerni do not know it yet—but their future begins today."

"I will need a lot of help, all the strongest men, as well as the stonecutter from the dun."

"Take what you need. You are my right hand in this. The orders you issue will be the same as mine."

They returned to the dun, ate and drank while they made their plans. Naikeri served them on the mound outside the door and listened but said nothing, not understanding what was being planned. When they were through Ason put on his newly polished armor and went to get his men. Inteb scratched diagrams in the dirt with a stick, then searched out the stonecutter.

"Your name?" he said. The old man glanced over his shoulder and to both sides to be sure he was being addressed, then looked at the ground. Inteb spoke more sharply a second time and the man squeezed his swollen knuckles and reluctantly said, "Dursan."

"Are there any in the dun other than yourself who can work stone?"

Dursan looked around for some release from this dark stranger, who spoke with such a thick accent that many of his words could not be understood. But there was no escape. He pressed his hands together and mumbled answers, finally and reluctantly admitting that there were two others who aided him in his work. Inteb sent for them. While he was waiting he ran his hands over the blue stone that Dursan had been working.

"Where does this stone come from?" he asked. "I've seen none like it on the down."

"Far away."

"I'm sure of that or I wouldn't have asked. Now try hard and give me a little more detail than that."

Under verbal prodding Dursan told him how the blue stones were brought from a distant mountain, where they waited to be seized by any warrior strong enough to do that. The story seemed true enough; the man did not have enough intelligence to concoct such a complicated lie. A warrior would take men with him, pull the stone down to the shore, then onto a raft of logs. It took a long time to paddle this out of the harbor and along the coast, because the ocean was wild there many times of the year. The sea voyage was ended when they reached the mouth of a river. Apparently the stone was brought up the river, across country and down another river. The Avon that passed nearby the dun. All in all a great labor. Inteb marveled at the things men do to assure their own importance.

"But why this particular mountain?" Inteb asked. "There must be good stone a lot nearer than that."

"It has always been done that way. They did it like that before we drove them out, in my father's time it was."

"They?"

"The Donbaksho. They used to keep cattle here, but

218

they don't know how to fight. Now *we* have the cattle and they give us the grain we ask for. They used to trade here—now we trade here. They used to have someone always on the mountain where the stones come from, watching for the Albi when they came from Domnann—you can see all the way across the channel from the top there. Now the Albi come here with their bronze and gold to trade with us, and we don't even need a watch on the mountain." Dursan snorted with pleasure over the superior fighting ability of the Yerni, then pointed to the large stone almost completely buried in the ground.

"See that, our speaking stone. Do you know how it got there? My father did that. It was the biggest standing stone the Donbaksho had, the chief's stone, and they all wanted to come and touch it. My father had the pit dug, pushed it over, buried it. Now we stand on it, stand on the Donbaksho."

Then Dursan's two assistants arrived, while the first of the Yerni warriors were already beginning to climb down the ladders and notched poles from the balconies above.

Very soon it was like a disturbed ants' nest. The warriors milled about, calling to each other, cradling their battle-axes and smoothing their moustaches. The women followed behind, keeping their distance, yet curious, too, as to the reason for this activity in the heat of the day. All they knew was that the Mycenaeans were going about the outer bank and hammering on all the doors with their swords, calling the warriors to the council fire. They came. Those who had pillar stones of their own leaned against the cool stone or sat in their shadows. Then Ason appeared, marching at the head of his Mycenaeans and, as always, the Yerni stared in admiration at this incredible sight. Men in bronze from head to foot, eye-hurting shining bronze, bronze swords in hand, brazen shields on their arms. Ason led them to the speaking stone, set into the ground within the ring of bluestones; they stood behind it as he stood upon it. When he raised his sword the noise died away enough so that his voice could be heard.

"I am standing on the speaking stone and I am telling you something. Today you will see a thing that you have never seen before. Today you will see a wonder that you will tell your children about. They will tell your children's children, and there will be no end to the telling. Today you will see something done that you know cannot be done. And after it is done I will tell you something that you never thought you would hear."

The rising hum of voices drowned Ason's voice and the crowd stirred with excitement. No one knew what the words meant, but everyone knew that something incredible was going to happen. What Ason said he would do he did, they had learned that much about the man. He called out again and they grew silent.

"Follow me," he said, striding away from the stone, with his Mycenaeans behind him, and out of the entrance of the dun. The Yerni warriors came next, pushing and jostling, shouting at each other, trying to stay close. The rest of the inhabitants of the dun, women and children, metal and wood workers, even the druids, followed after. Ason led them the short distance to the field of jumbled rock and climbed upon the great stone that Inteb had selected. The Egyptian clambered up beside him and reached down to take a heavy rock that Dursan lifted up to him. A hush fell as Ason spoke.

"Now listen to Inteb, who will do the promised thing for me."

Inteb rolled the round, greenish rock with his foot and pointed to it. The warriors strained to see.

"This is a maul," he called out, and they pushed and craned their necks as though they had not seen stones like this in the dun every day of their lives. "It is a hard stone, harder than any other. Dursan and the others use stones like these to dress the stones of the warriors. They do it like this."

He bent and strained to lift the rock—it was a third of

his weight—and struggled it as high as his waist before he dropped it. It smashed into the surface of the white stone with the familiar dull thud. Inteb rolled it aside and scraped up a little rock dust with his finger.

"This is what the maul does. Every time it strikes the larger stone it breaks off a few grains. After many blows a stone can be smoothed or grooved, or even hollowed away. It takes many days to smooth even the smallest stone, yet that is all that can be done. But not any more. Today we are going to do something new."

He slowly paced the entire length of the immense slab and back; every eye was upon him as he did this. He pointed down at the immense bulk and they listened with unbelief.

"Today we are going to break this stone in half, the warriors and I. It will become Ason's stone when we bring it to the dun. We will shape it and move it and raise it—and it will be the mightiest warrior's stone ever raised. There will be more after that, but I tell you only of this stone now. . . ."

Someone laughed and Ason leapt forward, pushing Inteb aside and stabbing his sword at the crowd so that the nearest drew back in fear.

"Inteb speaks for me," he called out with a deadly anger in his voice. "His words are my words. If you laugh at him you laugh at me. I will have the head of anyone who even smiles in my direction. Have you heard me?"

They had, well enough. The women covered their faces and many of the children ran away. The warriors stayed— they were warriors—but their faces were as expressionless as the stone before them.

"I will need only the strongest warriors to help me cut Ason's stone," Inteb said in the silence. "Each warrior will need a maul, and the heavier it is and the stronger he is, the more honor will be his. There are some mauls here and Dursan is looking for others."

Now it was a matter of pride and strength. The warriors

221

put their axes in their hair belts and went, shouting and pushing, to find the biggest mauls they could lift. Most of the stones they found were the wrong kind—only the hard green stone could be used—and they cursed and dropped the stones when they were told this, and went to find others. One by one, sweating and grumbling in the heat, they came back with the mauls. When there were more than twenty warriors who had them, Inteb called a halt.

"There is room for no more. The honor is for these warriors, who will do what no one has ever done before."

They swaggered about, then climbed onto the great slab with him, calling out boasts to the scowling warriors left behind. They brought the mauls with them. With the aid of the Mycenaeans, Inteb pushed the warriors into a line against the far edge of the stone. Shoulder to shoulder, they stretched the length of the slab, listening with pained attention as Inteb explained what they had to do. It was not complex, but they were not used to working together, had never done anything in unison before in their lives. It was a concept they found difficult to understand. He made them repeat the motions, over and over, many times before they got it right. Small stones, no bigger than a man's fist were passed up and they used these as they practiced. Inteb had drawn two charcoal lines the length of the slab, a pace apart, and he kept redrawing the lines as their shuffling feet obliterated them. There were mutterings of complaint over the stupid hot thing they were doing—but no one smiled. Inteb repeated the instructions with a voice rapidly growing hoarse.

"That's it, all in a line, your feet on that marked line. Not standing in front of it or behind it, but *on* it. Good. Raise your mauls, as high as your head, hold them there. . .*hold* them until I give the word, and all together, just for once, *drop them*!"

The small rocks clattered down, most of them on the marked line in an irregular fall, rolling about and some dropping over the edge to the ground. The watching crowd had been cleared back by the Mycenaeans, but small boys ran forward to retrieve the fallen stones and pass them back up. They were enjoying themselves, if no one else was.

"No, leave them there," Inteb ordered. "And throw the rest of the stones away. We'll do it now with the mauls."

There were excited shouts at this announcement, and the warriors called to one another as they kicked the small stones away and bent to pick up the waiting mauls. It was an impressive sight, the tall, sweat-drenched warriors, shoulder to shoulder the length of the great slab, with Inteb standing behind them. The crowd was silent.

"Lift!" Inteb called out and they bent and a ripple moved down the line as they straightened and the green mauls rose in the air.

"Hold, hold!" he shouted, since some of the warriors were slower than the others and one, cursing, dropped the stone on his foot. Then they were all up, high, higher. . . .

"*Drop them!*"

The great weight of hard stone fell with a rolling thunder, and the warriors jumped back.

Nothing happened. Inteb shouted hoarse orders above the growing murmur from the crowd.

"Not good enough, not at the same time, not on the line. Do it right or it can't be done at all, you great hulking dim-brained animals. Lift together, hold together, drop together. . .*drop!*"

Again, nothing—but a rising growl of anger from the warriors as well as the crowd. The Mycenaeans raised their weapons and shields, and Ason jumped up next to Inteb and paced behind the warriors' backs.

"Killers of dogs!" he shouted. "This is harder than killing. This is something you must do right—or I will slay you all. This you will do."

By force of will he kept them there, shouting aloud now

in protest, raising and dropping the mauls again—with no result. With the flat of his sword Ason drove back the men who tried to turn away, cursing them in three tongues, so that they once again grabbed up the mauls.

"Over your heads, you eaters of turds!" he called out. "High, higher, hold them there, all of you, do what I tell you, do it right, because this time they fall together and they fall on the line the correct way, bring them down. . .*now*!"

Shouting angrily, the Yerni warriors hurled the stones down with a crashing roar, and the solid rock beneath their feet shivered.

With a growing, crackling, rushing roar it sheared in half, fell away, a great broken slab that dropped and cracked, spraying fragments out at the screaming, running crowd.

Dumbfounded, the warriors looked down at what they had done.

The immense slab of stone had broken along its entire length, along the line Inteb had drawn upon its surface.

2

There are some things that are unbelievable. Even when they are seen to happen, they cannot be accepted. The warriors who had done this thing could not credit their labor with the mauls as having had any connection with the splitting of the great stone. It would have been easier to believe that lightning had struck down from the sky and done this thing; they had seen the carcasses of animals and riven trees that lightning had struck, so knew its strength. Just as they knew their own, and knowing this could not believe what they had done. They jumped down and pushed the crowd aside and stared with open mouths at the fresh white surface of the sundered rock, bent to pick up fragments of it from the ground. These they turned over and over and examined, tapping them, even touching them to their mouths as though taste might reveal something the eye could not see. But they were bits of rock, good solid rock, and could not be broken again. Some tried with the mauls, with no success other than a few bruised fingers and crushed toes. The stone which had given way and fallen apart before them was still stone; hard, intractable, enduring.

"Listen to me," Ason called out, standing alone on the rock above them. "This is a day that must be remembered; what was done here today must be remembered. Ason's great stone was cut this day. The council fire will be built high, and sheep and cows will be roasted, ale will be drunk and all the warriors shall sit by me."

This was greeted with roars of approval. When the shouting had died away Ason said, "Tonight, before these warriors, I shall be named the new bull-chief of this dun, which will be Dun Ason now."

There were more shouts at this, with dark looks only from the family of the dead Uala from whose ranks the new bull-chief should have been selected. They dared say nothing aloud, because the other warriors saw only honor and victories for the teuta led by a man like Ason. He was the strongest among them, the deadliest warrior, and now commanded great stones to be cleaved at his word. He would be a bull-chief men could follow.

"We could cut the other face now," Inteb said, the niceties of politics forgotten in the pleasure of once more working with stone.

"I think not," Ason told him. "There is enough wonder here for one day. The women must prepare for the feast, the druids have their work as well. Tomorrow will be a day for labors."

While the warriors had been away the Donbaksho had continued to bring their tithe of grain to the dun. The women had prepared it in the squat, wide-bottomed pots.

225

Because of the heat it had brewed and matured with bubbling efficiency. Now great quantities of ale were cooling in shaded corners. A fat-flanked cow was dragged to the killing area, bellowing at the smell of blood, its eyes rolling in agony. The first butcher, an ugly bondman with a fearful squint and great-muscled arms, swaggered over in his blood-drenched leather apron, his heavy stone hammer over his shoulder. While two men hung from the cow's horns he waited, then swung the hammer with practiced skill against the flat of the beast's head, just before its horns. It collapsed to the ground, dead instantly, where the old women severed its throat with sharp flint knives, catching the spurting blood in pottery bowls. Other beasts were dragged up, and the preparations for the feast got under way. Well before dark the first warriors were seated in their positions. The drinking had begun.

It was the druid, Nemed, who conducted the bull-chief rites. If he still bore any ill will towards Ason he was silent about it. Now he was wearing his finest robes, as well as a tall, cylindrical headdress that grew narrower towards the top. A wonder as long as a man's arm, made of beaten gold into which designs of lines and circles had been worked. He stood between Ason and the fire, arms folded, waiting as the crowd grew quiet. When they were silent he began his chant in a high, toneless voice that gradually deepened as he warmed to the subject. Much of the material was familiar, old lines repeated and used in different ways. This only increased the warriors' appreciation, rather than lessening it. They nodded at the parts they knew well.

Sound of thunder and rushing wind,
A crashing, a breaking,
Rock tearing, ground ripping,
Such sounds to deafen the ears.

The sounds that I heard were men at war,
Shield shock of shield against shield.
Axes striking and breaking,
Skulls crushed.

What fighting was done then,
Deep voices of heroes
And battling warriors, raging with anger,
Grim wild men, great bull-chiefs.

There was Ason,
In the midst was Ason, quick eagle,
Striking hound of gore, seeking blood,
Man of the long knife, bellowing bull.

Then they met,
Then Ason struck.
Cleft Uala's head,
Drove the blow to his navel—
Then a second cross-wise stroke
Brought him down in three pieces.

Nemed drew a deep wavering breath, loud in the silence, and shouted the remainder without stopping or even pausing:

Drenched with blood and gray with brains,
He cut away
> jaw from head,
> head from trunk,
> arms from trunk,
> bend from arms,
> wrists from bend.
> fists from wrists,
> thumbs from fists,
> nails from thumbs,
> legs from trunk,
> knees from legs,
> calves from knees,

> feet from calves,
> toes from feet,
> nails from toes,
> And he sent these limbs and parts
> Flying front and back like bees
> Buzzing about in the sunlight.

Loud shouts of appreciation followed this, and buzzing sounds that would not stop until Nemed had regained his breath and repeated the part about the bees again. There was more like this, often repeated, far more interesting to the Yerni warriors than to Ason. He could see no interest in the lying and the bragging that they all knew could not be true. It went on a long time, and Nemed built the tension carefully until the moment when he spun about and pointed at Ason.

"You have a question?" Nemed shouted.

"I have a question," Ason answered as he rose and stood before his henge. "Is there a different purpose for this day? How can this day be different from all the others?"

As he said this, two of the other druids dragged up a man who struggled weakly in their grip. A captive, imprisoned for what reason? Ason neither knew nor cared. The man was held with his back to Nemed who was handed a sharp bronze dagger. He nodded once and the prisoner was released, the druids stepping back. Before the man could take a step Nemed plunged the dagger into his back. A hard upward thrust beneath the ribs that penetrated his heart. The captive shuddered all over and fell, writhing for a moment on the ground as he tried to reach back for the dagger still in his body. Then he convulsed again and died.

As he fell and writhed on the ground in mortal agony Nemed stood over him, his face set and flintlike, reading omens from his thrashing, then the positions of his limbs after he was dead. The movements of a man already part way through the gate of death are far better augury than

228

clouds or the flight of birds. What he saw there must have satisfied him, because he straightened up and pointed carefully at Ason. He began the ritual questions that would make Ason bull-chief.

The thing was done.

"You rise with the first light, Egyptian," Aias called out from his perch on the ramp above as Inteb hurried by. Mist still hung over the plain; the birds were waking and calling.

"The first light of dawn can show things in a stone that are not normally seen."

"I know. It is in the shadows."

Inteb halted and looked up quizzically.

"For a boxer you seem to know a good deal about stone working."

"As a slave I learned a lot about a number of things that require a strong back and little thought. Boxing took me from that. I have been in the galleys, and in the stone quarry at Karatepe."

"Kizzuwatna sandstone," Inteb snorted. "You can chew it with your teeth. Come along and I'll show you what real stone is."

As the dawn sun burned away the mist it shone across the stone. Inteb hurried from one end to the other, mumbling to himself and marking quick strokes with his piece of charcoal. Aias watched, scratching and belching sleepily; he had not slept that night.

"This side should be even easier," Inteb said. "The stone is thinner, for one thing, and it will break cleanly away. The Yerni now know that it can be done, so it might be possible to get them to work together."

"A touch of the whip made from the skin of the water horse helps with that."

"Only with slaves and peasants, Aias. I wish I had a few here. An ax in the head is what I would get if I tried it with these Yerni. When the time comes for the final shaping I will have to find bondsmen, or perhaps the Donbaksho from the farms for that work. It is simple enough and requires only strong arms and the repeating of the same process from sunrise to sunset.''

When the boys drove the cattle out to pasture for the day they saw Inteb at the stone. Word was quickly passed. All the warriors who were sober enough to walk hurried out, led by the ones who had not had a chance to work a maul the day before. Laughing aloud they climbed onto the slab, smiling at Inteb when he cursed them for obliterating his marks, fingering the stone mauls, comparing their fine points like experienced masons. There was a warrior for every maul, and a growing crowd pushing close soon afterwards. Aias went to bring Ason for the spectacular moment.

''One cut for each side,'' Inteb told him when he appeared. ''This is ecnomical of labor and time, but is also a mark of skill that few possess.'' There was no conscious boasting in this, but only truth. Ason nodded agreement. ''The stone shall be wide at the base and will taper on each side as it rises, much like the temple of Ni-weser-re next to the Nile, or the pillars in the courtyard of Sahu-re. This is a much-admired line, and one I much prefer to the straight angularity of the walls and columns executed for King Khephren in his temple. That is not for you—even if I had the means here to work stone to that degree. Yours will be a living and warm stone that takes its unpolished form very much from the earth from which it springs. Now we begin.''

This time the warriors listened intently, straining to hear and understand, remembering that it could be done. The crowd of watchers moved far back and climbed on other rocks for a better view. Aias helped Inteb to place the men correctly and to order their movements. The practice with the pebbles did not take as long as the first time. One of the warriors shouted ''Ason abu!'' when they were told to pick up the mauls, all the others joining in the war cry.

High they held them, tensely waiting the word, and hurled them down at the given moment.

With a sharp crack the stone split, and the great jagged piece fell away.

The watchers were struck dumb for a moment, remembering the frenzied labors of the day before, not expecting anything yet. Then they burst into shouts and ran forward, pushing and milling about to examine this new wonder. In the middle of the broken stone, fallen away slabs and forgotten mauls, Ason's column lay neatly shaped and ready.

"Now to move it," Inteb said. "No excuses today about banquets, this work must be accomplished."

"Everything shall be as you say," Ason agreed. "Though how you intend to move this mountain is beyond me."

"But not beyond me, which is why I serve you. In Egypt stone working is older than the memory of man, or his writings. The art we practice is known to no others, and I am skilled in that art. But I need the proper materials and labor."

"Labor there is enough. The warriors themselves fight for positions to help. They will tire of this, I am sure, but there will be others to replace them, you have my word on that. What materials do you need?"

"Something unknown on this treeless plain. Strong wooden beams as thick as your leg or thicker. Lengths of logs, many of them, and rope, more rope than I have seen anywhere on this island."

"The wood is easy enough. The dun is made of wood, and you will have every splinter of it if you need it."

"Not all, not quite yet—"

"Then take my apartment. There are lengths of log that bridge the entrance that should suit you, the walls and floors as well. Do you wish it now?"

"As soon as it can be obtained."

The new orders were received with joy by everyone but the woodworkers and Naikeri. She cursed and threw things

231

at the people who came and began to tear at her walls, stopping only when Ason himself came to drive her out with the personal belongings. The woodworkers, many of whom had helped to build the dun with great labor and time, thought even less of tearing down their handwork. But it was coming down, whatever they felt, so they moved in and guided the destruction so it was done in the proper manner, the reverse of putting the building up.

Inteb stayed at the site and directed the digging out of cavities under the stone. Here, as everywhere else on the plain, the hard chalk lay just under the surface soil and could not easily be dug or shoveled away. Sharp-pointed deer antlers had to be driven into it with rocks, then levered sideways to crack out a piece of chalk. This process repeated as long as was needed. When the first beams and logs arrived, the pits were ready. Heavy stones had been pushed into positions before them.

"This beam is used as a lever," Inteb called out. "You do not have to know why, but a lever increases the strength of men and enables them to do things thought impossible. We will now use the levers to lift this stone. This will be done a little at a time. Each time the stone is lifted these logs will be pushed under to prevent it from falling back down. When it is tilted enough, these other logs will be pushed all the way under it. That will be the first step. We will do that now."

Once more aided by Aias, Inteb instructed the men on the great levers, putting their hands in the proper place, explaining over and over what they were to do. Aias and two Mycenaeans manned the chocks that had to be pushed under when the stone was lifted, since this required instant decision and action of a nature too technical for the Yerni.

There were twelve men on the three longest poles, eight men on the four shorter ones. They clutched the wood and waited anxiously while Inteb surveyed the arrangements. Then, on his ordered command, they threw their weight onto the levers. They of course did it unevenly, some hanging from the beams, others pushing in the wrong direction. One of the poles was rotten and cracked, dropping a half dozen men into the dust, where they were laughed at for their pains. Another pole was fitted, more explanations given, even a demonstration by six Mycenaeans as to how a pole should be pulled on. The Yerni spat on their palms and went back to their labors.

This time there were excited screams as the great slab trembled and tilted ever so slightly. The chocks were quickly thrust home. All work stopped again as everyone went to stare at the black opening, laughing and grabbing up the beetles and disturbed insects that emerged. Inteb waited until they had all seen enough, then ordered them back to work. The rock fulcrums were moved closer and changed for higher ones and, ever so slowly, the immense slab of stone tilted into the air.

"Enough," Inteb called out. "Bring the logs."

The Yerni were hesitant about coming too close to the stone, sure that it would fall back to the earth, or perhaps roll over and crush them at any moment. It was Aias and the Mycenaeans who put the logs under the stone as Inteb directed, until they filled the space beneath completely. Their round ends projected along the side in an unbroken row of circles. The sun was low, evening approaching, before Inteb approved of the arrangements and was prepared to lower the stone onto the rollers.

"Slowly," he called out, "a step at a time, the reverse of lifting it. If it breaks loose it will turn those logs to splinters when it falls. Then we will have to start all over again."

The creaking poles levered up the unimaginable mass and, one by one, the supporting chocks were removed. When the last one was taken away, all the weight came on the platform of loose logs, which groaned with the weight, and some of them, over irregularities in the ground, were crushed with loud snapping sounds. But the others held.

Inteb would not permit the excited Yerni to take more

time to run around the stone and admire it. They did it anyway, kneeling down and looking beneath it at the light on the far side. Under his direction more logs were placed on the ground before the small end of the stone, to form a solid mass of rollers. Inteb climbed up on the slab to direct the next step and Ason came to join him.

"We will move the stone," Inteb said. "Just a few paces today to see that it can be done, so that in the morning we can begin its path to the dun. Poles over here."

The great beams were once more angled under the slab, but this time at the large end, not the sides. On the given signal the men on the poles heaved and the great stone shivered.

"Again—harder!"

They pulled with all their strength, and the stone slab moved forwards over the first log, and then the second. The position of the levers was moved forward and they heaved again. Slowly, the last log emerged from the rear of the stone. The stone had moved forward twice the span of a man's hands.

"The beginning of the journey," Inteb said proudly.

3

News of what was happening at Dun Ason spread quickly to the other teutas, then by word of mouth to the Donbaksho farmers in the forest, on to the isolated Albi settlements. It was the dry part of the year; the crops had been harvested, the animals were well fed. There was time to see this new wonder in the world, and many came to do just that. Each day when the work began there was no shortage of observers and volunteers if they were needed. And they were. Bringing Ason's stone to its resting place was a great labor.

A track had to be smoothed across the open down to the gateway of the dun. More of the walls were sacrificed to obtain logs to be placed side by side to fill in the muddy spots and to level the ground. A smooth roadway now stretched from the field of broken stones the short distance to the dun—and along it the ponderous stone made its voyage.

Everything was organized now. Every bit of leather available had been gathered from the hides of cattle and wild horses, braided into ropes to tie about the stone. These were the anchor lines for two thick, long leather cables that stretched out ahead, well rubbed with fat to keep them soft and supple. Other leather ropes and plaited vines were attached to the stone near the front, so more men could haul at the same time. The mass of the stone was so great that if any progress were to be made, other than a simple crawl by using the levers in the rear, a great number of men would be needed. When they finally assembled to begin the move, their numbers were too large for the Yerni to count.

"My counting does not go that high either," Ason admitted. "Is all this needed?"

"It is," Inteb said with a calmness he did not feel. Would it really be enough? His calculations were accurate; he had gone over them many times. "To move the stone easily, to keep it moving steadily up the small grades here, we will need at least five hundred men on the ropes."

"A number beyond imagining," Ason admitted.

"It can be imagined. All the fingers and toes on a man number twenty and the count of five men is one hundred. We need the count of twenty-five men."

"It is still a very large number."

"It will be larger still. To keep the stone moving steadily we must have log men, two to each log, since they weigh as much as two men for the most part, and the count here will be two hundred. They must seize the logs as they emerge behind the stone and move quickly to the front of the stone, to lay them down ahead of the other logs. They act again as rollers when their turn comes. All of this must be organized to a very high degree. I will supervise the hauling team, Aias will make sure the logs are taken forward properly, while someone must ride the stone, supervise and order everything.''

''That is my position.''

''The highest, Ason, none other dare fill it. Shall we begin?''

Although they had started at dawn, the sun was nearing the zenith by the time the order to move was finally given. The ropes were laid out along the ground by Inteb himself, to be positive that the pull would come in the proper direction. The line of rollers stretched ahead of the stone, while men stood ready in the rear to seize them as they emerged. Inteb raised his hand and Ason called out loudly.

''We will begin.''

The men bent to seize their ropes, lifted them to their shoulders and stood there, awaiting Inteb's orders, as they had been directed. Inteb stood on a rock to one side to see that they were all in the correct position, then spoke the commands.

''Hold the ropes firmly. Lean forward. Do not pull yet, but lean forward so your weight is on the ropes. Feel that weight. Do not pull with your arms; your arms and hands are just for holding the rope—it is your legs that will do all the work. Now, crouch forward, bend your knees beneath you so that you are ready to push. Be ready now. . .ready . . . slowly as you can, straighten your legs, push— PUSH!''

They did. The ropes stretched and grew taut, and the logs beneath the massive stone creaked.

And then it shuddered and moved forward.

As soon as it did, some people fell, others turned to look—while the rest kept pulling with no effect, the veins standing out in their foreheads. Ason called out for them to halt and they did. The routine was repeated.

After many false starts the necessary coordination was achieved, and the stone moved forward with deliberate and steady motion. One log after another emerged from the rear to be grabbed by eager hands, lifted, and carried ahead to await the arrival of the stone again. The men hauling on the ropes sweated and strained; Inteb kept them moving, a slow step at a time—and Ason rode his strange stone ship through the entrance of the great dun and across its spacious interior to the prepared pit next to the council fire. When the signal to halt was given, some of the men dropped to the ground on the spot, while others called out for ale to slake their thirst.

Ason rested too, sitting in the shadow of the great stone, feeling it against his back, a part of him, eating the food that Naikeri brought to him. She wanted to talk about their new rooms but he waved her away. The stone filled his thoughts.

"Do we go on?" he asked the sweating Inteb, who crawled up out of the pit and dropped to the ground next to him.

"At once, while everyone is willing. I was making a final check of the dimensions, and all is as it should be, the stone will fit. You will notice that Dursan and his assistants have pounded the base, rounding it slightly. This will enable us to position the stone exactly, after it is in the pit, rock it back and forth, and even turn it if we must."

"By what magic will the stone enter the pit at your bidding?"

"No magic. Art. You will see that this side of the pit is cut in a sloping ramp. The far side is straight up and down. Those large stakes have been put in position against it, so that when the stone slides home it will not bring down the chalk on the other side, destroying all our labors.

What we will do now is draw the stone ever so gently forward so the base projects over the side of the hole and the ramp. When more weight is over the hole than is on the rollers, the end will swing down and the stone will slide in and seat itself."

"Leaving this great handsome thing standing at an angle half in and half out."

"You can see in your mind like an artist, Ason. You are correct. When it is down I will then bring it to an upright position against the far wall. We will hold it there while chalk and rubble are quickly shoveled into the hole to fill it and secure the column. Your first stone will be in place. The first upright of the henge that the druids call Mother Earth, the first planted."

Inteb had prepared the stone for its descent into the pit in other ways. As it had been brought closer and closer to its resting place, he had arranged that larger logs be used as rollers, so that the stone would be as far above the surface of the ground as possible. This was vital, as Inteb knew from experience, and he made many measurements and calculations before he would allow the stone to proceed, surveying it from all sides and squinting along it. He would not permit the operation to go on until the angle of approach had been moved slightly to one side. This proved to be harder than rolling had been, and there was much straining and cursing at the levering beams before Inteb was satisfied. Only then were the ropes picked up once more and the signal given to take up the strain as slowly as possible. The stone rumbled forward.

Moving alongside it, Inteb kept one hand on the stone, watching its progress carefully. The end was over the pit when he stopped the hauling. Two heavy wooden stakes were brought up. These were driven into the ground at the very edge of the pit, after the last log had passed that point and been pulled quickly aside before it fell into the opening. The forward movement was started again, and the pivot log crawled across the ground to the stakes, where it was stopped. But the stone kept moving, scraping across it, and the crowd murmured and pressed back as the massive end of the column moved out into the air, overhanging and shadowing the pit below. Further and further it went until the men on the ropes felt a shiver, so that they dropped the ropes and scrambled away. The stone hung there, its immense weight pulling it down, the chalk on the lip of the cutting crumbling and falling away, more and more, the pivot log next to it splitting and cracking as it was crushed.

With a sudden swooping rush the great length of stone hurled itself into the air, blotting out the sky, sliding down with a crashing roar to seat itself in the waiting socket.

The ground shook beneath their feet and a great cloud of dust rose up.

Tilted at an angle, like a giant's finger pointing at the sky, the stone was seated in its opening in the ground.

While the others celebrated and danced around it, Inteb went back to work. Pulling out his helpers from the mob and pushing them to their positions, with Aias at his side when a little violent persuasion was needed. Shear legs had been prepared days earlier. They were carried over and laid on the ground next to the straight side of the pit, opposite the angled stone. They were simply made, of four lengths of wood, but most cunningly designed. The shear-legs themselves were two tall tree trunks that were wide apart on the ground but angled towards one another as they rose, so that they crossed at the very top, and were tightly bound together there. An arm's length below this crossing, a short crossbar had been lashed into place between the two legs. Another, longer one connected them at ground level. The exact placement of these crossbars was essential to its operation. Before the wooden framework was raised, two pits were dug into the chalk for the bottoms of the legs so they would not be able to move about once seated there.

Again Inteb did what no other could do, laying out the ropes in the proper manner. A heavy log was lashed to the back of the angled stone just below the top. Ropes ran from the small crossbar near the top of the shear-legs and over this log to the ground. These ropes would first be used to lift the shear-legs into position. But before this was done, the hauling lines that would lift the stone were tied securely about the shear-legs, where they crossed at the top.

Lifting the great wooden form from the ground was a labor in itself. Two teams of men pulled on the ropes that ran over the log at the top of the stone, while others raised the top of the frame, pushing with poles when it lifted above their reach. Slowly the shear-legs rose until they were standing vertical next to the pit. The ropes that had been used to lift the legs were now lashed securely to the log behind the stone, and the lifting was ready to begin.

One hundred seventy-five men picked up each line. They would pull the top of the shear-legs away from the stone, and the lines tied to the short crossbar would pull the stone to a vertical position. If everything went correctly, Inteb ordered the slack be taken up on the lines, then walked about examining every detail before turning to Ason.

"We are ready," he said.

"Begin."

There was a great creaking from the wooden frame when the pressure came on it, as the men hauled with practiced strength. The great stone stirred from its resting point—then slowly heaved free of the supporting ramp and rose to the vertical.

"Stop!" Inteb shouted when the stone pressed against the flat wall of the pit. "Hold there, keep holding!"

They held, sweating and straining, as Inteb walked up to the stone and pressed a strange instrument to its surface. He had supervised its construction when the wrights had made it; none other than he knew its function. A half

240

section of a small log had been hollowed out to make a trough, almost a duplicate of the large chalk troughs, and this was secured to a vertical length of wood. There was water in the trough, and when Inteb pressed the trough and wood to the stone, he divined some mysterious knowledge from this water, perhaps as the druids read signs from the tortured positions of stabbed prisoners. Everyone marveled at this, even the gasping, straining men holding the stone in position.

Inteb was aware of the tension and knew there was a limit to the length of time they could hold the strain, but the column had to be vertical before it was secured in position. The water level told him all he needed to know. He had scratched a deep groove into the wood, and when the water level was at this mark the surface against which it was resting was vertical. With careful patience he made his measurements and ordered the men on the poles to push at the top of the stone, so it rocked on its base, to align it vertically. They pushed from one side, then from the other, then back to the first again. He shouted instructions at them, which Aias passed on with curses; the weakest men had fallen from the ropes, to be replaced by others, before he was satisfied.

"Now," Inteb called out. "Fill in the hole!"

Shouting with excitement, the workers shoveled the dirt and lumps of chalk back into the hole, mixed with rocks and broken mauls, anything that would fill the space. It rose quickly to the ground level, was tamped down with heavy logs and filled some more. When this had been done the second time, the order was finally given, and the exhausted men let go of the ropes.

The column stood by itself, reaching up into the air, casting a great pointing finger of a shadow across the dun, a shadow that had never existed before.

Soon after dark the moon rose, shone down on the banquet that was already well under way. This was a signal for more admiring of Ason's stone—it had never been seen by moonlight before—and a pacing out of the immense shadow that the moonlight threw. The most venturesome warriors came close to the rock and some even touched it; Ason stood with his back against it and feared nothing. Ale was brought to him there and he drank. There were no women at the banquet, other than those who served the drink, nor was their presence permitted at so important a function. Ason ignored the woman's voice calling to him, but he could ignore it no longer when Naikeri appeared, still speaking his name.

"Away," he called out, raising his hand to strike her if she came any closer.

"There is something you must know, something important."

"Another time."

"It is important now. Shall I come to you—or would you have me wait, away from the council ring?"

Ason jumped forward to seize her, but she escaped him. Angrily he followed her from the fire, until they were well away from the circles of men when she turned to face him. Her belly was large, pushing its mound up through her clothing. When he saw this he lost some of his anger, thinking about his son to be.

"I have word about the Atlanteans," Naikeri said. "Though perhaps they are no longer as important to you as your stone."

He turned to admire the column from this new angle, ignoring her waspish tones; women were often like that. "What have you heard of the Atlanteans?"

"They will march out of the valley of the mine to attack you here. A kinsman of mine is leading them."

For the first time in many days the stone was forgotten as Ason turned all his attention to her. With the excitement of the stone-raising, the Atlanteans had been out of his thoughts of late.

"Tell me all you know," he said.

"So now you have attention for me? Only when you need me do you even speak to me. At all other times you treat me as though I were as dumb as that stone you have there."

"Speak about the Atlanteans, woman," Ason said between his teeth. "You can flay me with your sharp tongue some other time. What has happened?"

In a sudden change of mood she went to him, her arms about his back and her face against his. "I wish only to help," she said. "What I do, I do for you, my king. There was no one before you, there will be none other than you for me, this I promise. I carry your son and this is what I want."

Not untouched, Ason put his hand to her hair and felt its softness against his ribbed callouses. Standing close like this she told him in a whisper everything she knew, everything she had done.

"The men of Atlantis are stupid and think only of slaves. Most of the nearby Donbaksho are gone. When they capture any now they put collars on them, lock them up so they cannot run away. But they know the Albi as traders who can help them, supply information as well as food and other things they need, so they do not enslave my people. Not yet. It is the cousin of my father Ler, a man named Turi—you saw him once in my father's house—who has been helping them. But he reports everything that he does, so I learn about it. The man Themis has been asking him to guide a force of men against you, but Turi has been afraid of being killed. Now they have given him many gifts, and he has agreed. He will bring them out—but his family will go north as soon as they leave, and other Albi as well, because he will take them through the forest to a spot where you and your men will be in hiding. He will be going ahead of the others, and you must let him escape. Then everyone else can be killed."

"When will this be?" Ason asked, speaking quietly despite the excitement he suddenly felt.

"In three days' time, in the valley you know, before the hills, beyond the meadows of Dun Ar Apa where we rested once. A kinsman of mine will meet you there to show you the path that the others will take, to point out the cousin of my father so he will not be harmed."

"No harm shall come to him—but I will not say the same for the Atlanteans. If we can surprise them, we can take them one by one, wipe them out. We must leave tonight if we are to reach the spot in time."

Ason returned to the banquet place and stood once more with his back against his stone, his mind working steadily as he thought about what must be done. The men of his own teuta were here, but there were many other Yerni as well. Maklorbi himself, thick-armed and gnarled, had come down from the north with eleven of his warriors. All had helped in the labor of the stone. There were warriors from Dun Finmog, while Ar Apa was here with many of his men. If all these warriors would fight together it would be the largest striking force he had ever had. They would accompany him, he was sure of that. He would give the bull-chiefs rich presents now so they would want to come. He would tell them all about the long column of soldiers going through the forest, how they could be attacked and killed, how their bronze armor and bronze weapons would be shared out afterwards. Not one warrior in ten now owned a bronze dagger for the taking of heads—how they would value a sword! He knew that this could be done. He would tell them how they would fight and win. They would follow him.

"Listen to me," Ason called out, stepping forward. "Listen to what I have to say." He waited until they were quieter, then told them what could be done.

They reached Dun Moweg just after dawn, where they drank and rested. When Moweg saw all the men, heard what was planned, he put on his ax and hair belt, took up his shield. All of his warriors there did the same. They were skilled hunters, so could appreciate the difference between attacking a heavily armed enemy on his own ground and surprising a column of men strung out through heavy forest. When the attacking force marched out of the dun soon afterwards it was much larger. They straggled out across the plain, the armored Mycenaeans first, with the men of Dun Ason just behind them. All of the others marched as they wished, singly or in groups, some taking parallel tracks while others lagged behind, then hurried to catch up. A great sprawling, disorganized mob of men, joined together only by greed and pleasure in battle and killing.

They came to the edge of the open down the following day. There, at the forest's edge, a small dark man was waiting for them. He came forward reluctantly to meet Ason, tremblingly aware of all the axes and swords.

"I am Gwyn, son of the aunt of Naikeri," he said quickly "I am the one who waits for you."

"There is nothing to be afraid of—it is the Atlanteans who should be fearful. Are they on the march?"

"A day behind me; they do not move fast in the forest. Along this same path. Turi leads them, and he goes in fear that he will be killed."

"His life is in my hands and I will hold it safe."

As his disorganized army straggled up, Ason climbed to the top of a large boulder. They gathered around it, Aias and the Mycenaeans closest with the bull-chiefs, while the warriors pressed in on all sides.

"This is the way the Atlanteans will come," Ason said. The men stirred and craned their necks to look at the opening in the forest wall. "The trees are thick here. There is that hill as well, which is difficult to climb, a stream and

245

a swampy area below. When they arrive, the Atlanteans will be strung out along the trail. We will be in the forest on each side. They will march by us and will not see us. You can do that because you are hunters, invisible if you wish to be. You will lie there, but will not attack until the signal is given. Not because I will kill any man who is greedy and attacks too early—which I will—but because it is the best way to surprise the Atlanteans and to destroy them all. They will pass between us, and when the leaders reach this spot I will give my war cry and we will attack. Every man hearing the cry will shout it out himself and attack as well.''

There were cries of agreement as axes were waved in the air. Ason led the way into the forest with the warriors close behind. This was their work—and they knew how to do it well. They were no longer boasting or swaggering; they walked in silence like great cats. Strong and deadly men, dedicated to battle and afraid of nothing. This great island was theirs and they ruled supreme. Now the men with bronze armor and weapons came and, though they respected them, they did not fear them. For they did not fear death itself in battle. They followed Ason and did as he bid, sinking into concealment in the places he pointed out, moving off the path and in among the trees. Down the hillside Ason went, with the men vanishing into the shade of the great trees behind him, to the swamp at the bottom. There was even more cover here among the reeds. The warriors bent them carefully aside instead of breaking them as they moved off into the muddy water. Ason watched while the last of them vanished from sight, then started back up the trail to the far end. His Mycenaeans were in the forest too, spaced out one by one where they could do the most good by attacking the Atlanteans singly. Drawing their attention so the unarmored Yerni could cut them down.

In the forest there was only silence. The wind moved the

branches in the treetops high above, but nothing else stirred. An army was hidden there, yet there was no sign of it at all. Silent as the trees themselves, the Yerni waited. Aias and Gwyn, waiting for Ason where the trail reached the open down, were the only ones to be seen. They moved off together between the trees, then settled on the cool moss behind the trunk of a giant oak. Gwyn crouched down while Aias dozed, muttering in his sleep, then jerking awake to look around. Ason sat with his sword in his hands and listened to the small sounds of the forest. The day slowly passed.

A distant shout.

Ason sat up silently, cocking his head to listen better, wondering if he had heard it. But the others were awake as well, listening just as intently. Then it came again, a man calling out something and someone else answering, far back down the trail.

"They are coming," Aias whispered, fingering his stone-headed sledge. He had seen the cattle butcher using it and had admired it, a short-handled heavy hammer of death. He had given a good copper pin for it. It was better than a sword, more like a fist, more to his liking.

The three of them silently moved closer to the trail, dropping behind a thick tangle of hawthorn, looking out through the heavy branches close to the ground. Another voice could be heard and, a moment later, the shuffle of feet. There was the first flicker of motion down the trail. An armored Atlantean came into view, walking just behind the brown-clad form of an Albi.

"The first one is Turi," Gwyn whispered.

They were here—and unalarmed. Which meant that the entire Atlantean column was strung out through the forest, in the midst of the hidden warriors. The trap was ready to be sprung. As the first Atlantean passed, Ason rose and stepped from behind the bush, then ran forward.

He was halfway to the trail with Aias right behind him

247

before one of the Atlanteans saw him and called a loud warning—drawing his sword from its slings as he did. As soon as he spoke, so did Ason.

"Run, you fool, run!"

The Albi ran even before the words were out of Ason's mouth; he had been expecting the ambush. The Atlantean who was guarding him was an instant slower, and his sword cut only air. He started to chase the guide, then realized that Ason was almost upon him and turned to defend himself. Ason swung his sword down and shouted as loudly as he could.

"Ason abu!"

Then his sword struck the Atlantean's shield as he pushed the other's sword aside with his own shield. Twisted his sword up into a belly jab, hearing the echo of his cry sounding down through the forest. *Ason abu*. As the words started from one man's mouth, another picked it up and another, from both sides of the trail. The attack was launched.

"Ason is here!" the Atlantean shouted, then choked as the sword caught him in the stomach, up under his breastplate, tore out his life.

Screams and the crash of metal sounded from the forest. Ason withdrew his sword and turned about to fight for his life. All of the nearest Atlanteans were ignoring the Yerni rushing towards them from the forest. They were attacking him. Five, six of them at once. Swords and spears and a barrier of shields. He drew away, slashing at them, until his back was against a tree.

"To me, to me!" he shouted, and his call was answered. Aias was there, his great hammer swinging, and the warriors of Dun Ason behind him. All Ason had to do was to hold.

He was the man the Atlanteans wanted, the man Themis hated, the one they had come so far to find. They attacked him in overwhelming force, battering at him.

248

One went down, then two—they were being attacked from behind, they could not hold out. A few instants more.

A few instants too many. A sword crashed against Ason's sword, all the weight of the man's body behind it, pressing him. Ason's shield was up to block another sword.

The spear thrust in over the shoulders of the nearest man, jabbing like a deadly fang.

Ason pulled his head aside, but not fast enough.

The bronze speartip, honed and sharp, caught him full in the throat and pressed home, through his neck, pinning him to the tree.

Blood filled his throat; he could not shout.

Everything ended.

5

Against the white-banked clouds in the pale sky the pair of hawks moved, soaring in lazy circles, each one separate, yet always close to the other. The male saw a movement in the grass below and halted in midair, hovering motionless under rapid-beating wings. He turned his head from side to side until he saw the motion again. There was something there. He closed his wings and fell downward like a stone, spreading his wings wide only at the last moment, with his great clawed toes out before him. Never touching the ground, he beat his wings and was up with something wriggling in his talons, his mate soaring close to see the captive mouse. They swirled away into the distance over the gray down, like leaves before the wind.

There were leaves as well, turned red and yellow-brown, pulled from the branches by the cooler winds of fall. They banked in the hollows, some even blowing far out across the plain to fall among the cattle cropping the sere remains of the summer's grass. To blow on again until they lodged against the woven lattice wall of the dun that rose solitary from the plain. The wind was not cold, not yet, but there was a crispness and a bite to it that presaged the winter soon to come.

Even the light touch of that moving air, the pale brightness of the sky, made Ason's red-rimmed eyes water. He blinked away the obscuring tears. The furs on the low couch on which he lay were soft and warm; softer furs lay across him. Memories of days and nights and unending pain came to him. He remembered waking like this, then sleeping again even before he knew he was awake. It had been a long illness. There was a low crooning, and he turned his head with caution to look at Naikeri who sat, cross-legged, nearby. She had the front of her garments undone and with her hand guided the fullness of her breast to the baby's mouth. It smacked industriously and made little kneading motions with its tiny hands. She rocked slowly back and forth while it fed, humming the wordless song. There was a sudden shadow in the doorway, and Inteb bent to enter.

"Awake, Ason?" he said, seeing that the other man's eyes were open. Ason nodded. He pointed to the cup of mead nearby on a wooden chest. Inteb handed it to him and he sat up on his elbows to drink it.

"You made it to the door yesterday," Inteb said, taking back the drained cup. "Shall it be outside on the balcony today?"

"He should not move yet," Naikeri said, shaking her shoulders angrily at the thought. Her breast fell from the baby's mouth and he gurgled and sucked air, then began to howl with hungry anger.

"He has the voice of a lion," Inteb said. The wailing cut off sharply as the baby began to feed again.

With Inteb's arm about him Ason managed to climb to his feet. Everything swam in circles when he did this, so he had to stand, leaning on the Egyptian's shoulders, until the motion stopped. Only then did he take a first shuffling footstep, then another. His legs felt strange under him, and he knew that the flesh had fallen away from his body. It would be rebuilt. He must begin now. Sweat broke from his skin with the effort but he kept going, one sliding step after another, through the connecting apartment to the inner door. Inteb kicked this open and they went out into the clear air, looking down at the center of the dun, at the hubbub of the daily activity. There were the animals and the playing children, the craftsmen laboring outside the door of their workshops, to catch the light, the hundred and one activities that were the life of the dun.

And something else, something new, that Ason had heard about but had not seen until this moment. His fingers dug into Inteb's flesh and he pulled himself up straight, smiling with pleasure at the unbelievable sight.

Where one great stone had risen from the ground the past summer, there now stood two. Matched and beautiful they rose, white and glistening. Two immense columns planted deep in the earth, stretching up towards the sky. At their bases they were close together, almost touching, but their sides were angled so they grew narrower towards the top, the space between them larger there. They were solid, strong, powerful; their presence spoke this message with firm majesty.

"Yes—" Ason said in a rough, hoarse voice, his fingers going up to his throat, touching the edges of the great puckered, red scar there.

There was more he wanted to say, much more, but the pain was still in his throat when he talked. Only a tiny memory of the immense pain that had bathed him for so long, but it was still there. And he was tired. Inteb helped him as he slid down slowly onto a wooden chest. He sat with his back to the wall, enjoying the light, warm touch of the sunlight.

"There is more done than you realize," Inteb said,

pointing to the summits of the stones. "If you look at the tops of the columns, you will see that they have been worked. I had old Dursan up there on a scaffolding for so long that he said he felt like a bird in a tree. But he is the only one who can do the fine finishing work. He lowered the tops of both stones so that a raised tenon remains in the center of each. This will be built just like the wood henges; they would do it no other way."

Ason blinked in the strong light and looked again. Yes, there on the top, in the middle of each upright, was the solid projecting bulge of the tenons, carved from the stone just as they were carved from wood.

"The lintel is almost ready to be raised, you can see them working on it over there by the wall. It was squared before we brought it in and now they are hollowing out the sockets for the tenons. I had a wicker form made—you should have heard the women scream when we made them climb the scaffolding to the top—an exact duplicate of the tenons on top and the distance between them. Dursan's men are using the mauls to hollow out the sockets so that the form fits into them. This is almost done."

"And by what magic. . .will you raise that great stone into the air?"

"An important question." Inteb paced the length of the balcony and back, his fingertips together before him. "In Egypt there would be no problem. One thing my dear country has more than enough of is sand. This can be shoveled, carried, heaped into a mound, made into a ramp or a roadway up which a stone can be dragged. That is not possible here. This white chalk is almost as hard as rock to break. We would labor for a year getting enough for a ramp. There is another way, but it would require wood, immense amounts of wood, almost a forest."

"Or a dun?"

Inteb turned slowly, squinting in thought, to survey the apartments and walls of the dun. "Yes, the wood is here.

252

But I might need all of it. And your people live here—what about them?"

"They can build houses nearby, just as the old warriors do when they marry. There will be no hardship. But before you tear down my dun, tell me, what is the need?"

"It is a technique we call raising. It is used inside tombs and buildings to lift large stones or statues into place. I will raise the stone with levers, just as we do when we lift a stone to put rollers beneath it. But instead of rollers we put a solid platform of logs beneath it like this." He held his hand out, flat, before him. "Now the stone rests on the platform and it is levered up again. When this is done a second log platform is placed across the first, going crossways, like this." He put his other hand flat on the first, fingers going at right angles. "This makes a sturdy support to work on, and the levering up continues, with more and more platforms being built beneath the stone, until it has reached the top of the columns. It is then pushed over and dropped into place. But, as you see, a great amount of wood is needed."

"You shall have it. My entire dun if needs be. Then I with have my stone henge and I will call a meeting of the five teutas here. I will have my strength back, enough to talk to them about what will be done, and behind me will be the strength of the stone. That will speak louder than I can." His face set suddenly into harder lines. "What about the Atlanteans? Any reports?"

"From the Albi, nothing. They stay away since the Atlanteans murdered many of them. Some even blame you."

"Naikeri told me this. She also said that it is not important."

"Probably not, but it does shut off that source of information. But the warriors who go to the mine to throw stones at them and shout insults report that the outer wall is even higher, and that a wooden palisade is being built across it.''

"Defense works. They know Yerni can't get past something like that.'' He hit his fist against the wall in sudden anger. "This wound. If I had not fallen we would have gone on and surprised them at the mine, finished them all at once.''

"None would march without your leadership. But don't forget that the Atlanteans we trapped were killed to the last man. Chased through the woods and pulled down like stags. There were heads for every warrior, armor and swords. It was your victory, Ason, and they know it. They will follow wherever you lead now.''

"I will lead them. This quaking body will be strong again. When I am, I will bring the Yerni together, unite them. But will my henge of stone and wonder be finished by samain, when the cattle are brought in and the traders arrive?''

"It will be, even if we have to work as I have done before, in shifts. By torchlight, someone always working. It will be done.''

"Then the word will go out now. The assembly of all the teutas of the Yerni will be held here. Here before the stones. It will be the beginning. Will they come?''

"They await only your word.''

"Then give it to them.''

6

There was a loud chuffing in the undergrowth, the sharp snap of twigs. The circle of men crouched low, spears pointed and waiting, muscles taut, ready to jump instantly. When the boar came out it could attack in any direction; fast, low and dark. And deadly. Its white tusks could rip a man open with a twist of the massive head, disembowel him or strip the flesh from his legs. This was the deadliest creature in the forest. And now they had driven it from its forest refuge into the open down, to temporary safety in the large clump of bushes.

"He's wounded," Aias said, crouching and alert like the others, but carrying his hammer instead of a spear.

"A scratch," Ason said, panting heavily. The hunt had been a brief one, but his first since he had been wounded. He was barely able to keep up with the others. His throat hurt as he gasped the air into his chest, but he ignored it. He was getting stronger, that was the only thing that counted.

"Boar, boar!" someone shouted from the far side of the bushes. There were excited cries and an angry squealing. More crackling in the brush and then, like a dark thunderbolt, the boar hurtled from under the bushes at the waiting men, towards the spears, twisting and dodging, its sharp hooves throwing up clods of dirt as it spun. With an angry squeal it spun about and raced towards Ason, hooking its tusks at his legs.

There was not time to spear it, just to leap aside. Ason did this, felt the rough hairy flank brush against him and heard the sharp cry from Aias, who leapt to meet the beast.

Fast as the boar was, the boxer was faster. The hammer chopped in a short arc and caught the beast in its shoulder with a loud crack, bowling it over. For one instant it was on its back, black hooves waving, and Ason lunged. As it rolled back, the spear point caught it in the side and plunged deep, almost pinning it to the ground.

It screamed in agony and fear, writhing and trying to snap at the spear, its red angry eye glaring at Ason. Then another spear plunged home and another. It kicked spasmodically and died.

"Your tusks," Aias said as Ason dropped to the ground next to the beast, breathing as loudly as it had done.

"The first blow. . .was yours," he said between gasps.

"The kill was yours, oh king. What does a slave need with tusks? I'll have the tail, a more fitting part."

Aias took his dagger and sawed the twisted length of tail off at the root and brushed smooth the tuft of hairs on the end. Then he stuck it in the back of his belt so it hung down behind. "Now I'll be safe in the forest," he said. "They'll take me for one of them."

The Yerni howled with laughter and slapped their legs, hit one another on the back. Even Ason smiled slightly, breathing slower at last. There was the sharp crack of stone on wood as one of the men chopped a sapling from a nearby grove. Another was lashing the dead beast's feet together with strips of leather. Aias prodded the boar's flank with a thick knobbed finger.

"Filled with acorns, rich with white fat. I can taste it already. Mead, ale, boar meat. This is a good land you rule, great Ason."

Leaning on his spear butt, Ason climbed to his feet as they started back to the dun. The others slung the boar from the pole and followed behind, laughing and bragging to each other, comparing the fine white curve of their moustaches to the sharp thrusts of the dead beast's tusks. And as they always did now when they came into sight of the dun, they marveled aloud at the changes. Any physical change was so rare in their lives that something as major as this had to be talked about over and over to fix it into reality.

It was a change. The palisade of tall logs had been taken down completely, as well as the rooms and apartments that were fixed to it. Now the dun was just a circular bank, cut by the entrance. The only building left was the workshop, which had not been touched. All about the embankment, in some cases pushed up against it, stood the buildings and shelters where the warriors and their families and the many workers stayed. There was some crowding, and occasional fights, but no real complaints from the Yerni warriors about this. A new dun would be built, Ason promised that, and they were comfortable enough. None of this really mattered. What was important, the thing that made Ason different from any other bull-chief, made them better than any other teuta, was the great structure in the center of the dun. The two stones that reached the sky, the third smaller stone now rising into the air, lifted by the Egyptian's magic. Once again there were shouts of amazement when they saw the great creation, though the rising balks of wood all but hid it from sight.

Inteb was waiting at the foot of the great timber construction when Ason came up.

"We are ready," Inteb said.

Ason led the way up the tall ladder to the top, past layer after layer of logs that were notched and fitted together into an immovable whole. On the platform that formed the top section lay the great stone lintel. Next to it and sitting on it were the workers who had raised it this far. Cut into the bottom of the stone, not visible now, were the two sockets that would fit over the upright tenons that projected from the top of the two columns. Ason admired these constructions, running his hand over the smooth bulge of their surfaces, realizing how much stone had had to be pounded away to leave them here.

"Notice the tops of the columns," Inteb said, coming up behind Ason. "Notice how they are scooped out so the lintel stone will settle firmly into place. It will not be able to rock or shift in position."

"A great work," Ason said with conviction.

Not too much of the summits of the great stones could be seen. The logs that made up the top three layers of the platform had been extended out to rest on the tops of the columns, as well as being held up by the platforms beneath them. Using the stones as supports, the platform was now much bigger, extending out over the stones.

"We will move the lintel now," Inteb said, ordering up

the leathern buckets of grease. Animal fat had been rendered down until it was thick as mud. Inteb himself threw down the first handfuls.

"I want it here, all the way across the platform and on these logs. Not close to the edge or you fools will be sliding in it and falling off. It is for the stone, not for you." He handed over the bucket and supervised the application.

When an even layer of grease had been applied, Ason and Inteb stood to one side while the workers grabbed up the long levers. Holes had been chopped in the top layers of logs, and heavy stakes had been driven into them. A thick log was placed against the stakes, running behind the back of the stone and leaving just enough room for the levers to be inserted. They pressed against this log and levered against the stone. When they were all in place, Inteb shouted the beginning of the chant that kept them working in unison.

"Seat the lever, seat it deep."

"*Bu*!" the workers shouted in answer.

"Weight on the wood and ready to pull."

"*Bu*."

"Pull now, pull, pull!"

"*Bu*."

Chanting together, they applied their strength, and the wood creaked beneath them. The stone slid forward a small amount. The chant went on until they had moved it far enough to get a smoothed section of wood in between their levers and the back supporting log. As the stone moved, more and more of the greased area came under it so that the going was easier. There was grease about the platform now, and Inteb halted the operation while he sent down for buckets of sand to throw on it. The men needed a firm footing to work—aside from the fact that a fall from this height would surely be fatal. Then the work went on. Slower and slower as the lintel approached the correct position over the supporting columns. Inteb ran back and forth peering under the stone, calling out instructions. It was levered from one side, and then from the end, while Inteb crawled about it and hung over empty space to check the alignment. He was finally satisfied and ordered a halt.

"One last step," he told Ason, wiping the sweat from his forehead with his arm, his hands black with grease and bark. "A supporting timber is removed from under each end of the stone, and in their place a stack of these flat boards, adzed down out of split logs, is substituted. When the stone is resting on the stacked boards, we lower it just as we raised it to this height—only in reverse. One end is raised, a board is removed, it is lowered onto the remainder. Then the same process is repeated at the other end. Light as a thistle the great stone will sink to its resting place."

He muttered a prayer to some animal-headed Egyptian deity as he turned to direct the final stage. It was the most delicate.

Once the weight was on the stacked boards the supporting logs were slid out from under it, dropped to the ground. Then, with careful efforts, the stone was levered up again just enough to pull out a board before being dropped back onto the others.

What ver went wrong happened very quickly. The lintel had been lowered so that the tips of the tenons were just entering the sockets in the stone. Ten men hung from the lever that held the stone, while two others steadied the planks and a third man withdrew the top plank.

There was the sudden crack of breaking wood and someone screamed.

The men on the lever fell in a tangle, the length of wood no longer supporting the stone. It dropped onto the pile of boards and the one board half removed, shuddered there for an interminable instant on the uneven support.

Splintering and crashing, the supporting pile bent and broke. The massive weight of the lintel dropped, fell heavily onto the stone column.

It struck with crushing impact and a crash as loud as thunder. Bits of stone flew out as the supporting bulk of timber swayed. A shudder went through the stone upright, Ason's stone, the first stone.

Everything moved, lurched sickeningly like the solid ground during an earthquake. Men shrieked and dropped, one falling from the timbers, sure that everything was collapsing, crashing down to destruction.

Time flowed slowly where it had rushed a moment earlier. Instants passed with the hesitant quality of drops of water falling from melting ice. The world trembled and moved.

Then everything was still. The horrified men stared into each other's faces, seeing their own terror mirrored there. But the movement stopped and they looked around them, numbed.

The boards at one end were gone. The lintel angled down from the precarious balance of the boards at the other end, to the solid stone of the column on which it rested. The tenon was out of sight and fitted neatly into its socket. The stones still stood.

Screaming, pained screaming drew them back. Inteb jumped forward.

"Supports!" he shouted. "Get them under here. Now. Before this other end goes. Jump, jump!"

The screaming went on. Ason saw that one of the workers had been under the stone when it dropped, his body and head smashed between the stone and the wood. He was silent. Forever.

But another man was still alive, shrieking in agony, over and over again as fast as he could fill his lungs. He had been pushing the board out of the way, and his arm had been under the stone when it dropped. It was still there, crushed, flattened, trapped between the massive stones.

After the accident the men were unnerved enough; the screaming did not help them to do the exacting work needed if a greater tragedy were to be averted. Ason understood this as he stepped forward and drew his sword from the slings. He reversed it and struck the man in the temple with the solid pommel.

It was like a flybite, unfelt in the greater agony, but the man did recoil and try to pull away, still screaming. Ason was not as gentle the second time. The bronze knob struck with a heavy thud, and the man was instantly still.

A little blood dribbled over the lip of the stone. But very little, so tightly sealed was the arm between the column and lintel. Most of the man's lower arm was trapped and crushed there, to within a handspan of the elbow. Ason tore one of the leather slings from his back and wrapped it tightly around the arm just above the elbow.

"Hold his body so he doesn't fall," he ordered the nearest man. He tested his footing, making sure there was no grease on the platform, then raised his sword above his head.

With a long downward chop, hitting true in the joint of the elbow, he severed the trapped arm from the body. Unconscious as he was, the man's body quivered when the sword struck.

"Pull him away and lower him to the ground," Ason ordered.

"Secure now, I think," Inteb said, trembling, his face pale. Ason put his arm about Inteb's shoulders.

"There are always losses; they should not bother you."

"For an instant there I thought—the entire thing. . . ."

"But it didn't. You build well, Inteb. The stone henge is almost finished."

"Blood. That arm, it will be in there forever, the bones."

"There is nothing wrong with blood to set the stones in place. There is a slave under each of the columns of the gates of Mycenae, put there when they were built to hold the stones firm. This should not bother you. Will the work go on now?"

Inteb pulled away, clutching his shaking hands together.

"Yes, of course. It must be done. Now, at this time. There is very little left."

Some of the men were reluctant to resume the work, but Ason showed them his bloody sword in silence; it spoke louder than words. Carefully, slowly, stopping and starting again many times, the boards were slipped from the other end, the stone levered lower until the last was removed. Stone grated on stone. Inteb rested his hand upon it.

"Here is your henge of stone, Ason, ready for samain. Something that has never been seen before. You will be king, Ason."

The men did not understand the meaning of all of this, but they understood what they had done. They shouted and called out their cries until they were hoarse. Everyone on the ground below did the same, except the man who had fallen from the top and lay crumbled and dead against the base.

7

Coming across the plain, the great dark form was clearly visible against the sky, rising above the circular mound. The buildings outside only served to contrast its looming size. The warriors from the other teutas saw it, shouted in amazement to one another, while their bull-chiefs fingered their moustaches and chewed at their lips. This was a henge. Albi with packs on their backs admired it; they knew the handling of stone from their great tombs, so appreciated it all the more. Donbaksho trudged many days, with trade goods or without, just to look upon it. Even wary Hunters wriggled across the down in the dark to seek a hiding place, where they could watch it for all of a day before returning to their swamps and forests.

In single file, the women as tall as the men, carrying packs as large or larger, the Geramani came west from their landing places on the coast and knew that there was something new in the land.

Samain. With the year drawing to a close and winter on the way, the teutas gathered. This was a time for cattle slaughter and feasting, trade and drink, time for the making of bull-chiefs and the burning of captives in the best manner. Time for everything.

Time for an assembly of all the teutas of the Yerni of the high downs. This had never been done before. It had been thought about over and over. But the bull-chiefs had warm gold and soft amber discs to wear to show that Ason wanted them. Each had been told that all of the others had agreed to come. This was a political suggestion of Inteb's, who had much experience in this sort of thing, and it decided any of the bull-chiefs who might have been wavering. How could one stand against the united power of all the others? They polished their ornaments and their bronze, and they came. They brought all that they had to trade with them. Many others, who would have traded at different duns, now came to Dun Ason. They came and they kept coming. Never in the memory of living man had there been a samain like this one.

Four henges had been built for the bull-chiefs of the four visiting teutas. Two on one side and two on the other, facing across the fire, with Ason's henge the tallest, at the head, between them. Ason had been generous. He had taken eight of the largest logs that had supported the dun. These had been planed and painted, sunk deep into the ground with a large crossbar above each. Now every bull-chief could sit before a truly majestic pillar-arch of his own, a henge twice as big as any he had ever had before.

While above them a henge of white stone loomed up like a mountain. It was a gateway to Moi Mell and the Prom-

263

ised Land, topped with a stuffed bull prepared by the new chief druid, and hung about with gold and weapons and severed heads. Unbelievably, it was stone, not wood. Stone as hard as any axhead. Stone. The bull-chiefs sat and drank in silence. For whenever they looked around, sooner or later their eyes would return to those massive stones, to look up, higher and higher at them.

In the newly built, round wickerwork building just outside the embankment, Ason was putting on his armor, polished and gleaming. As he tied the leather thongs, the baby, lying on furs on the floor, caught sight of the shining shield and crowed with excitement. Ason pushed it over with his foot so the tiny hands could touch the gleaming bosses.

"The bull-chief Maklorbi has been talking late at night to the druid Nemed," Naikeri said. "I have not seen it, but some of the women told me."

"I have no care for women's talk."

"You should care, because Nemed still talks to people in Uala's family and reads signs for them."

"The bull-chief is dead and can no longer hurt me."

"The living can when they consult with the dead."

"I do not fear the living or the dead, bull-chiefs or druids. I have a tooth that bites them all equally deep." He slapped the sharp blade of his sword as he said this, then slipped it into the slings.

"It does not hurt to notice these things. You have become bull-chief here instead of someone from Uala's family. They don't forget that they were once the highest. Now they are nothing."

Ason settled his helmet on his head, not bothering to answer as he left. The baby began to cry when the bright shield was taken away. Naikeri snatched him up and held him to her.

The other bull-chiefs were sitting before their henges. The meat was brought from the cooking fire when Ason appeared. He would make the first cut, take the hero's portion, then the feasting would begin. An appetizing smell of crackling flesh greeted him as the immense sow, smoking and round with fat, was taken from the fire and placed on the hurdles. She had been captured that summer and penned and fed heavily until she was round as a tree trunk. Her litter had long since been eaten, and now it was their dam's turn. Ason drew his dagger and tested the edge with his thumb.

"I am Maklorbi," the bull-chief from the northern teuta said, climbing to his feet. "I have marched a hundred and a hundred miles to be here for this banquet, and have brought a hundred men. I have more heads over my door than a hundred men can count. I have killed a hundred warriors in battle. I will make the first cut of the meat."

There was sudden silence after he spoke. He brushed at his moustaches and slapped his chest, a short but solid man, heavy with muscles that stood out gnarled as weathered bark. His arms were as thick as most men's legs. He was well known as a formidable warrior in battle. Now he was challenging Ason at his own fire. Naikeri had been right; here was trouble. Ason looked around at the silent faces and staring eyes and knew that he could not refuse the challenge. He did not want bloodshed, but it could not be avoided. Maklorbi would have to die.

"I cut the meat," Ason said, holding up the dagger. Maklorbi swung about to look at him directly for the first time.

"I am Maklorbi, and men fear my name. I sleep at night with the head of a bull-chief beneath my knee. I will cut the meat. I will sleep tonight with the head of Ason beneath my knee."

The challenge was there. Ason put away the dagger and slowly drew his sword from the slings. Maklorbi, still looking at Ason, pointed back over his own shoulder at the henge behind him.

"I have my gold, and it is here on my henge for every-

265

one to see. I have captured armor and helmets in battle, and they are here for everyone to see. I fought the men from the sea and captured these things. I fought as a Yerni fights, with my hair rope, my neck torc, and my dagger, my ax in my hand and my shield on my arm, my arms bare, my chest bare, my legs bare, my hair and my moustache white as a Yerni warrior. That is the way we fight. That is the way a bull-chief of the Yerni fights. We are Yerni.''

There were shouts of agreement from the warriors of Maklorbi's teuta, who slapped their hands against their legs with approval. Some of the other warriors in the circle did the same, but others murmured and looked about.

Ason stood silent as a sudden chill touched his skin. Now that it was too late to do anything about it, he knew what had happened. He had enemies and they had planned well. He still did not have his full strength after his sickness—while Maklorbi was the strongest of all the Yerni. In armor, with his sword, Ason could defeat any man. But now he had defeated himself. He had become a bull-chief of the Yerni and if challenged to battle he must fight as a Yerni; there was no other way. They fought in the nude except for a hair belt around the waist: without the armor they captured from Mycenaeans. If he were to remain bull-chief of his own teuta he must battle without armor. If he were to be king of the Yerni there was no other way. Heroic nudity. His enemies had planned his death well. All these thoughts went quickly through his head and he knew what had to be done. There could be no excuses that he was weak; a bull-chief could never be weak. There were neither excuses nor a way out.

''Maklorbi comes to my fire with a mouth that gapes open like that of a dog in heat,'' Ason said. ''Maklorbi wants to sit at my fire and cut my meat first, to eat the hero's portion. I will tell you what Maklorbi will get. He will not eat, ever again, he will not drink, ever again, for I will kill him, and with my knife take his head, and tonight his head will be beneath my knee."

As he said this Ason dropped his sword and his shield to the ground and tore the laces from his armor and his greaves. He threw these aside, his helmet as well, until he stood unarmed except for the dagger on the cord about his neck. Then he picked up the shield and slipped his hand through the loops on its back.

"I am Ason of Mycenae," he called out. "I am Ason of the Yerni of Dun Ason, and this is my henge. I am a killer of men. I will kill Maklorbi with an ax. I call to my friend Ar Apa of Dun Ar Apa and tell him I will do honor to his ax and will battle Maklorbi with it."

Ar Apa jumped to his feet and swung his arm in a slow circle so his ax flew across the fire, and Ason grabbed it from the air.

"Maklorbi abu!" Maklorbi shouted, clashing his ax against his shield and running forward.

"Ason abu!" Ason called out and stepped forward to meet him.

Ax struck shield and the battle began.

After the first blows it was clear who would win. Maklorbi was the stronger. With ax against ax little else counts. The stone head of his ax thudded against Ason's raised shield: Ason felt the shock of it in his arm. His own blow was caught and brushed aside. Even while his shield arm was aching from the first blow a second and a third rained down. Ason backed away but, relentless as death, Maklorbi followed him, his ax blows as continual and strong as though he were chopping down a tree. He was chopping down a man, for with each blow Ason felt the strength going from him. He panted with the effort to stay alive. His reactions were slowed and his shield tilted so that with the next blow the ax glanced off it and cut into his shoulder, drawing first blood.

At the sight of this all the watchers roared aloud and

Maklorbi stopped and stepped back, shaking his ax and shield over his head and shouting his war cry.

Ason felt the wound. It was not deep but it bled, and more of his failing strength seeped away with every drop. He would die—and he did not want to. Maklorbi spun about to shout his war cry again. When he did, Ason slipped his arm from the loops inside the shield and grasped it instead with his hand.

"Ason abu!" he shouted in his hoarse voice and leaped to attack.

Maklorbi braced his legs and stood waiting, smiling broadly so his yellow teeth could be seen. Ason swung a wide, full-armed blow that whistled about in a great wide arc aimed at Maklorbi's side. The bull-chief moved his shield out to catch it, and as he did this, Ason threw his own shield full into the man's face.

The edge of the shield caught Maklorbi square in the mouth, and he fell back bellowing in pain. Ason's ax bounced from the other's shield, then swung over in a quick blow that struck Maklorbi's right arm. The edge of the ax did not hit, but the weight of the stone was enough to strike the ax from Maklorbi's fingers.

Before Ason could recover and strike again, Maklorbi had hurled his own shield aside and dived forward, his fingers locking into Ason's throat.

The pain was overwhelming and almost drove awareness from Ason's brain. Through a haze he saw Maklorbi's face, mouth gaping, spitting blood and teeth. A roaring was in Ason's head as he tried to swing the ax, but the other was too close for him to use it. He let the ax drop, struck out with his fists, but it did little good. He was aware of shouts and loud voices, one familiar voice shouting louder than all the others—Aias bellowing something. Something about fighting, something he could barely understand. Then the meaning of the words penetrated the sickness and pain. Ason reached out his hands in obedience. Not to Maklorbi's throat, because in an even contest of strength

268

Ason would die, but to his head, to his face, his fingers crawling up to seize the sides of his skull. His thumbs to dig into Maklorbi's eyes.

Something that slaves did when they fought without weapons, something a warrior would never think of. Thumbs digging deep into eye sockets, gouging, blinding.

Maklorbi's battle cry turned into a cry of wavering pain as his hands dropped from Ason's throat and clutched at his ruined eyes.

Ason drew his dagger. In the same motion he plunged it up under the other man's ribs and into his heart.

Gasping for breath, his head swimming with a pain so great that his vision was fogged and he had to blink to clear his eyes, Ason bent over the corpse. While all the watchers shouted *Ason abu* over and over, he sawed through the neck until the head was separated from the body. He was red to his elbows with gore before he was finished. The dagger slipped from his fingers. Seizing the decapitated head by one long moustache, he straightened up and walked, step by slow step, to the great stone-henge. He threw the head down between the uprights, where it stared sightlessly out at the council fire.

"I am Ason, bull-chief of the Yerni," he said hoarsely, leaning back against the cool stone so he would not fall.

8

Ason drank thirstily of the ale, then mead rich with honey that brought some relief to his throat. Little by little the pain ebbed away. He saw the three remaining bull-chiefs drinking in silence while the great roast pig cooled on the hurdles. When warriors of Maklorbi's teuta came to take the body he stopped them and ordered them back to their places. Then Ason rose and went to cut the first portion of the meat. The headless corpse remained there for the rest of the banquet as a silent reminder.

Despite the presence of the body, humors improved under the onslaught of food and drink. In a little while there was much shouting and bragging across the fire. When it grew dark this fire was fueled with resiny pine logs, until it sparked and crackled and flames rose high into the air. By their light the stone-henge loomed even larger and more impressive. When the bull-chiefs and the warriors walked close to it none could resist the impulse to reach out and feel its grainy-smooth surface. Ason was not unaware of this, and when the proper time came he stood and touched the henge himself and everyone was silent.

"I am Ason. I have killed a hundred times a hundred men. I have killed bull-chiefs. I have killed Atlanteans. I have killed every animal that roves the land, caught every fish that leaps in the sea. I am bull-chief of this dun. I have built this henge."

The truth had more effect than any number of boasting lies. He had done these things. The great stones were here to prove it. Not a voice was raised in dissent.

"Today the five teutas of the Yerni meet together for the first time at samain. You are all here because you are bull-chiefs in your own duns, and that is the way it will always be. But we are something more. We are the Yerni, and together there are none who dare stand against us. I ask you to join me here in a union of the five teutas. I ask you to do this, here, in a dun of all the Yerni, a dun of a kind never seen before. Made of stone. If you join me here your wooden henges will be taken down and in their place you will erect a stone henge, just as I have done. This will be done."

They looked, all of them, at the wooden henges and at Ason's of stone, and in their minds they could see great stones rising in their places. This was something! Seated before his henge Ar Apa saw the stones. He shouted with happiness at the thought.

"Ar Apa abu! Ason abu!"

"Ason abu." More than one voice shouted it, and when they quieted Ar Apa called out again.

"Ason—will you be bull-chief of all the Yerni?"

Ason put his hands flat against the stone and said, "I will."

There were more loud cries at this and all of them seemed in favor of the plan. The bull-chiefs and their teutas would lose nothing by it—but would gain a good deal. There were other tribes to the north, beyond the forests, who raided for cattle here in the south. Now they could be attacked in force. There would be rich booty. And the henge, there would always be that. When they were most enthusiastic Ason called for quiet again, then pointed to Inteb.

"This is Inteb the Egyptian, the builder. It was he who shaped and lifted these stones for me. He will tell you of something else that will be done here."

Ason had been doubtful of Inteb's plan at first, but the more he thought about it the more appealing it became. He needed more than just the bull-chiefs' allegiance; he must have the warriors' as well. Inteb knew how to accomplish this.

"The five henges for the five bull-chiefs will be here." Inteb pointed and their eyes followed his hand. "Around them shall be a stone dun for the warriors. A ring of stones joined together at the top by other stones, with doors for the warriors to enter."

There were gasps, then cries of approval for this, and Inteb waited until they had quieted. "As the warriors of Dun Ason each now has his stone, so shall the most valiant warriors of all the duns have doorways in this stone dun. They will put the heads they have taken on the lintel above, during feasts will hang it with their prizes and

271

arms. This will be the dun of all the Yerni. In stone."

After this no one held back. There was shouting, war cries, axes were brandished while boasts drowned out boasts. In the excitement and noise Ar Apa came over and sat by Ason. They drank together. Ason returned the stone ax.

"You were there when I needed you," Ason said.

"You did good service with this ax and it will be remembered. But there is something I must ask you. Your Egyptian did not say how many doors there would be in the stone dun."

"No one asked him."

"That is true. But I have been thinking of my dun and the doors for the warriors and thinking of all the warriors here. This stone ring will be a very large one?"

"It will be, though not that big. The blue stones will be reset here and the ring built around them. There will be thirty doors in it, or so Inteb says. It will be a great labor."

"Is thirty a big number?"

Ason held up the fingers of his right hand. "This is the number five. There are five teutas." He added the thumb of his left hand to the others. "This is six. There will be six doorways for each teuta and six doorways five times is the number thirty."

Ar Apa frowned and scratched at the dirt with his finger. "There are more than six warriors in my teuta."

"There are. But only six will be honored. They will be from among your kinsmen, they will be the strongest warriors. To have a doorway will be a very good thing. Warriors will labor hard to be one of those six. They will work hard to help you. You will always know you can count upon their aid."

Thinking about this, Ar Apa nodded and almost smiled. It is sometimes harder to remain a bull-chief than it is to become one. There were rivalries and feuds within the teuta that never stopped. The six stone doors would help, they would help him very much. He went back before his henge and drank some more, glad he had come, thinking that an assembly place for all the Yerni was a very good thing.

Ason was happy to lean against his stones and drink quietly. He was tired and his throat still ached. Yet Inteb had been right. They were all with him. The henges would be built.

The warriors grew very drunk as the night wore on. Ason almost wished he could lie down and sleep, but he could not leave while the others were still here. Much later Inteb came and sat beside him and had some ale from his cup.

"There has been an accident," Inteb said. "The druid Nemed is dead."

"That is pleasant news." Ason touched his throat. "How did he die?"

"He was found on the ground with his head on a rock. He must have fallen and struck his head on the rock and died."

"What a thin skull the man had. I wonder if he could have had any help in embarking on this voyage?"

"Such things are always possible, I suppose. But no one will speak the thought aloud. He and Maklorbi plotted your death. Both of them are dead, instead, on the same night. I think the plotting will stop for awhile."

"I think so too. The druid must have a very large funeral with many funeral games."

Ason looked across the fire to the place where Aias sat. Had he been there the entire evening? He could not remember. The boxer was drinking from a cup that looked small in that great fist. A fist that could break a jaw and kill. Or a head? Perhaps it would be better not to know. The druid would no longer plot against him, and that was all that really mattered.

"I have amber from the north here, great Ason. Brought by trails through the dark forest and down the river Rhine and across the narrow sea to you."

Ason looked up to see that one of the Geramani was

273

bending over before him, opening a roll of leather on the ground. He sat on his heels behind it and arranged the display of lumps and plates of amber of all shades. "I am Gestum and I lead my clan."

Ason picked over the pieces, holding up the finest ones and looking through them at the fire.

"They are good. My workmen must see them."

"I know that. I only show them to you so we talk. There are many eyes on us. Do not reach for your red-stained dagger to have it drink at my heart when I tell you I have dealt with the Atlanteans."

Ason held up a piece of amber, but looked beyond it at the other man for the first time. He was tall, well dressed in a long cloak that was sealed by a curving gold bar, rich and heavy. The bar held the cloak away from his body, the bell-shaped ends of the bar peering brightly through the fabric. There were gold bracelets on his arms, gold as well on the bronze of his wide-horned helm. A short sword of bronze was in his belt; a bronze-headed ax was beside him on the ground. His cold blue eyes stared into Ason's and he was not afraid.

"You know I war with the Atlanteans?"

"That is why I am here, though others do not like it. I have said my people deal with the Atlanteans and that is because we must. They have camps and mines for tin on the lands in our valleys. They are too strong to fight. By aiding them we gain many things. We work our own bronze now, while our traders go along the rivers both east and west. We know of the war between Atlantis and Mycenae. That is a good thing. We know that you are a Mycenaean and have now united the tribes of the Yerni."

"You know a good deal," Ason said with no warmth at all in his voice. "Perhaps you learned a lot from the Trojan Sethsus and even helped him?"

"We did."

Gestum rose when Ason did, and they stood there face to face.

"I will not lie to you," Gestum said. "But I work only for the Geramani. We sold information and did work for the Trojan, were repaid and received tin. Now he is dead. You are the power in this island now and we will work with you. We can help each other."

At times there was little pleasure in being a king. Ason the warrior, knowing what Gestum had done, would have happily plunged his sword into the man's middle. Ason the ruler could not. Everything the man said was true. They could help one another and each would profit. Perhaps a way could even be arranged to get tin to Mycenae down the Danube. The gold of Dun Ason would pay for it.

"Sit and drink with me," Ason said. "I admire your amber."

"I will drink. I admire your decision."

9

"Ar Apa abu!"

All the warriors of his teuta shouted, as did the others who were there when the great pile of wood came down. The tall white form of the new henge was disclosed. It stood on the right of Ason's henge, built of the same stone, dressed and smooth. Ason's henge was the taller, that was only right, but they were both giants in the land. Across the dead council fire the untopped spires of another henge rose from the ground. When the shouting died the sharp ring of rock on rock could clearly be heard in the dry, cold air. There was a sprinkling of snow in the hollows, while more threatened from the slate-gray sky.

Ar Apa had no words—this was beyond words—but he danced from foot to foot with pleasure, swinging his ax about his head. They all knew how he felt. It had been a winter of unaccustomed labor, but only the bondsmen complained. To the warriors the bending of the intractable stone to their wills and bodies was a miracle that was renewed every day. They came from the duns of the other teutas, bringing the bondsmen laden with food for the winter. The animals had been slaughtered, meat dried, ale made. There was nothing to do until spring except hunt, and this working of the stone held more excitement than the wildest hunt. Fingers were bruised, feet crushed, four men dead already, but this was nothing. They fought with the stone and won.

Now there was another kind of fighting to think of.

"The Atlanteans are sending out hunting parties," Ason said. "I have had reports from the Albi, from the Hunters, as well, who watch the mine."

"They will be well armed and ready," Ar Apa answered distractedly, his eyes still upon the great stones.

"They cannot match the Yerni in the forest. We can surprise them—but we will wait until they are returning to the mine."

Ar Apa laughed at this. "Only you would have thought of that, Ason. Not only their heads and their swords—but their kill as well."

It was a winter long remembered, a winter well enjoyed. The labor on the stones was interrupted only by raids on the Atlanteans. Both were most satisfying. Until the Atlanteans grew wary, their hunting parties were easier to ambush and trap than the game itself, which produced the double benefit of meat and heads. It was a fine winter. When spring and the warmer weather returned, the warriors were loath to return to their own duns and their duties. They stayed among the great stones as long as they could.

The construction went ahead rapidly. Once the five henges were constructed, the men turned with equal enthusiasm to the erection of the outer stones, the doorways of the warriors. These doorways would eventually make a complete ring of stones, though they little resembled that now. Since each warrior chose his own place to enter and to face in some favored direction, the twenty-four completed upright stones formed a very ragged circle. Three together, three isolated stones, then a cluster of eighteen. Only six of the lintels that connected the upright stones above had been completed. These were harder to shape and fit—and to raise—and only five were in position, while a sixth rested on a rising frame of logs. The work progressed.

On a morning very much like many other mornings, the work was going ahead steadily just as it had since the first stone had been raised. It was then that Ason heard the shouts in the distance, as though someone were calling his name. But the shouts were lost in the voices closer by, on the top of the timber construction. The careful operation of lowering one of the lintel stones of the circle of doors was just under way. These stones had been shaped with great skill, not only socketed underneath at each end to fit on the tenon of the upright, but a projection had been left at the end of each lintel that would fit into an opening in the next. Settling these stones into place was an exacting operation. The shouts came again and this time Ason heard his name clearly. He turned, wiping the sweat from his eyes so he could see, and looked across the plain.

Three men were running through the entrance in the embankment. Two of them were warriors of his own teuta, and they half-carried between them the brown-clad form of an Albi. They had their hands under his arms to keep him from falling. His head bobbed about and he seemed to be in the last stages of exhaustion. It was Turi, Naikeri's cousin. One of the warriors saw Ason on the timbers, and cupped his hand to his mouth and called out loudly.

"Atlanteans!"

Ason sprang to the ladder and slid down it, two rungs at a time, turning to face them. They had been running hard in the heat and were all gasping for breath. The Albi had fallen to the gound as soon as they stopped.

277

"We found him this morning," the warrior said. "Out on the plain. Stumbling along, coming this way. All he would say is your name, and that the Atlanteans were on the way."

"I wish they would," Ason said. "We have lost enough good men trying to get over their wall. Bring that water over and we will find out what is happening." The Atlanteans could not threaten him, Ason knew that, yet he still had a hard knot of worry in his middle. Something must have happened to send Turi running all this way.

The exhausted Albi gulped at the water, drinking half. Then he raised the bowl with shaking fingers and poured the rest of it over his head.

"The Atlanteans march in this. . .direction," he finally gasped out. "Coming over the wolds, being led."

"We will welcome them," Ason said.

"No. . .more. . .more landed. They marched at once."

The hard knot was now a weight of stone. Ason shook the man so his head bobbed back and forth.

"More of them—how many more? Do you mean more ships? How many ships?"

"This many," Turi said, holding up the fingers of one hand and two fingers of the other.

Seven ships. Ason released him and he sank back to the ground. Seven ships. How many men in each? All of them armed, armored, fighting men of the sea king. Themis had commanded. That is why he had sent away the captured Mycenaean ship with such a small crew. That had been reported to him: he had paid no attention. To send back the tin, yes, but even more important to send for men. Ason was suddenly aware of his silence, and that the warriors were watching him.

"You," he commanded the nearest. "Go to the place where we get the stones. Tell the bull-chief Ar Apa and the bull-chief Moweg that I wish to see them at once."

The man left at once, passing the bondsmen and warriors who were hurrying up, aware that something was happening. Ason looked at them all and came to a quick decision. He called two of the warriors to him.

"Comn, you are a tracker of game and of men. Korm, I have heard that you could run a deer into the ground if you wished." He raised his hand in silence the instant boasts that sprang to their lips.

"Here is what you must do. I have been told that the Atlanteans are on the way here, more Atlanteans than you have ever seen before. They seek to attack us by surprise, but that is a game that two can play at. It is said that they come from the mine, over the wolds. Do you know that track?"

Both men did. He questioned them about it until he knew what sort of a track it was.

"They cannot march too fast, not with that many men, or through that kind of country. So here is what you two must do: You must take a skin of water and some meat. Leave and go down the track as silently as a hunting fox. You must not be seen. You must find the Atlanteans and follow them until they make camp for the night. When they do this, Comn must stay and watch them. Korm must return here to tell us where they are. We will march against them. Do you understand?"

When they had each repeated the instructions he dismissed them. They left at a run. Ar Apa and Moweg appeared, pushing through the excited crowd. Inteb had finished with the stone and descended from the wood, and was as curious as everyone else. There were no secrets here; all actions of the teuta and the warriors were decided in public.

"What of the Atlanteans?" Ar Apa called out.

"They come in force," Ason answered. "Ships have brought more men and they are on their way to attack us here, in our dun."

There were cries of outrage at this, and bloodthirsty boasts of what would happen to those who dared such a thing. Ason let them speak their wrath before he called for attention again.

"They have come a long way to die," he said, and there were shouts of agreement, which faded quickly so they could listen as the bull-chiefs talked. "They come through the wold and the going will be heavy. There is very little chance that they will be here before dark, so they will have to stop somewhere for the night. I have sent men to find the place where they stop. We must send for all the warriors to follow us. Then we must march at once with the warriors who are here. We will find the place where they are camped. Like the wolves, we will attack by night. We are hunters of the forest, we are hunters of men, we are killers of men. . . ."

His words were drowned out by excited war cries and the thud of axes against shields. The Yerni did not usually fight during the night, but they welcomed a battle at any time and shouted their enthusiasm.

The messengers were sent. Ason called to the bull-chiefs and they went with him to his house. Inteb followed after, the only one who showed any concern for the future. Naikeri was waiting for them, and Ason ordered her to bring fresh ale, meat and salt. They sat and Naikeri brought the trays to set before them. They dipped the meat into the salt and ate, passed the cup around and drank. Here, away from the crowd, Inteb was aware that Ason was as concerned about the future as he was.

"I am the one the Atlantean Themis wishes to kill," Ason said. They nodded their heads in agreement. Ason's battle and escape made a good story that improved in the telling. They had heard it many times, never often enough. "I will call him out and do battle with him before the warriors."

"No," Ar Apa said. "He is now drag-leg the cripple and no longer a man. He will not fight. We must fight them all."

"It is my battle."

280

"It is our battle," Moweg shouted angrily. "They come to our lands, they attack our duns, they seek the death of a bull-chief. Our battle." He bit savagely on the meat, his teeth crunching through the gristle. Ar Apa nodded agreement. So it was done.

"How many ships?" Inteb asked.

"Turi said there were seven."

"That is very bad."

"That is the way it is."

"Must you fight them now?" Inteb said.

Ason was surprised. "Of course. What else is there to do?"

"Many things," Naikeri cried and stepped back when Ason waved her to silence with a chop of his hand. "They cannot find you on this island if you do not wish to be found. What madness is it to go to them and seek death—"

"Be quiet, woman."

"—because death is all you will find. Other things are possible."

"This is the way it will be done."

The Yerni bull-chiefs chewed their meat and looked out of the doorway; women are not permitted to talk at such times. Naikeri called out to Inteb.

"Help me, Egyptian. No, do not help me; you will do nothing for that reason. But help Ason. You know nothing but twisted secret ways. Find another way to fight the Atlanteans. You can."

Inteb nodded reluctantly and turned to Ason.

"I know that women are of little importance to the Yerni, or to the men of the Argolid, for that matter. But in Egypt we are aware that through women different voices talk, and we listen. A way can be found to fight the Atlanteans other than by headlong combat."

"We surprise them at night and kill them," Ar Apa said.

"If that could happen we could hope for no better

281

result. But can you be sure? If all are not killed and they are as strong and as numerous as we think, they will still come on in the morning. . . ."

"This time I cannot use your counsel," Ason said. "This is a time for battle." The bull-chiefs nodded their heads in solemn agreement.

"Kill!" Naikeri screeched, and hurled the pouring vessel to the floor, where it broke and splattered ale in all directions. In the other room the baby complained lustily, then began to cry. "Kill. Do you know anything but killing? Is that all you can do? We of the Albi live without your wars and killing. We find that life can hold other things. Swords, axes, killing—is that all that the world contains?"

Ason was insulted by her words and actions and turned his back; the bull-chiefs all found the open door worth examining. Inteb spoke for them, angry himself now.

"It contains more—but if that were all it contained it would be enough. Mankind has a nobility that the lowest animals can never obtain. In the life of the warrior and in battle it reaches its highest point. That is something that you, a *woman*," he spoke the word like a curse, "will never understand."

"There is nothing to understand. It is a madness. Like the stag in the spring who fight and lock their horns and die fighting. Lock your horns and die—I don't want to understand. Die—"

Ason sprang to his feet. He seized her and dragged her from the room, pushed her through the door and sealed it shut behind her. Her words were like a curse, and there was a bleakness now that pressed against him.

"You are a warrior, Ason," Inteb said quietly. "The man of battles stands highest in the ranks of man. You stand highest of them all. Hundreds come running to follow where you lead. Where will that be?"

Ason touched his hand to the pommel of his sword.

282

"To battle, of course. If we must die, we will die as heroes and men."

10

From the top of the embankment around the dun, the figures could be seen coming across the plain while they were still far away, dark blurs on the horizon. The sky was low and solid with clouds, while from time to time lightning would flicker, followed by the deep rumble of distant thunder. Rain would be a relief—it was so hot and close. But it did not come.

As they came nearer, the dark shapes separated into groups of men making their way towards the dun. Warriors, all of them. Some with trophies, some with wounds, all of them tired. The first of them dropped into the shade of the buildings outside the embankment, calling out loudly for ale.

"What a battle," one of them found the energy to shout.

"Killed a hundred, took a hundred heads," another said, although his only prize seemed to be a blood-stained dagger shoved into his hair belt.

There was much boasting and swaggering, for that is the Yerni way. Inteb ignored it all until Ason and the other bull-chiefs finally appeared, coming in with the last of the men. They went to the center of the ring of stone to the great stone henges. Each sat before his own, gaining strength from the stone.

"Neither a victory nor a defeat," Ason said, licking the golden drops of ale from his lips.

"A victory," Ar Apa insisted. Inteb sat next to Ason and passed him the ale beaker.

Ason shook his head. "A victory is when the enemy dies or flees the field. We killed many—but even more still live and will pursue us."

"If we had had more men," Finmog said darkly. Ason agreed.

"If all the warriors had been there, the outcome might have been different. But many have not arrived yet. We attacked at night and we surprised the Atlanteans, that much we can agree on. But the attack was confused in the darkness, so they soon fought back well. Our warriors lost their way in the dark, or stopped for loot or heads, so the attack lost its push. We withdrew. The enemy still comes on. We must not deny these facts."

"It was a good battle; hundreds died," Ar Apa grumbled, and the others nodded.

"The next battle is the one that will be the important one," Ason said. They had to agree, although they did not like to do so. "It will be fought here, in this great dun of the Yerni, and many will die."

"More warriors are on the way from our duns," Ar Apa said. "They will be angry that they missed last night's battle, and will fight all the harder. We will all fight the harder for the great dun of the Yerni."

They were in complete agreement about that. It seemed to settle any differences of opinion. Most of them were asleep within a few minutes, as were the other warriors who had fought the previous night. Ason's head was nodding too. Inteb put his arm about Ason's grimy shoulders, smelling the acrid sweat and fatigue.

"Will we win?" he asked.

Ason looked about at the four bull-chiefs and lowered his voice.

"There can be no thought of winning. We must kill as many as we can to avenge the slaughter. And to help Mycenae. You must leave now, my Egyptian. Turi will take you to the Albi and you will be safe."

"Will you come with me?"

"I cannot."

"Then neither can I," Inteb said, holding his hands tightly to his knees so that their shaking could not be seen. "We have come this far together; I cannot leave you now. I can use a sword."

"Not very well."

"You speak the truth, Ason—even when it is hurtful. Not very well, but it will still be a sword. And I will be fighting beside you. We have journeyed a long way to reach this place. I do not wish to leave it without you."

"Nor I without you, Egyptian," he said, embraced him, then lay back to sleep. Inteb left to get his armor and weapons, meeting Aias at his door.

"I see you have armed yourself for battle, slave. Shouldn't you be fleeing?"

"I'll flee as far as you do—what is that sword doing in your hand?"

Inteb looked at it ruefully and shook it so it shimmered even in the dim light. "I wish I knew. My work should be for my Pharaoh, erecting great temples to his glory. So what am I doing here putting on armor to battle in this far-away place?"

"You follow a man, Inteb, the same one I do. You have paid a higher price. Mine was no price at all. I was a slave. Now I am a free man with honor. I can even talk to Egyptian nobles."

"Killing you will soon end that. You are a strange slave, Aias, with hard death in your fists. I reluctantly admit—though I will deny it if anyone asks—that it has been good to know you too."

After this there was very little to say. They went to stand on the embankment and watched the warriors coming across the plain, fewer and fewer now. The last stragglers and the men from the distant duns arrived. The afternoon was well advanced, the thunder still growling on the horizon, when the solid mass of the attackers appeared. Their warhorns could be heard, distant and small but soon

285

to grow louder; Inteb and Aias went down to the stone henges where the warriors grouped around the bull-chiefs. Ason stood before his henge and a silence fell.

"They are coming. We will stop them here. There are no city walls to fight behind but there is the embankment of the dun. We will be on the top of the embankment, and they must come up to us. Our axes will be ready. Ar Apa, take the men of your teuta and seize all the logs and pile them into the entrances that are cut through the embankment, so it will not be easy to enter that way. The rest of you—come with me."

Ason shouted the last words and the warriors echoed his cry.

"*Ason abu—abu*!"

They streamed to the embankment and to the top, and looked out at the marching ranks of the men of Atlantis.

They came on in three columns, with the greatest warriors at the head of the columns. Gold and precious gems decorated the bright sheen of their armor. The Yerni pointed to this and swore oaths that they would be wearing all of it before nightfall.

Thunder still rumbled, close now, as a thin rain began to fall. The Yerni welcomed this, turning their faces up to let it run into their mouths. Now the chalk of the embankment would be slippery and that much harder to climb. The Atlanteans came on, straight for the dun, calling out to one another, pointing to the waiting men and the great stones rising up behind them. They were almost to the embankment, dark, hard men in solid bronze with swords in their hands, when it happened.

Light burst and blinded them, and an instant later the roar of thunder beat at their ears.

Men cried aloud and looked, their eyes still burning with the tracery of lightning that had seared down from the sky to lick at Ason's henge. It had struck full upon it—but had not harmed that solid stone. Steam rose where rain had been before, and a cow which had been close to it lay gutted and dead at its base.

"An omen," Ason shouted above the roar of the rain. "An omen! Lightning itself cannot harm the henge of the Yerni."

The warriors stirred themselves now and beat their axes against their shields. It was a good omen; nothing could harm them. They shouted and threatened, and when the Atlanteans reached the foot of the embankment, they took the throwing stones from their places in the back of their shields and hurled them down upon the attackers. Men fell in the deep ditch, bringing others down who tripped over them, and then—shouting war cries with the horns bellowing behind them—they charged to the attack up the high bank.

On the top of the embankment the solid ranks of Yerni warriors stood as a barricade before the advance of the bronze-armored Atlanteans. There was a sound almost as loud as the thunder when the two hosts met and weapons crashed on shields.

And so the slaughter began.

In the rain, slipping and falling in the white chalk mud, the desperate engagement went on. For a short while the embankment was held, not so much by force of arms as by the fact that the Atlanteans could not climb and fight at the same time. But the uneven ranks of the defenders were soon breached. Once this had happened, the armored horde poured over this barrier and into the dun. The fighting broke into individual engagements, while in the center the bulk of fighting warriors retreated step by step through the rings of stones. Fighting all the way, dying as they retreated, back to the great stone arches of the henges, where the final desperate battle was fought.

Inteb was there, not through any strength of arm but because of the lack of it. He had stayed near Ason, and there were always others, stronger, who pushed past him to do battle. In this milling, screaming, dying mob he was perhaps the only observer.

He saw the litter being brought up, surrounded by rows of guards. He guessed that this must be Themis, crippled and carried to battle. Aias must have seen it, too, and recognized his onetime master and boxing student.

Swinging his great hammer, Aias plowed through the ranks of the Atlanteans. Not trying to kill them but only to drive them aside, until he reached within a few paces of the chair, shouting above the clatter of arms.

"Come out, Themis, you cowardly boxer. I could beat you anytime I wanted to, though I never let you know. Come out so I can do it now!"

Themis simply made a chopping motion with his hand; a slave is a slave. The Atlanteans closed in, and although some fell, at least one with a skull broken by a fist, they did their work quickly and efficiently. Aias went down as their swords plunged home. One fist rising up for an instant as they went about their butcher's work, then this dropped as well.

There were few defenders left among the stones. Inteb now had his chance to fight. He stabbed through at the attacking men and felt his sword sink home more than once. Then the circle of Yerni warriors was broken, and Inteb stood alone. His first sword stroke was easily parried by a massive Atlantean with black beard and blood-soaked armor. He struck out in return, driving the sword from Inteb's arm, cutting into his flesh at the same time. He pushed Inteb down with his shield, chopped at his body and legs as he fell, then trampled over him as he rushed towards Ason.

Ason. The Atlanteans pushed and almost fought one another to get at him. Inteb tasted salt blood in his mouth, and clutched at the other gaping red mouth of the wound in his leg, and looked up through the falling rain at the men bringing him to bay.

His back to the stone, Ason hacked at them, his sword

never stopping. Slashing it across an arm, darting under a shield to find flesh. Fighting, fighting. And losing against their numbers.

Their swords went up, came down. He vanished from sight beneath them.

11

Lying in the bilge of the Atlantean ship, Ason could see little other than the arch of the sky and the sweating bodies and legs of the galley slaves above him. His wrists were held behind his back in unyielding wooden fetters, his ankles sealed into an even heavier one. In heavy seas the stinking bilge water had washed over him. The rain poured onto his naked body, the sun burned it. Many of the sword cuts in his flesh were still suppurating wounds. His hair and beard were tangled and filthy. He had lain here every day of the long passage back to Atlantis from the Island of the Yerni.

It was the galley slaves who had kept him alive. Some of the nearest ones were from the Argolid, captured in battle, prisoned in the galley for life. They saw to it that he received his ration of water and tiny dole of food. At night they bathed his wounds with sea water and whispered to him of things they knew. Most of the time he did not know what they were saying, as the fever from his inflamed wounds burned at him.

The shouting and the heavy thud of the ship against stone woke him from an uneasy doze. His throat was dry, the sores on his mouth hurt as they always did. Atlanteans stamped down the gangway above and stood over him; hands lifted him and they cursed at the filth. Buckets were dipped over the side, and he was shocked to awareness by the cold splash of the water. The sailors doused him with it,

289

then rolled him onto his stomach while someone worked at the heavy fetters on his ankles. They fell away. For the first time in countless days he could move his legs freely. Now they seized him and dragged him to his feet, the world spinning dizzily at this unaccustomed position. Before he could recover, they pulled him down the gangway, where other hands took him and hauled him up onto the stone jetty, dropping him down onto it.

With this, the dizziness stopped and he could see. A ship landing of carefully dressed stone stretched out from the shore. A steep hillside of gray rock and flowering broom rose up behind it, where a stairway had been cut from its face. A litter was being carried up this, towards the palace that was set on the headland not high above. Red stone columns were visible behind the rows of high green poplars, the edge of a crenellated roof of stone bull horns. And above the colonnaded entranceway, the golden double ax of Atlantis glittered in the sun.

"On your feet," someone said. "We're not going to carry you."

In the end they had to, for there was no strength in Ason's legs after their long immobilization. He stumbled and fell until, grumbling and poking him with their spears, the Atlanteans dragged him up the stairs to the palace above. There were guards here, and hurrying servants, quick glimpses of paintings of fish and birds upon the wall as he lurched by. Dark halls and sunlight again, the pillars of the megaron, a fountain splashing, and Themis lying back upon a couch. When his guards released him and stepped back, Ason managed to remain standing, although he swayed like grain before the wind.

"Did you enjoy your sea voyage?" Themis asked, sipping at a golden beaker of wine.

Ason cleared his throat and spat upon the floor because Themis was too far to reach with the gobbet.

"Such barbarian manners. I thought you were a prince

in your land, and king to the Yerni? You act like a savage."

"Why didn't you kill me?" Ason asked, his voice cracked and hoarse.

"I started to once, and only Poseidon the earth shaker saved you at that time." Themis's voice rose to a screech as his precarious control on his temper vanished. "You struck me with a coward's blow. You will pay for that as no man has ever paid before."

When he did this his limbs twitched, and a thread of spittle fell from his lower lip. His hair, what little could be seen above the wrappings that concealed the gold plate on his skull, was gray. There was very little resemblance to the athlete and the boxer he once had been. Flesh had fallen from his body. The leg that he dragged was much thinner than the other. Ason looked at him with cold detachment.

"I don't think you are much of a man," he said. "I too wish one of us had been killed that day, since your life is now a waste. If you are going to kill me, do it and stop your talking."

"I will do what I wish! I will do, I will torture, I will do to you things never dreamed before. Bones broken, every one, your skin removed piece by piece, molten metal in your ears. . . ." The wail of his voice died away and he gasped for breath.

"Who is the barbarian now?" Ason said calmly, squaring his shoulders, using what energy he had to prevent himself from falling. "All you can do is talk of torture and revenge like some slighted woman. My Yerni, for all their bragging and boar's moustaches and drunkenness, are better men than you. I scorn you, Themis, you and your Atlantis."

Ason turned his back to Themis and faced out across the megaron to the sea beyond. It was warm and blue; the air smelled of home. There were strangled gasps from behind him, but he paid them no attention, looking instead at a great white gull that rode the air above the cliff, its wings unmoving, just its head turning from side to side. It passed silently, not far from him, and the dark eye looked into his and then it was gone. A hand touched his shoulder.

"Sit on this bench," the Atlantean said, a young man in gold-chased armor. "My kinsman, the good Themis, has suffered one of his attacks but will recover soon. When he does, I do not wish him to discover that you have hurled yourself over the edge and into the sea. Though I am of his house, I would probably suffer the fate he is planning for you."

The words were not harshly spoken, and Ason dropped wearily onto the cushioned bench. Two physicians had appeared and were bent over Themis, washing his skin with vinegar and water. There was a distant rumbling, more felt than heard. Ason turned to look out at the sea again. The young Atlantean had heard it as well and pointed off to the north.

"It is Thera again, growling in her bowels and spewing out smoke and ashes. You were there the first time this happened, and it has never been silent since. The people who returned are beginning to leave again." He frowned into the distance. "It is a bad omen, some say, because Thera is the royal island. But this island of Crete is much the larger and is still our home. These things happen."

"An omen that Atlantis is no longer as strong as she once was. That she has difficulty in the Argolid. . . ."

"Be silent, mountain man! What you heard from the slaves in the galley may not be the entire truth. We have lost some battles, but our ships still rule the sea. Our fleet is larger than it ever has been. Atlantis rules."

He broke off as there were shouts outside, and the sound of brazen horns. There was an immense flutter and running among the servants, and a clash of metal as a score of men in the finest armor tramped in, swords drawn. Themis stirred and the physicians drew back. Ason was

292

dragged to his feet. King Atlas strode heavily into the room, the members of his court flocking after him. There was blown spittle on his cloak. He slapped his chariot whip against his boot.

"Well, Themis, my son is home from his war. Your ship was seen; I hurried to welcome you. I feared for your health and your life in that pestilential land at the edge of the world. Now your father greets you."

Themis struggled to his feet and they embraced. Only Atlas, fat, old, gray of beard and furrowed with wrinkles, could see his son in this drab and twisted creature. Themis dropped back to his couch and Atlas sat beside him, following with his eyes the direction of the pointing, trembling finger.

"The Island of the Yerni is ours, father. The warriors who fought us are dead, the tin mine is bringing forth its gray metal for us, the one who put himself against Atlantis is my prisoner there."

Atlas looked at Ason coldly, then turned away.

"A worthy prize, Themis, though the force displayed against him was great. But you are a prince of Atlantis and command our ships. The thing is done. Kill the wretch and return to the court where we have all missed you."

"He shall die so slowly it will take years."

"Do what you will," Atlas said, shrugging the matter away. He stood and looked at Ason distastefully. "I wish his pirate of a father were here to be flayed next to him."

"Trouble in the Argolid, great Atlas?" Ason said, and smiled. "Can the mountain barbarians really prick holes in the thick hide of Atlantis?"

"Your barbarians have learned to fight in their unending squabbles with one another. They will be dealt with." He turned away.

"Or they will deal with Atlantis," Ason called after him, then laughed aloud. "You must fight us in the Argolid, and far away on the Island of the Yerni. Soon, perhaps, in other places. Until one day you will be dead,

Atlas. Then this broken stick of a son will rule. That will be the end of Atlantis."

"I shall kill him," Atlas shouted, swinging about and drawing his sword.

"He is mine," Themis screamed.

Ason laughed again, and almost in answer to his deep laugh there came a deeper rumbling from the earth beneath them. A rumbling that did not stop but kept on and on until the solid stone flooring swayed, while dust and painted tiles fell down from the ceiling above. A man nearest the sea pointed and shouted wordlessly, shrieking in terror. They ran to see. Themis followed, supported by the physicians; and Ason, forgotten by all except his guards for the moment, hobbled stiff-legged after them.

Here, on this ledge above the sea, everything could be clearly seen. The gray rock falling to the water below, the ship that had brought them tied at the jetty with the men aboard her clinging to the rigging and pointing. Beyond was the blue of the sea, the bluest water ever, with the white sails of a great Atlantean ship lifting and falling as it met the easy waves. Blue ocean stretched to the horizon to the north, where the island of Thera lay.

No more. No more the flames and smoke and inner rumblings. In a single, calamitous, mighty, world-shaking upheaval, the island had blown asunder, exploded in a single moment. A mountain of red-shot smoke—taller and larger than any mountain—reached climbing and boiling high up into the sky.

Then the wind and shock of the explosion struck, carrying with it the sound of the end of the world.

The blast struck them, whirled them about and sent some of them crashing to the floor. Ason leaned into it and did not fall. In an instant it was past, the echo of its sound still in his head. Men were groaning and calling out in fear while they climbed to their feet again. Atlas stood with his hand to his chest, his blanched face a tortured mask. Themis gasped for air as his physicians held up his sagging form. Men shouted and cursed and pointed at the thing that traced a white line on the horizon.

A wave. A wave such as the world had never seen before. A wave born in the heart of the volcano.

The center of Thera was a mountain, the mountain was a volcano—and it had erupted. In a single gargantuan upheaval it had exploded, sending the rock and soil and people, homes, trees, everything, exploding out ahead of it. All crushed, broken, incinerated by the lake of molten rock that lay within the volcanic chamber. Lava that now burst out and destroyed the island above it and every living thing upon its surface.

Where the mountain had stood with its molten core of lava, there now remained only a scorched crater, a caldera in the ocean from which the contents had been vomited forth. Red-glowing rock reaching to the floor of the ocean, even lower, empty of anything other than poison fumes, with the waters of the ocean a shivering wall all around.

Until the waters fell. Until a deluge of falling ocean filled that monstrous opening in the sea, pouring in, hissing into steam that was lost in the fall of more and more water, until the caldera was quenched and full.

And then the sea gathered all its weight and surged back. A wave was born in the eruption and the caldera that rose higher than the highest waterspout. A wave that could not be called a wave, because the word is too small, a surging mass of matter that was a new thing on the face of the earth, an ocean rising above an ocean. A wall of water that was half an ocean in itself, that rose up higher and higher and higher. Then moved out with a speed faster than any living creature.

One moment it was a white line, just a tracery, then it was thicker, a broad white line, and an instant later it was a white wall. It stretched from horizon to horizon and it thundered down upon them. They gaped with terror and could not move nor take their eyes from it. In this ultimate moment of life, only Themis, maddened by life and tortured with unending pain, could possibly think of anything else. He seized a sword from the limp fingers of the nearest warrior, tearing it from his hand. Turned towards Ason mouthing incomprehensible words with his frothed lips. Dragging his leg like a stick of wood, he staggered forwards. Until he came between Ason and the terror of the sea, and Ason was aware of him.

Almost disdainfully Ason kicked out and struck him in the good leg with his foot, and sent him tumbling to the floor. No one saw, or if they saw, cared.

It rushed, it grew, it was impossible. It was there. A wall of raging foam and green water that rose up higher and higher into the sky and did not stop rising. The Atlantean galley turned to flee and was struck and destroyed in an instant, vanished from sight. No ship could live in this sea. At first the water looked higher than a ship's mast, then they realized that it was as high as the palace perched on the cliff above the water. Then it was higher, much higher, looming over them, with white spray thrown in clouds from the face of its walls, rainbows touching color from the spray.

The roaring louder than sound.

Ason laughing, unheard.

Blotting out the sun, a darkness of water coming straight at them with no top to it.

Ason shouting aloud as men fell and twisted and screamed before it, Ason standing to face it and shouting unheard as the water harder than stone struck them all and ended all in an instant.

"Die Atlantis—die!"

ENVOI

The small, dark-skinned man came first, the brown of his clothing the same brown as the tree trunks of the forest they had just passed through. A bronze-armored warrior walked at his side. A man no longer young but still upright, and bearing easily the weight of a horsetail-plumed helm, the richly decorated breastplate and greaves, the long sword in his hand. Behind them more and more armored warriors emerged from the forest in loose formation, coming on steadily despite the burden of their armor and packs, calling out to one another, singing songs. The column emerged like a writhing golden snake that wound across the plain, more than a hundred men.

When the sun was at its highest they stopped to eat and drink, then moved on again, after only the shortest rest. By midafternoon the brown man who was guiding them pointed to a mound on the plain ahead. There was the smoke of cooking fires rising from it, the gray forms of immense stones at the center. The march continued, with the men shouting to one another about this strange sight in this empty plain. The mound was a ring-shaped embankment. They went towards the opening that had been cut through it, crowding through this entrance.

Rough huts and small wooden buildings had been built against the inner wall of the embankment. People were in the doorways, looking out with frightened eyes. Some men appeared with stone axes, but drew back further and further as more armored warriors appeared. Their leader ordered them to halt and went on alone to the ring of capped stones, with the even greater stone archways in the center. There were five of these, massive and brooding. He felt dwarfed when he stood before them looking up at their height.

"You will see nothing like them in the rest of the world," a voice said and he turned quickly, his sword ready.

A raggedly dressed man, as small and dark as his guide, hobbled towards him. He let his sword fall. There was an old scar on the man's face that pulled at his cheek, an even deeper one on his leg that forced him to walk painfully.

"You are not of Atlantis," the man said, his clear voice and good diction out of place in his tattered form. "Tell me who you are and why you come here, if you please."

"I am Phoros of Mycenae. These men are Mycenaeans for the most part, though some are from Asine and Tiryns and other cities of the Argolid."

"Then I bid you welcome, warm welcome. I thought your face familiar; we met once. I am Inteb the Egyptian."

"The builder?" Phoros looked closely and shook his head. "You resemble him in some ways. Yet, still. . . ."

"Still, many years have passed and many strange events have overtaken me. Shall we sit? My leg is not good for much. Over here, on that long stone in the ground. It was called the speaking stone once and we can speak there. Speak, yes we shall."

Phoros shook his head again as he followed Inteb's limping progress. The way the Egyptian talked, his senses seemed as scarred as his body. They sat and looked up at the stones that rose above them.

"I did this," Inteb said, and there was more strength in his voice now. "I raised these stones for Ason. This place is Dun Ason of the Yerni."

"Where is Ason? We come seeking him. There was trade with a tribe to the north of the Argolid, the Geramani, who carried messages from him to King Perimedes."

"You are too late."

"There have been wars; travel is not easy."

"There are always wars, it is what men seem to do best. There was a war here, with the Atlanteans. I fought in it, these are noble wounds you see here. It was a great battle, even though we lost."

"Ason was killed?"

"No, captured, though he killed many before they took him. I saw him carried away, wounded and unconscious. I heard later that he was still alive when the Atlanteans left, and he was taken in their ship. He is surely dead by now."

"When did this happen?" Phoros asked, speaking softly so that his excitement would not be seen.

"When? I have lost track of the months." He looked around him. "This must be the dry month of Payni, by Egyptian reckoning. It would, then, perhaps be thirteen months since it happened, in the month of Epiphi."

Phoros rose to his feet and paced back and forth excitedly.

"We hoped to find him alive, but I think that even Perimedes knew he must be dead. We knew the Atlanteans had come here in force; that is why I came with seven ships. But they are gone now, the few at the mine now dead. Ason must have been taken back with the others, to Atlantis."

"Where else would Atlantean ships go?" Inteb said testily, rubbing at his leg.

"Where indeed? With good sailing they should have reached Atlantis in time. My cousin Ason is dead, but he died nobly. He died knowing that Atlantis would die as well."

"You are talking in riddles and I am very tired."

"Then listen, Egyptian, you knew him—"

"I loved him."

"Then know how he died. The world has changed. There was a day of fire, the sun turned red and black, the earth shook, and in Mycenae ashes fell from the sky. Here is what we discovered when we went down to the ocean: The water rose up and washed into the sea all those cities on the shore, waves such as no man had seen before, destroying cities as far away as Troy. Every ship at sea sunk, every coast ravaged. We built new ships and armed them and sailed to Crete. Thera, their holy home, is no more. Their coast is wiped out and their ships sunk. Mycenae now rules in Atlantis and in the Argolid; mighty Mycenae on her rock far from the sea has descended and now rules them all."

"I do not see."

"Don't you? Don't you see Ason taken to Atlantis, dying there with all of his enemies, knowing that their death would mean life for Mycenae? He would know victory."

"He is dead. It matters not how he died. He left this, these henges of stone. They will live after him and be his memory. Men will see them and know that something great happened here. You will return to Mycenae?"

"Yes, soon. Perimedes must be told."

"Will you take me? I think I have served Mycenae well. Now I wish to see green Egypt again. I will pay for my passage with something worth more than treasure to Perimedes. His grandson."

"Is this true? Ason married?"

Inteb grinned crookedly. "Married by local custom, to a princess of her people. She and I both loved Ason, so in the end learned not to hate one another. She kept me alive. Ason's seed already lived in her, but I could not return the life she gave to me. She is dead, along with the daughter who would also have been Ason's. But his son lives. There, behind the stone, watching us, bolder than the Yerni children." He raised his voice and called out.

302

"Atreus. Come meet your kinsman."

The boy came forward slowly; if he was afraid he did not show it. Already wide-shouldered and strong like his father, with his same steady gaze.

"I have taught him the Mycenaean tongue," Inteb said. "In case this day should ever come."

His thoughts wandered then, and so did his attention. He would be leaving here soon. Although Egypt pulled him with golden memories, he knew that part of himself would always remain in this place. These great stones were Ason's. If any part of Ason lived on, it was here. Inteb limped slowly among them, touching their cool surfaces with his fingertips, hearing dimly the war cries of the Yerni warriors, the crash of weapons on shields.

It was all over. He must leave. His dragging footsteps brought him to the single stone where he had labored so long. What magnificent hard stone this was. His hand went out to the face of the column. With his own hands he had done this. With stone mauls, swung until his fingers bled, and with a broken bronze sword for a chisel, and sand, hammered until the metal was worn away. But the harder the stone, the longer the inscription would remain.

"Ason," Inteb said. This was the stone before which he had fallen.

He moved his fingers to trace the dagger he had so painfully incised and abraded in the stone. The square-hilted, long- and narrow-bladed dagger of Mycenae. The royal dagger that was Ason's.

The royal dagger of Mycenae.

Filled then with fatigue, Inteb turned and limped away, a small figure among the great ones of the stones. Turned his back and walked away from them a final time.

Left them behind, Dun Ason, the Island of the Yerni.

Left behind the Yerni, dispersed and slaughtered, their power broken.

Darkness fell then and lasted a long, long time.

AFTERWORD

I

This is a violent and bloody novel—as it should be, given the history of the European Bronze Age. The world of 1500 B.C. *was* like this, or so we are told in the epics of Homer. To be sure, Homer glorified the bravery and courage of a warrior class that was not the only element in heroic society, but it was the leading one. The qualification is well understood by all students of the Homeric question. They wonder, for example, what could be the meaning of upwards of 20 or 30 bronze rapiers found in a single Mycenaean grave. What did this person *do* for a living? It is only cautious to ask. There is much poetic exaggeration in the epics, paid for by their royal patrons, which may or may not relate directly to Mycenaean relics. Yet despite any exaggeration, the age of Stonehenge is undoubtedly the age of heroes as well.

Our novel opens with a quotation from the *Critias*, the main part of Plato's account of what was surely the world's first world war. On the one side were the united Greek city states of the Argolid. On the opposing side was the king of Atlantis, King Atlas in this narrative. He was the founder of the Atlantean empire, called the Minoan by historians, an empire destroyed in battle with the Mycenaean Greeks, at long last sinking beneath the waves of the Aegean Sea it once dominated.

The war engaged nearly every ancient land from the walls of

Troy to the river wilds of Central Europe, from the little garrisoned palace towns of Mycenae to the glories of Atlantis itself.

It was a war over a resource as precious as the one that names our own Petrochemical Age. Not oil, but tin. Without tin, there could have been no Bronze Age. For at the very dawn of metallurgy it was evident that copper alone was too soft to make durable tools and weapons. Tin was essential, but almost impossible to find. Yet when combined at a proportion of one to nine, it transforms the abundant, more malleable copper into hardened bronze. Too much tin, and the bronze is too brittle, like the raw hardening agent itself; too little, and the bronze is too soft, like the copper it melds with. But it is scarce; the more so for the ancients, who didn't dig deeply for it as we do, but who searched for nodules of cassiterite in naturally open tin streams. There are none of those nut-like nodules of tin oxide left anymore, the surface of the earth having been picked clean a long time ago.

In this novel we have described the ancient conditions of prospecting and the crude old methods of smelting. Nothing is invented here; that is the way it was done—with tin smelting, bronze forging, ship sailing, stone working, Stonehenge erecting, everything. What is described by way of technology and engineering is in every detail based on sure knowledge and experimental archaeology.

As for character motivation, the competitive effort to obtain the exotic metal was made by the very type of hero and man for whom it was most important, the Bronze Age king and his warrior followers. The two sides went far outside their home waters to get it, and swept all manner of peoples into their conflict. The Atlantean side passed out of the Mediterranean into the Black Sea, and halfway up the great river Danube that feeds it; that is where their tin workings were. The other side went the western limits, through the Straits of Gibraltar and up the Atlantic coast to Britain, there to work in the tin lodes of Cornwall.

That other side was Mycenae, and in the course of the war, nearly three thousand and five hundred years ago, Stonehenge was built, *had* to be built. It was the necessary thing to do, the defensive thing against Atlantis.

This is history? Yes. A true story? Yes, in that no facts are left out to aid the plot, none invented. This is no historical novel, but a novel *about* history. Never do we go beyond the possibilities of what *could* have happened. The only fiction is the lives of our characters and their movements; the cultures they represent and their interaction are graven in stone. Our adventure story comes out of that. Consider some of the facts.

II

In 1953 there was discovered at Stonehenge a dagger carving on the inner face of one of that monument's five trilithons, likened by its finders to a type of dagger known from Bronze Age Greece, in the royal burials at Mycenae. A Mediterranean link to the building of Stonehenge was inferred on the spot, as the front-page headlines about this remarkable discovery attest, and the date for that connection was given, for good reason, at about 1500 B.C.

The date was arrived at this way. First, the association was made between the highly distinctive dagger carving and a weapon of that type found buried in the royal cemetery of Mycenae, within the city walls near the Lion Gate. Also among the items of grave furniture are Egyptian trade goods, including pottery, which has a precise chronology, its changing fashions being datable in relation to the solar calendar of Egypt and the historical records based on it. So, Egyptian pottery of about 1500 B.C. is found associated with bronze daggers in the shaft graves of Mycenae. The configuration of the daggers closely matched that of the carving about four feet off the ground on the inner face of stone number fifty-three at Stonehenge. Therefore, this phase of the monument, with its massive trilithons and sarsen ring, is contemporary. Soon after this connection was made, the date was confirmed by radiocarbon methods, using organic material (as must be done) in the form of an antler pick found at the base of one of the other stones. Years later, the radiocarbon calendar was revised, with the result that all dates were pushed back in accordance with a new and rather complex standard of calibration. Stonehenge was now fixed at 2000 B.C., which meant the building phase in question occurred five-hundred years before the rise of Mycenae (and all the other palace towns of the Argolid, which as a group take their cultural name from this main citadel). Therefore, the monument had to be a strictly local accomplishment, leaving the dagger carving inexplicable.

Lately, however, archaeological thinking has come around full circle. The carving won't go away, and there is an actual Mycenaean dagger from southwest Britain in the vicinity of the tin lodes there, as well as an ingot of Mycenaean stamp, not to mention the ribbed gold cup from Rillaton in the same region—again like those in the shaft graves—so there still must be something faulty with the radiocarbon method. It is weaker than the Mediterranean link. We may conclude that a Mycenaean presence was indeed felt at Stonehenge in 1500 B.C.

Another event of about the same time was a volcanic eruption on the island of Thera in the Agean, sinking the metropolitan center and royal city of the Minoan sea kingdom otherwise known as Atlantis. Despite all the mystery mongering that has been done about Atlantis, this once-legendary realm of Plato's is no longer a mystery, and has been identified by archaeologists ever since 1909 with the Minoan Thessalocracy, also a headlined discovery, at that time. The staid old news, now forgotten in the wake of more recent occult fancy, remains current in the professional literature. So much for the effort of scholars to educate against the eruption of nonsense. Yet the facts are, Atlantis was a sea kingdom whose principal island bases were Thera and Crete (the small round and the large rectangular ones of Plato), it existed at the time of the landed Mycenaean confederation, and it was the rival of this other.

Based on these facts, the novel proposes that the dagger carving at Stonehenge, not to say the monument itself, came to be there as an incident in the long war between Mycenae and Atlantis. Fantastic? Not in the least. Plato's testimony as to the existence of Egyptian records of the war with Atlantis is quite unremarkable to historians. What is fantastic is the Atlantis of the mystery mongers. Based on nothing more than a mistake Plato made in his dates, the mystery is easily penetrated. Because of this obvious copyist's error, concealed by those who wish to make something else of it, a super-civilization for Atlantis has been posited at a time when men everywhere in the world still were in the hunting and gathering stage of human history. Plato got the story from Solon, who got it from Egyptian priests. The priests had it, according to Solon, that Atlantis was destroyed 9000 years before his visit, when he came to Egypt to study library documents in the care of the temple of Sais on the Nile delta, Sais being the capital city of Lower Egypt. That would place the event some time around the end of the Pleistocene geological epoch or Ice Age. No human culture anywhere had as yet made the revolutionary transition from Old Stone Age food collection to New Stone Age food production, much less erected an urban culture on a yet-to-be Neolithic farming base. No Egypt then existed, and no priests to record the event. Atlantis, like Egypt, was a Bronze Age civilization, with sailing ships and commerce, metallurgy and court artisans, stately palace buildings and temples, and monumental public works. Solon must have transcribed thousands for hundreds, an easy mistake to make in reading Egyptian numerals. The priests meant 900 years before Solon's time. This is more like it, and would place the event near 1477 B.C., the year estimated by geologists to be that of Thera's eruption.

The novel begins three years before that, the time it took our Mediterranean hero Ason, prince of Mycenae, to get Stonehenge built in the cause of his father's war against Atlantis.

The Egyptians of the delta region had good reason to record the destruction of Atlantis; apparently they were shaken by it, feeling the earthquakes, tidal waves and fall of dust caused by Thera's explosion, huger than that of Krakatoa. It is even thought that the Pharaonic army, in pursuit of the Israelites in their Exodus, fleeing across a sea-level desert bordering the delta region, was an army of Thuthmosis III, and that it was inundated at just the right miraculous moment by a tsunami wave, sweeping southward out of the Aegean. But Egypt survived. The other main island of Atlantis, that of Crete, did not. Its great palace buildings at Knossos were knocked down, and the subsequent history of Crete is Mycenaean, as we know from the change of script in the palace records. For the Mycenaeans, the fall of Atlantis meant an opportunity to occupy and rebuild Knossos in a thrust across the eastern Mediterranean that carried them all the way to Troy. The fall of Troy in its turn is the end of the Mycenaean adventure, remembered in Homer.

III

From Homer, we are led to the other Bronze Age cultures of Europe, that of the Ûnetice, located in what is now Czechoslovakia (whence come our Geramani), and the Wessex culture of southern Britain (that of our Yerni, builders of the final phase of Stonehenge). Mycenae, and Ûnetice and Wessex north of the Alps: these are the high points of development in Europe. The Minoan culture of Atlantis is a variant of the Mycenaean—more sophisticated, no doubt, but they were well matched in the war between them that Plato reports; like contests only with like. Both kept palace records on unbaked clay tablets, nothing but business accounts. Mycenae, however, has its echo in the poetry of Homer, composed around 750 B.C., some centuries after the collapse of the culture it celebrates, following the advent of the Iron Age and the beginnings of Classical Greece. Nothing like this epic literature has come down to us from central Europe or Wessex but, as we shall see, there is a way of knowing that Homer is their poet, too. The heroic life of a Bronze Age warrior-nobility applies to all these places, be the weapons bronze swords (Mycenae and Ûnetice) or stone battle-axes (Wessex). The latter, after all, are copies of metal axes; the Wessex warriors (or Yerni) favored precious types of stone for their double-edged axheads, stone that would polish up to a metallic sheen in the imitation of bronze.

Parallel to the heroic tradition in Europe is the civilized one of the Near East—Sumer in the Tigris-Euphrates valley and Egypt in a narrow strip along the Nile. Both traditions are developments of the Bronze Age, each in its different way. Both, of course, evolve out of the Neolithic, a food-producing economy based on plant and animal domestication. This may lead to either settled village life or to pastoral nomadism. The latter is the heritage of ancient Europe, warrior herdsmen coming out of the East, the so-called Battle-Ax folk whose home, the ancestral home of all Indo-European peoples · before their movement outward in all directions, was the steppeland of southern Russia, the Ukraine. These Battle-Ax folk, these original Indo-Europeans, had at the start been a Neolithic people of the mixed farming type before they went pastoral and mobile. Why this happened is a puzzle.

Partly it is due to the soil conditions of this region. When the first farmers made clearings for their fields there, the trees did not regrow, forest land turned into steppeland, and soon hoeing and herding became nothing but herding. At the same time, they had been influenced by the existence of a civilization to the south of them, the Sumerian of ancient Mesopotamia, which, incidentally, they almost destroyed in the process of becoming the nomadic, warrior herdsmen known as the Battle-Ax folk. Their chosen weapon was the stone battle-ax, and this is but a copy in stone of the Sumerian war-ax cast in bronze. Or rather, it is more accurate to say it is copied from a metal axhead made as a trade good, sold to Sumeria by a special community of wealthy smiths located in Caucasia, one of the world's first two metallurgical centers (the other being located in Croatia on the slopes of the eastern Alps, embedded with ores of both tin and copper).

After waves of migration and conquest, with the aid of horse-drawn wagons and war chariots in the later ones, they arrived in western Europe and Britain, still attached to the old stone battle-ax, even after they themselves had mastered metallurgy. But they went elsewhere, as well. Speaking an undivided Indo-European tongue, which language in time differentiated into Sanskrit, Greek, Celtic and a hundred others. Moving in on the Harappan civilization of India they became the city-smashing Aryans (whose epic is the *Rig Veda*). Moving into Greece they became the Mycenaeans (whose epic poet is Homer), and into the rest of Europe they became the proto-Celts. The Battle-Ax folk are thus the common ancestors of the Mycenaeans and the Wessex warriors (our Yerni) who built Stonehenge. In the latter case, however, charioteering had not yet crossed the Channel, and did not until Iron Age times.

Coming into Europe, they settled down as a warrior aristocracy among the pre-existing Neolithic villagers there, forming a layered tribal society divided between warrior heroes and agricultural producers. The resulting political order of a heroic society is known as a chiefdom, with elective chiefs, not dynastic kings, heading up the authority structure. King Perimedes was not really a king, nor was Mycenae really a city (no more than was a Yerni dun), but merely a palace enclosure in which Perimedes sat as a redistribution chief, taking in loot gathered by war and piracy, keeping a large share for himself and giving out the rest as gifts to his retainers and warrior followers, and as diplomatic gifts to rival chiefs. It is this diplomatic exchange, however, that brought him to the verge of true kingship and dynastic striving, an evolution forced by the war with Atlantis and the need for political unity throughout the Argolid, in one "empire" under one "over-king." Things never got that far elsewhere in Europe, as alliances were fragile at best. Everywhere it was a case of dealing in precious metals, of a chief leading his warrior band in a quest for them, and in the sport of war and the thrill of revenge, brightening his authority thereby.

The heroic chiefdoms of barbarian Europe contrast with the civilized polities or true kingdoms of the Near East. There, kings and pharaohs dealt also in the precious metals of the Bronze Age, but did so as big businessmen, ordering trade on a large scale. This is partly to be explained by the fact that the alloys of bronze, copper and tin, were not to be found in the realms of Sumer or Egypt; they had to be sought in Europe, and indeed, metallurgy began there. The main business of these ancient kings, therefore, was the search for copper and tin, and it carried traders, prospectors and even military adventurers far from home. What they acquired for their king was necessary for his carpenters, sculptors, jewelers and soldiers, all attached to his court. This offers another contrast with the European chiefdoms, in which warriors were not army men but formed a nobility, and craftsmen were itinerant, the heritage of the traveling tinkerman. A more striking difference, the kings of Sumer and Egypt resided in true cities—including the full round and roster of urban life as we know it—and not merely aristocratic compounds. These drew their support from the Neolithic villages of the surrounding countryside by way of taxation, indeed grew directly out of them. City life and state organization, with an elite-focused high culture in command, are just what chiefdoms lack, and those of Europe finally fell when the penetration into Europe went beyond trade, when the Iron Age successors to the ancient Bronze Age kingdoms moved on to the business of territorial annexation.

This brings us directly to the expansion of the Roman empire and Caesar's conquest of Gaul, in which he speedily defeated warrior heroes given to individual combat with troops trained for mass murder. Useful to us, he described what he came to vanquish, and also drew on some older eye-witness accounts made by other classical authors. Preeminent among these authors was the Greek ethnographer Posidonius, who died in 51 B.C., the time of Caesar's own commentaries. Posidonius gives us a description of the Keltoi in Gaul, the people we know in classical history as the Celts. In archaeology, they express the last horizon of the pre-Roman Iron Age, the so-called La Tène culture.

The Iron Age, in its Roman development, includes not only cheap iron for weapons and tools, but also the alphabet, coinage, free craftsmen organized in guilds, and a state tied together with a system of horseback-riding postmen. Cheap, mass produced swords and armor destroyed the monopoly on force held by the old Bronze Age nobility equipped with expensive metals, and made organized armies possible; alphabetic writing destroyed the monopoly on literacy held by priestly scribes serving Bronze Age kings; and coinage made small business possible, beyond that of kingly dealings in bullion; as did cheap tools make possible the guild-protected independence of artisans. Thus giving the new rulers of the Iron Age a much different kind of polity to administer, imperial in scope.

La Tène Europe beyond the Roman frontier, however, was not much different from the social order of Bronze Age Europe that preceded it. Posidonius gives us a picture of Celtic warriors armed with iron swords not for military but for heroic combat, and in Britain Caesar found them using chariots as did Homer's heroes. No dynastic kingdoms are reported, much less any imperium, and artisans were independent not for any guild organization of their own, but for their itinerancy, working under the patronage of local chiefs as they chose. Priestly men there were, the druids; they used no system of writing, but they did monopolize oral literature, including the memorization of the genealogies and the glories of their chiefs. Without iron weapons, we have the analog of Homer's Mycenae. Even the large confederation of chiefdoms under territorial war leaders which Caesar describes as having been organized against him, may be seen as a response to a common enemy, as Atlantis was to the warring citadels of the Mycenaean Argolid under our fictional King Perimedes (whose prototype is Agamemnon in contest with the Trojans). They gave up their mutual raiding and cattle stealing only for that. These are the same warrior herdsmen who built Stonehenge during the British Bronze Age; their shaft-holed, double-bladed battle-axes of stone and their stolen finery are buried with them in their grave mounds all around the place, about 460 of them within a two-mile radius. If the Celts held tribal assemblies in their cemeteries, in the midst of their dead heroes, then Stonehenge was erected in a similar setting for a like purpose. In fact, the Wessex warriors associated with that monument, and also the central European warriors buried with their bronze swords in the grave mounds of Únětice, are known in the archaeological literature as the "proto-Celts." Yerni and Geramani alike are poor cousins of the Homeric heroes. To project back certain basic elements of the Celtic Iron Age culture into the life-ways of their immediate Bronze Age ancestors is not unreasonable. By looking at the Celts we can learn about the proto-Celtic Wessex warriors (or Yerni), for whom we have no oral nor written historical testimony.

IV

Eye-witness accounts of Celtic life and custom recur in Greek authors such as Strabo the geographer, Diodorus Siculus the historian, and above all, in the priceless ethnography of Posidonius. Strabo said of the Celts, "They are madly fond of war, high spirited and quick to battle." No doubt the Yerni were much the same, and that is how they are depicted in this novel.

The last surviving stronghold of Celtic culture was that found by St. Patrick in fifth-century Ireland, a belated Indo-European culture of the Homeric and *Rig Veda* type, complete with chariot-riding, cattle-reiving, war-making and loud-boasting heroes whose chief virtues were courage and violence, and with an oral literature that praised such doings. Christian monks recorded this epic literature, including the *Táin Bó Cúalnge* (toin vo *ku*-ling-ee). The title means, "Cooley's Cattle Raid."

The warrior aristocracy and its deeds of raiding and fighting are the only fit subjects of literature in the *Táin*, as in Homer. Diodorus, in fact, when describing the habits of the Gaulish Celts at a feast, makes an explicit Homeric reference.

Beside them are hearths blazing with fire, with cauldrons and spits containing large pieces of meat. Brave warriors they honor with the finest portions of meat, just as Homer introduces Ajax, honored by the chieftains, when he conquered Hector in single combat: "He honored Ajax with the full-length chine."

Posidonius witnessed the same thing. What he describes, the Irish tales dramatize.

The Celts sometimes engage in single combat at dinner. Assembling in arms they engage in mock battle-drill, and mutual thrust-and-parry, but sometimes wounds are inflicted, and the irritation caused by this may lead even to the slaying of the opponent unless the bystanders hold them back. And in former times, when the hindquarters were served up the bravest hero took the thigh piece, and if another man claimed it they stood up and fought in single combat to the death.

In the Irish hero tales, the champion's portion is the *curadmir*, the best cut of the meat. It is literally a bone of contention. For who *is* the bravest hero present? In *Mac Datho's Pig*, one warrior after another claims the right to carve the pig at a feast; each man in turn yields to a rival after a dialogue of boasting and abuse. Finally the Connacht champion, Cet mac Mágach, is about to carve the roast after having put several Ulstermen to shame. Then Conall Cernach enters the hall, and there follows the very same scene that Posidonius witnessed a thousand years before in Gaul. What better testimony for the archaism of Irish tradition! In it, La Tène culture lives!

While he made ready for the pig and had his knife in his hand, they saw Conall the Victorious coming towards them into the house. And he sprang on to the floor of the house. The men of Ulster gave great welcome to Conall the Victorious at that time. It was then Conchobar threw his helmet from his head and shook himself in his own place. "We are pleased," said Conall, "that our portion is in readiness for us. Who carves for you?" said Conall.

"One man of the men of Ireland has obtained by contest the carving of it. Cet mac Matach."

"Is that true, O Cet?" said Conall. "Art thou carving the pig?"

"It is true indeed," said Cet. . . .

"Get up from the pig, O Cet!" said Conall.

"What brings thee to it?" said Cet.

"It is true," said Conall, "I will be the challenger. I will give you competition," said Conall, "for I swear what my people swear, since I first took spear and weapons, I have never been a day without having slain a Connachtman, or a night without plundering, nor have I ever slept without the head of a Connachtman under my knee."

"It is true," said Cet, "thou art even a better warrior than I; but if Anluan mac Máqach (my brother) were in the house, he would match thee contest for contest, and it is a shame that he is not in the house to-night."

"But he is," said Conall, taking Anluan's head out of his belt and throwing it at Cet's chest, so that a gush of blood broke over his lips. After that Conall sat down by the pig, and Cet went from it.

Mac Datho's Pig is one story from a body of heroic narratives, including the *Táin*, known collectively as the Ulster cycle. The point of reference in all of them is the king of Ulster, Conchobar, equivalent to the Myceanaean king Agamemnon in Homer. His champion is Cuchullain, the Irish Achilles. The Irish Trojans are the men of king Connacht, one of whom is Cet mac Mágach. The *Iliad* is in fact a good guide to the life of the Celts of Gaul and Ireland. Homer's Mycenae is essentially an Indo-European culture transplanted into a Mediterranean setting, but not an urban one. Cattle are a staple form of wealth, the aim of much fighting and raiding in the Ulster cycle; the measure of wealth in Homer, a captured set of armor is worth from nine to a hundred head of cattle, a prize well worth the risk of battle.

Perhaps the chief difference is that while the Ulster cycle delights just as much in court ceremonial as does Homer, Homer likes to depict ceremonies in progress, while the Irish bards prefer ceremonies in collapse. The most noble Irish heroes abandon their dignity to a youthful, rough-and-tumble melee despite the abundance of ritual niceties, especially in the feasting hall, the center of court life. Celtic feasts in Posidonius and the ancient Irish tales are peopled with swaggering, belching chieftains endowed with a strong arm and a big mouth, adored by an equally impossible following of adolescent gangsters, all hands twitching to the sword-hilt at the imagined insult, all greasy, mustachioed lips curling with snarled threats, boasts, and bombastic self-dramatization. Such may have been the rude barbarian builders of Stonehenge. Certainly the Irish tales are closer to them than Homer but we must also remember that Homer, no partisan of civic society, is just as much the celebrant of heroic society.

Coarser than belching and bombast in the novel is the Yerni practice of human sacrifice. Here too Celtic custom has been suggestive, and the most spectacular episode in Caesar's commentaries is his account of human sacrifice in Gaul.

> Some tribes build enormous images with limbs of interwoven branches which they fill with live men; the images are set alight and the men die in a sea of flame.

Strabo describes both stabbing and cremation as forms of human sacrifice.

> They used to stab a human being whom they had devoted to death, in the back with a dagger, and foretell the future from his convulsions. They offered their sacrifices not without a Druid. There are also other accounts of their human sacrifices; for they used to shoot men down with arrows; and impale them in their temples, or making a large statue of straw and wood, throw into it cattle and all sorts of wild animals and human beings, and thus make a burnt offering.

This holocaust, whose victims were war captives, recalls various Irish stories in which houses are burned down around the victims of a blood feud. In one case the sacrifice is interrupted by the appearance of a supernatural woman leading a cow which she directs to be offered in substitution. The story has a parallel in

319

the Aryan traditions of India, where in time human sacrifice had been abandoned for animal surrogates, but not among the Irish branch of Indo-European culture. Caesar himself found nothing extraordinary in the real thing among the Celts. For him, Gaul had merely retained the archaic practice of human sacrifice once at home in his native Italy until the first century B.C., although he could not know that Indo-European warriors had introduced it there at the time of their much earlier invasion. Upon that the Roman state arose.

Yerni headhunting also has its Celtic model. Here is an account by Diodorus of the Gauls in battle:

> For their journeys and in battle they use two-horse chariots, the chariot carrying both charioteer and chieftan. When they meet with cavalry in the battle they cast their javelins at the enemy and then descending from the chariot join battle with their swords. Some of them so far despise death that they descend to do battle, unclothed except for a girdle. When the armies are drawn up in battle array they are wont to advance before the battle line and to challenge the bravest of their opponents to single combat, at the same time brandishing before them their arms to terrify their foe. And when someone accepts their challenge to battle, they loudly recite the deeds of valor of their ancestors and proclaim their own valorous quality, at the same time abusing and making little of their opponent and generally attempting to rob him beforehand of fighting spirit. They cut off the heads of their enemies slain in battle and attach them to the necks of their horses. The blood-stained spoils they hand over to shield-bearers and carry off as booty, while striking up a paean and singing a song of victory, and they nail up these first fruits upon their houses just as they do those of wild animals they lay low in hunting.

The match between this and episodes in the Irish sagas is perfect. The warriors of the *Táin Bó Cúalnge* go into battle in chariots, and the challenge to single combat is as central there as it is in the *Iliad*. The hero Cuchullain in his two-horse chariot, with his charioteer Láeg, and armed with shield, spear and sword, is a Celtic warrior right out of Posidonius.

The custom of headhunting appears again in Strabo, who sees it as

> a trait of barbarous savagery which is especially peculiar to the northern peoples, for when they are leaving the battle-field they fasten to the necks of their horses the heads of their enemies, and on arriving home they nail up this spectacle at the entrances to their houses.

Celtic society is a heroic society of aristocratic chiefdoms; warfare is its business and severed heads, a dominant theme in Celtic art, are trophies won in that business. So too in the Irish epics.

If in the light of archaeology, classical histories, and Indo-European epic literature we rightly interpret the Celts of La Tène Ireland, they reveal the cultural landscape of Bronze Age Britain in 1500 B.C. at the time the proto-Celtic Yerni built Stonehenge. La Tène culture died out in Gaul at the beginning of the Christian era, and in Britain at the end of the first century A.D. The Irish La Tène is of Gaulish origin, and it would have died out in about A.D. 150 had the Roman conquest extended far enough. It didn't. Rome never came to Ireland, at least not with legions. La Tène, the last archaeological horizon of the pre-Roman Iron Age, lived on there in isolation as the oldest surviving relic of Celtic culture, to be discovered by St. Patrick in the fifth century A.D.

Then Rome came to Ireland with monks, who later recorded a heroic literature whose bardic transmitters had drawn on an oral tradition going as far back as the Irish adoption of La Tène culture in the fourth century B.C. The Celts themselves first emerged as a separate people in Western Europe as soon as the Battle-Ax folk arrived and set up their chiefdoms there, their cow-chiefs winning sovereignty over the local Neolithic farmers. On the way, they picked up a knowledge of bronze from metallurgists in Croatia who, like those in the Caucasus, long had made a living by trading their goods with the Near Eastern civic societies. Thus the European Bronze Age begins with the emergence of the proto-Celts, although metal goods at this time are quite rare (the

Yerni wear their bronze daggers as jewelry) and the chosen weapon, favored by sentiment and tradition, is the stone battle-ax. Not long before 1500 B.C. these newly formed Celts enter southern Britain, and dominate the local farmers (the Neolithic Donbaksho of the novel); and their monument to chiefly power is the Stonehenge whose ruins we see today. Pre-Christian Ireland, in the Iron Age condition remembered by the bards, is only little more than 1,000 years later than that, not a long time in the history of conservative cultural traditions. Remember that the distance between Posidonius and the Irish epics is even less. We have only to subtract Iron Age technology from the Irish tales to find the social and political condition of the proto-Celts. In the Ulster cycle both Conall and Cuchullain use iron swords; and one or two references to the ogham alphabet, devised under distant Roman influence, occur. But Irish heroes still ride war chariots, not horses, chariots like those Bronze Age weapons described by Homer for Mycenaean times. Take away iron swords, and the Irish hero tales describe the doings of Bronze Age warriors. Take away more, the chariots, and what is left is barbarian Europe of the Bronze Age, the very condition of proto-Celtic chiefdoms in the Wessex district of southern Britain at the time the Yerni built Stonehenge.

Furthermore, as remarked earlier, Stonehenge is located at the center of an immense cemetery. Here in single grave mounds are buried the warrior heroes of Stonehenge society, laid to rest with their stone battle-axes, bronze daggers, beer jars and looted finery. The location itself tells us the function of the monument, that it was a tribal assembly place, as we may deduce from the example of the classical Celts, whose assemblies of chiefs and warriors invariably met in cemeteries. Assemblies among the pre-Christian Irish, we know from the hero tales and Christian law-tracts formulating ancient custom, merged with periodic fairs where chiefs proclaimed laws and poets praised chiefs, and where all freemen were attracted by a periodic market as well as by sports events, including horse racing. These open-air gatherings, appropriate to a nonurban people, were often held in the midst of ancient tumuli, or near sacred well shafts into which severed heads were thrown.

There is no difficulty whatsoever in reading back into the proto-Celtic culture of the Wessex warriors gatherings of like purpose, during which new chiefs were selected when the old were superannuated or killed in battle. Indo-European traditions everywhere have it that the king or chief is elected from a council of nobility of which he is a kinsman. In the oldest substrate of the ancient Brehon Laws of Ireland the range of kinsmen for this purpose included four generations—so much more cause for contention! Genealogical reckoning is important to the validation of leadership, the one indispensable subject of any oral tradition in aristocratic chiefdoms for which there must be a specialist occupation. The Druids of Gaul were carriers of this role, ancient by the time of Caesar, as he himself remarks. They were also responsible for computing the rota of annual festivals and assemblies for a ritual calendar. The old tribal round of life among the Wessex warriors, called Yerni here, may very well have its echo in the ritual year of the classical Celts.

The two main seasons reckoned by the Celts were the cold and the warm, marked at their outset by Samain (pronounced sahwin) and Beltine. Beltine is a pastoralist festival, starting the summer season when cattle are driven from winter quarters into open grazing. On our calendar it is the first of May, but the Celts marked it on the preceding night. Relics of the Celtic way of counting nights and not days have survived in our use of the terms "fortnight" and "senight" and in our Christmas Eve, New Year's Eve, and Allhallow's Eve. Beltine means "Bel's Fire," after one of the oldest of the Celtic gods, Belenus, known throughout the continent, but it is in Cormac's *Glossary* that the chief events of Beltine are recorded. Cormac is the ninth-century Archbishop of Ireland, who glossed the meaning of obsolete words in Gaelic. Cattle on their way to summer grazing grounds, and men as well, are driven between two fires kindled close together by Druids, who pronounce the purpose as a preservative against disease for the coming year. Other fires were kindled during Samain for sacrificial purposes, with children and beasts as victims, if Cormac can be believed. If so, it would not be fantastic to recall the holocaust of men and cattle in burning wicker figures described by Caesar and Strabo.

Two other Irish seasonal festivals are Imbolc (first of February) and Lugnasad (first of August). Imbolc corresponds with the Feast of Saint Brigit on the Christian calendar, whose name is cognate with the Sanskrit *Bhrati*, "the exalted one," another example of cultural continuity over the whole Indo-European domain, from Aryan India to pagan Ireland. Imbolc means sheep's milk, and thus is the name for the lambing season when the ewes begin to lactate. Lugnasad means feast of Lug, a god associated with ripening crops, and not with a pastoralist economy in the midst of transhumance, which is when his feast date falls. The festival is obviously an imported one of later agrarian settlers to Ireland. Lug is well known as the name behind Lyons and other continental towns.

The most outstanding of the truly archaic festivals is Samain, the reassembly or gathering of the tribe at the end of the grazing season. In pre-Christian Ireland, the regular annual assembly was the *oenach*. This was the chief event of Samain, the autumnal reuniting of the *tuath*, or tribe. The *Book of the Dun Cow*, part of the Ulster cycle, says the *oenach* was

> that period of time which the Ultonians devoted to the holding of the fair of Samain in the plain of Murthemne every year; and nothing whatever was done by them during that time but games and races, pleasure and amusement, eating and feasting.

These fairs were attended by people from various clans within a tribe and sometimes by people from different tribes, their eternal wars with each other held in suspension by a sacred armistice or "sword truce," as in the Olympic and Isthmian games of Greece. If the fairs of ancient Ireland serve as historical memories of an Indo-European tradition of which the Wessex culture is a part, tribal forums held at Stonehenge would include not only feasting and sporting events, but marketing. Feasting, of course, would be part of the autumnal cattle round up, but marketing would play an emphatic role, given the position of Stonehenge at the crossroads of important prehistoric trade routes; it is common-place in the anthropological study of primitive economics to find trade located within a wider social, often festive, context than in the case of our own specialized marketing practices. Moreover, the building of the structure itself, season by season, would con-stitute yet one more of those festive activities. The whole affair would be held under the direction of a strong-armed, drunken, beer-drinking, beef-eating battle leader, his authority given supernatural sanction by the Druids, drawing on the ancestral spirits of the war dead in their grave mounds of assembly all around. This is evident from the old Irish word *oenach* itself. It means first of all "a reunion" (hence a popular assembly or gathering), but also "a burial ground," that is, the place where an assembly is held. To ignore the fact that Stonehenge is built in the midst of a vast burial ground, in which generations of warrior herdsmen and chieftains are interred, with their weapons and stolen treasure, is to dissociate that monument from the most important feature of its setting. Much loose speculation has resulted.

V

Therefore, what we know of the Celts, and of barbarian Europe south of the Alps in Homer, tells us that Stonehenge is nothing if not a monument to heroic society. It cannot be an astronomical observatory, as Gerald Hawkins has it in his 1965 work, *Stonehenge Decoded*, for calculating summer and winter solstices and for predicting eclipses; this is to project Babylonian concerns of the fourth century B.C. and onward into the very archaic past, not to say our own scientific ones.

Besides, the pastoralists of early Europe looked to the ground for important signs, the change in the grass for their cattle with the onset of winter and the onset of spring, Samain and Beltane on the Celtic calendar, Halloween and May Day on ours. Samain marked the pagan new year, the turn to autumn when the Celts brought home their cows to keep those they could winter on forage, and to slaughter and feast on those they could not. That carnival (when the souls of the dead also came home) was Christianized as Allhallow's Eve in Charlemagne's Europe about A.D. 813. New Year's Eve had by then already gone over to an event of midwinter on 1 January, following the Roman example, fixed astronomically in keeping with a state-regulated agricultural calendar adopted from the days of Rome's earliest civil existence. In light of this difference between the civilized and the barbarian societies of old, we are permitted to think of the pastoral Yerni as having their assembly time on Halloween, and so it would have been for the grand gathering of warriors from the five different Yerni chiefdoms at Stonehenge.

The established Mycenaean connection only gives us an opportunity to dramatize it in the person of Ason, who sees to the building of Stonehenge as a means of confederating the Yerni—to give their warring chiefdoms a political center and common assembly place, and thus deflect them from their competitive raids on his father's tin mine to the west in Cornwall. It was an act of heroism in the war between Mycenae and Atlantis, but the outcome was finally decided by the blowup of Thera. Uncompleted, Stonehenge fell into the ruins we see today.

VI

What ruins they are! They are the second most popular attraction in all of Great Britain, after the Tower of London, visited by nearly 1,000,000 tourists a year. Actually, this has being going on with increasing numbers ever since the eighteenth century, when in 1740 William Stuckeley they antiquarian published *Stonehenge, A Temple Restor'd to the British Druids*. This is the book that not only first popularized the monument, it imprinted Druids indelibly on the British national consciousness. Stuckeley of course meant the Druids of Celtin Britain that Caesar described, not the Ancient Order of Druids he inspired with his writings. With no justification they seized on the white robes and the rites of nineteenth-century Freemasonry, and may still be found parading about the place i midsummer (the same time of year that fascinates the manic astronomers). For some reason, in order to discredit these mock Druids, it is quite the intellectual fashion to dismiss the *real* Druids as having anything to do with Stonehenge. Stuckeley, of course, had no idea how old the monument really is, but he had a shrewd insight into the nature of the society that built it, one in which shaman-like priests, or Druids, served the political order of a warrior society. And although he stressed "temple" where we stress "forum" or a kind of parliament, it is clear that if priests and warriors held joint sovereignty over a producing class in Celtic times, the same must have held in proto-Celtic times. If there were Bronze Age warriors at Stonehenge, and they are buried all about with their battle-axes, then there must have been Bronze Age Druids to go with them. That's the pattern of the layered societies of the Indo-European chiefdoms from India to Ireland, Brahmins in Aryan India, Druids in Celtic Europe. The social structure Caesar described in Gaul is the same one reflected in the Irish hero tales, which again is the same for the Punjab district of India at the time of the Aryan invasion. This latter is reflected in the hymns of the *Rig Veda,* which celebrates the Aryan conquest at the very moment the last phase of Stonehenge was erected. Thus Druidic priests, warriors, and Neolithic husbandmen make up the social order of chiefdoms everywhere in the Indo-European domain. To summarize:

	Aryan India	Celtic Gaul	Celtic Ireland
Priests	*Brahmana*	*druides*	*drui*
Warriors	*Kshatriya*	*equites*	*ri*
Producers	*Vaishva*	*plebs*	*aire*

What is more, the word for Druidic wisdom and knowledge is cognate in all three languages, Sanskrit, Gaulish and Old Irish.

The Sanskrit word *veda,* as in the title of the Vedic hymns, means "knowledge," or rather, to be literal, it means "vision" or "sight" and is related to the Gaulish and Irish words for wiseman or Druid.

The *Rig Veda* is the most sacred book of Hinduism, finally recorded by British colonials in the early 1800s, after centuries of oral transmission from the date of composition by the Aryan invaders of Northwest India, wreckers of the Harappan civilization. The book's language is Sanskrit, dead for all but the Brahmins, who conserve it in recitation as well as (lately) in scripture. They are the praise poets or druids of the Aryan tradition, still singing the glories of warrior heroes come to the Punjab, now gods. The *Rig Veda* is, in fact, a compilation of 1,028 poems in praise of various deities, chief of whom is Indra, the same chariot-riding, bolt-hurling thunder god who is Jupiter with the Romans, Zeus with the Greeks, and Thor with the Scandinavians. Indra is the apotheosis of the Indo-European warrior chieftain. "He sweeps away, like birds, the foe's possessions." It is "He under whose supreme control are horses, all chariots, and the villages, and cattle." Above all, he is a "city destroyer," as is Odysseus, who bears a special title of honor, *ptoliporthos*, "Sacker of Cities." Indra hurls thunderbolts in his divine moments, otherwise fights with bow and arrow from a chariot.

> With all-outstripping chariot-wheel,
>   O Indra, though far-famed, hast overthrown
>   the twice ten kings of men
> With sixty thousand nine and ninety followers.
> Thou goest on from fight to fight intrepidly,
>   destroying citadel after citadel with strength.

Rig in Sanskrit means "laudatory stanzas," and *veda* means "knowledge," cognate with English "wit," which, at bottom, comes from the Indo-European root for "to see." It is therefore cognate also with *video*. The word for what we see on TV springs from the same root that names the sacred lore of the Hindu Brahmins, and that names the Celtic Druids as well.

Celtic wisemen were tagged by Caesar after the plural form of their self-name in Gaulish, *druides*, that is, they who see three times. The derivation is *id* or *wid* ("vision" or "wise") with an intensifying prefix *dri* or *tri* ("three"), hence "thrice wise," and the same with Gaelic *drui*. The number three, as a matter of fact, is an intensifier in all Indo-European languages, as in French "*tres*" and in English "terrific."

The power of three is vested in the divine triads of the major Indo-European divinities, such as Brahma, Siva, and Vishnu in the Hindu tradition; Zeus, Poseidon and Pluto (or Hades) in the Greek. They stand for a set of universal principles governing sky, earth and underworld; those of creation, destruction and preservation. The trilithons at Stonehenge may have symbolized the same cosmic principles, one for each stone. Such meaning would have been assigned to them by the class of Druids associated with the Wessex warriors, whose political monument

Stonehenge is, in accord with the religious overtones of its architecture, it being the centerpiece of a well-planned necropolis.

The doings of our novelized Druid, called Nemed, is altogether in keeping with his classical counterparts. The function of Druids, and Brahmins, in heroic society is to legitimate the political authority of the warriors over the producing class, to preserve the genealogies of the chiefs, if not sing their glories, to sanctify the tribal assembly place, to keep the ritual calendar, and conduct sacrifices and read omens. That Druidical rites in La Tène Europe called for human victims, killed by stabbing and holocaust, is well attested by Posidonius, a fact that today's mock Druids and their romantic apologists squeamishly avoid.

The novelized warriors, the Yerni, are no less authentic. That is to say, they are cast as warrior heroes, not as soldier warriors. In the epic literature, heroes are likened to wild beasts. Cuchullain is "the hound of gore." Homer's warriors are "ravening lions" and "jackals." Indeed, the heroes themselves take for a long self-image what they believe to be some outstanding attribute of ferocity in wild animals. The physical description of the Gauls by Posidonius is instructive. Posidonius writes:

> The Gauls are tall in stature and their flesh is very moist and white, while their hair is not only naturally blond, but they also use artificial means to increase this natural quality of color. For they continually wash their hair with limewash and draw it back from the forehead to the crown and to the nape of the neck, with the result that their appearance resembles that of Satyrs or of Pans, for the hair is so thickened by this treatment that it differs in no way from a horse's mane. Some shave off the beard, while others cultivate a short beard; the nobles shave the cheeks but let the moustache grow freely so that it covers the mouth. And so when they are eating the moustache becomes entangled in the food, and when they are drinking the drink passes, as it were, through a sort of strainer.

La Téne art commonly features the upturned Celtic moustache and backswept hair style, stiffened, no doubt, by lime as Posidonius reports. Cuchullain's hair is said to be three-colored and standing up rigid, so that apples falling from trees are impaled on its spiky points. This description matches exactly the limed hair of the Celtic warrior. It is worth passing notice that the eyes of warriors in La Tène sculpture are portrayed large and bulging. Perhaps they are the eyes of a pastoralist, gazing upon far horizons, like those of "far-seeing Zeus" in Homer's words.

The Celtic moustache in La Tène art is modeled in shape after the tusks of the wild boar. This would not be the first culture to use the symbolism of the hunt as an index of valor in war. The lion, the bear, and the eagle still have their place in the heraldry of all western nations. Hunting, the sport of kings, is little fun against animals of no dangerous challenge. Odysseus was wounded on Mount Parnassus while hunting the wild boar, gored in the thigh. Boar's tusk helmets are mentioned in the *Odyssey*, and fragments have been found buried in several Mycenaean sites. Roman legionaries wore helmets topped with a crest of bristles made of horsehair, but the only animal with a standing mane the helmets could have imitated is not the horse but the wild boar. The two distinctive features of that animal in Celtic scupture are its high mane and its long, curved tusks. The long, curved moustaches for which the Celtic warrior is famous, not to mention his swept up head hair, is evidentaly intended as an ensign and battle emblem of the boar.

The difference between the Celtic moustache and the Roman helmet is that the former is a growth of the warrior's own body and the latter is an attachment taken from the body of the animal symbolized. The moustache is consistent with an oral culture, the helmet with a literate one. In a culture that lacks the written word, the only word is the spoken word, the only memory is un-written memory, as recorded in body decoration. The human body, with its boar-toothed moustache and boar-bristled hair, is made to stand for something else, as a symbol; that is, as a reminder and emblem of the tribe's militant ferocity. The boar-maned helmet of the Roman soldier is government issued equip-ment, symbolizing the mission of an organized army of the state, to which the heroics of the individual warrior are deracinated for systematic butchery of the enemy by the numbers. When Roman helmet met warrior's mask, trophies of severed heads yielded to captured real estate; warfare as the personal achievement of prestige and wealth through killing and looting was swamped by the legions of Caesar, who fought in the name of territorial annexation. Feud and foray is for warriors, conquest for soldiers.

At all events, only warriors in Celtic society were allowed to wear the moustache. The Druids were required to shave it off but grew beards. Today's mock Druids, wearing both (usually false), have got it wrong. Wrong, too, is the snobbery that refuses to see proper Druids associated with Stonehenge. They go with the package in proto-Celtic as in Celtic society.

VII

Visitors to Stonehenge come to see only what in the novel Inteb built, the trilithons and the sarsen ring. But these big stones constitute but the final phase of the monument, known as Stonehenge III, dated (once again) to 1500 B.C. on a site whose building activity actually begins 900 years earlier. Before concluding this Afterword, some mention of that history cannot be omitted.

The original inhabitants of Britain were food collectors of the hunting and gathering type, living in forests that covered the entire land. Sometime in the fourth millenium the food producing revolution arrived in the form of Neolithic migrants from across the Channel. They made clearings in the forest for their fields, their browsing cattle causing further erosion of the tree cover, producing the open downs we see today. The result for the first farmers was that their Neolithic mixed economy took on a pastoral bias, leaving little room for the hunting and gathering aboriginals, but they survived right on down to the time of Stonehenge III, and are the novel's Hunters. Their mobility and their knowledge of trails in the back-woods gave them a new lease on life as traders, dealing not only in forest products but in jadite for axheads and in Irish gold and bronze.

Meanwhile the emergent pastoralists, known as the Windmill Hill folk, were building earthworks of a type called causewayed camps. These are located on the tops of modest hills (the type site is Windmill Hill) and are formed of two or three concentric ditches interrupted by a number of causeways. They seemed to have been gathering places for isolated homesteaders during the autumnal cattle round up, and thus the Samain holiday we have as Halloween may be older than Celtic and proto-Celtic tradition, making it easy for the coming invasion of Battle-Ax warriors to fit into the local landscape. Before that happened, however, the Windmill Hill folk reduced the complexity of their causewayed camps and built them on lower ground as a single encircling ditch and bank with only one causeway leading into the interior. These are known as henges, Stonehenge being the most notable of many for the sarsen structure within it.

Stonehenge I is a mere earthwork of this sort, to which the Windmill Hill builders added the Aubrey Holes (they are cinerary pits) and the Heelstone, and started the custom of interring their dead in the vicinity under barrows. In this case they are long barrows, containing family or clan burials, the round barrows of the single dead coming with the heroes.

The first heroes were the Beaker folk, about 800 years later, and it was they who made the additions we know as Stonehenge II. The Beakers (named after the large beer jars buried with them and their bronze daggers and archery sets) are the Battle-Ax folk in their western European expression, after having picked up the technology of metal working from artisans in Croatia, who specialized in it strictly for trade. Henceforth the Beakers continued their westward migrations with their own smiths in their employ. They moved not only into Britain but onward through the Iberian Peninsula to the Atlantic coast, with some doubling back in a reflux movement. In Iberia they seem to have run into another group of metallurgists, or so one theory goes, and we have tried to accommodate it, as it is the only one that explains the presence of the bronze workers in Ireland with whom the Hunters trade in supplying that metal and gold as well to the Yerni in Wessex (who get metal goods also in direct trade with the Geramani from Únêtice). This metal working population slowly crept up the Atlantic coast of Europe, starting with a primitive copper technology, then sailed on up to Ireland, the novel's Domnann. They were traders and prospectors, originating somewhere in the Mediterranean area with distant Mycenaean connections, before they settled down in alien lands. Their tombs, huge upended boulders capped with massive slabs of undressed stone called dolmens, are the only mark of their passing. But in Domnann, they reinvented bronze.

The island on which Ason is wrecked is covered with their dolmens. Known as the Scilly Islands, it is today not one island but several, now the sea level is higher. The tomb builders, the Albi of the novel, lived in what is now Cornwall and Devon, site of the remote tin streams the fictional King Perimedes was forced by his war with Atlantis to exploit. Uncle Lycos, in search of tin for Mycenae, had only to prospect the Albi copper mines; the two metals are at times found in association.

At all events, the Beakers at Stonehenge erected an almost complete double circle of bluestones (which may or may not have been hauled from Mt. Prescelly in Wales—this matter is hotly disputed by geologists), and the people they dominated were the Neolithic and pastorally inclined farmers of the Windmill Hill culture, whose remnants are the Donbaksho—the deracinated builders of Stonehenge I. This, about 100 years later, is the setting of Ason's arrival. Beaker culture had flourished and evolved into that of the Wessex culture, which is associated with the dismantling of Stonehenge II and the erection of Stonehenge III, with the monumental sarsen stones (of strictly local origin) we see there today. Both Beaker and Wessex warriors are buried in the surrounding round barrows. This cemetery is as much a part of the monument as its standing stones.

VIII

In fact, the stones themselves and their arrangement take on a funerary symbolism quite in keeping with their situation at the center of this huge burial ground. It by no means follows, however, that Stonehenge is the temple of a mortuary cult. The sepulchral features of the trilithons in particular, borrowed from the interior design of the surrounding tombs, may just as well sanctify an open-air setting for tribal politics. Think of Christian churches as a setting for the coronation of kings. Bishops and kings, Druids and cow-chiefs—the pattern of relationship is continuous in western culture. A monument belonging to the sepulchral class, in terms of architecture, may come to represent the war-and treaty-making powers of chieftainship; political authority is backed up with supernatural values with the aid of religious experts, the Druids, by way of their tomb-side tendance of the dead and everything else of cosmic and otherworldly significance. Hence the funerary architecture of the trilithons, associated with a cult of the dead, in a political monument.

Trilithon—a structure consisting of two pillars and a lintel across the space between them, named by William Stuckely, five of which stand within the sarsen ring at the center of Stonehenge. They may represent a triad of cosmic principles, as remarked before, the power of three in the Indo-European gods of creation, destruction and possession. Indo-European chiefdoms from India to Europe were layered in terms of priests, warriors and peasant producers, and their wisemen everywhere invented departmental gods to express the social reality of these different strata, thus explaining society to itself and making it work. In Aryan India, the god of the Druidic priests (who formulated and taught this explanation) was Brahma, that of the warriors was Siva, and that of the producers was Vishu. Brahma the creator, Siva the destroyer, and Vishnu (the one female deity in this triad) the sexual possessor. In the mythology of northern Europe they are Odin, Thor and Freya. In all these and other cases they represent wisdom, force, and wealth: the instructive wisdom of the priests (Brahmins or Druids), the destructive force of the warriors, and the erotic fertility of wealth in possession of the Neolithic peasant's plants and animals. Long after the Indo-European chiefdoms disappeared as actual social structures, the gods remained as mythical ideals, as in the Medieval social idea of the three estates, clerics, knights, and people.

At all events, the mythology is very ancient as a means of analyzing and understanding the cosmos at large, and so it must have been at Stonehenge. There, in one of the heroic round barrows, has been found a chief's mace of authority in the stylized form of a battle-ax, its head of rare and precious stone, its wooden handle (now rotted away) adorned with rings of bone cut jaggedwise as if they were motifs of the lightning flash. Thor's hammer! Battle-axes long have had specific gods attributed to them in all branches of Indo-European mythology, the god of thunder is himself a warrior. He is known by many names: Thor, Donar, Jupiter, Tauranos (the Celtic Zeus), Teshub (the weather god of the Hittites), and Indra. The famous hammer of Thor, called Mjollnir, representing the destructive power of the heavens, thunder and lightning, is nothing if not a mythic transformation of the battle-ax. Such is the cosmic connection of the Wessex warriors, mediated by their Druids.

So much for the sky, but the underworld too is a Druidic concern. At Stonehenge, structures exactly like the trilithons, only smaller and with a wider doorway, occur inside the long barrows as transept entrances, that is, as gateways to collective burial chambers leading off from a main gallery (there being only one such chamber underneath the round barrows with their single burials). The most notable nearby sepulture of this construction using large stones, called a megalithic tomb, is the West Kennet long barrow. It is a five-chambered cairn, with rooms behind its five transepts or trilithon-shaped doorways, for the burial of five different family or clan groups. It is a tomb of Neolithic time, and was as central to the Wessex region then as Stonehenge III later came to be. The five trilithons there seem to indicate a similar kind of social organization. Megalithic tombs all over the British Isles mark out social territories, enforcing claims to the land by supernatural means. The barrows are more than tombs for the dead, they are spatial guides for the living. At their forecourts is the garbage of annual feasting, no doubt done at Samain and all that implies. If Irish folklore allows that spirited fairy folk live in these mounds, it is a memory of jolly picnics that also worked as ghostly warnings in the defense of hallowed tribal lands. The big cemetery at Stonehenge, however, tells more. Evidently it was the focus of intertribal alliances over a wider region, for other than local dignitaries are buried there, the artistic details of the grave furniture are traceable to five different regions. The five trilithons are the outward signs of the same political geography. The archways leading into the different chambers of the megalithic tomb have been magnified and placed outside; the trilithons are stylized transepts, representing the five dynastic cow-chiefs who met in council to do their intertribal business at Stonehenge, a parliament of heroes. Each chief stood in front of his respective portal, speaking for the full force of his lineage, and with the living memory of his ancestors behind it, as it were, spoken for by his genealogy-reciting Druid.

This picture leaps to the imagination soon as one looks at the map. In addition to Stonehenge, four other major cemeteries are located in the Wessex district, five in all. Each is associated with a megalithic assembly place. From north to south they are Lambourn on Berkshire Downs, at Avebury on Marlborough Downs, at Stonehenge on the Salisbury Plain (the biggest cattle grazing area of them all), at Cranborne Chase at Oakley Downs in Dorset, and at Dorchester, also in Dorset. These places correspond to our five Yerni chiefdoms, those of Dun Maclorbi, Dun Finmog, Dun Uala (later Dun Ason), Dun Moweg and Dun Der Dak.

Five trilithons, five cemeteries. One trilithon, at the heel of the horseshoe-shaped layout, is bigger and taller than the other four; and the Stonehenge cemetery is bigger than the others. Great archways, which once led to burial rooms within the chambered tombs of different kinship units, now lead outward to chiefly families united by tribal alliances and by a common cemetery on the quasi-dynastic burial grounds of the dominant partner. Regional burial groups, with distinctive grave goods from each locality, show this clearly.

These relationships suggest that the five trilithons in some way stand for rival powers over the five ancient grazing areas of southern Britain, brought together for a "sword truce" (the phrase occurs in the Irish epics) under the influence of one preeminent war leader. In the novel, that forceful person is Ason, doing his father's business in the war with Atlantis. But he takes on the task, inserting himself into local squabbles, by way of using the local religious ideology for the sake of political unity. His architect, Inteb, understands the meaning of the wooden structures the Yerni call "henges," wooden trilithons their Druids have erected to shelter the war speeches of their chiefs. Such a thing is quite permissible to imagine, because the stone trilithons we know are constructed on the principles of carpentry, with tenons on top of the pillars and mortise holes cut in the underside of the lintels. This is a wood working technique transferred to stone, and the explanation for this oddity is that the transepts of megalithic tombs were once made this wooden way before the use of stone was tried, and were later where stone was scarce.

To put the matter in the language of ancient Ireland, as ever a vital comparision, one "overking" at Stonehenge must have held hegemony over four "underkings." In Irish mythology, five has both a scared and a political meaning. The number is related to the fivefold division of Ireland, its four quarters and its *axis mundi*, turning where the central authority sits. Perhaps the doorways in the sarsen ring at Stonehenge represent the portals of lesser warbands, allied to the Big Five, drawn in from the periphery to join a consolidated forum as the Stonehenge project proceeded, season after season.

While one may only speculate on the parliamentary function of Stonehenge, it is less difficult to guess at the symbolic meaning of the spatial layout of the trilithons themselves. The five of them are arrayed, to the modern eye, in the shape of a horseshoe. This is a significant perception. The horseshoe, in popular superstition, is a good luck charm to be nailed up over the barn door, and as such it is the heritage of Indo-European pastoral society. The horseshoe acquired its good luck symbolism precisely from its resemblance to the upcurved horns of the bull; and the custom of nailing up an upside-down iron horseshoe is a substitute for mounting the horns of a steer, still a custom where they are available. The Celts wore an ornamental set of horns around the neck in the form of a golden torc, which to our eyes looks like a golden horseshoe. The horseshoe-shaped array of trilithons, then, is a symbolic set of cattle horns.

The remains of both horns and hooves have been found at some Neolithic long barrows around Stonehenge. The possibility that heads or even stuffed carcasses were set up atop them is something to consider. According to Herodotus, the grave mounds of Scythian kings were surmounted with stuffed horses. This in the Indo-European homeland where the horse was first domesticated (but at a much later time than were sheep, goats, pigs and above all, cattle, by Neolithic settlers elsewhere).

The horse was a widespread game animal in the Pleistocene, in post-glacial times it was largely restricted to the Eurasian steppes. The Battle-Ax folk trained it not for riding but for pulling wagons and war chariots. The one was used to haul the goods the chiefs captured with the aid of the other. Mounted warriors and knights did not appear until a new breed of horse of sufficient strength had been bred in late Roman times. Its use for commercial draft and plow agriculture came even later. In the novel, the Yerni still *hunt* horses, as the domesticated variety had not yet entered Britain with the Beaker folk.

All the same, admiration for the horse by Europeans has outlasted that for cattle. A man of honor at long last was not a cow-chief, but a "horseman," that is, a *cavalier*, a *chevalier*, a *ritter*, a *caballero*. And with the advent of the automobile, the honor object has been switched from horse to car, pastoral mobility on wheels. Yet before the horse, the honor object was the cow. The heroic aristocracy of the Indo-European chiefdoms we know so well in Homer owes its wealth to cattle in a tradition as old as the original Battle-Ax people, in whose undivided language before the migration *pecunius* means holding property in cows; the word for "war-band" means a horde seeking cows, the root word for "protection" means to guard cows, and the title of the chief is "cow-chief," from whom the measure of hospitality is the slaying of cows for guests.

All of the above is by way of advising the reader to restrain from laughing when we depict stuffed cows atop the trilithons at Stonehenge. Our Yerni are not foolish. The picture makes a lot of sense, when you come to think about it historically. Already noted are the cattle horns and hooves found on the upper surfaces of the long barrows in the Stonehenge necropolis and elsewhere. The masses of ox bones found at the forecourts of these same barrows may suggest that the animals slaughtered there served as more than a carnival for the living. In Celtic mythology, the afterworld is a Land of Promise; it is Moi Mell, where the dead warrior will feast upon unlimited herds of beef; not to say drink from ever-full pots of beer. It's always Miller Time in the Moi Mell. If Stonehenge is an open-air tomb, in terms of architecture, we might very well expect it to be adorned with cattle emblems, whole carcasses or perhaps only horns. These would have been fixed to wooden dowels set three inches deep into the lintel tops of the sarsen ring, holes recently discovered—although the astronomers prefer to see them as holders for celestially aligned sighting wands. We prefer to see them as holders for bovine esoterica, perhaps even gilded horns or copper-sheathed replicas.

Symbolic cattle horns are traceable all the way back to the European Neolithic at its widest extent. The most famous example is the horn motif in the decoration of Cretan palace buildings, repeated end to end along the edge of every rooftop like so many golden crenelations. The palace culture of the Cretans or Minoans is a non-Indo-European evolution out of the same Neolithic base, and so again, nothing is invented here in the picture of Atlantean architecture.

Still we might ask, what is the intellectual *content* of this bovine symbolism? The answer can be found in Democritus, in his explanation of how horns grow on animals. Behind this ancient work of natural history lie beliefs and assumptions about the natural world even more ancient. Horns, Democritus believes, grow out of the head because the life-substance of the body is drawn to the head and the brains; what grows out of the head is an issuance of whatever is within the head, an out-cropping of the life-substance. Horns grow forth, watered by the same body moistures that are lost at death, and which are supplied to the "the dry ones" (a Homeric reference to the dead) by means of libations. Horns, then, are outcroppings of the stuff of life that is concentrated in the brain. In the Indo-European languages, the words for horn and brain are cognate (*cornu* and *cerebrum*, for example). The horn of plenty, detached from the head and which supplies the Celtic otherworld with beef and beer, is another embodiment of the same procreative and re-generative power that causes the growth of horn in the first place.

The symbolic set of cattle horns built into the horseshoe array of trilithons at Stonehenge is most appropriate for a meeting place where the cow-chiefs of different war bands assemble to deliberate alliances and then celebrate them once formed. Cows are an important possession, the object of raiding and a measure of wealth. What could be more important to the heroes of a pastoral society than control over cattle? And what symbol more fitting than the *horns* of cattle, the very outgrowth of power and the life-substance itself? Warriors want booty and expect their chief to lead them to it; the *Rig Veda* verily howls with their "resolve to win a cow, to win a steed." What are they to do when their battle leader wants instead to form alliances and not make eternal war on each other? What is the sport in that? Where the loot? This was Ason's problem when he took over Dun Uala. He had his architect, Inteb, build the trilithons, symbolic gateways to the nether world of Moi Mell. Each chief in tribal forum, standing before his own, thus won the supernatural clout (with the added promise of chiefly largess in *this* world, drinking and feasting) to bring his contentious warriors into line. Now the chiefs themselves were to follow an "overking," the Prince of Mycenae, whose own ambition was to keep the Yerni off his father's back. In that he manipulated the local culture in a way whose result is the tourist attraction we know as Stonehenge. That it was never completed is an indication of how fluid was the political nature of chiefdoms, how shifting the tribal alliances in a warrior society on the very rim of the Homeric world.

IX

Just as the unavoidable violence was essential to tell a realistic story of this period, so is it necessary to avoid any reference to astronomical theories and other unacceptable explanations for the construction of Stonehenge. To even consider an astronomical explanation is to be ignorant of Homer, not to mention accepted archaeological realities. Society in ancient Britain at the time of Stonehenge III was not civilized, that is to say, not a civic society. It lacked cities, even a sufficient agricultural base for the support of cities, much less urban specialists like astronomers and mathematicians dependent on writing and library archives. The Britons who built the final phase of Stonehenge were a pastoral people known to archaeology as the Wessex warriors, a proto-Celtic branch of the Battle-Ax people identified with a zone of Indo-European occupation stretching from India to Ireland and from northern Europe to the Mediterranean. The battle-axes of the Wessex warriors are interred with them in the vast burial grounds of Stonehenge; their deeds of combat and cattle lifting echo in the oral literature about various other Indo-European warrior heroes, as recorded in the *Iliad*, the *Rig Veda*, and the *Táin Bó Cúalnge*. Homer's *Iliad* was set down in the eighth century B.C. on the basis of an oral tradition recalling the Myceanean heroes of Bronze-Age Greece in about 1500 B.C. The *Rig Veda* recalls the invasion of civilized India by battle-loving, city-sacking, cow-stealing Aryan charioteers at the same time, in an epic poem faithfully transmitted orally by Brahmins until recorded during

340

the British raj. (Thirty-five centuries and not a syllable changed!) And the *Táin* recalls the heroic character of rival Indo-European chiefdoms that survived in Ireland, isolated even from the Roman conquest, until reached by Christian missionaries in the fifth century A.D. We are indebted to the monks who in about the seventh century recorded the *Táin*, for they have provided us with an oral tradition that, incredible as it may seem, opens a window on the proto-Celtic past and blows life into the bones of the Wessex warriors who died in 1500 B.C., roughly contemporary with Homer's Mycenae. If Mycenae, the most advanced of the European heroic societies,. is an unlikely place for a solar and lunar observatory and eclipse computer, how much more so barbarian Britain at the very same moment of historical time.

The Stonehenge of the astro-archaeologists (or the archaeo-astronomers, they haven't decided which they are) is in fact a fiction. To present Stonehenge as a scientific instrument cannot be done without fudging the archaeological data, for it must be made to appear that the monument was built at one time, for one purpose, by one people. In reality, it was built over a period of nearly a thousand years by three different cultures, the Windmill Hill, the Beaker and the Wessex. Astronomical Stonehenge is a conflation of these three building phases. Indeed, the Four Stations of Stonehenge II (a rectangular arrangement of stones and mounds) cover up some of the Aubrey Holes of Stonehenge I, yet all parts are supposed to be integral to a single device. What is more, the idea is dubious on statistical grounds alone. Douglass Hettie, who teaches mathematics and theoretical astronomy at Edinburgh University, determined this in his recent book of 1982, *Megalithic Science*. Of the 240 alignments Hawkins investigated at Stonehenge, 48 could be expected by chance to line up with something of solar or lunar significance, yet he found only 32 significant orientations. Chance in excess of design! (On recalculation, only 25 of these have errors of deviation under the $2°$ of azimuthal arc Hawkins fixed as the limit for claiming astronomical orientation—a generous limit widely exceeded.)

Our own fiction, we hope to persuade you, is closer to the truth of the historical Stonehenge, which might better be called Cowhenge.

Leon Stover, Ph.D., Litt. D.
Professor of Anthropology
Illinois Institute of Technology

SUGGESTED READINGS

Prehistory

Stuart Piggott. *Ancient Europe*. Chicago: Aldine, 1965.
Derek Roe. *Prehistory*. Berkeley: Univ. of California Press, 1972.
Andrew Sherratt, ed. *The Cambridge Encyclopedia of Archaeology*.
  New York: Crown, 1980.

Atlantis

A.G. Galanopolis and Edward Bacon. *Atlantis: The Truth Behind the Legend*. Indianapolis: Bobbs-Merrill, 1969.
Sinclair Hood. *The Minoans*. London: Thames and Hudson,
  1971.
J.V. Luce. *The End of Atlantis*. London: Thames and Hudson,
  1969.

Mycenae

George E. Mylonas. *Mycenae and the Mycenaean Age*. New Jer-
  sey: Princeton Univ. Press, 1966.
Lord William Taylour. *The Mycenaeans*. London: Thames and
  Hudson, 1964.
Emily Vermeule. *Greece in the Bronze Age*. Chicago: Univ. of
  Chicago Press, 1972.

Celts

Myles Dillon. *Celts and Aryans*. Simla: Indian Inst. of Advanced
  Study, 1975.
T.G.E. Powell. *The Celts*. New York: Praeger, 1958.
J.J. Tierney. "The Celtic Ethnography of Posidonius." *Pro-
  ceedings of the Royal Irish Academy* 60, sec. C, no. 5, 1960,
  pp. 189-275.

Irish Sagas

Tom Peete Cross and Clark Harris Slover, eds. *Ancient Irish Tales.* New York: Henry Holt, 1936.

Kenneth Hurlstone Jackson. *The Oldest Irish Tradition: A Window on the Iron Age.* Cambridge: Cambridge Univ. Press, 1964.

Cecile O'Rahilly, ed. *Táin Bó Cúalnge.* Dublin: Dublin Inst. for Advanced Studies, 1967.

Southwest Britain and Wessex

Aileen Fox. *South West England.* London: Thames and Hudson, 1964.

Stuart Piggott. "The Early Bronze Age in Wessex." *Proceedings of the Prehistoric Society* 4, 1938, pp. 52-106.

J.F.S. Stone. *Wessex.* London: Thames and Hudson, 1958.

Stonehenge

R.J.C. Atkinson. *Stonehenge.* Harmondsworth: Penguin Books, 1960.

Colin Burgess. *The Age of Stonehenge.* London: J.M. Dent, 1980.

Leon Stover and Bruce Kraig. *Stonehenge: The Indo-European Heritage.* Chicago: Nelson-Hall, 1978. See review by Anthony F. Aveni in *Archaeology* 33, no. 4 (July / August), 1980, pp. 64-5.

Astro-archaeology

Kenneth Brecher and Michael Feirtag, eds. *Astronomy of the Ancients.* Cambridge: The M.I.T. Press, 1981.

Gerald Hawkins and John B. White. *Stonehenge Decoded.* New York: Doubleday, 1965.

Douglass C. Heggie. *Megalithic Science: Ancient Mathematics and Astronomy in Northwest Europe.* London: Thames and Hudson, 1982.

Druids

Nora K. Chadwick. *The Druids.* Cardiff: Univ. of Wales Press, 1966.

Stuart Piggot. *The Druids.* London: Thames and Hudson, 1970.

Ward Rutherford. *The Druids and Their Heritage.* London: Gordon and Cremonesi, 1978.

George Dumézil. *The Destiny of the Warrior*. Chicago: Univ. of Chicago Press, 1970.

Gerald James Larson, ed. *Myth in Indo-European Antiquity*. Berkeley: Univ. of California Press, 1974.

C. Scott Littleton. *The New Comparative Mythology*. Berkeley: Univ. of California Press, 1973.